Cayce West Columbia Library

9502 9100 255 5759

New
3-20-18

FIC KEN

Kendig, Ronie, author.
Fierian

FIERIAN

CAYCE WEST COLUMBIA
BRANCH LIBRARY
1500 AUGUSTA ROAD
WEST COLUMBIA, S. C. 29169

Also by Ronie Kendig

FIERIAN

ABIASSA'S FIRE

BOOK THREE

RONIE KENDIG

an imprint of
GILEAD PUBLISHING

Published by Enclave Publishing, an imprint of Gilead Publishing, Grand Rapids, Michigan

an imprint of
GILEAD PUBLISHING
www.enclavepublishing.com

ISBN: 978-1-68370-106-4 (print)
ISBN: 978-1-68370-107-1 (eBook)

Fierian

Copyright © 2018 by Ronie Kendig

All rights reserved. No part of this book may be reproduced or transmitted in any form or by any means, electronic, mechanical, including photocopying and recording, or in any information storage and retrieval system without prior written permission from the publisher.

This is a work of fiction. Names, characters, places, and incidents are products of the author's imagination or are used fictitiously. Any similarity to actual people, organizations, and/or events is purely coincidental.

Edited by Reagen Reed
Cover design by Kirk DouPonce
Interior design/typesetting by Beth Shagene

Printed in the United States of America

To Reagen Reed,
Editor Extraordinaire, who wrangled
this beast-of-a-final-installment into something
readable and enjoyable. You truly have a gift
for editing [epic fantasy], even if I did nearly drive
you to the brink of insanity. Thanks for your
patience and wisdom. Ready for the next series?
Mwahahahaha.

The People of Abiassa's Fire

House Celahar
Royal Family of the Nine Kingdoms
seat of power located at Fieri Keep in Zaethien, Seultrie

Zireli Celahar – (zĭ-rel'-ee) king of the Nine Kingdoms; the "Fire King"

Adrroania Celahar – (ăd-rō-ăn-ya) queen of the Nine Kingdoms

Kaelyria Celahar – (kā'-leer-ee-uh) daughter of Zireli and Adrroania

Haegan Celahar – (hā-gen) son of Zireli and Adrroania

Zaelero Celahar – (zah-lĕr-ō) Haegan's forebear; first Celahar to become Fire King; fought the Mad Queen and restored the Nine to the ways of Abiassa

Asykth Family
Northlands seat of power at Nivar Hold in Ybienn

Thurig Asykth – (thoo'-rig) king of the Northlands

Thurig Eriathiel – (air-ee-uh-thee-el) queen of the Northlands; wife to Thurig

Thurig as'Tili, "Tili" – (tĭl-ee) eldest son of Thurig

Thurig as'Relig, "Relig" – (rĕh'-lig) second eldest son of Thurig

Thurig as'Osmon, "Osmon" – (aws-man) youngest son of Thurig

Thurig Kiethiel, "Thiel" – (thē-ĕl) youngest and only daughter of Thurig; love interest of Haegan Celahar; one of four companions Haegan joined on the journey to the Great Falls

Klome – (klōm) stable overseer

Aburas – (ah-boor-ahs) second in command of the Nivari, the Asykthian guard

Legier/Legier's Heart

Aaesh – a servant

Aselan – (a-seh-lon) cacique of Legier's Heart

Bardin – (bar-den) member of the Legiera

Byrin – (by-rin) right hand of the cacique; brother to Teelh

Carilla – (ka-rill-uh) worker in the cantina

Entwila – (en-twill-uh) one of three Ladies of the Heart

Hoeff – (hoff) giant who practices the herbal arts

Ingwait – (ing-wāt) matron of the Ladies of the Heart

Markoo – (mar-koo) member of the Legiera, quiet

Teelh – (teel-uh) member of the Legiera; brother to Byrin

Toeff – (toff) giant who works with the cacique

Wegna – (weg-nuh) – an Eilidan reader

Tahscan Warriors

Vaqar Modia – leader; brother to Anithraenia, queen of Tahsca

Adassi – Vaqar's right hand

Dwaith – older member of the Tahscans

Jadrile – brother to Haandra

Haandra – sister to Jadrile

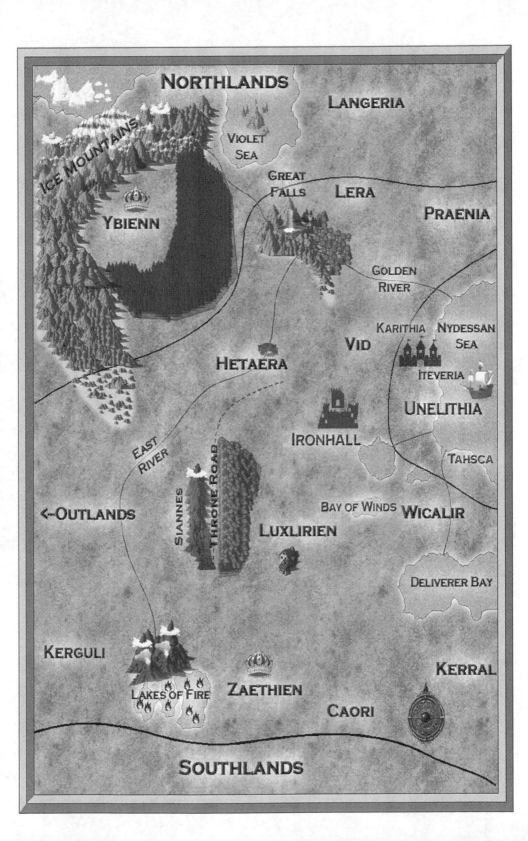

1

Darkness crouched heavily, ambushing them in the night. Tucking the moonslight behind a thick veil, clouds forbade the contingent from advancing across the plain at anything faster than a crawl, for fear of falling prey to an ambush. Yet survival required they travel at night over the open terrain, guided by the unfaithful moonslight and Sir Gwogh's urgent instructions. Following Colonel Marz Chauld single file, Thurig as'Tili guided his destrier, whose sharp black ears flicked in every direction, pinning against the black poll whenever one of the Jujak bringing up the rear drew too close. The colonel had sent four men—their fiercest, fastest—to scout ahead.

Which meant they were guarded by less than the fiercest and fastest. Temptation squirmed through Tili to wield, to draw the ample heat from the air and cast light ahead. Just for a second. Enough to catch the path and keep them safe.

Foolish. They would not be safe outside the night. Even a little light could cost them plenty, including their lives. But he was tired. His muscles ached from the last two days of riding from the Citadel, fleeing Poired's army.

The Southlands around him were scorched. Thousands dead, and those who yet lived had stumbled in a beaten daze toward the only sanctuary that once existed—Hetaera. Now even it lay as rubble beneath the boots of Poired.

Despite the hours that had passed, his thoughts were still anchored to that fateful day. To the boy who'd died in his arms, his blood soaking into the leather of Tili's gauntlets. Into the mantle he now wore but had never anticipated nor wanted. Yet wants were of no consequence when the hope of the kingdom lay before a warrior.

"*Tsst!*"

At the signal, Tili drew up his horse. Heart backed into his throat, he listened around his pounding pulse. 'Twould not be the first time they'd stopped in fear of an imminent attack, only to have a wild dog cross their path.

But no . . . This time Tili could sense something in the air. Something that hadn't been there before.

"Form up on the steward!" came Chauld's shout.

In a crash of thudding hooves, grunts, and stirring dust, a circle of horses and well-muscled men drew around him. Annoyance plucked at Tili's pride—he'd been the commander of the Nivari in Ybienn. Second only to his father, King Thurig, he had been tasked with protecting, not being protected. By the flames, he knew not why Abiassa had chosen him for this venture. Nor did he dare question Her. 'Twould do no good. He'd tried already anyway.

As the dust settled, he strained to see the scorched land beyond his small contingent. What threat could be so terrible that it could survive this desolation?

But even as the question sprouted in his mind, he heard it: the steady rumble of distant hooves.

Tili closed his eyes, forced himself to shut out the darkness, the fear. To focus solely on what was coming. He reached beyond the thundering hooves and sensed only silence. A quiet unlike the peace he had known in Nivar, this silence hung heavy with the anticipation of violence.

Again he reached out and this time felt heat wakes, isolating the numbers. His alarm rose with the count. "Too many." His mutter was answered by the nicker of a destrier. "Twenty. Thirty. Perhaps more."

"Blazes," someone muttered.

Here Tili could wield the Flames without fear of reprimand or mockery—the desperate lands were beyond propriety. Beyond Citadel-sanctioned hierarchies. The Nine Kingdoms had crumbled beneath the oppression of Poired and Sirdar of Tharqnis. In the name of protection, more folk accepted the violence of wielding.

Is that this hour?

The approaching roar grew until, in thunder and swirling dust, the riders fell upon them. It seemed as hundreds, herding their tiny circle tighter and tighter, like a noose constricting a neck. Horses and warriors shifted nervously. Uncertainly.

Fear drenched the air, heating bodies and slowing reaction times. Tili gritted his teeth and tightened the leather reins in his hands. "Whoa," he murmured when his destrier stamped a hoof.

"Halt! Declare yourselves!" Chauld shouted.

Dust and noise seemed to yield to the colonel's command as the horde came to a halt, but Tili and his men remained packed in on all sides by bodies and beasts.

"Who speaks?" a gruff voice demanded from the darkness.

Thwap. Flap! Thwap! Thump.

At the strange noises, Tili tensed, expecting an arrow in his chest. But nothing came save a ripple of the air above his head, pulling only his gaze upward. A moment later, a dull glow spread over the faces of the twenty men and horses surrounding them. Eyes on the thick, black—yet not black—banners that unfurled above every third man, Tili felt the knot of tension in his chest loosen a fraction.

"Fool!" Chauld snapped. "You'll alert—"

"Shielding," Tili muttered, impressed at both the perfection of the illumination—clear within the small bubble surrounding them but stretching no farther than the outermost horse—and at the perfection of the military formation the riders held. His father had spoken of shielding, but Tili had never seen it in action. Those outside this bubble would see naught save the darkness the shielding mirrored.

The leader nodded with a grim smirk.

"General Negaer."

"Steward Tili." Negaer inclined his head, then motioned to his men. "We are at your service, sir."

With a snap, the soldiers tossed open their cloaks, a move that flipped the black-as-night cloaks to an inspiring, glaring white.

"Pathfinders," Tokar whispered in awe from behind.

Tili frowned. Haegan's friend had come far in the short months he'd trained with the Nivari and Jujak—Tili had even been rather grateful for his presence the last two days—but his mouth had yet to find discipline.

"What of Hetaera? Have you abandoned your post so quickly?" Chauld groused.

"Careful, *Colonel*." Negaer glowered, no apparent love for the other officer. "Hetaera is lost."

Though Tili had guessed it already, the news struck like a physical blow. The Citadel—lost. How many had died? How many still suffered under the cruel reign of that monster Poired?

Belatedly, Tili realized the general had turned his attention back to him. "Steward, if you continue on this path, you will encounter Sirdarians. It is my advice that you shift southeast—aim toward the Bay of Winds."

"That's more than a hundred leagues off course," Chauld objected. "And the lands are peppered with mercenaries."

Negaer ignored the colonel. "Whatever course you choose, 'twould be an honor to serve you, sir."

Tili's eyebrows rose, mirroring his surprise. "Serve me? Are ye not needed—"

"The Nine need a ruler." And their legitimate ruler, Prince Haegan, was missing, supposedly having fled to Iteveria. "As with the shielding banners, we have means to protect and supply you, as well as the determination to see you safely to Vid."

Tili glanced around at the twenty men. Did the general truly believe so few could make a difference?

"That is my responsibility, tasked to me by Sir Gwogh," Chauld objected.

"Sir Gwogh." Negaer sat straight, his visage unaffected despite the venom dripping from his words. "You are a reputable officer among the Nine armies, Colonel." He motioned to the half-dozen Pathfinders flanking him. "My men speak highly of you. They say you are reasonable and well versed in the codes of warfare."

The words held a placating tone, but there was thin undercurrent of challenge. It reminded Tili of the lectures Father had given, grooming him for the throne. And always, there came a smack at the end—whether literal or figurative, it stung the same.

Chest puffed, shoulders squared, Chauld took the bait of the supposed compliments.

"Tell me, Colonel," Negaer said, the tone one of remonstration now. A superior to a lesser. "What armies does Sir Gwogh command?"

Chauld drew back ever so slightly, apparently realizing the smack intended. Gwogh was an accelerant. He did not command the armies of the Nine.

The general seemed intent on making his point aloud. "I believe the accelerant's authority is limited to the Ignatieri." Negaer angled his head to the side, to the Pathfinder at his right hand. "Colonel Rhaemos, to whom do we answer?"

White cloak catching the pale blue glow of wielding, the much-younger colonel remained impassive, his face like granite hewn from the rocks of the Cold One's Tooth. Though fewer than thirty cycles, the colonel had an eternity in his eyes. He'd seen much. Done more. "The Fire King."

"We have no king," Chauld growled, his anger evident.

"Nay!" Negaer's response crackled through the night, his gaze scanning the gathered. He almost seemed bored. "We have a *king*, Colonel." He nudged his mount closer to Chauld, the blaze in his eyes a stark contrast to his grim expression. "Uncrowned. Missing. But no less our king."

Blanching, Chauld trembled, both in fury and aghast at his mistake. "I—"

"The general is right," Tili said, intervening, unwilling to endure further humiliation of any fighting for Abiassa. "Ye have a king. And we ride to him"—he looked at Negaer—"not Vid. As Steward of the Nine in Haegan's absence, I accept yer service and that of yer twenty."

Chauld snorted. "What good is twenty except to get us spotted more quickly?"

The slightest hint of a smile broke through Negaer's façade. He flicked a finger to Rhaemos. A whistle riffled the air.

Tili drew in a quiet breath as tiny bursts of light flickered in the distance. Fifty more. A hundred. The height and distance made it impossible to tell if the sentries were on hills or just very far away. They were all equidistant apart. A perimeter. No, a second perimeter, for around Tili and his men stood the twenty Pathfinders, their bearing hard and resolute.

Even before this display of shrewdness and might, Tili had known better than to refuse the protection and experience of Negaer, the general who'd founded the elite Pathfinders, who could track as well as Nivari or Legiera, and fight better than any other soldier he'd met on the plains or mountains. "Whether twenty or fifty"—Tili's gaze again considered the farther-out sentries—"I welcome yer help, General."

Negaer seemed to relax. Another whistle went out and horses shifted. Even with the subtle glow of a touchstone, Tili almost didn't see the two Pathfinders who sidled up on their destriers and settled in as though they belonged there.

Blond hair streaked with gray, the general nudged his horse in front of Tili's. "It is an honor, Thurig as'Tili."

"I—" A yawn cut off Tili's words.

Speculative eyes considered him. "When did you last rest, my liege?" Negaer's smile bore both rue and concern.

"Rest is a luxury." In truth, Tili could not recall his last full sleep, though it had certainly been before the burden of the mantle found his shoulders. But he was not alone in bearing it. "All with me are tired," he said, not wanting the attention or worry. "We have grave concerns before us. Most have not slept—"

"Nay," muttered someone solemnly. Tokar. "Some *have* rested. He has not."

Negaer's gaze shifted behind Tili as he gave a nod. "That would explain how we so easily set upon your caravan."

Tili cursed himself. If he could not care for a contingent of ten, how was he to steward nine kingdoms? "I will rest when we are safe." He nodded. "We should move."

"Then we ride to safety," Negaer said, pulling his massive horse around as a long, low whistle tweetled.

A series of commands, which sounded like stiff wind or creaking reeds, sailed through the air. Touchstones doused. Flaps of the shielding banners thwapped closed. The line of horses advanced, chasing the fading light at a clip that belied the dead black.

Relief spread through Tili, drawing with it a large measure of exhaustion. He'd not allowed himself to sleep, knowing they were being hunted by Poired's army. Also with the knowledge, whether spoken or not, that Haegan had left his people and armies abandoned. Tili would not be that man, would not close his eyes and do the same injustice to the people of the Nine.

He would make Father proud. Lead admirably. Assure Haegan had a throne to ascend to. Then Tili could return to Nivar, to his siblings and parents. To his own glorious, blessed bed.

The nicker of a horse drew him up—and only then did he realize his eyelids had closed. He adjusted in the saddle. Somewhere along the way, they had been joined by wagons, presumably carrying the provisions and gear Negaer had mentioned. Their rumble made Tili think of far-off thunder.

"My liege?" the Pathfinder escort on his left whispered in concern.

Anticipating the next question—are you well?—Tili cleared his throat. "How much farther?"

"Not much, my liege."

Even as the words met his ears, Tili felt his destrier dip down. He leaned back to balance. They were riding down a steep slope into a shallow ravine.

Negaer called a halt and ordered them to set up camp.

"Is it safe here?" Chauld asked.

As if in answer, several light sources flared, dull but adequate. A small copse of trees huddled around them, sagging against the heat and wind. They seemed as exhausted as Tili—and as dehydrated. The whole of the kingdom was parched.

Tili dismounted. His knees threatened to buckle when his boots hit the ground hard, but he refused to yield to the aches in his thighs and back. There were many no longer alive, so he would be grateful for the pain of a hard journey. He reached for his bedroll.

"My liege."

He shot a glare over his shoulder.

A Pathfinder inclined his head and motioned to his right. "You should rest by the fire."

A bloom of hazy blue fire roared in a circle of stones. Tili's heart pitched at the sight, frantic it would draw the enemy. But his groggy mind remembered the flicker of shielding banners. 'Twas fathomless that there could be so much illumination beneath the banners, yet pitch black beyond.

Still. He must talk with Negaer. Plan tomorrow's strategy. Discuss Haegan and plot their effort to locate and retrieve him. "I would speak with yer general," Tili said, shoving his bedroll under one arm. "There is much to tend to before we can close our eyes to the danger."

Where had Tokar gone? He searched the shapes around them. A cluster of men stood near the fire. He glanced beyond. Then behind. "Have ye—" When he shifted back to the front, Tili blinked.

The once-gangly youth who had fouled every match in the training yard at Nivar Hold, now stood shoulder to shoulder among the best of the men. When had that happened?

"My liege," the Pathfinder prompted. "This way."

Surprise spiraled through Tili at the cluster of tents that had sprung up off to the side, out of sight and earshot of the fire pit. When his guide held back the flap of the largest one, he saw a long table with a map already spread upon it. To the right of it sat a cot piled with soft pelts and pillows. Suddenly, the aches in his backside gnawed greedily at his will, longing for the comfort of rest.

Nay. Duties first.

Negaer strode into the tent and nodded at Tili, then approached the table. He was followed by Major Draorin, one of the men who had accompanied Tili out of Hetaera, and a Pathfinder with a steaming cup in hand.

"To ward off the aches." The general's smile was deep and inviting as he motioned to the cup. "Drink while we talk."

"What is it?" Warm drink on the belly might fast put Tili to sleep.

"Warmed cordi, sir," the Pathfinder said.

"Nay." Tili rubbed his brow. Warm *and* fermented? He'd be out in a blink. "I thank ye, I—"

"It's not fermented," the Pathfinder assured. "We have no use for such luxuries."

"You'll need its hardiness for our talk," Negaer prompted, planting himself on a bench inside the tent. "Come. Talk. As a keen steward, I know there is much on your mind."

Plying my will . . . ? To what end? Did they not serve the same throne and Abiassa? He accepted the cup and lowered himself onto a chest, grateful for the uncomfortable press of wood against his backside, keeping him awake. "Nice tent ye have." Again, he eyed the cot.

"Glad you like it, but 'tis yours while you are under our protection."

"I couldn't." Yet he could. In so many ways.

"No false humility here, my liege. 'Tis yours."

Tili considered the man, his blond-gray hair and weathered features. The hard lines had clearly been carved into him from years in the sun, from a life devoted to violence of action, but there was also a gentility, an honor behind those hazel eyes.

Beside him, Major Draorin stood respectfully and offered a subtle nod that somehow encouraged Tili. Though he'd met Draorin only two days prior, he had quickly understood his worth.

Tili gave a nod. "I thank ye." He tipped the cup to his mouth and the scent of spiced cordi swirled around his nostrils. Silky warmth slid down his throat and coiled through his chest and aching muscles. Soothing. Comforting.

He had no sooner finished the drink than the general was grinning. "Better?"

"Indeed." Tili licked his lips.

"'Tis not much," Negaer said, "but should suffice until more suitable provisions can be prepared."

"It will serve well enough for now." Tili fisted a hand over his mouth to hide the yawn stretching his jaw muscles. "Now, I would have us discuss the route and contingencies for locating the prince."

"But of course," Negaer said, sipping his own steaming cup.

A strange . . . headiness lilted through Tili's mind. Unfamiliar, a thwapping noise distracted him. Tent flaps? He glanced there and found them tied back. So what then?

Beyond the opening, a banner snapped. On its dark field, a raqine flared beneath the tri-tipped flame.

Beneath.

Ybienn beneath the crown. When had they had time to make such a thing? That the sigil of Ybienn should be subordinate to the Nine cloyed at him. Yet he saw in the design that it was not simply beneath. The wings of the raqine supported the flame. Supported the crown. Allies.

Tili raked a hand over his face and stifled a yawn, his limbs like lead. His eyelids drooped.

"I would beg your patience a little longer, my liege." Negaer indicated where Rhaemos had entered with another map and spread it across the table.

As Tili struggled to his feet, Chauld stalked through the tent opening, followed by Tokar. Two Pathfinders took up positions behind their general and captain as the officers gathered around the map-strewn table. Strange. Though he had been ready to command his father's army in Nivar and Ybienn, here Tili felt like he did at six years old when he'd sneaked into his father's war council meeting. Like an intruder.

"We continue southeast toward the bay, just north of Caori's border, and bank northward into Vid before heading east," Negaer said. "Here, here"—he stabbed a finger at several red Xs on the parchment—"and here are Sirdarian strongholds."

"We must avoid them," Colonel Chauld said.

Annoyance played along Negaer's furrowed brow. The colonel's comment was more open dialogue than instruction—of course they must avoid the Sirdarians. Poired and Onerid would take too much pleasure in gutting their contingent. "Aye," Negaer finally growled. "Avoiding them brings us to the prince faster."

Negaer motioned to one of his men, who stepped out, and returned with another steaming cup, which he delivered to Tili. "My men know the terrain. Already we have scouted it and feel it best provides a path to success for this mission."

Considering the proffered cup, Tili knew he shouldn't—'twould be too warm going down, too soothing—when sleep already beckoned. Still, he accepted it. "General, I side with ye on this. Anything to bring us to Vid sooner."

"And to Haegan," Tokar spoke up, receiving a stiff glare from Negaer for having spoken out of turn.

Tili sipped, secretly relishing the heat that coaxed the pain from his muscles. The fight from his body. Exhaustion plied against his strength. Fighting the heady invitation to slumber, he planted his hands on the map and stared down at it.

Why was it so blasted hot? Heat radiated through night, the product of an unusually warm spring and the fact there were no nearby trees or springs. It made him long for Ybienn's cooler temperatures and lush vegetation. But then, in the last week or so, everything had made him long for Ybienn—the contending had ended in a nightmarish attack by incipients . . .

Nagbe.

"I agree," he forced himself to say. "Through . . ." What was the name of that place?

Crushed as the image of the broken body of a young boy lying on the table far below the Citadel filled his mind, Tili rubbed his forehead. Nagbe had been dealt a deathblow by General Onerid, Poired's right hand. Ultimately, however, Tili had been responsible for the boy's death. If only he'd failed the final test—which he technically never completed because they had been attacked on Mount Medric—and left the boy in the cave. If only he'd brought the ruby from the cave and not the boy as well, then Nagbe still would be alive.

The foolish thought drew him up straight. Or maybe that was the grief he avoided. The truth was, they would have all been slaughtered, along with everyone else in the Citadel. The boy would have died in the cave, alone, instead of in Tili's arms.

He pointed. "The . . . thity." Why was his tongue thick?

He blinked and Draorin stood over him. Tili drew back, startled at the stealth of the long-legged major. Then the great man tilted sideways.

The tent blurred into nothingness as a voice rumbled, "Good rest, Steward."

2

"I cannot believe ye *invited* them!" Thurig Kiethiel stared down the great Ematahri warrior with a mix of revulsion and shock. If she knew what was good for her, she would yield her anger and don contrition. But she had never obeyed those impulses. "Do ye wish to bring all the Flames down on yer head?"

The tall, broad-shouldered warrior had been born and reared on the land. Wildness lurked in eyes tormented like the stormy sky. As did all Ematahri, he wore his dark hair long, tied back and braided down his spine.

Cadeif flexed his jaw, and a bare pectoral muscle streaked with paint twitched. As he fisted his hands, tight red bands strained against his biceps. Those dangling cords had been dipped in the blood of his enemies and marked him the leader of his people. All reasons she should stop antagonizing him.

"You think I am to take counsel from a traitor?" he growled, his lip curling.

Surprise roiled through her at his harsh words. Where was the consideration he'd long given her? The affection?

Cadeif stomped closer, rage perched on his corded shoulders. "You think I will trust the one *I* protected with Kedardokith, yet who repaid my gift by bringing the Lucent Riders against my people?"

"Lucent—" Thiel stumbled back, nearly tripping over a thick, gnarled tree root. "I–I didn't bring the Riders."

Well, not technically. That had been Haegan. But not technically him either. They'd come *because* of him. He didn't bring them. There was a difference. Was there not?

"They *came*," he roared. "They judged!"

Thiel's breath caught. "Wh-what do ye mean *they judged*?"

Cadeif swung his arm, and the back of his hand connected with her temple. The blow sent her sprawling.

Her ears rang as she stared up at him, stunned. Hurt. Digging her fingers into the litter of the forest floor, Thiel took a second to compose herself. "Please. Listen to me—"

"I do not answer to you!" He spun away, muttering something in the Ematahri language to Zoijan, his right hand.

She caught snatches of their words, but not enough to understand. His body language told her plenty. Being struck in the head filled in any gaps. He hated her. Though she should have expected it, it left her baffled, grieved.

Never quiet about *his* hatred of her, Zoijan stood over her with a dark smirk. His expression sent a shiver through her as he reached for her—

Chortling ripped the air, startling them and shoving Thiel's shoulder-length hair into her face. They turned to where Chima stalked toward them through the forest, head low. Beside her walked Laertes, and behind him, Praegur. Hackles and meaty jowls lifted, Chima bared her razor-sharp teeth. Challenge set in her fiery eyes as she glowered at Zoijan. And . . . had her eyes changed color? A red hue burned like an ember.

Zoijan's knuckles whitened as he gripped his sword.

"A threat against me is a threat against her." It wasn't a whole lie. But he probably didn't know that each raqine chose *one* person with whom to bind. That person had full protection because they were connected deep, some said through the Void. But it wasn't Thiel that Chima would protect. At best, she tolerated Thiel.

Zoijan lowered his sword. Casting a wary glance to the raqine, he motioned to Thiel. "Up." As Ematahri bled from the trees, he nodded to the others. "Bring them."

With a grateful nod to Chima, Thiel came to her feet. Chima again chortle-growled when a warrior grabbed Thiel's arm. Though he flinched, he did not relent. "Walk."

They wove through the dense vegetation to the encampment.

"How long have ye been in these woods?" she asked.

Only the near-impossible-to-hear crunch of his steps answered. That and the thrumming of Chima stalking them on a parallel path through the forest. They broke from the line of trees into a clearing, and there she found the familiar setup of the Ematahri camp. As well as their cold, bitter glares.

• • •

WEST OF LUXLIRIEN

"Defeat." Boards creaked as Sir Gwogh paced the upper room of the tavern, stricken that he had been so unprepared, that they had so wholly failed Hetaera, the Citadel, and Abiassa's people. Three weeks had passed since the Contending was disastrously cut short on Mount Medric. He and the few others remaining of the Council of Nine had accomplished next to nothing. Three weeks of sending scouts, who never returned, and waiting for information that never came.

A shout arose from the street below. He paused at the dusty half-moon window and stared across the smoldering village. A lone Jujak rode toward the tavern. Gwogh watched the man's progress. Noted the tight way he rode. "He's injured."

"It's Qaocit," Kelviel said. "The scout we sent west."

"He had ten men with him!" Falip Wrel exclaimed, his white hands fluttering to his throat.

Gwogh looked at him in distaste and wondered, not for the first time, if they had made the right choice in Wrel. The Council newcomer was always a little excitable—a less-than-ideal trait in these troubled times.

"He will need a pharmakeia," Kelviel noted.

"There's not one for leagues," Gwogh said. "We will have to do."

"Child, prepare the cot there for him," Kedulcya said to her attendant, Elinia, a winsome young woman of seventeen with raven hair.

The three watched the Jujak rein in outside the half-gutted tavern, then turned as heavy boots thudded on the wood floor below. Two villagers helped Qaocit up the steps and into the room they'd converted into a miniature command center.

"On the cot," Kedulcya instructed as she and Elinia scooted aside.

"Sir Gwogh," Qaocit said around a grimace as he was lowered to the stretch of hide and wood, "the Sirdarians are encamped at the Throne Road crossroads."

"Encamped?" Gwogh drew closer. "You are sure?"

Qaocit lifted a bloodied hand from his side. "Caught a bolt from an incipient before I could gain enough distance. They pursued, but I lost them along a ravine—which was once the River of Shadows."

Kedulcya and Elinia knelt beside the soldier and began ministrations, first cutting away the stained green fabric of his uniform.

"What number?" Gwogh asked.

Qaocit breathed a dark laugh as his gray eyes came to Gwogh once more. He shook his head. "Hundreds, if not thousands. I could not count them, but they were as ants filling that gorge."

"Thousands," Kelviel hissed to Gwogh. "How? How can there be so many here already?"

"They have been razing villages for over a year. We have too long focused on finding the Fierian, and the enemy has stolen right into our midst." Grieved, Gwogh stroked his beard.

"But finding the Fierian was important."

"Aye," Gwogh said. "Imperative. But we should have divided our efforts sooner. And now, now we must gather the remnant."

"Agreed," Falip said. He seemed to have control of himself again, and his face had settled into a thoughtful mask.

Gwogh considered the newest Council member. What thoughts churned through his mind?

Kedulcya worked steadily on Qaocit's injuries, lifting an eye on occasion to the others.

"They aren't moving," Falip said slowly, seeming to let the thought gain substance, "because they are gathering. The crossroads is a four-corners site, the meeting of the Northlands, the Nine, Outlands, and Southlands." His lips thinned. "They are there to gather strength and numbers."

Gwogh's mind turned toward the girl and the Counselor. He'd sent them there as much for safekeeping as for them to persuade the Ematahri. Was he too late? Had he been wrong?

"I beg your mercy," Elinia said, hands full of bandages and ointments her mentor had prepared, "but if the enemy is there, between us and the Ematahri, what of Praegur—and the princess and boy?"

"Aye," Gwogh grunted.

"Praegur is the Counselor. He's divinely connected. We need him," Kedulcya said, panic etching itself into the lines of her face. Her brow tangled. "Gwogh—"

He nodded. "Aye," he said once more. "We must retrieve them all. Kedulcya, go with Falip. Once you have the three, journey east on the south side of the Shadow River as fast as you can—check the cities of Zardohar and Daussi for survivors. Gather any accelerants or villagers who can fight. I will do the same along the northern routes, checking Fraelik and Lirwen. I'll venture also to Zaethien and so on, until we are gathered back at Vid with an army to support Haegan's rise."

"Rise?" Kelviel snorted. "He fled. He left us—"

"He will find his strength. She will help him—and we are an extension of that. Feed not your fears, Kelviel. Feed your fury against the Dark One."

• • •

CASTLE KARITHIA, ITEVERIA, UNELITHIA

Fires burning bright.

Water cold and brittle.

Smoke thick and choking.

Voices loud and quiet.

Haegan Celahar gripped his temples, curling in on himself. Burrowing beneath the thick blankets, he growled, willing the dichotomies away. Silencing the chaos. But it didn't work. Somehow, his attempts to quiet the raging storm only strengthened the howl within.

"Release the Fierian! Release the Fierian! Release the Fierian! Release the Fierian!" The voices roared through the night. Through the day. Through first rise. Twelve bells. The great feast. On and on. Maddening. Reassuring.

For the last fortnight it had echoed, making demand of . . . someone. It was startling at first. He'd spun around, searching for the voice, the owner, but only found the quiet beauty of the Infantessa's palace. "Pray, did you hear that?" he'd asked of Thomannon. Of Trale. Of servants. Even of the great queen herself. Alas, none heard the voice demanding someone release the Fierian. All dismissed his questions as readily as they would an annoying insect crawling over their hand.

That was enough to drive him mad, but then there existed a second voice, hollow, tinny, and insanely quiet, piercing his every thought. Though but a whisper against his soul, it called—no, *screamed* to him. The whisper that punctuates the thrum of the heartbeat like respiration.

Haegan curled tighter. Groaned. There was nothing worse. If only *that* would stop, then he—

"Haegan . . ."

This, *this voice*, proved cruel and tormenting. A ghost vaulting from his failed past. "Father." A moan, miserable and raking, clawed through his chest. That voice haunted him with unrelenting fervor.

"Prince Haegan," Thomannon said firmly. "Twelve bells meal is served."

Ignoring the servant would only elicit anger, which invariably brought a beating—not with hands or fists, but through more of that voice. He'd had plenty. Most days. Most meals. Because he cared not if he ate. If he lived. If he died. Existence no longer mattered.

Hands gripped his arms, tossing him from the bed.

"Release the Fierian."

The Fierian.

Why did that sound familiar? The word displeased the Infantessa. She'd flown into a rage more than once at the voice's demand.

Haegan blinked. Looked at the patterned rug beneath his fingers. How had he gotten here? Why?

"You must eat, Prince," Thomannon intoned dully. "The Infantessa wills it. If you do not, you will not be strong enough to sit at her table."

Her table. *A place of honor that I never had at home, where I was relegated to the tower to hide the affliction.* "Of course," Haegan muttered, climbing onto all fours. His limbs trembled beneath his own weight. He could not disappoint her.

But as he crouched there, staring at the swirls of the carpet, something . . . something important—

"Prince!"

Haegan shook his head and lumbered to his feet.

A robe wrapped his shoulders. "There now, Prince. The table awaits."

Haegan stumbled across his bedchamber into the receiving room, where a table boasted a dozen different delicacies. *I was never so elegantly served in Fieri Keep.* He owed her great thanks. "Where is she, the Infantessa?"

When Haegan blinked, he found himself staring at a bread roll. He lifted it, disappointed that it was hard. When had he sat in the chair? He abandoned the bread and lifted his soup spoon, only to realize the room was too dark to see the contents of the bowl. "Is it dark, Thomannon? I can't see—"

"No, Prince. There's plenty of light."

Haegan blinked again, and there was light. "Ah." Odd. A hunger stirred in him, but not for food.

Wasn't there something he was supposed to do? Something important . . .

"Haegan, help me!" The insistent words dug through his deep thoughts. Gripped him tight. He knew that voice. A familiar voice. Once strong—

"Father," Haegan whispered.

"Your father?"

Haegan dragged his gaze to Thomannon, who stood to the side, waiting with an apathetic expression. "My father?" Why had the servant brought him up?

"My prince," Thomannon said quietly, "your father is with Aaeshwaeith Adoaniel'afirema."

Pain snapped through Haegan's head. With a groan, he gripped his temples, trying to stem the violent roaring. His ears hollowed against the excruciating sensation. He blinked rapidly, feeling as if he'd popped up in a lake with water running over his ears and eyes.

Swallowing, he glanced around. Where was this dirty, dusty place? But more importantly—"What did you say?" That's what caused his head to ache.

The tall servant jerked. It seemed he'd realized or seen something terrifying because his face went white.

Haegan frowned, straightening as if he stood on a great plain, unencumbered. Hauntingly alone. But even as he waited there, he remembered sitting at a table, eating. Yet the table seemed dirty and unused for months, years. Where were the platters of food?

What was he doing here?

This was . . . wrong. It was all wrong.

Wasn't it? He didn't belong here.

Yet I belonged at Fieri Keep and had been put in a tower, shamed.

As the waters of confusion rushed back at him, Haegan turned a glare to the servant. "What did you—"

But it was gone. His thought. His . . .

He looked at his hand. A spoon. There was a spoon in his hand.

Was I eating?

3

Old bones did little to help with stealth, but after a week of trudging across scorched lands to get to this place, Kedulcya would not let that stop her. She slunk through the dense patch of trees at the far end of the gorge with Elinia. In the lead, Falip hissed and drew up short, sidestepping a tree. Kedulcya and Elinia did the same, Kedulcya's heart loud in her own ears. Curse their eagerness to get into the camp—they had nearly missed the sentry on patrol.

Too close. As she saw the brawny Ematahri step their way, his gaze searching the shadows where she hid, Kedulcya made a tiny gesture to Elinia. Then, raising her hand, she stepped into the open, haloing the warrior in a bubble. At the same time, as they had practiced over and over, Elinia flicked a dart at the warrior's temple, strangling his cry of alarm. The tension and his weight shifted as he went limp in the bubble. Kedulcya grunted, struggling to keep from dropping him.

And then the burden lifted. Balance rushed in, and she met Falip's steady gaze as he, without effort, assisted her in lowering the warrior to the ground. She nodded her thanks and released the halo, then Falip and Elinia dragged him aside.

"We must hurry," she whispered and started deeper into the forest. It took them another fifteen minutes before they reached the edge of the Ematahri camp. A twenty-foot radius gaped between the trees and the huddle of tents.

"There," Elinia said, pointing to where thin white saplings formed two cages. One held the girl. The other the Counselor and the boy.

Kedulcya nodded to Elinia. "Spark them—gently—to alert them to our presence."

The raven-haired girl focused her wielding and threw a dart at Praegur, who sat with his spine pressed against the wood. Arms folded, legs crossed, he looked to be asleep. The spark flew quick and true, pricking his arm. The Counselor swiped at the spot but didn't rouse, no doubt thinking it an insect.

Kedulcya indicated for the girl to repeat it. This time, the spark was brighter, which meant sharper.

Praegur grunted and flinched, slapping at his arm and no doubt seeing a small black dot. His gaze shot to the trees, so Falip peered out just enough to reveal their presence.

The Counselor unfolded his arms, then shook his head. A moment later, another sentry who had worn the path around the perimeter walked into view. Chest bare, breeches stained and dirtied, he patrolled with power and confidence.

They would need to time this perfectly. And that couldn't happen on this round. She touched Elinia's arm to stay her, and they both slunk back into the shadows, farther out of sight.

"You spark," she said to the girl, then to Falip, "You catch him."

Both nodded. Then waited as the sentry made the wide circuit. In that time, Praegur had risen and gone to the adjoining cage where Kiethiel looked to him. And though Kedulcya could hear nothing, the Counselor must have spoken, for the princess turned her gaze—only for a second—toward the trees. Then she was on her feet, talking to Praegur, shaking her head. Frowning.

"What are you doing there?" someone shouted, sending Kedulcya and the others into hiding once more. A guard stalked toward the cages. "Get away from her!"

A massive shadow grew beside Kiethiel and became the great raqine. Kedulcya felt herself shudder at the sight of it. By the flames, she hated those beasts, though she knew they were created by Abiassa as well. If she never rode one, it would be a lifetime too soon.

The Ematahri pulled levers and a section of the cage opened—and the young boy moved willingly into the one with the princess.

A knot formed in Kedulcya's stomach. Why were they relocating the lad?

"You. Let's go." They pulled Praegur from the cage and a warrior grabbed his arm and led him past Kedulcya and the others, right into the woods.

To relive himself, she guessed.

"Go," Kedulcya hissed to Falip. "This is our chance."

They sped after Praegur. It might take longer—they'd need to return for the boy and princess. But they could secure the Counselor. And no matter what Gwogh said, Praegur was the point of this endeavor.

They scurried after the two and found them less than fifty paces outside the camp. The man shoved Praegur forward, motioning for him to hurry.

Falip rushed the guard and hooked his neck before he could cry out, snapping him with a bolt and dropping him to the ground.

"The girl," Kedulcya said. "We must hur—"

"No." Praegur's voice was filled with authority. "She will not come."

Elinia gaped. "She has to. She's the Fierian's—"

"She will not," Praegur repeated. "And she said if you try, she will betray your presence to the camp. Her purpose is here with these people. She will not give up yet."

"But the boy—they are both important." Kedulcya stilled, anxious for them. Angry at them. Annoyance flared. The girl had been headstrong for a long time. She glanced toward the camp and through a copse of trees to the cage. Saw Kiethiel staring back through a sliver of space. The girl inclined her head, then shifted away.

"She does not get to decide," Kedulcya bit out. "She—"

"Stop! Sound the alarm! They're—"

Falip sent a fiery dagger at the warrior, felling him even as he turned to run. "Now!" he shouted. "We must go!"

"This way," Praegur said. "To the ravine."

Falip pointed in the opposite direction. "But our horses—"

"Are too slow," Praegur said as he fell into a lope, then a full-out sprint.

With no choice but to follow, their group ran with all their might after the Kergulian who'd been chosen by Abiassa. Kedulcya would trust him. Her legs quickly grew tired. Strangely, it dawned on her that she trusted the Counselor more than she did the Fierian. That was something she would need to amend.

As they broke into a small clearing, Falip grunted. "Great. Now we die in sunlight instead of shade."

Hope vanished. Dread rushed over her, cold and forbidding. There was nothing here but a downy field, fed by a struggling stream. How could she have been wrong? She looked to the Counselor, who shielded his eyes and looked to the sky.

She followed his gaze. Dots blipped, then grew larger. As did shouts and threats from the trees.

"Raqine!" Elinia squealed.

Praegur shared a smile with her, their excitement spilling over to Kedulcya.

She marveled. Again. "But how . . . ?"

Praegur shook his head. "I know not. Only that I wished they were here when I saw you in the trees."

Two of the great beasts descended, and Kedulcya realized Abiassa was going to force her to eat her words. To flee, they would have to ride those beasts.

One, amber coated and amber eyed, landed beside Praegur with a firm thump and satisfied trill. Praegur touched its side, as if thanking the great animal for the rescue, then mounted. He held out a hand to Elinia, who slid atop the beast with little effort.

Should she just die here? Was it better than riding—

"Kedulcya," Falip shouted from the other raqine. "Now."

Swallowing her anxiety, she mounted the beast. They lifted and she squeaked her fright, then clung to Falip like a babe to its mother as they canted to the right then veered away, the furious objections of the Ematahri falling away with the roar of the wind.

●●●

CASTLE KARITHIA, ITEVERIA

"Your bath awaits, sire," Thomannon said.

Haegan dragged himself from the bed, feeling every ounce of exhaustion and aches from the festivities the night before.

Standing on the thick-carved rug, he hesitated. What festivities? Laughter and chaos rang through his head like a gong, but it was a blur—a painting doused with water, colors running, bleeding. Making it impossible to decipher one thought from another. One memory from another.

Surely there had been a party. Why else would he feel so wrecked? When Haegan left the comfort of the carpet, he hissed as frigid marble bit his feet. He hurried, anxious for the heated waters. He nodded to Thomannon and waited for the manservant to leave, then stripped and stepped into the steaming enclosure.

Silky waters rushed over his head and shoulders, enveloping him in warmth and luxury. Strength seeped into his muscles and ligaments. Each day, he lingered here more, savored the rejuvenation longer. In fact . . .

Haegan reached for the knob and twisted it hard right. The panel above shifted back. Water exploded over him in a torrent, allowing more of the falls- and ocean-fed waters to drown him. Pound his body.

Palms against the marble wall, he leaned into the deluge with a moan. Let the water pummel tension knots from his shoulders and neck. He sighed and let out a long, pleasured breath. *Brilliant.* His head felt clear for the first time in . . . ages.

Just a few more days and then the ball.

Wait. Hadn't that ball come and gone?

Water sliding down his face, he stared at his feet, groping for a memory that seemed just . . . out of . . . reach.

No, it's only been a few days. He'd arrived to visit with the Infantessa and return home with a new alliance forged between Iteveria and the Nine. No need to battle Poired. They could talk and live in peace.

But memories, distant yet growing sharper as he focused on them, told him perhaps more than a few days had passed. How long then? A week? A fortnight? Nay, 'twas not that long. Yet how could he explain Trale as a friend now? They'd shared laughs and barbs over the nights.

Nights. More than one. More than a few, he was certain.

Why could he not remember? What ailment seized him? Haegan tilted his head back, frustrated that his brain felt immersed in a vat of murky muck. Blinking, he stared up at the panel that directed the curtain of water.

A dark shape danced on the glass.

His heart hiccupped, and he shifted away. Smeared the water from his face, glancing around. His heart tripped at the thought of someone seeing him in such a state. Where had it come from? He scanned the room, then the glass—

There! Again. Dread coiled as he latched onto the shape. A reflection. Of what? A man. Holding something massive. A stick? *A sword!*

Haegan swung around. Eyed the large arched windows and beyond the balcony. Out over the sea. The city. Nothing. Just the dazzling white set amid a vast emerald forest. Was he going mad?

What then was in the glass? He looked back up at the spot where he'd last seen it. Heat shot through his chest.

The reflection was still there.

"This makes no sense," he muttered as he stepped closer to the panel. Water rushing over his body as he stared up. How could it be there, and yet not . . . out there? Droplets splashed his cheek. He turned to the windows once more. This time, water drenching his vision, he saw. Saw the man in the distance. He pushed his sodden hair from his face, blinking, disbelieving. His eyes lied to him. That man would be . . . monstrous if he was truly that size. Impossible.

"Fierian, you are needed."

The call, the voice, so pure, so hot, coursed through his chest and down into his stomach as if fed by the water itself.

Fierian.

Yes. A strange certainty hit him. He was the Fierian. How could he have forgotten? He scratched his jaw. The fuzz there drew his attention. Nay, not fuzz. Beard. But . . . this much growth told him he had not been here a week. Nor a fortnight. Nausea swirled. Months?

No no no. This could not be.

But how could he argue the facts, the evidence? If it'd been a month, then . . . Grief gripped him. Such negligence! To have so wholly abandoned his course. His calling. His gift.

He must leave. Leave now. How could he have done this? Been so careless? "Have mercy, Abiassa!"

Urgency speared him. In a near panic, he shoved open the glass door, grabbed his robe, and wrapped it around him. Hurrying across the marble floor, he was careful not to slip. His feet hit plush carpet.

So nice. So soft.

It was nice of the Infantessa to provide me a home. To provide friendship. She treats me so well—much better than I was treated in Fieri Keep. Was it not better to be treated well than scorned as a cripple?

A shiver ran through him. He glanced at his still-wet chest and the towel around his waist. What was he doing?

Something . . . outside. An ardent current of emotion pulled at him. Forced him to look out the windows of his room. The waterfall. No, the sea. The sparkling waterfall cascading down the great cliffs to the sea below was so beautiful.

Besides, who could like the smoky skies around Seultrie?

"Sire?"

Haegan whipped around, some scant impression of a dark shape still lurking in his mind as he met the servant's confused expression. "Thomannon." He glanced over his shoulder. Something . . . What . . . ?

"May I help you, sire?"

"I . . ." Haegan coiled his hand into a fist. *What was I doing?*

"Your clothes, sire, are laid out on the bed."

Haegan looked at the tidied bed where a clean, crisp doublet waited. "Of course." Was he going somewhere? "Thank you."

• • •

LEGIER'S HEART, NORTHLANDS

She lay at his side, wrapped in pelts and warmth. Aselan, cacique of the mountain-dwellers, outcast of his own blood, widower, now bound to a princess. Bound by the sacred rights of the Eilidan.

Gently, so as not to wake Kaelyria, he rubbed a strand of her very long, white-blonde hair between his fingertips, which itched to touch her, confirm for the thousandth time that this was no dream. She was his. She had chosen him during Etaesian's Feast. Come with his dagger and a world of beguiling in those ice-blue eyes.

He had argued at first. Told her she knew naught of what she offered. That she was too young, he too old. That he would not war with the thinbloods over her. A lie that sat bitterly on his lips. Truth, he could scarce believe she had come to him that night. That she'd chosen him. Beauty against the black of the mountain—him.

"I can feel you watching me," she murmured, eyes closed. "Still think I misunderstood?" Silken strands spilled across their bed, haloing her porcelain face.

"I think ye've shown me, but I might need more convincin'," he said, his innuendo anything but subtle. He leaned down and gently kissed her shoulder.

She brushed long fingers across his beard. "Although we've known each other but a short while," she whispered as she rolled onto her back, "it seems I've known you all my life." Her kiss was warm, inviting. Intoxicating.

Aselan pressed his lips to the hollow of her throat. With a soft moan, Kaelyria curled into him, sliding her arms around his shoulders as he trailed kisses up her neck, along her jaw, and captured her lips. And once more made her his bound.

Afterward, she lay smiling at him. Touching his beard, as she had grown fond of doing. "Ingwait asked about heirs again."

He kissed the spot near her ear, cupping her face. "'Twill happen in its time."

A low rumble sounded from the floor. Aselan's gaze jerked to the icehounds at the foot of the bed. Duamauri flipped up onto all fours and stood facing the wooden door, growling. Hackles rising.

Drawing the pelt to her shoulder, Kaelyria eyed the hounds as well. "What is it?"

Even as she asked, he heard steps approaching their chambers. "Stay," he ordered the hounds as he slipped into trousers.

"Cacique!" came the shout of Byrin, his first.

Grabbing his leather tunic, Aselan swept aside the pelt curtains that divided his sleeping chamber from the main area. "Come." He threaded his arms through the sleeves as the burly man entered with two others. Alarm coursed through him, noting Byrin's dark expression and the soft movements of Kae behind the curtain. "What is it?"

"The Rekken!"

Aselan stilled. His pulse slowed. Yet sped. "Where?" he breathed, already fearing the answer.

"The Spine."

He pushed his gaze to the rock ceiling, as if he could see across the Cold One's Tooth and the rugged length that ran around Nivar and up to the Violet Sea. He should not be surprised, yet shock pummeled him into action. He snatched his peltcoat. "How have they come so close without an alarm being raised?"

"I know not, but there can be but one answer."

Their farthest scouts were dead. "Ye found them then?"

"Nay, no sign."

Aselan swallowed. The journey from the Violet Sea up to the Spine took more than a month. That meant . . . "The feast." He stuffed his feet into the hide boots. "They used Etaesian's Feast against us." And not just the feast, but the distraction of the men as they got acquainted with bounds and family life. "Gather the Legiera."

Byrin nodded. "In the hall, waiting. But do ye think ye should be goin' out with . . ." His gaze shifted to somewhere behind Aselan. "Ye have more to consider now."

Kaelyria. He felt her presence before she glided up beside him, knelt and assisted with the straps to secure the pelts. "Even my father, king of the Nine, went to war with his men," she said, her voice soft but sure. "I would expect no less from Aselan."

"I beg yer mercy," Aselan said, touching her cheek.

Though she put on a brave face, tears swam, turning those pale irises to ice.

"The hounds will stay with ye."

"Are you sure?" she asked, glancing to Byrin, who seemed just as surprised.

"I'm going to the nest."

"The *nest*?" Byrin balked, his ruddy face reddening. "Are ye mad?"

"I need an aerial view. If there are Rekken on the Spine, where else are they? How close? How many? They seek to attack and we must be prepared."

"If they see ye—"

"I will use care," he growled back. But the danger existed—if anyone saw a raqine come from the tunnels, they could find their way to slaughter the entire nest. "The Rekken have taunted us and Nivar too long. If they are invading, we must know when and where."

"Pharen will no' be happy to see ye waking him before his sleep is over."

"I fear our alarm has already awakened the great beast." Aselan started for the door, then hesitated. Glanced back to Kaelyria. "I'll return." About to leave, he spotted her scarf and snatched it up.

"Something to remember me by?" she asked, a wistful smile on her lips.

Aselan hesitated at the sentimentality she read into action. Yet—

"Aye," Byrin said, pushing him onward.

Thin shoulders straight, she clasped her hands and gave a nod. Duamauri slid up next to her and pressed his flank against her leg. Kae rested a hand on the icehound's shoulder. It was a perfect memory, save one thought—would they ever have a child? And would she survive the birth? His first bound had not.

The haunting memory chased him into the cold passage and past the corridor to the great hall, where a din of nervous chatter filtered out.

"Why did ye stop me from telling her?" Aselan asked.

"What?" Byrin said. "That the scarf was for a raqine so they do not detect her scent and mistake that for another raqine, which would make them think you've abandoned them? Which would make them attack you to defend their territory."

"Aye. That."

"Ye are too thick-skulled to be quick where gentlefolk are concerned, and we don't be needin' any more trouble from the Nine." Byrin huffed as they rounded a corner. "Ye go north then?"

Aselan nodded. "I'll pass over Nivar as well. Be sure there is no danger there."

"Ye just want to be sure the Jujak aren't comin' to take back their princess."

"She's my bound now. They'll be takin' her nowhere." Aselan rushed up the iron steps and down several more passages, making his way to the secret entrance to the raqine nest. Two more turns and he'd be there, so he let out a low whistle. The hearing of a raqine bonded to a rider was not hindered by distance. The great beasts were in tune and intuitive. He ducked behind a large tapestry of Zaelero II and his siblings. Took the switchback maze. And stepped into the musty, earthy nest.

Not two feet from him, bright yellow eyes glared back. Head down, lip curled, Pharen challenged impatiently. Aselan inclined his head, acknowledging the raqine's position. He held out a palm. "I should have known ye'd be waiting." Not the other way around. "Sorry to end yer hibernation early."

Pharen's chortle had a soft tenor, twitching his blue-black fur. He slunk closer, nudged Aselan's hand with his snout, and breathed his acceptance. With a shriek, he suddenly tossed his head. Shook it. Harder. Reared back, eyes now glowing red-gold.

Aselan swallowed hard at the rejection.

"He be smellin' the Mistress on ye," Byrin said.

"Aye." Holding out Kae's scarf, Aselan stood still, confident, as the raqine circled him, sniffing. Showing fear would give Pharen room to refuse him altogether. Confidence told the great winged beast there was nothing to fear.

Pharen muzzle-punched him in the back.

Aselan stumbled forward with a laugh. "Jealous, are ye?"

With a grunt, Pharen shook his head and neck again, then started for the tunnels that led outside. Relief washed through Aselan at not being thrashed. He trotted to keep up with the beast. And the jealousy that had surged through the raqine now rose through Aselan—at those who defiled the Spine to spill blood and steal lands. Upon them, he would deliver vengeance.

4

Vaqar Modia pressed a knee to the coarse surface, rocks biting through his trousers and into the scarred flesh of his leg. Head draped with a wet cloth, he closed his eyes. Closed his senses—at least, he tried. Desperately, he reached for respite. Chose gratefulness for the dampness of the cloth and the land's isolation, far from villages. Far from the reek of the curse.

Peace. He breathed the moisture. Fire flared in his chest, and he touched once more the mark at his side. "Obeisance and fealty first," he said through gritted teeth. "Mind and body last. Her will forever." At least he did not have the torture of scent at the moment. *"Aaeshwaeith Adoaniel'afirema,* I am your servant."

A heat wave warned him of a presence. Instinctively, he stiffened as the scent washed over him, drenching his senses. Spiced, heady. Recognition sparked. Awareness flared with a hefty dose of fear regarding the one who arrived without sound. Vaqar's muscles constricted, but he forced himself to be still and kept his eyes fastened on the charred road.

"Vaqar, Her Servant," the authoritative voice spoke, "I would have your gaze."

He'd heard some had lost their sight for gazing upon one of the Lady's Guardians. Yet they obeyed and were called beloved. He would obey, too.

Vaqar lifted his head, peeking over the edge of the cloth. Let his gaze travel up the light-riddled form to the glorious face.

"Ride west, Vaqar, to the Bay of Wind's westernmost edge."

The towel flapped against his mouth. He sucked in a breath, the cloth suffocating. He snatched it off, only then realizing three things: He now stood alone, the towel had dried, and the air hung rancid.

As my soul, Aaeshwaeith. You know me, yet call me.

Scents of his people assailed him. Anger. Bitterness. Lust. Greed.

With a growl, he cupped the burn in his side and climbed to his feet. He stood, taking in the scene around him. Where great walls once protected the well, now only scraps of torn tarp hung between remnants. Rock gave way to dirt. Horses grazed on tufts of grass that forced their way through cobblestones. Granite steps and columns that had at one time gathered thousands beneath the porticoes and into its coliseum, now stood alone in the unrelenting elements. The treasury office reminded him of himself—a vicious cut struck down half the side wall, just as a blade had left an indelible scar across Vaqar's temple and brow.

Deep betrayal. Like the cut, which had required the skill of a pharmakeia—who complained the entire time.

A hint of laughter pressed between the weighted shoulders of his soldiers. Two knelt playing lots. Most, however, had propped themselves against walls and draped their heads with wet cloths, a method they'd discovered to shield themselves from the assailing scents. A few slept on their sides, arms over their faces. Protecting. And there sat Adassi, arms folded over his chest, which rose and fell evenly in a sound sleep.

Quietly, Vaqar made his way to him and nudged his man's leathered boot.

"What is this?" groused Adassi, coming awake.

"He visited me again." Vaqar squatted against the wall, the stiff cloth between his hands. A terse, bitter scent smacked of disgust. He growled, flaring his nostrils. "Think you this was my choice?"

"Nay," Adassi growled back. "But each time *he* visits, *you* follow. *We* follow."

"Would you stay and have the mark burn you senseless?"

"Better than fighting a plague of scents." The much older Dwaith snatched the cloth from his face. "I would go back to Tahsca, to my bound, to the quiet life of raiding—"

"And being miserable," the more agile Jadrile mumbled.

"You've always been miserable," Haandra taunted her brother as she lay curled on her side, arm shielding nose and mouth. She was the only female among the fifty-three who'd fled Tahsca.

"Aye, miserable," Vaqar repeated lowly, annoyed with their grumbling. "We none of us wanted to spill blood to survive."

"Mayhap," Dwaith said, "but you did not seem to mind when the empress dispatched you."

Grinding his teeth did little to allay the frustration coiling inside Vaqar.

"Aye, he didn't mind—anything to be out of her sight," Adassi said. "We all went ready enough. Do not blame him."

"We must remember who our enemy is," Vaqar warned. "It is not the Westerners, who are as ignorant and complacent as they are pale." He sighed, heart heavy. "And it is not one among our company."

Dwaith threw down his cloth. "This place is too blazing hot. I want the Oasis of Shandalhar."

"The oasis is dried up," Adassi reminded him. "Thanks to that desecrator himself, Poired, there is nothing to return to in Tahsca. The empress has bedded the Dark One and our homes have been ransacked."

"Aye, because he was told of our gift," Jadrile said.

"More like a curse," muttered Dwaith.

"I thought the empress liked you, Vaqar," Haandra said.

Annoyance churned, mixing with his frustration and the fire in his side. "Anithraenia loves two things—herself and power. I served no benefit to her." Forever he would be reminded of her position and his. He pushed to his feet, bent over the well, and dipped his cloth in the murk. When he lifted it, the putrid odor burned his nostrils. Anger. Jealousy.

He stormed to his horse, tying the black-and-gold threaded cloth over his mouth and nose. "Scarve up." When he grabbed the reins, a bitter smell hit him. Warning came with that smell. He responded, trusting the scent more than anything, including himself. Vaqar spun, drawing his dagger fluidly from its sheath, and brought the blade to the throat of his attacker. He stared at familiar gold eyes.

Swift as lightning, Dwaith shoved his arm away.

Vaqar anticipated the move. He had not only height and size on the older man, but also training. Agility. He hopped back, ready. "I would prefer to ride with you than bleed you, but the choice is yours."

Dwaith, stripped of family and position because of this *gift*, stared back with a mixture of fury and defeat. "I can't do it any longer. I can't."

The smells. The confusion. The memories. He understood. Were it not for the vision of the Guardian, he might have been the one trying to slit the throat of anyone who crossed his path. But they would travel west as the Guardian said. And perhaps, She would grant them release from the pulsing in their veins.

Anger waned at the torment in the man's expression and words. "I know," Vaqar muttered as he sheathed his dagger, then spread both hands to the side. "But neither am I your enemy. I am plagued as well. We will sort it." He turned to the others, his immediate circle of friends and warriors. His fifty-two. "We will learn to control this . . . in time. How to shut down the flood. To focus on the one flower floating in the sewer. How to turn it against our enemies and deal them a deadly blow. We are Tahscans!"

"By the sword! With the sword!"

Shouts rang through the empty city in which they'd taken refuge. Another entity gutted of life and happiness.

But the Guardian had promised . . . promised this was a gift, though it had the reek of a curse.

5

An old man sat beside him, too feeble to lift the silver fork to his lips.

"Oh, come now," the Infantessa crooned to the new guest on her right. "Surely you know Prince Haegan."

Wide eyes came to Haegan, then a shaky smile riffled through the man's beard. "O–of course. I . . ." He laughed. "I just thought him younger."

A trilling laugh that needled Haegan's nerves coursed from the Infantessa. "Oh, Councilman Breab. Not everyone can be as young and pretty as I."

"Of course, Infantessa." The old man's gaze flickered. "But aren't you the least worried about the Guardians—"

"Silence!" Her shrill command could have cut stone. It sliced right through Haegan's head. His heart. He doubled, clutching his chest.

"Oh dear," she crooned. "See what you've done, Councilman? You've sickened our prince with your doubt and wickedness."

Haegan hauled himself up straight. *I am a prince. Maybe not a good or useful one. After all, Father abandoned me.*

"Perhaps you should retire for the evening, Prince Haegan," she said.

But wasn't it still day? "Yes," he said, already folding his napkin. "I should rest." *I'm so tired. More than ever before.*

Escorted through the halls by his manservant, Haegan found he needed a little more support than usual. *I'm so weak.*

Thomannon guided him into his bedchamber and, as usual, turned the locks on the door. "I will lay out your nightclothes, sire."

Haegan stood on the thick rug and stared out the window. Something . . . a memory . . . a thought . . . flickered. Sparked. Haunted. Like a bad dream he'd awakened from, losing the fragment as soon as he tried to recall it.

"Would you like warmed cordi, sire?"

"I . . . I'm not sure," Haegan said, his thoughts dulled, slow.

"It's your favorite."

"Oh yes." *It's my favorite.* "Please." His gaze shifted to the bathroom. "And a bath, Thomannon. No, a shower."

"Sire? In the evening?"

An urgency gripped him. "Please." Haegan stalked to the bathroom, shedding clothes, an urge compelling him into the shower. He cared not that Thomannon had yet to prepare or warm the water. That no towels were set out. Water. He cared not. Just . . . the water. *Please, the water.*

Stepping into the glass enclosure, he felt a surge of excitement. Reached for the handle. Turned the knobs. The stream rushed over him, flattening his curls against his eyes and face. As the droplets warmed, so did he. So did his thoughts, clearing as if a fog lifted from Deliverer Bay. Again, he planted his hands against the stone wall and closed his eyes, water kneading away the exhaustion.

He had been so tired. So . . . He shook his head, swiping water from his face.

"Sire?"

"Leave the towels," Haegan commanded, without looking over his shoulder at the servant.

"But sire—"

"There!" Annoyed, he pointed to the bench lining the window. "Leave them—"

Again, a large form loomed in the distance. Riveted Haegan's gaze to it. *What are you?* The answer hung out of reach.

"Sire?"

"Go!" Haegan growled. "Leave me to peace and quiet," he said, staring at the enormous being. Why did he have a sword? He'd seen him before. But this time, the great one wore a terrible scowl.

Voices skittered in and around his mind, haunting. Torturing.

I am weak.

He'd heard the accusation so often in the last few weeks. Or had it been longer? Felt it in his bones. Felt it cut courage from his heart. Breath from his lungs. But this time . . . it wasn't his voice.

He didn't understand. That didn't make sense.

"Because you are weak!" the hissing accusation came again.

The thought wasn't his own.

Then whose was it? "I am losing my faculties," he said, sliding against the wall and crouching beneath the pummeling downpour. He cradled his head. It was almost like the water soaked through his muscles, seeped into his soul.

Yes, please. Wash it away . . . Wash it all away.

What he wanted to wash away, he wasn't sure. Just didn't want to be this person, this Haegan anymore. So weak. And yet . . . His gaze fell to his arm, his biceps. He wasn't weak. The muscles were strong. Not as Father's or Negaer's or even Prince Tili's, but enough. Then why was he always so tired?

"Release the Fierian!"

Haegan started, his gaze snapping to the window beyond the shower enclosure.

"No!" a shriek came from somewhere.

Though heat fogged the glass and the enormous man was far off, Haegan saw without difficulty. Saw glowing eyes that locked onto him, drawing him to his feet once more. Fire roiled, pulling him. Calling him. Something in that man clutched at the frayed tendrils of Haegan's courage. He slapped a hand to the glass that separated them. *Help me. Please.*

"Free the Fierian or face Her wrath."

Voices assailed him. One after another, thumping against his own weak thoughts. Breaking him down, robbing him of even his ability to stand. *Please, no more. Free me. Help me,* he begged the warrior standing on the shore. He leaned against the glass wall as cold water hit his back.

"The fight is yours, Fierian."

Cold water? But steam rose. Panes fogged.

"No! Leave him—he gave himself to me."

"Haegan, help me, sssss . . ."

"Release the Fierian!"

He gave himself to her? How? When? Images, once scattered and floating in the dense fog of his mind, coalesced into one memory: leaving the Citadel, walking away with Trale and Astadia Kath, willingly entering the Infantessa's castle. Not caring if he ever went back.

Those thoughts had not been his own.

No. They had been his. They *were* his. They had been birthed from a single grain of doubt. Like a virulent, self-propagating weed, flourishing beneath the cultivation of sweet words. Her wielding.

Inflaming.

Slowly, numbly, Haegan glanced down at his hands. Blue light warbled around his fingers. Wielding.

He was Haegan. Prince of Seultrie.

Weak. Cripple—if not of body, then of mind.

No. He shook his head, still using the shower wall for support. "No." Those thoughts tasted familiar. They were his own, but . . . not wholly.

"Haegan! Son!"

Jerking straight, he looked around. "Father?" Turned a circle, searching.

"Sire?"

Haegan ignored Thomannon and probed the corners. "Where is he?"

"Haegaaaannn!"

From above. Haegan looked up but saw only the ceiling. "Father!" he shouted, palming the glass. "Where are you?"

"Sire," Thomannon rushed forward, his face a blanket of worry. "Sire, please." Begging. The servant was *begging*, throwing wild, frantic glances over his shoulder. He reached quickly for a towel. "She'll hear you. Please—I beg of you, stop. Here." He extended the towel. "Come out. Dry off. You need rest."

Rest.

His gaze once more rose to the window and out at the trees. Leaves. They had leaves. It'd been winter when he'd journeyed here. Early spring, actually. Scowling, he turned back to the servant. "How long, Thomannon?"

The man's weathered chin trembled. "Sire—please. Just come out and dry off."

The trees had budded. Leaves rustled on the wind. "Spring. Or summer?" Tears welled in his eyes. "How long, Thomannon?"

Defeat sagged against the elder servant. "Nigh two months, sire." He lifted a single shoulder in a shrug. "I know not how long precisely. It was too depressing to count."

"My father—"

The gray-haired servant whimpered, grieved gaze rolling to the ground. "She won't . . . I can't." He lifted his head, shaking it frantically. "Please don't—"

Haegan fisted a hand, arm rotating, the wielding a natural extension of what arose within.

Eyes widening, Thomannon took a step back.

The warbling grew brighter. Fueled him. "Take me to him."

"I can't—"

Flames roiling, Haegan said, "Do it or—"

"Very well." Thomannon flashed his palms in a placating manner. "I'll take you." He held up the towel.

Haegan moved to the door and opened it. He took the thick cloth, dried off, and paused when Thomannon offered nightclothes. "You're to take me to my father."

"Of course. But if she finds you, I can blame it on you sleepwalking again."

"Again." Haegan met the man's eyes. "I've done it before?"

Freezing, the servant nodded.

"Where did I go?"

"I . . ."

This had happened before, but he recalled none of it. Was he so weak—

You are *so weak!*

And why did he care about his father?

He left you in that tower . . .

"No," Haegan hissed, realizing doubts were again throttling his courage. "I . . ." The water. He pushed his gaze to the shower.

"Did you want to go to bed, sire? You were so tired."

Yes, tired.

No! No he was not tired. But his limbs ached. His heart struggled . . . somehow, he'd climbed into a pit of doubt and self-loathing again. He felt it. Felt the difficulty in arguing with . . . His gaze flipped to the servant. "You tricked me," he said around a pound of lethargy.

Because you are so weak!

"You should rest, sire. You'll feel better in the morning."

"No . . ." The water. He let the sight of the shower drag him closer. Another step. Another. Each weighted as if he moved a cornerstone. "I'm tired." His heart lurched, recognizing the inflaming of his thoughts. Urgency sped through him. "No," he growled. "I'm. Not. Tired." He threw himself toward the enclosure.

Something wrapped around his legs.

He pitched forward, and his face rammed hard into the marble floor. Blood gushed from his nose. He cupped a hand over it, turning back, feeling the restraint even still. The servant lay across his legs, clutching him. "Release me!"

"I beg your mercy," Thomannon said, tears in his eyes. "I beg your mercy."

At the grief roiling out of the older man, Haegan slumped, confused. His thoughts tangled. Maybe . . .

Too tired to fight.

Tired of fighting.

What was he fighting anyway?

Why was he on the floor?

6

THE COLD ONE'S TOOTH

Aselan pressed his chest to Pharen's spine as the enormous raqine leapt from the den. A terrifying second of weightlessness sucked his breath before thunderous flaps snapped the cold air and pulsed along Aselan's abdomen as they rose over Legier. The dusting of winter's last stand mingled with the yawning breath of dawn and coated them in a fine mist that sparkled in the early light.

Rumbling, Pharen arched his back. His movement to lift them higher rubbed Aselan, who focused on searching for the Rekken. With snow still covering most of the mountain, it should not be hard to find the invaders or to ascertain their number.

A shadow glided into his periphery. Ebose flew closer, bearing Byrin. Though his man was supposed to stay behind and protect, it bolstered Aselan to have a second pair of eyes watching. The scouts had reported the Rekken on the Tooth, so they would fly north, staying high to avoid dropping shadows or hints that they were aware of the attack. Better to keep the enemy unsuspecting. Let them think they had the advantage.

With the sun rising, they angled farther west before aiming north, beginning their search on the still-shadowed western slope of the Tooth. They then made their way over the peak and eastward to avoid inadvertently casting raqine-shaped shadows right on top of the enemy.

They rode in silence for nearly a half hour, the cold chomping into them. Gliding on the currents made it easier on the raqine, but colder for the rider. Legier's bite was a threat, even with pelts and hides.

Byrin pointed to the side.

With a nod, Aselan used his knees and subtle pressure from his palms to guide Pharen along the southernmost rise of the Tooth. As they maintained altitude and speed, he leaned down, peering over the ridge of the wing as the terrain slid past. Pristine, a mottle of dark green against white, it was a beauty he would never take for granted. But something snagged his eye.

"Hyup," he huffed to Pharen, pressing his hands and knees against the raqine's sides.

With a chortle and rumble beneath Aselan's legs and hands, Pharen flapped his wings twice and pulled up, higher . . . higher. They came around and repeated the course, Aselan urging the raqine into a glide. In seconds, they were over the spot—and he saw it. Through light-falling snow and dew of morning—a puff of snow.

Movement. Someone down there had leapt for cover.

Aselan cursed. After the care they'd taken not to be spotted . . .

Using hand signals, he notified Byrin to circle back and watch for movement. Aselan would continue north, searching for more Rekken, while Byrin would attempt to sight and identify the person trekking along the Spine. They separated and Aselan relaxed as he and Pharen scouted.

They'd gone no more than a few leagues when they left behind the heights of the Tooth and passed over lower elevations, where the beauty of winter gave way to the sludge of spring thaw. The dark color stark and—

Aselan's gut clenched, realizing it wasn't the mountain below him but an entire army. Hundreds.

He swallowed. Hard. How . . . ? Why?

Even as he urged Pharen around, the blue-black glint of his fur blurred with the sea of Rekken. They'd made the turn when a whistling pierced the air. Aselan's heart climbed into his throat as he recognized that sound—arrows!

"Hyup hyup hyup!" he shouted, but the raqine had already sensed the threat and banked left. Then right.

Flapping hard, Pharen shot upward.

Aselan clenched fur to stay mounted, but the vertical climb made it seem as if the Tooth clutched his legs, pulling him down. He growled against gravity's grip and held. But with each snap of Pharen's wings,

Aselan felt himself slipping. His thoughts flipped to Kaelyria. If he died . . . what then? What would she have? Who would be her ally?

Ally? He cared not—he did not want to leave her. Their time together had been short but the best he'd experienced in many years. To his amazement, he loved her.

Pharen wavered and screeched.

Something was wrong.

Even as he had the thought, he felt the raqine level out high above the Tooth. The ride had become choppy and faltering. Aselan glanced to his left and saw the problem—an arrow had pierced Pharen's left wing. He was losing blood and altitude.

Could they make it back to the nest?

Pharen's sudden descent answered the question. Aselan gripped tight, knowing he must guide the raqine to safety. And this far from the nest without the ability to fly, there was only one option.

No. There had to be another. Anything else.

But it seemed Pharen knew the truth of the situation, because he folded his wings in and dove. Headlong for Nivar Hold.

• • •

LIRWEN

Barreling toward the huddle of Sirdarians who had pinned down a ragged band of Jujak protecting some villagers on the outskirts of town, Tili reached out with a clawed hand, then coiled it, twisting as he drew it back to his side. He threw the fiery bolt with a growl. It struck the first armored soldier then splintered, scattering Sirdarians as they dove for cover. Tili swung his leg over the cantle of his saddle and effortlessly dropped to the ground, then sprang forward, thrusting with one hand, extracting with the other as he collided with the first Sirdarian.

Around him, Negaer's men fought the scarlet-clad enemy. Steel sang. Blood flowed.

He drew his sword, far preferring the earthy reality of steel to the ethereal giftings that had landed him in the middle of this insane battle for a kingdom not his own.

A particularly large Sirdarian came at a villager in a flurry of rotating arms and bands of fire.

Tili startled at the agility. It was almost graceful, in a terrifying, haunting way. A scream punctured his thoughts, reminding him of what he fought for. He speared the man in the leg, making the incipient stumble.

Surprise streaked the man's face, then he turned to Tili. Sneered. Flicked out a half-dozen daggers—one from each finger it seemed.

Deflecting with one hand required a bit of a dance. Tili again wished for more formal training in the wielding arts, but it had been forbidden in the North. He could but pray his father's decree would not mean Tili's death.

Fire seared his cheek. Though he refused it attention, Tili felt another bolt bleed his calf. He shifted his weight and thrust back. But his flames were diverted effortlessly. The incipient advanced.

Tili tripped as a bolt crackled against his ankle.

Steel sang and sliced the incipient's neck, dropping him.

From the fallen man's right, Tokar held out a hand, which Tili gladly accepted and struggled onto shaky legs. "Are they all so skilled?"

Cocking his head toward the body, Tokar grunted. "He was a Silver. Trained by Poired himself. They're especially cruel and swift."

Shifting his gaze to the dead incipient, Tili noted the silver cords.

"They're dressed down to disguise themselves as they move among the villages, eliminating any threat to Poired's advance. Gathering accelerants in the hopes of turning them, and killing everyone else, especially Jujak."

Wiping the blood from his face, Tili shook his head. *Have we so little hope of success?* "Thank ye for—"

"Steward!"

Tili pivoted and found Negaer trotting up on his horse, leading Tili's.

The general's sweaty face was flecked with blood, dirt, and grim determination. "We've rounded up another ten Jujak. Apparently they've been guarding three-dozen or so villagers here since Hetaera fell. This is the third attack they've faced this week."

A few more soldiers to fight. Many more mouths to feed. But he could not leave them behind. He nodded, swiping a hand over his beard. "Gather supplies and let's clear out before more Sirdarians or Silvers"—his gaze again hit the blade-garroted man—"arrive."

"Agreed," Negaer said. "But with sick and wounded, the pace will be too slow for—"

"Take cover! Take cover!" someone shouted. "Raqine!"

"Poired!" another choked out.

Tili instinctively shoved his gaze skyward rather than take cover. Raqine might be feared in the Nine, but they were a familiar sight in the Northlands. Yet he was reminded that there weren't any raqine this far east. Stalking to the shelter of a single-story structure, he looked again to the white-blue expanse above.

"There," Tokar said, pointing west.

Two shapes slid across the hazy sky and approached the razed village.

"Archers!" Negaer shouted.

"Wait!" Tili called, watching as the great winged beast circled. "They're not attacking!" They were landing. His heart thudded at the patch of red on the belly of the smaller one. He breathed a laugh. "Draed!" His gaze skipped to the other. Rippling red fur revealed blue roots. "Umoni!" He cupped his mouth and did a raqine call. Though they could never be called, they often responded to the trilling sound. And the two did—they arced in their descent to hover over him.

Wings tilted skyward, sharp claws pointed to the ground, the raqine alighted with a solid thud on either side of him. Relieved to see the two, he wondered—

"Praegur!" Tokar rushed forward.

"No!" Tili's shout was lost to the bellowing yowl from Umoni and Draed, who took the sudden burst of movement as a threat. Draed dropped his front paws and bared his teeth in a ferocious growl, sending the newly minted lieutenant scurrying backward.

"*Never* approach a raqine like that," Tili barked, noticing the four people the raqine divested onto the street of Lirwen. An old woman, a young woman, Haegan's friend and counselor, and a man. Where was his sister? His pleasure at the raqine's familiar presence receded. Gwogh had said he'd sent Thiel to the Ematahri with Praegur and the boy, Laertes.

"Steward," the old woman said as she slid clumsily from Umoni's back, "while I am glad to see you are still alive, I am disappointed to find you have made so little progress."

Irritated with her condescension and the insinuation that he was failing in his duties, Tili inclined his head only slightly. "Councilwoman." He glanced at Haegan's friend. "I beg yer mercy, but how do ye have the raqine? They—"

"Ask me not, young steward. It was not my doing." She nodded to Praegur. "The boy said he wished it and they came."

Tili redirected his questions to the dark-skinned boy, face wreathed in innocence but eyes burgeoning with wisdom. "Ye brought them?"

He nodded, as if he'd done nothing more amazing than don a tunic.

"Praegur is the Fierian's Counselor," Kedulcya said. "Abiassa knew he must return to the Fierian, so she sent the raqine to ferry him there."

"Then why stop here?"

"Because we cannot risk the raqine," Kedulcya said, looking to the beasts. "They are needed for the final battle. The more they fly, the more risk of them being shot from the sky—I heard even your general call for archers." She looked around the gathered soldiers. "Where is Sir Gwogh?"

"Gwogh?" Negaer asked, joining them. "Why—"

The woman nodded sternly. "He said he would come this route. We must gather accelerants and Jujak and make for Vid, so the Fierian has an army to use."

"We have seen no councilmembers nor accelerants," Tili said. "Councilwoman, what word from the Ematahri? Where is my sister, Kiethiel?"

After a long pause, Kedulcya held his gaze, resolution touched with pity in her eyes. "The Ematahri play host to Sirdar. I and my companions were sent to retrieve our emissaries. Your sister refused to come. You have my sympathies, Steward."

Tili took a step forward, anger shooting through him. "What do ye mean, refused to come?"

"Thiel had work yet to do. She is in Abiassa's hands," Praegur said, and Tili took note of the finality of his tone. This was the one that didn't speak, wasn't it? And yet he spoke. To Tili. Said Kiethiel wasn't done. Something whispered to accept the words. To trust Thiel to her path.

"Hey, can someone call off this . . . thing?" Tokar muttered, drawing their attention.

Draed had skulked closer to the young lieutenant, hackles still up and clear irritation homed on Tokar. Heat wakes rippled over his spine. His fur shook, as if he were trying to shed Tokar's existence.

"I'm afraid ye've made a bad impression," Tili said.

"Yeah, well, so did he." Tokar arched away from the catlike creature that prowled closer. And closer. "Blazes, Tili, call him off."

Tili scoffed. "Ye can't call off a raqine."

Now, Draed pressed his nose to Tokar's breeches. Then dragged his damp snout up the man's leg and side.

"Tili . . ."

"Just stand very still. Let him inspect ye. He needs to trust ye."

"Yeah, that's not happening, I'm pretty sure," Tokar muttered as the snout rose to his chest, staining his green tunic darker with heated, moist breath.

Draed's ears flattened as he came nose to nose with Tokar. The beast took several deep breaths.

"Blazing thing looks ready to sear the life out of him," someone muttered.

Drawing his head back, Draed took in a sudden draught.

Oh no.

And with a lurch, he sneezed.

Tokar fell backward. Landed on his back, his face full of steaming, sticky, milky-gray ooze.

Draed shook his snout, flinging more snot as he turned from the crowd and stalked back to Umoni, who sat watching with squinted eyes, observing the way Draed defended her. Almost amused.

Laughter bubbled around the crowd of Jujak and villagers as Tokar picked himself and his pride off the ground. Wiping his sleeve over his face cleared some of the goo but did nothing to remove the humiliation.

Tili bit back his smile, but their gazes connected and betrayed him.

"You *knew* what he was going to do!"

"Not until it was too late."

"I hate those things!" Tokar growled. He accepted a cloth from a villager and worked to clean his face.

"Steward, we must make for Vid."

Tili glanced at the Councilwoman, then at Negaer, who knew their true purpose. Gwogh had said their mission to find Haegan would be a secret, but he had not imagined it would be kept from the Council. "Begging ye pardon, Madam Kedulcya, but ye were there in the base of

Mount Medric when Gwogh sent me after the prince. We"—he glanced to the others—"make for Unelithia as instructed once supplies are gathered and the villagers ready."

"Then I ride ahead after we reach Caori."

"I can afford no man to guard—"

The woman turned a steely gaze on him, and suddenly he felt like a boy again. "You mistake me, Steward. I ask neither for your permission nor help."

• • •

HETAERA

Smoke rose in lazy tendrils from the ruins of Hetaera. The only unscathed structure remaining in the great city, the Spire of Zaelero seemed an odd and ridiculous sight amid the ruin. The sun taunted the depressed city as the smoke spirals wavered, affording a sliver of light to break in and stab the spire's golden orb, then throw its glare into the eye of the downtrodden. Curling smoke came not from burning buildings, which had been gutted weeks ago, but from the continual pyres upon which the diseased dead were disposed. Included in their number were many Jujak left to defend the city and slaughtered with glee by the madman who'd stolen power.

Drracien Khar'val stood at the window, hands clasped behind his back, feet spread shoulder-width apart. Never had he imagined the great Citadel would fall so easily. That the home he'd known for nearly ten years would collapse in defeat.

He sensed the rear approach and hoped—no, *willed* the intrusion not to happen. But with a swirl of red and burnt-earth smell, Poired joined him. His shape, a mirror of Drracien's—not just in height, but in the way they stood—made Drracien want to drive a fiery bolt through the Dark One's heart.

"It has been three weeks since we took the city," Poired hissed.

"And your very skilled Maereni, the most vicious of your fighters, still haven't found Gwogh."

Acidic eyes turned on him. "You sound pleased."

"Amused," Drracien corrected. "Gwogh and the Council of Nine will continue to be a problem if you cannot subdue them. If you had allowed me to—"

"Your place is with me."

"It was not always. You abandoned me."

In a blaze of Poired's fury, Drracien flew backward. He braced for the impact—a second too late. Pain exploded across his shoulders. Punched the breath from his lungs. He dropped hard as darkness snatched his vision.

In a wind-torn thought, Drracien lay on a blackened surface, staring up at Poired, who crouched over him, hand on his chest. Eyes blazing red. Face gaunt and hollow—not the old man with short-cropped hair, but an incorporeal conglomeration of black wisps and flayed flesh. Searing agony wormed through his chest at the touch of the man who'd given him birth.

Drracien gripped the tormenting hand in both of his and pushed.

"Get up." Poired's command scraped at his ears.

Blinking, he complied with the Dark One's words, which seemed to have hands that moved Drracien outside his own will. On his feet, he looked around. Found more of the same flayed-flesh beings. "Where—what is this?"

"The Void." Poired's hulking form glided across an unseen floor or road.

As he moved farther away, strangulation closed around Drracien's throat. Only then did he realize the other beings were clawing at him. With terror, he jerked free and scrambled—and yet he didn't. His moves were muddied. Sluggish.

"Stay close or be lost to eternity."

Rubbing his throat and arm, he glowered. "Might have said that before they strangled me."

"You are my heir. They will not harm you."

"They strangled me!"

Poired stopped sharply. Spun. Glowered. "This is the Void."

"And is that supposed to mean something—beyond being terrifying?"

"We are not corporeal here."

Light-headed at the words, he glanced at his own hands, surprised to find them as frayed and flayed as the rest. Surprised to see distortions of color bend around them. If he was not in a body here, then . . . "I don't need to breathe."

Poired inclined his head with an arcing brow and started moving again. This time faster. Steps clipped, intent.

"Is there a hurry?"

"We lost her for several weeks—she ran after upending everything I had worked toward for the last decade. The Maereni have located her."

"Ah. Then they're good for something." Drracien knew better than to mock the Maereni. "Wait. Located who?"

"A traitor," the Dark One spat. "A vile witch who has conspired against me from the start, though I have provided for all her needs. Though we had an arrangement. She has sacrificed her soul on the altar of her arrogance to think she can outrun me."

"A lover's quarrel." Drracien snorted, his stomach roiling. Uh . . . He placed a hand over his abdomen and glanced down. Did he even have a stomach here?

"Do not be so childish. I have no need for love. It is a wasted effort. We have one goal—to deliver his will to this rotting planet."

"Why? Why are we doing his work?" He motioned around them. "Look at the power we have!"

Poired spun. At the sudden move, his frayed flesh swirled in vapors around him, forcing Drracien to stop short or tumble into—through?—the Dark One. A gnarled hand reached toward him. "We have no power without him." Then he smiled. "You are a quick study. I knew you would be. Saw it in your rapid advancement at the Citadel." Which was far too creepy, to think about the Dark One monitoring his academics. "Soon you will not need me to walk the Void. Your transference is nearly complete."

"Trans—" Agony ripped at Drracien. His ears popped and he stumbled forward, finding himself corporeal once more. He turned his palm over, surprised at the way the fading . . . faded. The way his flesh solidified and the surroundings took on greater density.

Alarm kicked his gut when he realized they were no longer in the Citadel overlooking the city. They now stood in a hovel. One that reeked of waste and rot. He dared not move, afraid he might trip back into the Void, but he darted a look around. A large fireplace. Table with two chairs, one broken. A moldy lump of bread on a broken plate. Murky water in a tin cup. "Where are we?"

"This home—"

"No." Drracien again took in the place. "No, *where* are we? As in, this isn't the Citadel. I *know* the Citadel, every alley and nook."

Amusement glinted as the Dark One smirked, then gave a slight nod. "Caori."

"Caori?" Shock pushed Drracien back a step. "But that's a hundred leagues from the Citadel!" He shoved his hair from his face, grappling with the reality that they'd traversed two countries in the span of a few minutes. "Why?"

Morning light caught the gold fibers of Poired's overcloak, its sleeves and hem and collar embroidered with flames and strange symbols. In fact, every inch of the cloak had been embroidered with black thread. Symbols upon markings and markings upon symbols. That ebony stitching made the red and gold threads stand out even more with his nearly white hair. "You mean," he said as he opened a tattered book sitting on a table and let the pages flutter closed, "why have I brought *you* here?"

Drracien gritted his teeth. "Another lesson, then?" It seemed the Dark One felt he must cram lessons Drracien missed from the last twenty years into the fortnight he'd been with him, teaching him, instructing him, making Drracien into his own dark image.

"Isn't that what all of life is?"

"We learn from mistakes so we do not repeat them." It had been a mistake to follow Haegan. In doing so, he'd been so intent on keeping eyes on the prince, he'd noticed too late the Maereni sent to retrieve him.

"A noble concept, but flawed." Poired stilled, stared into the space between them, then gave quick signals to his guards. He'd detected someone's presence. He had an uncanny ability with that. "Mistakes are made when our loyalties are divided, when our attention is divided."

Hardness edged into his expression, tightening the knot in Drracien's gut. Loyalties. Attention. What was Poired afraid would distract Drracien? The way he watched him, the intensity roiling through his eyes told Drracien he should know. He should have anticipated the answer.

"Everything always has a purpose with you," Drracien said. "So—yes, why am I *here*?"

Poired smiled. "You're going to dispatch a traitor to the Void."

Dispatch. The beings that had clawed at him—were they the dead who'd been dispatched? The thought made his skin crawl. "You mean kill." But who? His mind rent the moment, recalling the words from the Void. "The woman you mentioned." But *what* woman? The Dark One was not known to have dalliances. He himself said love was a wasted effort, especially when busy destroying the world.

When his gaze struck a coat hanging limp on the wall, Drracien recoiled. Nondescript tattered material meant nothing. Revealed nothing. It was the twisted metal that stabbed the lapel. Nausea swirled as ice sped through his veins. He swung his gaze to Poired. "You can't—"

A scream severed his objection. Thuds and shouts preceded shadowed forms on the other side of the opaque window. The door flung back and four Maereni dragged in a writhing woman—no. They weren't touching her. And none were wielding. Drracien's gaze moved to the Dark One. With a nearly lazy effort, he held the woman beneath a band of wielding. He sneered and yanked her forward. Her face smashed against the wood floor.

With a strangled cry, Drracien recognized the woman.

Elara Khar'val. His mother!

Palms sweating, he froze. *Please.* The word clawed through his mind, his chest, and dug into his heart. *Please.* But to voice it—utter the plea and she would be boiled out before his very eyes. There would be no chance. No salvation for her. No perfectly spoken words to buy her life. She would die.

Yet if he allowed Poired to murder his mother—"Please."

"Please!" she cried out, her beseeching wail colliding with Drracien's and drowning it. Swallowing it.

His heart thudded as he stared at the bent woman and half wondered if Poired had heard his betraying plea. Shame beat him that he worried more for himself than the woman destined to lose her life.

Ash-colored hair, peppered with age and dirt, hung in tangles that shielded her face. Head shaking, she sobbed so deeply it heaved her shoulders.

"Killing her," Drracien said, his voice a tightly controlled tremor, "does not remove the attachment. She is my mother. That cannot—"

Elara went closer to the warped wood planks, a strangled yelp spiraling up from her.

"*Raising* you does not mean she was your mother." Calloused, unfeeling words, meant to temper Drracien's attachment to the woman weeping on the floor. "I brought you to her as a babe after your mother, a woman I knew before the war, died giving birth."

Uncertainty slashed Drracien's resolve. He considered his mother— Elara. She hadn't given birth to him? Is that why she had never favored him with affection? He snapped his gaze to the Dark One. To the roiling irises. "She raised me. She tended my needs."

"Did she?" Poired circled her, the hem of his long black cloak—much like the one Drracien now wore—floating above the heat wake matting his mother's hair to her scalp. "Will you tell me that she gave you clothes? That she paid for scholars and tutors? That you ate the choicest meats?" Hatred flared through the man's features. That straight nose, so like Drracien's. The fiery eyes that seemed to change with wielding. The slight yet muscular frame.

Gaze falling on his mother, Drracien hesitated. He hadn't learned to read until he'd entered the Citadel, then he'd devoured every book in reach—all the ancient, musty texts. Clothes? Most were inches too short or torn, the castoffs of others. That is, until he'd entered training.

Training.

"You." Disgust slashed him as he lurched toward the Dark One. "You sent Aloing to bring me to the Citadel. He colluded with you?"

"No." Poired's jaw clenched then relaxed. "I could no more stand that pompous, self-righteous accelerant than the next incipient. But when one of my Maereni reported you stealing from the baker and butcher, I investigated. I . . . encouraged the High Lord with a hefty donation to the Citadel."

So it *had* been him. Drracien had wondered how he'd ended up at the Citadel when he'd so expertly hidden his gifts.

Poired's leather riding boots shone beneath the embers of his wielding as he rolled his fingers at Elara. "Tell me, witch. What did you do with the coins I sent? You spent them on the dregs and those brats of yours."

Dolin and Dati. His brother and sister.

"They were your brats, too," she hissed. "That money was my payment for enduring your stench!"

With a flash, she slid across the room and slammed against the stone hearth. A crack sounded through the room. She screamed as her body crumpled against the wood.

So, his siblings *were* his siblings, even if they only shared a father.

"She betrayed me, failed me, and stole my money for years before I learned the truth." Eyes narrowed, Poired stalked toward him. "She was paid handsomely the years you were in her home, and you had naught to show for it save a severe work ethic, calloused palms,"—he lifted Drracien's hands—"and a hunger that drove you to crime."

He remembered the hunger. The desperation to eat. To fill the growl in his gut that seemed like a desecrator clawing out of his belly. Painful. Weakening.

"Does this anger you?"

It did. But what did it matter now? Drracien slid a look in his mother's—Elara's direction. There, amid her trembling, he found wild green eyes beneath stringy strands of dirty blonde hair. Her gaze darted from him to Poired.

"Why?" he found himself asking. "Why did you deprive me?"

She shook her head, drawing in her hands as she gathered herself into a sitting position.

"You'll lie to him as well?" Poired's words were quiet, amused and yet furious. "When he stands with me. When he knows the truth of what you've done?"

"I . . ." She shook her head, looking more like one addicted to the roots than a woman in possession of her faculties. "I wanted—"

"You *wanted*?" Drracien found himself towering over her. "*I* wanted! I was starving and all I wanted was food. Five years old, scurrying with the rats through tunnels to find a scrap."

More headshaking denials. "It wasn't—"

"I might understand that you did that to me. I wasn't your child. But to do that to the twins . . . your own children." Drracien liked the twins—they were good kids. "To what end? To torture us with starvation?"

"So you wouldn't end up like him!" she spat.

"Starve us. Demean us." He noticed the warbling wake from his fingers and didn't care. "Disgrace us and yourself. All to *what*? Teach us not to be evil? Is this not evil, what you have done to those who depended on you?"

"N-no." Shaking fingers stretched toward him. " P-please. I . . ."

"How many times," Drracien growled, "did Dolin and Dati *beg* for food? How many times did I hold Dati while she cried herself to sleep for the hunger that ate at her? How many times did I steal and end up having the constable bring me home?" Breathing grew hard. Warbling tingled his fingers. He focused the heat. "And you would beat *me*. To teach me, you said."

Her face blanched.

Fear.

Yes. Good. "You should be afraid." How had he gotten close enough to smell her breath? Her foul breath. He pushed from his crouched position back to his feet, animosity tumbling through him.

"Ask her about the money you donated to them from your allotments as a student of the Citadel. Anonymously, I believe, but your money all the same."

Heat stabbed between Drracien's shoulders. How had Poired known about that?

"Does this hovel look like one your money has paid for?" the Dark One asked. "Where did she spend the money you sent?"

Anger, hot and violent, surged through Drracien. But he fought it. Knew Poired sought to drive his rage.

"Please!" Elara cowered. "I only—"

"Ask her where the children are now."

Alarm pierced what little remained of Drracien's control. Stricken at the fate they could have met, he searched the hovel. No children. No doll. No food. No sign of them.

Sobs wracked the woman's skinny body. This was not his mother. This was not even the woman who raised them. This was a shell of a person. He straightened, the warbling strong and beating his cloak against his legs.

"End her. Now!" Poired commanded. "End her betrayal."

"Where are the children?" Drracien demanded. "Dolin! Dati!" he shouted, looking toward the lone room separated by nothing more than a ripped sheet. With a lunge, he surged around Poired. Hurried to the room, angry he had not thought of the twins sooner. Not noticed their absence. Slapping aside the thin barrier gave him little pleasure. The space lay bare, save a pile of straw and a sheet with dark stains.

They're dead.

"The Scourge has claimed many victims," Poired explained casually.

"They're *dead*?" Drracien demanded as he stormed toward Elara, who shouted and threw herself backward. Only then he realized the flames roaring off his fingers. "Are they dead? Where are they?" he said, his voice a razor-sharp whisper as he crouched over her.

She only stared. Gave no answer.

He speared her with a vicious spark.

With a yelp, she flopped against the dirty floor, cradling her side. "I don't know!"

"They are your children! How can you not know if your own children are dead?" Fingers clawing the air, he drew back. "Tell me! Tell me where they are!"

Wagging her head, she cried. "I don't know."

Screwing up his face, he drew his hand backward and pulled in a massive wake of heat.

Her green eyes widened, tears marking dark rivulets down her face. "No no no! I don't know. I promise!"

"Your promises mean nothing!" He pulsed her, the heat slamming her head back against the boards with a sickening crack that yanked a yelp from her. "Tell me!"

"They were taken."

"Taken?"

Curling in on herself, Elara surrendered to her pain.

"Where?" he growled, pulsing heat waves over her, reddening her cheeks and blistering her face. *"WHERE?"*

"The mines," she wailed.

He stumbled.

Slaves. Children using their bare fingers to dig out near-molten rock to make more swords, more armor for Poired's army.

His heart jammed against the thought. Rage roiled. "I gave you money! Every month!" Wielding focused, he hoisted her from the ground so he could look into her eyes. "I gave you *every* coin I had. And this—*this* is what you do to them?"

She sobbed.

"They. Were. Innocent!"

"No—"

Drracien unleashed his fury.

Spine arched over the floor, she howled as heat boiled through her.

7

Brittle blades of wheat swayed, scritching against his trousers as Tili crouched in a narrow crook. 'Twas the only vantage that gave him the slenderest of peeks at both Hetaera in the northwest and Vid in the far northeast. This bump in the land, which the locals had named Lake Mountain, had neither lakes nor the height to be called a mountain. Not like those he'd grown up beneath. But the name had been given because the hill in this sad scrape of land was no more than a few leagues west of the Bay of Winds. Which was a lake. Not a bay.

Tili scrubbed his scalp and let out a sigh. He'd never understand thinbloods.

Propped against the rocky incline that spilled down onto the more even terrain of the plains of Vornesse, Tili squinted. Pressed his sight as if he could reach far beyond the Citadel, straight through Baen's Crossing, the Black Forest, and up into Ybienn. He closed his eyes, forced himself to remember the chill, which was hard when sweat plastered his tunic to his spine. To recall the scent of pines and winter's breath.

Father, that I could have yer counsel . . .

A word. Instruction. A laugh, even. Maybe a remonstration. He'd take any of it, just to hear a familiar voice. What would Father think of him slipping away from his detachment to seek solace? To find . . . direction.

Days passed without progress in reaching Haegan, then a week. Two. Three. Their band had twice come upon and absorbed stragglers who'd abandoned villages, and three times engaged small contingents of Sirdarians bent on pillaging the land. Praegur, the girl, and the Council members were still with them, to the chagrin of the soldiers, who grew tired of the councilwoman's insistence on cutting north. Negaer, thankfully, had handled her. There seemed to be some history between the old pair. When Negaer lost his temper and shouted that they were doing their best and did she have a better way to deal with packs of enemy between them and their goal, she had finally taken his frustration for what it was: evidence of genuine effort.

The dangers of driving north—lack of food, lack of water, greater risk as they edged closer to the route Poired had used in his razing—grew with each passing day. Food stores were dwindling and their number rising. They'd gained two-dozen Jujak in the last week alone, a surviving remnant from hundreds, and countless civilians. How fared Ybienn and the Hold? There, he had looked to his father for counsel on all matters, as obligation demanded of the commander of the Nivari. Who commanded Nivar's elite now? Aburas most likely, though the old goat hated command.

"I'm too mean. If it's me orders I be shovin' at them, they'll hate me. But shovin' yer orders—I can be mean and still do that." Tili felt himself breathe through a smile at the memory. Truth told, he had never seen a man better suited for command than the burly colonel. So, it must be Aburas.

What of Relig? Did his bride yet carry a Thurig heir?

An ache wormed through Tili, bitter, sweet. Cruel. His gaze scanned the gnarled fingers of the leafless trees. Shrubs with prickly leaves that would probably survive a cauldron. Drought. Barrenness. Was this his life now? Where was the good, the beauty?

"The only time protecting the realm is pretty is when I'm with yer mother." His father's near-facetious words rang in his head. Tili may not have his father in person, but he would always have him—his words—within.

"May I do ye proud, Father," Tili whispered.

A sound rattled, stilling him. He cast his gaze—and only his gaze—down and to the side, listening. He eased off the rock, his senses awakening, pulling out of the past.

That noise—a distant rumble. Riders. Many of them. The sound was distinct and worse, threatening. Who would be riding out this far and in this number?

Tili whirled up and around the rock he'd used for support, trained on the approaching thunder. He slunk along the shoulder-high barrier. Technically, they weren't in enemy territory, but boundary lines had vanished with Poired's decimation of the Nine.

He slipped down one level of the incline. Along another of jutting rocks and defiant shrubs. Between the scraggly branches, he spied movement a league off but not well enough to identify uniform or sigil. If there was one. Tili nested in a rock gap. He stared down the hill separating the mounted army on the north from his mismatched contingent of Jujak and Pathfinders on the south.

It was a sea of red bleeding in from the east. "Sirdarians." From Unelithia, Tili guessed. *We are so close to their blades. So far from help.*

Steps crunched behind him and Tili spun.

General Negaer climbed the path, his broad shoulders momentarily spanning their encampment below. Even as the general set boot on even ground, two shapes morphed from the shadows.

Adrenaline spiked at the sight of the two Pathfinders, Tili realized he had never truly been alone with his thoughts. He raked the two men with a glare, both in awe that they'd so stealthily paced him and in frustration that they had not granted him solitude.

Negaer nodded toward the clearing. "You've seen them, then."

"Sirdarians. At least a hundred."

"Seems they've infested every inch of the Nine," he groused, his weathered face a stone mask. As usual. Where was his concern? His worry for those under his command? Those depending on him? Nearly seventy men were encamped at the southern base of Lake Mountain. Hands behind his back, Negaer eyed the north. Why was he not worried?

"Should we not make for the trees again?"

"No need."

"No—" Wait. Tili took in the general. Hands behind his back. Keen hazel eyes assessing. He stood like one monitoring sparring matches, as Tili had over the Nivari training yard. So what did Negaer know or see that Tili had not? He set aside his discomfited response and turned his attention north.

Sirdarians flooded down the lip of the valley toward stone ruins that littered the ground. Great buildings had been brought to their knees beneath the ravages of time.

"Little Hall," Negaer said. "It was the last trade stop south of the mountain and before Baen took back Wicalir from Unelithia. Named Little Hall because it was commissioned by the Baron of Ironhall, Glomain the Great."

"Ironhall—I read of it." Tili bit his tongue, refraining from sharing the true histories, which many of the Nine did not adhere to. But Ybienn, Baen's daughter and the one from whom Tili's line had been born, commissioned the building of Ironhall for her husband.

"That will break your heart," Negaer said. "One of the first cities Sirdar attacked—and with a vengeance. It has long been in ruins. I remember visiting as a lad."

"Ye were there?" Disbelief coiled around Tili's mind.

"Careful now, young steward. That sounds like you're saying I'm old." Negaer pointed to Little Hall. "There are hundreds of refugees hidden in the catacombs and buildings."

A scream stabbed the hot air as someone shot across the path of the Sirdarians. Blinding white, a streak spiraled from the contingent and struck the woman. Smoke and fire consumed her.

"They have an incipient," Negaer muttered. And for the first time, concern creased his brow.

"A Silver?"

"I think not." Negaer considered him. "Silvers are always incipients, but incipients are not always the Dark One's elite fighters."

Tili nodded. "Should we go—"

"Nay. Watch."

Screams and shouts went out as the Sirdarians leapt from their horses and swept across the ruins. Tili's gut cinched. "I pray yer mercy, but I was not made steward to watch innocents slaughtered."

"Look at them," Negaer said, a curl in his lip, "so blazing arrogant. Confident they will not be opposed, let alone defeated."

As if obeying the general's command, the Sirdarians dismounted, formed lines in the crumbling city, and waited as their leader trotted down the center on his mount, then swung around to face his horde.

"Oppose them?" Tili scoffed. "They have no chance. Few would dare."

"And today," Negaer said, "you will meet those few." He nodded. "*Watch*, Steward."

Anger surged through Tili, but as his gaze hit the ruins, rocks came to life. The organized brutality of the Sirdarians fell away. Cloaks tumbled, looking like blood filling the streets. Glints flickered and glared through the hot afternoon, more than one searing Tili's gaze and forcing him to look away.

Tili leaned closer, confused. "What . . . ?" The Sirdarians—"Half lie dead!" How? It had been but two heartbeats. Bright bolts of light shot up. Then went wild, straight into the heavens. Another bolt. A glint. Then the focused light suddenly came straight toward Tili.

"Down!"

It happened in the space of a blink. Tili crashed against the wall of rock at the same time it rumbled and chunks fell at his feet. He widened his eyes at Negaer, who was smiling as he craned his neck out the gap again, then smiled even bigger.

Tili followed his attention. The Sirdarian commander was no longer mounted. He stood on the steps to what had once been a palace or government hall. Beside him a black-and-red cloaked incipient. And in the street, wading in the blood of the Sirdarians, a half-dozen men with enormous curved blades. "Tahscans."

"Aye, as they ever be," Negaer said.

Even as the general spoke, one of the Tahscans climbed the steps. The incipient wielded, but three other Tahscans strode with the leader, brandishing blades that somehow deflected the fiery darts and defied logic.

"Impossible," Tili muttered. "Accelerant flames melt steel."

"Not Tahscan steel," Negaer said with a grin. "They have the steel. They're fierce and skilled—organized. They fight better than any army I have seen, even my Pathfinders. I've used many of their techniques, but they never share all of their trade craft."

"I want to meet them," Tili said.

"Nay." Negaer pushed away from the gap and started back for camp.

Tili stalked after the general. "They have tactics, steel—all would help us win this war against Poired!"

"If we want our heads on our shoulders come dinner, then we ride wide around them, be grateful the Lady saw fit to have those Tahscans deliver us from the hand of the Sirdarians—who would have discovered us—and forget this moment happened."

"I never thought ye to be one to run and cower, General. Fear isn't like ye."

"This isn't *fear*!" Eyes blazed as he spun and faced Tili. "This is wisdom. You know the Ematahri?"

Tili flinched. The general knew well the Ybiennese had had encounters with the Ematahri, that the leader had given shelter and who-knew-what-else to Tili's sister.

"Tahscans make those forest savages look like children!" Negaer said, nostrils flaring.

"We have a common enemy."

"No. Not a *common* enemy. We have the word in common, aye—but only because they see everyone not of Tahsca as an enemy. Outsiders are a threat, and their new queen is close friends with the Infantessa, who has made the young queen her puppet."

"If they are outsiders, why are they in the Nine?"

Negaer cocked his head in thought as they reached the command tent. "That I don't know." He scratched his beard. "We are farther southeast than any Jujak or Pathfinder has been in a full cycle of the moons. But we don't dare test their patience."

"Ye do fear them."

"I respect them, and their privacy. And you'd do well to do the same." He grabbed a decanter of cordi juice and poured some into a tin cup. "Have you ever seen anyone cut down an entire contingent of Sirdarians so effortlessly? And you want to turn their eye here, to the only representative of the Nine left to speak of?"

"Haegan—"

"Is the Lady knows where." Negaer threw back the drink in one big gulp and wiped his mouth.

"Give care with yer words."

"There is great care in them, I promise you that," Negaer said. "What I speak is not ill, but truth."

"It's true, then?" Tokar asked, rushing into the tent, flushed with excitement. "The Tahscans?"

Seated, Tili propped his elbows on the table and held his head. Light flickered and the air stirred as others entered the tent. He lowered his arms and sat back, staring out the open flap. Remembering the glitter of steel as the Tahscans so efficiently dispatched the Dark One's horde.

"What will we do against them?" Tokar's voice held anxious hope as he looked to Praegur, whose eyes seemed wider than usual. "The Tahscans."

Rhaemos moved closer to his general and stood tall, proud. "We make for Vornesse?"

Negaer's gaze flicked to Tili. "As planned."

Tili shook his head at the thought of continuing the same futile effort to reach Haegan. They'd been pushed farther and farther south since this journey began. Yet they had potential right here, weapons capable of leveling the playing field. Warriors who could train them. Help them gain ground instead of lose it day after day.

And was not Tili Steward of the Nine? Should not Negaer consider his counsel and take it, regardless of his own personal feelings?

Yet Tili could not discount the wisdom. Nor the skill that had two Pathfinders pacing him on Lake Mountain. He was not so brash as to disregard the man's experience. But . . .

"Is it not yours to do the will of the Steward?"

Tili peered up from his seat at Draorin. Though he was not as broad-shouldered as Negaer or the elder Grinda, who had remained behind with a contingent in Hetaera, he possessed an athleticism Tili knew not to undervalue. Though he must have at least forty or fifty cycles, his hair was as dark as Tili's and his brown eyes, which shifted to Tili, radiated authority.

"The risk here is enormous. 'Tis my duty to advise the steward as I see fit," Negaer said.

"Aye," Draorin said. "No one of us doubts your intention, nor your ability."

"Then what do you doubt?" Rhaemos growled.

Negaer steadied him by catching his forearm.

Again, Draorin turned to Tili, who somehow sensed the strength the man possessed course through his own limbs. Strangely, it brought Tili to his feet as the realization dawned that this was not Draorin's fight. Nor Chauld's, who was oddly absent.

This battle belonged to Tili. To stand for what he believed to be just and right. "We doubt not anything about ye, general, nor the Pathfinders," Tili said.

Tension hung like thick smoke between them, roiling and coiling around the strongest and the weakest. He must show himself confident, but was it stronger to yield and defer to Negaer?

"Have ye considered," Tili said, surprised at the words about to come out of his mouth, but they rang truer than any other option before now, "the possibility that Abiassa has placed us here to cross paths with the Tahscans?"

"Seeking Abiassa's will is the job of the Fierian." Ferocity sparked in Negaer's eyes. "Mine is to protect the representative of the Fire Throne, be he the prince or be he the steward."

"Protect," Tili repeated quietly, firmly, seizing the advantage Negaer had unwittingly established. "But not command."

The man's beard twitched as he, too, realized he'd been ensnared by his own words. He conceded with a cockeyed nod. "You know well."

Tili lowered his gaze. "I respect yer wisdom, General Negaer," he began carefully. "I may not have yer experience nor yer years in the service, but I have commanded the Ybiennese army and led the king's guard—both positions given me not because of the blood in my veins but the fire in my heart. It has guided me and never failed me." The words burned through his lungs. "And it will not this time. We *must* attempt to speak with the Tahscans, especially now that they are at our very door."

A shrill whistle shot up outside the tent. Four large strides carried Rhaemos to the flap, where he fixed his gaze intently on something in the distance. He spoke to the side, "Word from the scouts. Trouble." He stepped back.

The quick, soft noise of a runner preceded a lanky young Pathfinder. He rushed up to Rhaemos, taller by a head, and whispered, his gaze never leaving his captain's face. Quick words exchanged, then with a clap on the man's shoulder, Rhaemos pivoted. Hurried shouts and calls assailed the air. The camp flew into a buzz.

Rhaemos's gaze found Tili. "It seems, Steward, you are about to get your wish."

8

Her bed lay cold for three nights. Byrin had returned two nights past, saying he and Aselan had split to scout the approaching Rekken. But Aselan had yet to return. Which could only mean one thing: He had fallen.

The thought chilled her and played havoc with her mind. Would he die as her father had? Would he leave like Haegan?

Foolish thought, that. Haegan had gone to claim the Fire Throne, as was his right. She'd heard the report that he had been forced into Contending. An ironic twist of fate, considering Haegan's longstanding penchant for peacemaking. She could only imagine how that ended. Surely there had been a decision. Weeks had passed. Why had word not come?

Kaelyria slipped on the leather duster that nearly reached her toes, and secured it with a braided belt. She smoothed a hand down it and paused at her belly. How long before she knew if she carried a child? Here, she had women to advise her on the ways of the Heart. But personal, intimate conversation . . . She ached for her mother, for someone to speak to about womanly things.

She felt alone. Truly alone.

Duamauri and Sikir came onto their haunches expectantly as she turned toward them. She smiled at their responsiveness and eyes so keen she was sure they could speak. Mayhap in their own way, the icehounds did communicate, much like a raqine.

Duamauri's ears twitched.

Sikir let out a soft growl.

Thud! Thud!

Kae's heart skipped a beat at each knock, and realized it was not her the hounds had reacted to, but the approach of whoever beat against the door. She released the bolt and slid the door across the steel rod.

Hoeff stood with a wooden tray and steaming cup.

"You are acknowledged, Hoeff." She inclined her head and removed herself to the chair and table in the corner, knowing she must give wide berth for the giant. Though as she sat, Kae could not help but wonder why Hoeff and his twin Toeff had not left the mountain when the other Drigo followed Haegan. The reports—still so hard to believe—made her worry over her brother.

"Mistress drink," Hoeff said, sliding the tray onto the table in front of her. "Mistress heal."

As the hounds settled back onto their pelts, she gave a lone nod to the Drigo healer and reached for the cup. "Hoeff, can you . . ."

The heavy-lidded giant grunted and motioned with his thick fingers toward the steaming cup.

With a smile, Kae lifted it to her lips and sipped, knowing compliance might make conversation easier. "Hoeff, may I ask a question?"

"Yes, mistress."

"I heard of the Fierian summoning the Drigo at Baen's Crossing."

With a sigh, Hoeff swiped his thumb across his sweaty brow with something that sounded like a soft growl.

"Why did you and Toeff not respond and assist him? Did you hear it—or how is it the Drigo even knew? Or even Coeff?"

Again, he swiped his brow. Was she making him nervous?

"I beg your mercy if my question is impertinent."

Again, he reached forward and nudged the cup in her hands, and obediently, Kaelyria swallowed the bittersweet concoction. She could not deny its medicinal effects, swirling strength and warmth through her limbs and body.

"She not call us." His voice was like tumbling rocks.

"She." Interesting. "You mean Abiassa." Kae shifted on the edge of her seat. "Then She—the call, it is from Her. But how do you know She didn't summon you?"

"She gifted Fierian to call those he need. Only Thelikor summoned."

"Thel . . . ?" It sounded like a name of some sort. "Who is that?"

"He lead his clan. One clan one army." He nodded, as if she should understand. One giant no doubt was the equivalent of a hundred men.

"But my brother is fighting the Dark One. How can he need only one clan against an army of darkness?"

"Fierian gone."

Kaelyria stilled. "Gone?" She swallowed hard. "What do you mean, gone?"

"I hear Fierian summon." He swiped his thumb over his brow again. "But not summon me. Only Thelikor. Then I feel it—cold. Empty." Another shrug. "Fierian gone."

"Dead?" She tried to keep the rising panic and the shrillness in her voice under control. "Are you saying my brother's dead?"

"Hoeff, ye are acknowledged." A voice gruffed along the walls and Kae's nerves, drawing their gazes to the door where Byrin stood. "Tend yer duties, please."

Kae came to her feet as Hoeff bowed, then folded himself through the door. Agitation worked through Byrin's jaw, evidenced by the twitching of his thick beard. "Ye would do well not to ask the giants for news of yer brother, Princess."

She lifted her chin. "It seems they are the only ones willing to provide any." Surely he had something important to say if he was here. She worried the end of the leather belt, waiting.

Byrin's brows were terse and thick as his gaze skipped around the cave.

"You're avoiding my eyes."

"I be avoiding yer emotions."

"Emo—" Kaelyria pulled herself straight. "Is something wrong? Is Aselan hurt?"

"I've no word of the cacique, but with his raqine and abilities, he be fine." He glanced at her hip where Aselan's dagger hung, a sign of her position and his protection.

"Then why fear my emotions? I know you were not . . . pleased I claimed his dagger."

"Ye know nothing of me thoughts, Prin"—his dark eyes hit hers—"Mistress."

She stood before him, tall and straight as her mother had taught her. She might not wear a crown or the title of princess any longer, but leading a people was the same whether in a palace, mansion, home, or cave. And if his concern was not over Aselan, then she could only guess one other possibility. "What do you know of my brother, Byrin?"

The rigidity in his posture softened. "It is as the giant said: He's gone."

She jerked forward. "Dead?"

The icehounds were on their paws again, growling at Byrin, who scowled at the oversized hounds, then at her.

Bolstered by the hounds and aggravated with having to pry the information from Byrin, she braved the question. "Then my brother is dead?" A breath staggered from her lungs.

Though hesitation held his answer hostage, there was a tenderness, a rawness in his expression. "'Tis worse."

"Worse?" she scoffed. "How can anything be worse than death?"

"I not be knowing the details or truth. But there are rumors."

She held her peace, more to steady her raw nerves than to feign strength—which her wobbling legs betrayed that she did not have.

"Some say he fled the Citadel. One rumor has him in league with the Rekken—"

"The Rekken!" She turned away and moved to the chair again, relieving herself of the inordinate task of standing straight and not trembling. "Don't be absurd. Haegan would never do that. How could they even suggest such a thing?"

"Because Thurig would na' give him his only daughter."

Kiethiel. Haegan had spoken of her. Even Aselan had spoken of Haegan's attachment to his sister. And the king of Nivar refused him. It would wound her brother, certainly, but that wouldn't drive Haegan to betrayal, to turning traitor.

And yet . . . he seemed so ready to find any path besides the one Abiassa had set him upon.

"Then there is the other rumor, an insidious one, that he has taken up with the Queen of the Falls."

"Queen of *what*?"

"The witch who rules Unelithia and Iteveria."

"Infantessa Shavaussia?" Her voice pitched at the ridiculousness of the rumor and its ignorance. "She's no witch."

"Aye," he said with a sharp nod, "she be, and one with a black heart, they say."

"Haegan may be many things, mayhap driven by compassion but not idiocy." Conviction tightened her chest. "The Nine and Iteveria have long been neutral, and there is no advantage in a match there."

"And what advantage is the match between ye and the cacique?"

Heat climbed into her cheeks. She lowered her gaze. "The only advantage is that I now have a home."

Byrin eyed her, something darkening his expression. "Is that it, then? A home. That is what this means to ye? What he means to ye?"

"You twist my words cruelly. I meant that Legier is my home, that—"

"Home. Again ye say *home!* But what of 'im? What of all he has sacrificed takin' ye to his bed and givin' ye his protection?"

"And is that all it means to you—that he took me to his bed?" Her own words humiliated her. "I am his bound! I am your Mistress!"

"Oochak!" *Clack! Clack!*

They both started, glancing at the door, where an old woman stood, grinning gap-toothed at them with a large, thick stick gripped in her gnarled hand.

Byrin muttered something as he barreled from the room and down the passage.

Grateful to be rid of him, Kaelyria struggled to keep her composure as the old woman fixed her with a glittering stare. Had they met before? Using the table and the back of the chair, she climbed to her feet. "Hello. I don't believe—"

"Ah, but ye do, daughter of Zaelero!"

"I beg your mercy." What madness had claimed this woman? "Might I have your name?"

"Why would ye want that when ye have yer own?"

Kaelyria curled her fingers into fists. She'd had enough of annoying visitors today. This—this is why she had kept to their cave since Aselan had taken to the skies.

The woman, who had seemed bent and weak but a blink past, now straightened and shook the stick at Kaelyria. "You believe he left to escape you. You believe you made a grave mistake. You believe Abiassa has left you as She left your father and mother on the steps of Seultrie, dead—"

"Silence!" Kae hissed, tears stinging her eyes.

"But ye are much mistaken. She has ye right where ye are supposed to be. Fear not the darkness nor coming emptiness."

• • •

NIVAR HOLD, YBIENN

Pain speared Aselan as he shifted his leg, the break bound and secured. Trying to stem the ache did nothing but force him to groan and grab his thigh. When Pharen landed at the hold, it had been a clumsy, labored effort, which pitched Aselan into the south wall, snapping his leg. Beyond the window came the annoyed chortling of his raqine. Three days penned so his wing would mend enough to fly—for the great beasts would continue on otherwise, further injuring themselves.

Aselan shifted on the bed, hating the comfort, hating the cool mattress, which only bespoke Kaelyria's absence. Several weeks had passed since the Feast, and still he struggled to believe he had not dreamed it all.

"Finally awake, are ye?"

He jerked his gaze to the door, surprised he'd not heard it open and even more surprised to see his brother filling the frame. "Relig." He shifted, wishing himself out of bed and clothed so he could stand before his brother. "Come to gloat?"

Relig crossed the room with a swagger. "It would be quite easy, but no."

Aselan hesitated, but family dynamics were not his concern this hour. "I asked for a hawk to be—"

"'Twas sent." Relig stood over him with an impassive expression.

He looked to his younger but taller brother. "Where is Father? I must speak with him about the Rekken."

"Ye saw them on the Tooth?"

"Aye, hundreds. Poised to attack." He nodded toward the raqine den. "Took Pharen to scout the passes and saw a band closing in on the hold. I must return to the Heart."

"Both ye and yer raqine are broken. Ye won't be traveling anytime soon." He remained aloof, a stranger to Aselan, who had known his brother younger, more rash, less courteous. "Father sent Aburas and his ten up to rout the enemy."

"Aburas? Ten is not enough. There are scores more Rekken." He scowled. "What of Tili?"

Relig's eyes widened. "Ye haven't heard?" He swiped a hand over his mouth. "He's been named Steward of the Nine. Off somewhere in the south, battling Sirdarians and incipients."

"The *Nine*? What has he to do with ruling there? Is Prince Haegan dead?" Aselan did not want to bear such news back to the Heart. Kae would be devastated.

"Missing. It's said he went to Iteveria."

Missing was better than dead, but perhaps not by much. "Why Iteveria? He seeks alliance?"

Relig's nonchalance faded to regret. He shrugged. "There is no definitive answer, so 'tis not my place to speculate."

"Not yer place? If Tili is gone, then the throne falls to ye if Father is ill or injured. 'Tis absolutely yer place to speculate."

With a relenting nod, Relig sighed. "'Tis said he went with two assassins."

Aselan barked a laugh. "They think that slip of a boy is an assassin? He couldn't sneak up on a deaf hog!"

"Mayhap, but 'tis said all the same." Another swipe of his nose.

That's when Aselan saw it. The ring. And recalled the wedding he hadn't been invited to. An opportunity lay before him to bridge the gap that had grown in the cycles since he left for the Heart. "And how is yer bound?"

Relig's face brightened. "Brilliant. She carries my heir—the pharmakeia confirmed it yestermorn."

Aselan's heart warmed . . . then ached. He extended his hand and clasped his brother's forearm. "'Tis good news, brother." He smiled, or tried to. "Father will have his line secured for another generation." That task had been his at one time. Even though he'd been in the Heart, losing both Doskari and their babe . . .

"Not going to taunt me for taking Tili's bride?"

Confusion spread through him. *"Tili's* bride?"

"Father intended Peani for Tili, but he is as wild as raqine and refused her. It was fortunate, for she and I had a mutual attraction. If Tili hadn't stepped aside . . ." Relig's expression shifted and he drew up his shoulders, considering Aselan for a moment. "What of ye? The great feast has passed, if I remember correctly. Did they convince ye to take a bound this time?"

Relig was far too perceptive, always had been. Aselan steeled himself to lie . . . and failed. He looked at the thick blanket over his legs, unable to deny Kaelyria.

"Freeze the flames!" Relig exclaimed with a laugh, the last of his reserve melting away as he slapped Aselan on the shoulder. "Does Mother know?"

"No," Aselan growled, "and we will keep it that way."

Relig hesitated.

"'Tis not their concern, since I am disowned." Aselan shifted, tossing aside the blankets. "Help me to my feet. I must meet with the king."

His brother huffed. "Elan—"

Cold anger gripped Aselan, as if the glimpse of camaraderie had only deepened the pain of his family's rejection. "Delay me not, Relig. I know ye wish me gone—"

"Wrong, brother." Relig gripped Aselan's arm and pulled him upright, then held him still. "I was hurt and angry when ye chose a foreigner over the whole of yer family. I wanted ye to stay."

Surprise rooted Aselan. He stared at the stone floor, refusing to meet his brother's eyes.

"Stay now."

"I cannot, Relig, even if I were still welcome here. I have a bound to consider again, the Rekken are at our door, and the Heart must prepare. If Father will not receive me as his son, he must receive me as a representative of people under his rule." It was the only way to make his voice be heard. No king could refuse a representative.

"Elan, please—"

"I may have come at the will of a crippled raqine, but I must go to Father with what I know out of concern for Nivar, for my brothers and sister." His chest tightened with unexpected emotion.

"Thiel is not here."

Aselan chanced a look. "Pray, she is well?"

"We know not. We received word that Gwogh sent her to the Ematahri six weeks past. There has been no word since."

Would his sister never break free from those savages? The more reason to speak to the king. Bracing against the pain in his leg, he reached for the staff, no doubt left beside his bed by the pharmakeia who treated him.

"Elan, don't. This isn't the way to heal things."

"There is no way to heal when he refuses me an audience." Clumsily making his way, Aselan hobbled out of the room and down the hall. Veered left to the library, where his father was known to take afternoon appointments and tea. The doors were closed, but his father's booming laughter carried to him. Egged him on.

Aselan pushed the doors open wide and found Thurig sitting with a cup in hand and his feet up. Across from him sat another man, some dignitary no doubt.

His father's ruddy face went crimson.

"Father." Aselan hadn't addressed him as such in years. "I'm sorry it was too much trouble these past three days for ye to receive me. Ye should know the Rekken are on the Spine. They are headed toward Ybienn as I speak. But ye go ahead." He nodded fiercely to the cup in his father's hand and gestured to the other man. "Continue yer revelry. When yer people are cut down in the streets, at least ye'll be too drunk to know."

Thurig came to his feet, as did his guest. "If ye will excuse me, Duke. We can continue this later."

After the other man ducked out of the room, Aselan felt some of the fire leave him. He leaned heavily on the staff. "What has happened to the father I knew, that ye could so cruelly and thoroughly turn against yer own people?"

"Ye have no notion of me, Elan, though ye sit in accusation and take pride in doing so."

"I crashed here on Pharen after seeing Rekken on the Spine!"

"Aye!" Thurig bellowed. "And I have dispatched my guard to deal with them."

"No, ye have killed yer guard." Aselan clutched the staff tightly in frustration. "There are hundreds. Yer ten Nivari will be slaughtered." He shook his head, then straightened, though all his weight was on his good leg. "Prepare the Nivari and citizens. The Rekken will be upon ye within days. They are already knocking at the doors of the Heart, and if they take it, there is nowhere for my people—our people—to flee. No safe haven in Nivar."

Dark eyes studied him. "What would ye suggest?"

Aselan hesitated. Considered his father. Was he in earnest? He would hear him, his thoughts? Or did he mock? "Begin preparations for evacuation."

"Eva—" His father balked but turned to the great fire pit, where flames danced and crackled. There was a long silence, then, "Is it as bad as that?"

Breath stolen at the weight in his father's voice, at the fact that he actually listened, Aselan nodded, though his father couldn't see him. "'Tis. I would ask, Father, that ye allow the Heart to empty into Nivar and evacuate with the Ybiennese."

His father pivoted, scowling.

"If they are caught in the mountain by so great a number, the Heart will hemorrhage."

The stern expression held fast for several aching seconds. "Aye. Send them."

Relief thudded into Aselan's chest. "Thank ye, Father. And may the Lady have mercy on us all."

9

Palming the glass server that stretched along the wall in the small dining alcove, Haegan stared to his right. Toward the bathroom. Past the glass walls. To the spigot. Above it to the panel that released the water of the falls. Hunger churned in him, despite the spread of food beneath his nose. 'Twas a different sustenance he craved.

But what?

Why was his mind such a mottled bed of muck?

"Haegan."

But the shower. He wanted to return to the water. He wasn't even sure why. Just knew that the warm stream brought something he was missing. Mayhap something he was forgetting.

If you forgot, how could you remember?

"Haegan!"

He blinked and cast a look over his shoulder to the small table. A man sat there. Bearded. Limp against the back of his chair. His eyes sagged. Trale was half the man he had been. What had happened? What changed?

"Haegan, come sit," he said, his voice scratchy and weary.

"I'm hungry."

"Then sit so Thomannon can fill your plate!"

"Thomannon?" As if speaking caused the man to manifest, Haegan felt a presence at his side. He started. Then gave a smile as the man's face bled into focus. "Oh, yes. Right." But again his gaze strayed to the bathroom. "I want a shower."

"In the middle of our meal?" Trale barked a laugh around a chunk of bread. "Don't be absurd. Sit down. Eat. Talk to me. I'm lonely."

"Trale Kath is never lonely," Haegan said, though he wasn't sure how he knew that. "Your sister."

Trale blinked. Stilled as his gaze met Haegan's, as if some distant memory hung between them. "Sister," he grunted, as if testing the word. "Astadia." He shrugged, looking out to the falls. "She left me. Serves her right, whatever happened to her."

"Of course." A plate slid in front of Haegan, and Thomannon stepped back casually. Though the food was surely delectable, something in his stomach churned. A . . . weight. A nagging. As if something was . . . wrong. Terribly wrong.

Abia—

"Sir." Thomannon spoke quickly, quietly. "Would you prefer something else to eat?"

"N-no. I . . ." A shower would help. He'd feel better after. "Perhaps a rest, and a shower."

"I'm afraid the Infantessa is rationing water now, sire."

Trale again laughed. "Rationing water! She's so clever and looks out for her people."

"But there's a waterfall and a sea outside," Haegan said, his gaze drawn to the rushing water.

Rushing water.

Why was that familiar? He reached for his glass of water but misjudged. The crystal toppled over. Water rushed toward him. Water rushed over his hand.

Rushing . . . The spilled water slid into his lap.

A servant girl appeared behind Trale. She was short, young. Ash-colored hair framed a vibrant face.

Wait! That face. "You," Haegan said, looking over Trale's shoulder. "What are you doing here?" He'd seen her before, but not here. The servant from the Heart. Aaesh.

Hands clasped, she smiled, and it seemed the entire sun burst through his being.

Trale lifted his arms. "Eating! Same thing as you!"

"Sire, you should go change and dry off. I'll clean this up."

"I asked what you're doing here," Haegan growled.

"Serving," she said quietly. "You called me."

"I did?" He barely recalled the word—the name that had seeped into his thoughts in the form of a prayer, interrupted by Thomannon.

The manservant inclined his head. "Fresh clothes are in the boudoir, sire."

Haegan considered him. Beady eyes bored into him, though he wasn't even looking at him. Wait. That didn't make sense. Then again, there had been little sense made in the last few days.

No, weeks.

It was weeks, wasn't it? Why did he think that?

As Haegan left the table, Trale used another piece of bread to slop up gravy from the porcelain plate. He slapped a hand in the air. "You and your books! After years in the tower, you'd think you'd have had enough of books."

In his bedchamber, Haegan found the fresh clothing and quickly changed. When he emerged, the girl was there again.

"Do you feel like reading now?" she asked.

"Reading?"

With a gentle smile, she motioned to his bed.

As if she had somehow dusted a musty, unused corner of his mind, he recalled the ancient text he'd hidden in the mattress upon his arrival on the first day. Haegan became absorbed by the way the girl's eyes swirled with encouragement.

The Kinidd.

Warmth speared his head and drew him up straight. Images of an ancient leather-and-gilt book swam in his thoughts. The way Gwogh— *Gwogh!* When he had last thought of the aged tutor . . .

The tutor who betrayed and tried to kill you.

He hadn't tried to kill him. He'd tried to protect him.

And nearly killed you in the process.

But Gwogh had been so . . . afraid of the text. "I think I'll read," Haegan said.

Thomannon frowned. "Would you like a volume from the library?"

"Please." Haegan waited until the manservant left, then hurried to the mattress and reached between it and the lower supports. There, he felt the rough edges of the volume. Pulling it out, he eased a leg over the mattress. *Kinidd* in hand, heart pounding, he tucked the ancient book out of sight.

Moments later, as Thomannon was clearing the tables and sending the dirty dishes out with a servant, a guard appeared with a book. The man-servant accepted and delivered it to Haegan. Knees bent and feet planted on the mattress, Haegan placed the book on his lap. He waited for several long minutes until Thomannon had his back turned, then slid the *Kinidd* onto the other book. It was smaller, but only marginally. If the servant came near, he'd spy it. Haegan propped a pillow against his leg to better conceal the contraband.

His gaze drifted down to the ancient scrawl. At first, it made no sense. Lettering looked like the noodles that'd been on his plate all too often. But slowly, the shapes straightened themselves into recognizable letters . . . then words. Sentences. Verses.

> *Hidden beneath cooling waters, where once he was freed;*
> *drawn by thirst and aches so cruel, exposing the need*
> *to obediently and violently stand between life and death,*
> *living and dead*
> *first and last*
> *then and now.*

Though he wanted to read more, his gaze kept flipping back to that first line. *Hidden beneath cooling waters, where once he was freed.*

Cooling waters.

Hidden.

He looked again to the shower. Thomannon had once dragged Haegan away from the shower. Apologizing.

Rest, Fhuriætyr . . .

Where had *that* voice been all this time? Why had it now resurged?

Aaesh was there again. "Because you called."

He had, hadn't he? The word his heart had completed when he'd been cut off.

"Are you well, sire?" Thomannon asked as he bent over the table.

"A little tired, I think," Haegan said, sliding the *Kinidd* out of sight, and grateful his words had not been a whole lie.

"A nap, then?"

"Aye," Haegan said.

"Rest well, sire."

Thomannon picked up the wet clothes Haegan had cast off, then strode out. Haegan remained in the dark, afraid to reach for the ancient text and be discovered. Lying on his side, he held the text close, as if somehow the words could bleed into him. Strangely, he felt strong for its closeness. Or mayhap for its words.

Haegan could stand it no longer. He shouldered the blanket higher and rolled his fingers, bringing a dull blue glow to the text. He fixed his eyes on the Verses. Though he read page after page, he kept returning to two of the poems.

> *Hidden beneath cooling waters, where once he was freed;*
> *drawn by thirst and aches so cruel, exposing the need*
> *to obediently and violently stand between life and death,*
> *living and dead*
> *first and last*
> *then and now.*
>
> *Begged and summoned, he once steps into that tearing plane;*
> *existing not only in one but in two, this terrorizing refrain*
> *as he stands obediently and violently between life and death,*
> *living and dead*
> *first and last*
> *then and now.*
>
> *Making war on enemies of Aaesh and freeing enslaved minds;*
> *releasing from prisons of their own making,*
> *and then he finds himself standing obediently*
> *and violently between life and death,*
> *living and dead*
> *first and last*
> *then and now.*
> *Forever.*

And the other, a bit more daunting.

> *Father and heir, torn apart in cruel haste,*
> *The greater left below to ruin and waste.*

The people wandering and lost
Cry for release from the dungeon's taste
By her reckoner, his strength replaced.

Howling in their ears come the screams of night,
Their own rebellious hearts exposed to light.
The people wandering and lost,
Drowning in their pride and chained in fright,
Though many captured, none in her eyes so slight.

Even Her champion struggles with his own chains,
Resisting and refusing, he has created his own fanes.
The people wandering and lost
Lay at his feet, eyes upcast with hope that he reins
In his insipid doubts by words seared into his veins.

Beneath the water cool and rushing fast there came
Hope, fire, and fury with but a singular, holy aim:
The people wandering and lost
Find freedom at last, chains severed with their shame
Beneath blue-white cleansing of Aaesh's Chosen Flame.

In the hall of iron and blood he takes his stand
With races past and present to reclaim their land.
The people wandering and lost
Give witness as the one birthed from darkness
Decimates the poisoned and perverted line of Tharqnis.

What he would give to have Gwogh here to help sort the Verses. To glean understanding and wisdom. His mind was a muddled mess, but he flipped back once more and committed to memory this:

Father and heir, torn apart in cruel haste,
The greater left below to ruin and waste.
The people wandering and lost
Cry for release from the dungeon's taste
By her reckoner, his strength replaced.

Strength replaced. The Reckoner. *Fhuriætyr* was another word for Reckoning, right?

So . . . me.

But that last part—strength replaced. How? How was he to regain his strength?

And how long had he been here? Or a better question: Why had he been here so long? He could answer neither. Nor why he, with this book in hand, felt freed from that which had clogged his brain and will. A greater fear worked through him—he hadn't cared. He wanted to stay. He'd *wanted* to be here.

Vulgar, vile atrocity!

Hidden beneath cooling waters, where once he was freed. The words whispered through his mind. No, not his mind.

Abiatasso.

The realization made him pull in a sharp breath. This was bigger than Haegan. Bigger than his mind. "Abiassa . . ." he whispered, unsure what to say next. Where to begin. Because he was suddenly and fully aware of where the blame rested for the nightmare that had engulfed his life and devoured his days—on his own shoulders. "I walked away from You. Now, I'm trapped." By his own pride. His own ego. His own doubts. "I beg Your mercy."

A warm breeze trickled through the room. Haegan peeked over the covers, afraid Thomannon had returned. But his heart started when he saw the servant girl. "Aaesh . . ." A collision of thoughts and words and names cracked against his head. Knocked the breath from his chest as he held her gaze.

Aaesh.

A servant girl who existed, yet didn't, according to Aselan. Who now stood before him.

Aaeshwaeith Adoaniel'afirema.

A name Thomannon had uttered once and nearly fled the room afterward. Not just a name. *Her* Name. A name in the Verses.

"You're Abiassa."

She smiled.

"But why?" He crawled over the bed to the edge, closer to her. "Why have You let this happen? Why have You not freed me?" He looked out the window, the lights of Iteveria glittering in the falling darkness. And yet, bright-white columns dotted the perimeter.

No. Not columns. Beings. Deliverers!

Panic clutched him. "Free me of this madness, please!"

"I cannot do it for you, Haegan."

"But You could have stopped them, stopped me!" Desperation spiraled through him, both to be free and to never have had this happen.

"Then it would not have been your choice, and from free will comes the greatest good of all." Aaesh still resembled the young girl, yet she had an eternity of wisdom and maturity. "Your will, your future became buried in each choice you made, Haegan. From fleeing the great room at Nivar, to leaving the Contending to travel with Trale and Astadia to this place."

Haegan hung his head. She was right. He'd known it. "How? How do I get free of this?"

Sorrow seeped through her glory. "Do you remember in Legier's Heart when I asked what if your anger were not merely your own?"

"Aye," he said, lowering his gaze as he remembered all too well his encounters with Her in the Heart. How he'd been irritable, impudent. Chastised Her for not knowing Her place. Grieved at his own arrogance and pride, he wanted to burrow beneath the covers. "I beg Your mercy. I had no idea . . ."

"It is what you do when no one sees that matters, Haegan. Your anger in some instances was justified, for it was not yours alone. Look with new eyes at those around you." Her words were soft but compelling. "It will not be easy, what you see. You must fight because you have so terribly lost your way. It's time to find your way back."

"How? Show me! I—"

"The *Kinidd* will show you."

"My thoughts," he realized. "My thoughts were clear when I was reading."

She inclined her head. "The Verses are my gift. Just as embracing your place as Fierian imbues you with physical strength, so does the *Kinidd* work the heart."

Glancing at the book, he wondered at that. Amazed at the fact that he thought clearly when he read them, because . . . they were Her touch. "But how—" When he lifted his gaze, She was gone. He threw himself from the bed. "No. Wait!" Spun in a circle, bereft. "Please! I need You, Abiassa. Show me. Speak to me! I'll listen." Grief clawed at him and

Haegan crumpled to the carpet. Tears blurred his vision. Anger spiraled through him.

He hated this place.

No. He hated that he'd been held captive. His pride brought him here, but she—*Nydelia* had kept him here.

Inflaming. She'd inflamed every negative thought.

But being a scourge is not what I want.

He didn't want to be hated. He didn't want to be . . .

Haegan blinked. Again! It'd happened again. Thoughts inflamed. Fear of hurting others seized upon. How? How had Nydelia known? He looked up and around the room. At the ceiling. At the door. At the— corner. Thomannon.

The man's eyes widened.

Haegan hopped to his feet, surprised to find his strength there. "You."

Thomannon shook his head.

"You're inflaming—"

"I have no ability to wield." But the eyes. Thomannon's eyes betrayed him.

Anger churned like the tidal pull of the moons on the ocean. Building. Curling up and toward him. "How long have I been here, Thomannon?"

The man gave a hurried shake of his head. "Please—"

"I asked before and you betrayed me. Think not to do it again. Answer plainly—how long?"

"Six weeks since your arrival."

Crushed at the pronouncement, Haegan fisted his hands and pressed them to his forehead. *Fool! Coward!* "What has happened in the Nine?"

"I know not. I stay here. I keep you."

"Keep me?"

The man's face went as pale as the moons.

"You *keep* me?"

"It was for your own good."

Indignation writhed through Haegan. "My own good?"

"If she—if she felt you were a threat, she would have killed your father and you."

Haegan jolted. He couldn't breathe. Couldn't move. Couldn't think. "My father?"

Your father never cared for you. Why care for him?

It was true. His father had left him to rot in that tower.

A strange, bitter taste hit his tongue. A spark of realization came with it—inflaming. It was happening again. How long before he succumbed this time? Became the useless twit he'd been for the last two months?

Wait, wait, wait.

What had he gotten angry about a second ago? Shoulders braced, head down, he stared at the twisting pattern of the hand-carved rug. Searched the fibers for the truth that had slipped so easily from his mind like water through his fingers. It was there. He could feel it. Like a jewel hidden just beneath the surface of a murky pond. What was it . . . ? Precious. Important.

"Father." Haegan pulled in a breath. Lifted his gaze to the manservant and stared at him through a tight brow. "Where is my father?"

10

Tili smoothed his tunic, aware he was not outfitted to meet the warriors as a commander nor as steward.

"Here." Negaer lifted a jacket from his case. "At least look the part." He held out the richly detailed garment, and Tili's eyebrows rose in surprise. The general shrugged. "Never know when you might have to eat with a duke. I find it pays to be prepared. Saves the bother of fussing tailors."

Tili slipped into the fine garment, then went to the tent opening and peered out, anticipation buzzing in his gut.

Rhaemos offered him a cup.

Tili hesitated, remembering the clobbering headache he'd awoken with the last time they'd given him a drink. He narrowed a look.

The Pathfinder snorted. "That was weeks and leagues ago. Have you not forgiven us?"

"Forgiven," Tili said with a nod as he accepted the drink and tossed it back. "But not forgotten." He felt refreshed, but something still nagged at him, like an itch he couldn't reach. Glancing down, he fingered the brass buttons and intricate stitching along the cuffs and stiff collar that mirrored the crest emblazoned over his heart. The emblem—that of the Fire King—was wrong.

The message was wrong. After slipping out of the coat, Tili handed it back. "Thank ye, but no. We are fighting to stop the same enemy. That is the ground I meet them upon, not as a superior or nobleman."

Hesitation held the general, but then he relented. "As you wish."

Negaer, Rhaemos, Draorin, and Tokar grouped up around him. He knew not where Chauld had gotten to. Together they stepped from the shade of the tent and straightened. Tili's pulse sped a little more than expected at the sight of the Tahscans as they plowed a path through the camp with their horses, shorn heads, and steel swords arcing at their backs. Casually comfortable in their bloodstained tunics and trousers. Dark eyes peered from above cloths that concealed noses and mouths. Of what fashion was that? Corded muscles marked their preparedness, their ability to eliminate any detected threat. But it was their unwavering confidence that arrested Tili.

"They ride as if this were their camp," Rhaemos grumbled.

"Aye, and it will be if we make a mistake," Negaer warned. "Steady."

As the Tahscans approached, their line thinned until a group of six fanned out before the tent.

"Interesting," Negaer mumbled as the six remained mounted in front of Tili. He continued in a side-whisper, "The three with shaved heads are Malkijah—the royal guard."

The revelation thickened the blood pumping through Tili's heart. "Why would they send royal guard into the Nine?"

"Bravery? Idiocy?"

"That we have in common, too," Tili muttered as he stepped forward, flanked by Draorin, Rhaemos, and Negaer. "I am the Thurig as'Tili, Steward of the Nine. Name yourself."

Nervous chitters raced through the camp, and Tili realized his mistake—the declaration to name themselves was a tradition and custom of Northlanders. Not the Nine.

Four dismounted, including the three Malkijah. They stood, glancing around at the Pathfinders, who had closed ranks. A stream of foreign words fell off the tongue of a Tahscan with long black braids dangling over his shoulders, his chin lifted proudly toward Tili.

Rhaemos translated. "He greets you in the name of the Tahscans and Vaqar."

Negaer leaned to Tili again. "I know that name—Vaqar is the commander of the royal guard. Fierce, bloody fighter that one."

In awe, Tili remembered his father's tales of the Tahscan's exploits ruling the eastern seas. "Yet he has braids," he noted. Which meant the man feigning to be Vaqar could not be the commander Negaer knew or his head would be shaved. So he was lying about something—was it his name, his position? The bigger question—why?

He cared not. Right now he must convince this Tahscan that he was worthy of conversation and not the *tsing* of his blade relieving Tili of his head. "Ye are welcome in our camp. Please join me within."

Tension rolled like a sandstorm through the desert, filling every crevice and needling their nerves raw as the four Tahscans strode—faces still masked—toward the Command tent.

Inside, Tili reached the head of the table and placed his hands on the chair. When he saw the eyes of Vaqar spark, Tili acknowledged the annoyance, then removed the chair and placed himself at the second chair on the side, enabling protection on both sides.

Vaqar said nothing but took the chair directly across the table, his braids knocking against the wood as he leaned forward. He was immediately hedged in by two more Malkijah, and a third stood behind him, translating just as Rhaemos did behind Tili.

It annoyed Tili more than he cared to admit that they insisted upon the cloths covering their faces. This was a custom he had not heard of before, and found it vaguely insulting. "It is unusual," he said, "to find a Tahscan so far . . . west and on dry land."

The translator's brown eyes glinted with appreciation that he was not accusing them of crossing a border. He repeated Tili's words in Tahsci to the Malkijah, then, added Tili's next question: "Are the coverings necessary?"

The Tahscans didn't move.

Finally, Vaqar spoke, and Rhaemos said in Tili's ear, "They are for our protection."

"Yer protection." Interesting. Tili had a split-second realization. "Because what ye are doing here is not official business of the crown." When the words had been translated, all four sets of eyes struck him in question and he shrugged. "Ye greeted us not in the name of yer queen, Anithraenia."

The men flinched even before the words had been translated—likely they had recognized their queen's name—but none more than the translator. He seemed unsettled, and when he spoke to Vaqar, he said far more than seemed justified by Tili's simple observation.

"'Tis not my intention to put ye on the defense," Tili said, noticing Negaer and Rhaemos shift as well, "only to be plain. As ye can see and no doubt have learned from yer able scouts, we are alone."

Negaer cleared his throat, clearly displeased Tili revealed that intelligence.

"As are ye," Tili continued, letting the implied threat hang in the air for a few seconds, watching.

Vaqar did nothing. Simply stared back, his eyes inscrutable above the veil. The Malkijah followed his lead.

Tili glanced at the translator. "It's a long way from Tahsca to be slaughtering Sirdarians."

The man's left eye twitched, a tiny movement, before he spoke.

Vaqar's snarled reply betrayed volumes, even before Rhaemos translated: "It is never too far to slaughter those animals. What business have *you* in this land, Northlander?"

Tili gave a quiet snort that he'd been identified. He eased forward, resting his threaded fingers on the table. "Vid is a Nines realm. I am its steward. Ye're in our land."

"This land is razed and infested with Sirdarian wickedness," the translator said, coming forward without first repeating Tili's words and waiting for Vaqar's response. "That makes it no one's land."

Tili tilted his head at the translator. Considered the man for a very long moment. He didn't flinch. Didn't look away. Tahscans didn't flinch. They were trained to face death, not only head on, but screaming and swinging steel.

"According to yer translator," Tili said, dropping his eyes to the man with long braids, "this land now lies unclaimed. Tell me, which prince claims it?"

Vaqar frowned, scowling. "Which prince?" he asked, as though confused.

Shrugging, Tili sat back. "I am a prince. And ye are a prince." He sighed, rubbing his eyes. "Now, which of us would claim this land, Vaqar of Tahsca?"

"Me, of course," the man answered.

"No." Tili shoved to his feet.

Vaqar glanced to the side, then leapt up, his chair toppling as the others reached for sabers. The air sang with blades freed of scabbards, stonelights catching the glint of steel. Belatedly Rhaemos translated Vaqar's demanding words, "You think you have more right than me?"

Two. Not all three Malkijah had reached for swords. Translator or not, he was royal guard, charged in the protection of his honor and realm.

Tili had been right. "Than *ye*?" He smiled at Vaqar and shook his head. "No." He tossed back some cordi juice, ignoring the wavering blades and loyalties. "When those Sirdarians ye killed do not return from their mission, more will come. When that happens, 'twould be good to be allies rather than enemies. Would ye agree?" When no one answered, irritation scratched at the back of his neck and good graces. He considered each Tahscan slowly, carefully. "When ye speak plain the truth, discussions will continue."

In the instant he turned toward the tent opening, something happened. Something fatal. A mistake. An error. Tili wasn't sure what, but the Tahscans came alive. A shout went up. This time all four blades flashed.

One snapped to Tili's throat, halting him. He lifted his chin carefully to avoid losing his head. He slid his gaze to the wielder—the Tahscan translator—but did not meet the warrior's eyes, nor any of the Tahscans', for they had all turned their attention to something behind Tili.

"Where did he come from?" the translator breathed, then unleashed a flurry of frantic Tahsci.

Tili eased from the blade and glanced back. Naught but Draorin stood there. "Remove the blades from my men or ye will not leave here alive," he said, doubting his threat could be fulfilled.

To his surprise, the Tahscans complied. Tili strode from the tent without looking back. His nerves thrummed at the possibility that he had read this wrong, read the warriors wrong. A dozen paces from the tent, he spotted Chauld hurrying from the north, sweaty and harried. What was he doing in that direction?

"*What* was that?" Negaer hissed at Tili before turning a glare on Chauld. "Where have you been?"

Chauld balked at the question and focused on Tili. "What's going on?"

"Later," Tili growled.

"Maybe if you'd been here," Negaer growled, "you would've seen the steward you were supposed to protect nearly get run through."

Chauld paled.

Tili heaved a sigh. "Aye, but something upended their anger."

"They looked to be terrified of Draorin," Tokar said. "Why?"

Tili frowned as Draorin emerged from the tent with the Tahscans.

"What in blazes?" Rhaemos whispered as the officer joined them, taking up position behind Tili.

Unease and something . . . *other*, stronger, prickled his nape with awareness that there was much more transpiring here than he had been privy to. Was there danger from his own appointed guardians?

"Steward!"

Tili let out a shaky breath as he eyed the four, unsure who had spoken.

"The translator," Rhaemos told him.

Tili straightened. "I said we would speak when ye chose truth, Tahscan."

The translator nodded to the warrior with braids, who reached up and dug his fingers into his hair. He yanked off a wig, revealing a shorn scalp glistening with sweat.

"Blazes," Tokar muttered.

The translator approached as he removed his face cloth, revealing distinctive double wave arcs beneath his right cheekbone.

"Blood and fury," Negaer muttered, half in awe, more in fear.

"You are a brave prince to challenge four Tahscans," the man said as he stalked forward, his face dirty and mottled with the blood of their enemies. "So great a number of soldiers in your camp, yet only you surmised our ruse. Impressive." Dark eyes homed in on Tili with amusement. His bearing promised his ability to dispatch any challenger. The large man considered him for several thundering heartbeats. "*I* am Vaqar, firstborn son of Vasthuili, second-born heir of Tahsca."

"Commander of the Tahscan fleet," Tili said.

"No longer," Vaqar said, his expression weighted. "You are far from home, Thurig as'Tili."

"As are ye, Vaqar," Tili said, his pulse slowing to a near-normal rate.

"I will leave the scorched land to you, Prince," Vaqar said with a smirk.

"You have no interest in our land?" Chauld asked, his voice piqued.

Vaqar held the colonel's gaze for several long seconds, his expression betraying nothing, then he returned his focus to Tili. "We have no interest in land—not yet. We only seek to rid this world of the Sirdarian stench. Consider it a bloodlust. There will be no rest for us until they are vanquished."

"Then you will return to your homes," Negaer suggested.

"We have no homes. No families. The queen slaughtered them when we stood against her."

Surprise caught Tili. "Ye stood against yer own queen?"

Vaqar's eyelids grew heavy with repressed emotion. Whether anger or disgust couldn't be discerned. "We were affected by the inflaming, but then . . . we were given a gift by Aaesh. That is when we tried to stop them. Rout the enemy. Anithraenia is no longer my queen." He fixed his attention on Tili. "Steward, my men and I have one goal—to eradicate the Sirdarian stench."

"As ye have stated."

"I would ask something of you that I have no right to ask."

"I am listening."

Vaqar's bright gold gaze flicked over Tili's shoulder as he said, "I would have your trust, Steward."

"His trust?" Negaer scoffed, frowning. "You only just met—"

Tili held out a hand, mentally back stepping and remembering who stood behind him. A strange sensation buzzed his neck and sped down between his shoulders. "Ye have it, Vaqar."

"What?" Negaer hissed.

Vaqar's eyes never left Tili's as he gave a nearly imperceptible nod. In less than a blink, he slid his hands to the hilts of his blades and took a marginal step back. The air sang with the fury of Tahscan steel, the sound ringing in Tili's ears. His face warm.

Why was his face warm?

By the time shouts went up, Chauld's body thudded to the ground, pouring his lifeblood into the parched soil.

11

HEART OF LEGIER

Weariness perched on his shoulders as Aselan limped to the pelt throne, relieved to be home but disconcerted at the change in his father. Was it genuine change? Might there might be a reprieve in his anger? Or had the mighty King Thurig recognized that alliance with the Eilidan was more beneficial than old grudges when faced with a war?

"'Bout time ye got back."

Leaning on the staff he'd brought from Nivar Hold, Aselan turned and found Byrin stalking toward him.

"Ye're injured," his man groused. "Is that what delayed ye so long?"

"Aye. Pharen took an arrow and threw me when he landed hard at Nivar. We both needed to heal before we could return."

Byrin's eyes widened. "Nivar. Bet that went well."

"Did ye not know? They sent a hawk."

Shrugging, Byrin pursed his lips. "None came."

"Strange," Aselan said, then heaved a sigh. "We must plan. The Rekken are closing in on the Heart."

"I saw them on the Spine, after ye split off from me and Ebose. I been preparin' the Legiera."

"That is well. The Rekken outnumber our fighters, and they're coming, determined to take our homes and lives."

"What says Thurig about the Rekken?"

Aselan paused. "He sent the Nivari out, but I warned him it wasn't enough." He placed a hand on Byrin's arm. "Old friend, we need to discuss the real possibility that we will be forced to flee the Heart. Gather the Ladies, then the men later."

To his credit, Byrin did not argue, only set his mouth in a grim line and nodded. "What of the Mistress?"

Aselan frowned. "What of her?"

"Have ye seen her since returning?"

Aselan glanced down.

"See? There be the thing that worries me—ye not knowing the way of the gentlefolk. She'll be none too happy ye're here making war when she's in yer cave worrying a crevasse into the floor. Ye should be thinking 'bout her—"

"She's in me thoughts every bleedin' minute," Aselan growled. "When Pharen took the arrow and stopped accepting my guidance, I feared I'd never see her again. That the Rekken would attack and I could do nothin' to protect her."

"That may happen some day," Byrin said. "But she's there now, waiting and worrying. And what if she's got yer child in her? And ye're torturin' her."

Aselan scowled at the insensitive topic.

Byrin chuckled. Thumbed a hand over his shoulder. "Go see her."

"We have to make plans. The Legiera need to prepare to set out. We cannot stay here."

"Aye. Plans will be made. Go to her."

• • •

"Mistress," came a gnarly voice.

Kaelyria stiffened to find Wegna in the doorway again. "How may I help you?"

"Yer brother," Wegna said.

"I have no knowledge or awareness of anything related to my brother, save that he is apparently missing at this time."

"Aye," Wegna said. "But ye do realize yer role in all this, aye?"

Guilt hung like heavy chains around Kaelyria's neck. She turned away, agitation squirming through her belly, roiling.

Duamauri and Sikir rumbled a warning at the old woman.

"If by my role you refer to the Transference—"

"I do not."

The old woman's firm pronouncement surprised Kaelyria. She turned, abandoning guilt and stepping into confusion. "Then . . . I beg your mercy, but I do not understand."

"'For the sake of the sister, the Fierian offers his life.'"

Kaelyria shook her head, a balmy sweat coating her face and chest. "No . . . I am here in the Heart, with Aselan. I am neither threat nor help to Haegan or any in the Nine."

"It is written," Wegna said, her voice snarling, though there was no animosity in her expression or words, "'From the mountains comes she who carries hope and healing within her, the heir to unite the realms.'"

Kae scoffed. "I beg your mercy, Wegna," she said, her heart thundering a little harder than it probably should. She'd seen the first spotting of her cycle just that morning, "but I am wanted by no realm—"

"But it is ye," Wegna insisted. "I read the books and the words from the *Kinidd*."

"I assure you, it is not me."

"But it must be!"

"It is not!" Kaelyria snapped. "I carry no heir! And I beg you to leave off and torment me no longer for my all-too-apparent failure and disgrace."

A shape appeared in the doorway.

Kaelyria's heart tripped and her breath whooshed out. "Aselan."

Brow knotted, he looked to the old woman. "Good day, Wegna," he said, shifting aside and pointing her out of their dwelling and down the passage.

Kaelyria spun away, sick with regret and grief, and weak from . . . everything. She cupped a hand over her mouth and fought the tears.

"Kae," came his soft, whispered voice along her nape. His hand slipped to her waist. "I'm sorry she upset ye." His arms closed around her, pulling her against his thick chest.

Surrendering to his embrace should have been a relief, but it was only a reminder. Of things painful. Of a father's hug she'd never feel again. Of the first time Aselan held her. Of the nights they'd been locked in an embrace. Of the reality that she still did not carry his child.

"It will happen," he muttered, his lips grazing the ticklish spot beneath her earlobe.

She turned and hooked her arms around his neck, crushing herself to him. "I was so worried when you did not return." Breathing deeply, she caught his scent and felt her worries fading.

"I beg yer mercy," he muttered. "I injured myself when we crashed at Nivar."

She pulled back and glanced at his leg. "What happened?"

"A break, but 'tis mending."

Kaelyria eyed him, saw the burden in his blue eyes. "What is it? What did you find?"

"The Rekken are on the Spine," Aselan said quietly. "The Legiera will take to the skies on the raqine. The women and children will go deeper into the Heart."

"We are to hide?" She frowned, drawing closer. "And what, wait?"

"'Tis safest. We must stop the Rekken, but if they breach the Heart . . . The women and children must reach safety."

"Where is safety?"

"The ancient tunnels lead to Ybienn. I have been there, spoken with my father. He will shelter our refugees. We will return to the Heart when it is safe."

She felt something twist inside her. His words contained so much. He'd been to see his father, the man who had disowned him? She wanted to ask about it, but sensed the time was not right. "But the Heart has never been abandoned."

"Untrue. The original settlers abandoned it once during a collapse that flooded the passages." Aselan lowered himself to the bed, the tightening around his eyes evidence of the pain in his leg. "But ye are right in that no other cacique has ordered an evacuation."

Kaelyria watched him, wary. Nauseated at the chaos and fear. She went and knelt before him, resting her hands on his knees. "You are wise to protect the children. The Heart is sacred, but it's only a location."

"So I would tell myself. But if we have not the Heart, what have we?"

"Each other."

"But 'tis our *home*. They have been here for centuries."

Realization dawned—he thought he had failed his people in making them leave their home. It was their identity, their existence. She knew she'd never understand fully because she had been here but a short while.

Though she loved it and the people, it was not home, as much as she ached for it to be. As much as she ached to be all that Aselan needed. And even his moving away, his emphasis of *home* made her wonder if she belonged here. The thought rippled through her. She shook off the foolishness. She chose this. Chose *him*.

Kaelyria stood. "This is not your fault, Aselan."

"But—"

"You can no more control the enemy's movements than you can steer the will of Abiassa." She ran her fingers over his beard, smiling down at him. "You are the best man I've known, and your heart for these people—*your* people—tells me you have done everything possible."

"'Tis an easy answer I will not accept," he said, his tone grieved. "It has been too easy to remain beneath the mountain and pretend the war did not exist."

"Aselan," Kae said, softening her voice as she braced his shoulders. "Your heart wills that the Heart remain safe, but ye cannot control all the elements and movements of every realm or race in this world."

His hands came up to her hips, and he rested his chin against her belly so that his face tipped up. A smile twitched his beard. "Ye said 'ye.'"

Kae blinked. "Did I?" She smiled, sinking down beside him on the bed. "I guess you're rubbing off on me, though if my mother were alive to hear such poor linguistic skills . . ."

"Poor linguistic skills?"

"Aye," she said with a laugh. Then leaned against him. "All will be well, Aselan. We'll come back to the Heart and life will go on." Something in her squirmed at those words, some premonition that they were not wholly true. Surely Abiassa had not delivered Kae here to die. Or given her love only to rip it from her hands. A sudden and alarming dread spread through her, as she stared up into the bearded face of the man she'd come to love so deeply in such a short time.

He kissed her gently. "If ye believed what ye spoke, I might have hope."

• • •

CASTLE KARITHIA, ITEVERIA

Searing heat blasted the back of Haegan's head. Knocked him forward. Another hit between his shoulders, shoving him face-first into the marble floor. Shards of pain exploded through his head and mouth. On all fours, he glanced toward the door, tasting blood.

Three blurry shapes lurched. He whipped his hand in their direction, glaring white enveloping his vision. Something rammed into him. Punched him backward. His world went dark. Whether it had been seconds or minutes that passed, he came to as a blurry form hovered over him.

Haegan moaned.

Heat pressed against his temple and a weight fell into his palm. A hand came to his head.

Pain erupted through his temple. "Augh!"

Darkness again prevailed.

• • •

Haegan thrashed against the veil that blocked him. Kept him hostage. Strange. So strange. He was not unconscious. Trapped. Like being stuck in body-shaped box. He clawed his way out, seeking the coolness that trickled across his face.

"Easy," came a warning.

Haegan stilled, confused. But then pushed again, desperate to be free. Light cracked at last. He struggled harder against the dizziness that swallowed him and burst free.

He was abed. Alone. He could hear voices. There—at the door. He hoisted himself up, his hand slipping on something. When he glanced down, surprise hit him—the *Kinidd*. Thank Abiassa they had not discovered it when they put him in bed.

"I'll be back shortly," came a stern voice. "Do not let him leave this room."

"You're sure he won't remember?"

"I blocked it. He won't remember him."

Remember who? It didn't matter. He could remember later. Right now, he had no time left. He had to free himself. Now. But . . . how?

And why? Was it so bad here?

Groaning silently, he gripped his head. Yes! Yes, it was bad here.

Hidden beneath cooling waters, where once he was freed.

Cooling waters . . . The shower! He rolled from the bed, still holding his head. Willing himself not to listen to the inflaming that swarmed his mind. Anger roared through him. He was sick of this. Sick of being captive. Sick of being manipulated!

He caught sight of the *Kinidd* and tucked it under his arm before hurrying into the bathroom. Shut the door. Turned the lock and pivoted—then swung back. He held his hand over the handle and wielded, melting the metal. He threw himself into the glass enclosure and spun the lever.

Even as water splashed over him, Haegan remembered the sacred text. He'd ruin the pages! His heart thudded. The words would soon be gone. But he couldn't leave the water or his thoughts would grow muddled.

Abiassa, help!

An idea took hold as he recalled the words from the *Kinidd*. He used his finger to trace his forearm, drawing on the Flames and searing the Verses into his flesh. Hissing against the horrid pain, he fought the nausea. The screaming plea of his body to stop the agony. He could *not* lose the words. Could not lose the hope. He needed a way to remember.

He carved his arm, scream-moaning as the lettering bubbled his flesh. Tears streaming, water pouring, he seared the next line, heart tripping at the ink bleeding down the page. It was blurring too fast. Too fast! He'd lose it.

"Stop him!" came Thomannon's shrill shout from the other side of the door.

There were two verses. Two. Two that were the answer. He ripped them from the book and held the first one over his arm, tracing them. Melting them into his flesh. Sweat beaded on his brow. His stomach churned at the agony. He kicked against the glass shower, but didn't stop.

The door rattled.

Acrid, the smell of burning flesh—*his* flesh—stung his nostrils. He cared not.

Aaesh told him to find a way. This was the way. *She* was the way—Her words, written to him.

"Father and heir," he muttered as he committed the second page of

Verses to his other arm. His body rebelled, hurling his lunch onto the stone floor. Trembling, he fought the weakening. Pain was winning. Defeating him. Just like the Infantessa. Sobbing, he slumped down. Shielded the *Kinidd*.

How? How did he free his father when he could not think outside the water? He could not stop. Could not yield. Finger shaking, he started again, the water strangely cooling, healing. Forearms. Abdomen. Wherever he could burn the words.

The door splintered open as Haegan wrote the final script into the crook of his arm. Thomannon and a guard stood there, gazes dropping to his marred flesh. Mouths open in shock.

Enough. He'd had enough. Haegan staggered upright, steam rising off his arms and body as he let the tunic fall to his hips once more. He lifted the *Kinidd* and tucked it beneath his leather belt at the small of his back. His long hair dripped into his face as he beheld the intruders. "Where is my father?"

"B-below," Thomannon stammered.

"Not helpful." Haegan drew back a clawed hand, wielding.

Thomannon threw up his hands. "In the dungeon. But you can't get down there."

"Even if you did," snarled the guard, "Thane would kill you."

Something grew in Haegan, something strong, virulent. Furious. He placed a palm against the glass. "You—"

Crack! Shhhhick!

Beneath his fingers, the glass spiderwebbed into a thousand tiny pieces. Integrity compromised, glass rained down with a tinkling *whoosh*.

Haegan sucked in a breath, and for a moment, all three were frozen, staring from his still-poised hand to the shards at his feet. The display emboldened Haegan. Infused him with reminders of who he was and what he possessed. It was a choice. Linger on the doubts and fear. Or seize the gift of Abiassa.

The guard lunged at him.

Instinct awakened. Light, bright as morning, flared through the room and seized the guard. And then he was . . . gone.

Surprise rippled long enough for Haegan to realize he had ended the man's life with wielding. He grieved the loss. But turned to Thomannon.

The older man shook his graying head, tears rolling into his trimmed beard. "I beg your mercy. She made me—"

"My father." In his sodden clothes, Haegan stepped from the shower. "Take me to my father."

"I can't. She'll kill me."

"Your death is assured. But the choice is yours: by Nydelia's wicked hand"—he rolled a flame around his fingers—"or by the swift justice of Abiassa, if you refuse me," Haegan vowed, the visions and nightmares of these many weeks ringing horrifically in his ears and mind. All this time . . . all this time she held him.

No more. "Now take me to him."

· · ·

EMATAHRI CAMP

Clutching the wooden bars that formed a prison, Kiethiel rattled them. "Release me at once!" But her words, foreign to the Ematahri and annoying to the Sirdarians, blended into the crinkling warmth of the dense forest foliage.

"It ain't worked the last firty times," Laertes said. "Don' fink it will dis time either."

Palms to her forehead, Thiel twisted and slid down, the saplings scraping her spine. "Gwogh sent me here to get help, and I've . . ." She shook her head. "I've ruined it."

"T'weren't nothin' to ruin. Him what wears the blood didn't give ya a chance. He frew us in here and locked the cage." His dirty blond hair hung shaggily in his innocent blue-green eyes.

"I should have gone with Praegur. Or at least sent ye. I will never forgive myself if something happens to ye." Thiel groaned. "I can't believe Cadeif is aligning with those desecrators," she groused, staring at the encamped Sirdarians. "Are they every blazing place?"

"Haegan'll find out they have yeh here and get mad, and he'll come whomp 'em into the ground," Laertes promised in his youthful ignorance. He didn't know Thiel and Haegan had argued when she'd challenged his petulance over being the Fierian.

She pressed her head back and sighed, closing her eyes. "Do ye think he will ever accept what he is?"

"He has to. He's the Fierian. He's got t' burn the land for the rest t' happen."

Though every muscle ached from the weakness of inactivity and the limited food afforded them, Thiel lifted her head. "The rest?"

Laertes nodded. "Yeah, the Lakes of Fire will turn t' water and the deserts'll breathe bounty."

Thiel snorted.

"It's true," Laertes snapped. "Me mam told me the story every night when I was li'il." He scooted across the cage to her. Though ten years her junior, Laertes had grown a lot in the last year. "'Twas the only hope for Caori, the south, and the outlanders. It says deserts would bloom an' there will be sheets of rain and clouds of moisture what hangs over the deserts, and flowers long dead come back, and the south would prosper again. A desert to a paradise." His eyes were pleading, hopeful. "It has t' happen—it's the only chance to see me mam again."

Thiel struggled to hope his mother was alive, that the so-called prophecy could come true. "A desert into a paradise, eh?"

He nodded eagerly.

"Well," she said with a sigh, cradling the boy beneath her arm as night pushed its coolness into their bones, "I never expected to see a Drigovudd . . ."

They drew closer and snugged in to offer each other warmth and comfort. She also had not imagined spending weeks in a cage. And Chima! The great beast curled in the corner snoring—*snoring!*

As if knowing the silent objection was lobbed at her, Chima chortled and adjusted, coiling in on herself. Her feathery wings haloed her furry body in a silent repose.

"Beast," Thiel hissed quietly. "Why aren't ye breaking us out of here?"

"I ain't never seen her get mad enough t' do something like that."

"If Haegan were here, she would," Thiel grumbled.

"Aye," Laertes said around a yawn as he lay on the ground, arm bent beneath his head. Thiel arced around him and did the same.

Haegan, where are ye? If he was able, he would come for her, save her.

But that just made her worry because he hadn't come. Which meant he was in trouble.

Tili. Where was her brother? He might chase her through Nivar Hall with a spoonful of honey in hopes of getting it in her hair, but he loved her as any brother would. He was also as protective as the night was long. So there—another worry. Where was he? Why hadn't he come?

Or had they, and somehow the Ematahri put them off? Tricked them? Killed them?

Defeated by her own thoughts, Thiel sank into her dreams and the coldness. Ached. Bones ached. Thoughts ached. Heart ached. Even when she had been on her own before, at least she'd been with Cadeif. They'd been friends.

"You were mine!" he had declared the last time they'd been among the camp, when Haegan retaliated and wiped out one of Cadeif's clans. The Ematahri had demanded a blood price. Cadeif demanded Thiel stay.

Their only salvation then had been the Lucent Riders. Deliverers. Two sent to free Haegan.

Two. Had Abiassa's Guardians known then that the Ematahri would align themselves with the Sirdarians?

"Bring her!" The barked order snapped through Thiel's thoughts and the weight of near-sleep.

As thudding feet drew closer, she glanced around. Ruldan and Raleng, the twin warriors, stalked to the cage. Fierceness glowered from their ridged brows and hooked noses.

"Up!" Raleng commanded as his brother released the cage lock.

Thiel eased from Laertes, who was rousing at the commotion.

"Wha—"

"Quiet," Thiel whispered, motioning for him to stay. "'Tis well." Though she knew not the truth of her own words.

"Now!" Raleng grabbed her arm and jerked her up.

A low, heated growl came from the corner.

They both turned, feeling the brush of hot breath on their backs. Chima rose, and with an elegance that belied her size, she unfurled her wings. They expanded, filling the cage. Her eyes glinted—first gold, then the red of warning.

Raleng's iron grip on Thiel's bicep tightened. "Tell her to stay back."

"Ye know nothing of raqine if ye think I can order her about. They only do Abiassa's bid—"

Jav-rods slipped through the cage slats.

"No!" Thiel threw out her hands toward the warriors—not Ematahri. Silvers. "Fools! Anger her and ye'll have the whole nest on ye."

Narrowed eyes glittered from Colonel Jepravia, who commanded the encamped Sirdarians. "You know a lot about the creatures, Princess." Dark hair shorn to his round skull, he exuded hatred that made her skin crawl.

Thiel snorted, even as Raleng eased her from the cage. Chima's fiery eyes never left Thiel, though one strong flap of her wings—a taunt—sent Jepravia stumbling back with a startled gasp. "Ye know nothing! They are independent of all man and suppositions. They answer to Her will alone."

"Wrong," Jepravia said. "It's written they answer the Fierian as well."

How did he know what was written? "And is not the Fierian the will of Abiassa delivered?"

"You know your Verses."

"The Desecrator, it seems, is not the only one who has read them."

"I love an intelligent woman," he leered.

"Ye don't know the meaning of love." Her words were meant as a taunt, a jibe, but the vile colonel merely watched her as the twins secured the cage and ushered her toward the main tent.

Jepravia sent a sidelong sneer to the Ematahri. "I want proof that he has bed her this eve. If he does not break her now before she undoes all his work, Cadeif will feel the full measure of my wrath, and I will break her myself!"

His oily threat followed her into the main tent. Most of the warriors had gathered here, as they had so many months ago when Haegan was pitched at the archon's feet.

Bodies and smoke thickened the air and formed a stranglehold around her throat. She swallowed as they marched her through the crowd and shoved Thiel to her knees at the dais, where the archon and someone else sat ominously in similar thrones.

She peered up—and felt a sharp prick at the back of her neck. Hissing, she dropped her gaze, all too aware of a blade or jav-rod pressed there.

"You brought a violent beast into our camp."

The voice was Cranna's, an old hag who'd turned Cadeif against Thiel and convinced him that anything between them would be the destruction of the Ematahri. She'd been why Thiel had fled so long ago. Why Cadeif let her go and did not give chase. But because of Haegan, Thiel returned to their camp those many months past, and the hag warned Cadeif that Thiel had returned to bring about the violent end.

And then the Lucent Riders came. What happened after the Deliverers sent her away with Haegan?

"To be clear," Thiel said, "Chima goes only where she senses Abiassa wants her. If I guided her one way and she felt compelled another—"

"With your presence," Cranna barked, "there is an obvious threat from the Nine, from Nivar, and from the mountains."

"Mountains?" Thiel's voice cracked, thinking of her eldest brother. "There is no threat—"

"Break or kill her, Archon," Cranna said, shaking her craggy head. "It is the only way."

Thiel swallowed. *Break* wasn't a nice term. Yes, it sounded less . . . final than killing, but it wasn't. She'd seen them break people. She didn't worry about the Sirdarian general's idea of breaking. But an Ematahri's? She shuddered. People became hulls of what they'd once been.

"Cadeif—Archon," she said, correcting herself in hopes of gaining his ear. "I came to warn ye, but as ye so aptly pointed out when I lan"—*no, don't mention Chima*—"arrived, ye are aware of the condition of the lands and the"—her gaze hit the contingent of blood-red uniforms in the corner—"*presence* of certain armies. Since ye have heard my missive, sent by the Council of Nine, I would beg ye release me, so that I may remove the so-called threat from yer camp."

Cadeif's brown eyes were molten, the planes of his face hard and angular as he sat rigidly on his throne. He'd always been fierce with his large, powerful build and little hidden behind dyed leathers. Where once there had been warmth in his rich, dark eyes now lurked . . . something darker. More ominous.

Thiel swallowed hard, realizing this was no longer the warrior she'd called friend, the one who'd protected her, sheltered her. Kedardokith. The ritual of accepting a person, claiming them in an act of protection. He'd claimed her beneath that tradition when she stumbled into their camp, bloodied and beaten. Scared. Scrawny. He'd trained her. Laughed with her, taught her the Ematahri ways. Then Cranna.

The hag had convinced Thiel that Cadeif's path was better without her. Despite her fondness for the man who eventually became archon of the Ematahri, Thiel must confess she never loved him. Not like she did Haegan.

"The traitor is where she belongs," Cranna crooned. "At your feet. Your property to do with as you please."

As he pleased? Thiel's heart thudded a little faster. She considered the old woman and her malicious sneer, then Cadeif, who slumped in his chair, hand propped over his mouth as he stared back with hard, unrelenting black eyes. His skin was so dark, the firelight skittering over sculpted muscles in his chest and arms. But the darkness of his expression . . .

Why had she ever thought she could convince this warrior?

She hadn't. But Gwogh had said she must. "I know not why I thought ye would listen," she whispered, then looked again at the Silvers clustered far too close to him. "But I never thought ye capable of this madness, aligning yerself with bloodthirsty savages. They've wiped all that's good from the land."

Cadeif launched out of his chair with a roar. "And what of Fut and Fortari?"

Thiel arched back to look up at him, but again felt the prick of jav-rods at her nape, which steered her onto her feet.

He stopped short of knocking her to the ground. "You came with that scourge, and the Lucent Riders killed two of my best men. Because you"—his nose pressed into her cheek—"brought him here. To my clan. You shamed me. Shamed this clan. We gave you food. We protected you. We *claimed* you."

A thundering shout from the warriors rattled the tent beams.

Adrenaline coursed, leaving her limbs trembling and weak. "I . . . please—I didn't know—"

"Please," he repeated, his breath hot against her face. "Yes, Etelide. Beg." His nostrils flared and his lip curled. "Take her to my tent."

Another raucous shout went up, this one shrieking and mocking. Raleng and Ruldan dragged her back violently, lifting Thiel off her feet.

To his tent? There was only one reason they would do this. "No!" she shouted. Writhed. "Cadeif, please!"

"She begs for him," came a sick taunt.

The twins hauled her through the camp, past curious onlookers. Pulling her, their hands bruising her arms.

Thiel thrashed. "Please—please, no. Ruldan, ye'd never want this for yer sister."

"You're not my sister," he snarled, throwing back the flap of the archon's luxurious tent. Pelts, lounges, and pillows embraced a fire pit in the middle. Beyond, drawn-back tapestries revealed a feather bed, torchlight glaring at her.

Two female slaves froze and dropped their gazes.

"Out!" Raleng barked at the younger slave, yanking Thiel inside. Then to the other slave, "Wash and prepare her for the archon's bed." He cast her forward.

"No," Thiel said, stumbling, her fingers grazing one of the pillows. She spun around, reaching for a dagger she no longer had. Futility snaked through her. "This isn't right."

"You belong to him," Raleng growled. "Kedardokith gave him *all* rights." His thick, strong hand swung toward her. "You accepted before the clan. Then you shame him, endanger everyone who protected you, including me! Fut was the fiercest warrior and most loyal to Cadeif. You robbed us all when you left the second time."

Ruldan scowled. "It's a wonder Cadeif never took what was his in the first place." His beady eyes hit the slave. "Get her ready. If she gives you trouble, we'll be outside."

"Etelide."

When Raleng spoke her Ematahri name, Thiel felt defiance rear.

"Resist, and the slave will be punished, too."

Sharing a wide-eyed look with the girl, Thiel hesitated. Defeat clung like water, weighting her courage. It was one thing to endure beatings, but it was entirely another to cause someone else pain. As the slave girl came at her an apologetic look, Thiel struggled between defiance and dejection.

She forced her mind from the preparations. Away from the thought of what was coming. The ministrations were far too thorough and humiliating, especially when she scrubbed Thiel from head to toe with scented water, then stuffed her into a gown with many sheer sections. "Please," Thiel whimpered. "Is there another dress . . . ?"

The woman gave a quick shake of her head, nodded to Thiel's hair, which had finally grown below her shoulders. She had it shorn to conceal her identity while traveling the Nine with Praegur, Tokar, and Laertes.

The servant guided Thiel to a chair and went to work on her tangled knots.

Another woman entered with a tray of a steaming drink. She offered it to Thiel, who refused, knowing she'd most likely throw it all up again. The woman persisted. Pressed the warm cup into Thiel's hand. "It help you forget."

Thiel considered the drink. Did she want to not remember? No, she wanted to, so she could *never* forget what he'd done. What he forced.

Tears blurred her vision.

Hands framed hers as the woman lifted the cup. "Drink. Trust me."

Chin quivering, Thiel allowed the woman to guide it to her lips. She tasted it, felt the strange, tingly sensation. Hesitated. Then gulped.

The woman nodded, her features marked with sadness. "It better this way."

Thwap!

The women gasped and jerked back, then dropped their gazes and bowed.

At the sight of Cadief's formidable frame hovering there, Thiel came to her feet, unsteady. Nervous. She mustered the remnants of her courage and shut out the strange chill from the half-sheer gown.

"Leave us." His deep voice rattled down Thiel's spine, heating her face.

She fisted her hands and stayed in place, staring at the fire. Gritting her teeth did not steel her, for she twitched when the tent flap closed. She froze, sensing him drawing closer, his shadow stretching toward her, slowly, intentionally.

She wanted to hear his voice. Wanted him to talk, tell her this was a joke. "Ye are stronger than this, Cadeif—than them. The Silvers are using ye." Could she talk politics and intrigue to distract him so he wouldn't violate her? She closed her eyes, willing courage where there was none.

The heat of his presence pressed in on her.

Her heart thudded anxiously as his breathing grew heavier, closer. "Please," she whispered, shaking her head.

His hand slid around the back of her neck.

Thiel shot out a hand to brace herself, and nearly cursed when her palm met his firm, sculpted chest.

His grip tightened. He tugged her forward. There was something in his eyes. Something she couldn't understand. Something she'd not seen before. Something that scared her.

"Please, Cadeif . . . please don't—"

His mouth was on hers, hungry. Demanding.

Thiel stiffened. Placed her hands against his abdomen. "No." She'd seen his anger before, and she dared not tempt it, but neither would she be bedded by him. It took effort to pry free of his grasp. She stumbled away and felt the wood pallet of the bed at the back of her legs.

When he moved in again, a wild look hardening his gaze, she jerked her face away. "Stop. Don't do this."

Rage exploded through his expression. He reared, his hand landing with a cruel blow. She fell across his bed and he was atop her.

12

"Subdue them!" Negaer shouted.

Before Tili could comprehend the actions, the death of the colonel, a sea of white and green overcame them. Rushed Tili in one direction and the Tahscans in another. Jujak and Pathfinders alike barreled over the warriors.

Men shoved Tili backward, a flood of warriors filling the small void and protecting him. Yet no further blade flashed. The still-mounted Tahscans sat unmoving. Tili struggled against the hands pulling him away, trying to see. To understand. To move beyond his shock.

Nay, he understood full well—Vaqar had killed Colonel Chauld. Right in front of him. The warmth he'd felt on his face? He dragged his hand over his cheek and stared at the crimson staining his fingers.

Shouts pounded Tili's ears as he glimpsed, through the tangle of his own warrior's legs and arms and steel, the lifeless face of Marz Chauld forever frozen in antipathy. He'd never known what was coming.

Neither had Tili.

Ye fool, allowing them into the camp, thinking ye could tame them. Ally with them.

But thoughts, facts began to churn through Tili as he recovered, Draorin and Tokar pushing him into the Command tent, where they secured the entrance. Numb, baffled, Tili moved to the table. He wiped his hands on his tunic and stood over the map, fingers grazing the edge of the wood. What had he missed? How had he not seen the true nature of the Tahscans?

Vicious. Negaer had tried to warn him.

"Why would he kill the colonel?" Tokar asked, his thoughts mirroring Tili's. "And the lightning speed . . . Blazes, he could have taken you as well."

Tili looked at him sharply.

"Perhaps there is something we should learn from the Tahscan," Draorin offered, his gaze speculative but also warning.

"What?" Tokar snorted. "How to steal into a camp and kill the enemy in broad daylight? They must be fools."

"Guard yer words," Tili snapped at him, nodding to Draorin. "He's yer superior." He met the colonel's eyes and stilled. Saw something vast, wise.

Listen to him.

Tili had been slow to pay that voice heed before. He would not now. "Have ye a guess why Vaqar acted thus against the Nine? I would have ye speak freely, Draorin. I need yer counsel."

Shoulders relaxed, gaze serene, Draorin cocked his head. "Perhaps he does not act *against* the Nine."

Tili frowned, turning that idea over in his head. "If Vaqar didn't act against the Nine, then what would ye call killing Chauld? Ye would trust a Tahscan over a Jujak?"

"In the war against Sirdar, I would trust those who have surrendered their will to Abiassa over anyone, Nine or otherwise." Draorin's words were laden with reminder. "It is easy to lose sight of the true battle when exhaustion and weariness turn allies to enemies and enemies to allies. There is only one truth that remains unchanged."

Tili felt the answer in his bones. "Abiassa."

Draorin nodded. "We must not forget nor abandon that truth in the course of our fight to stop Sirdar's army."

A half-dozen Pathfinders, stark in their now-dirtied white cloaks, delivered four Tahscans into the tent. Where Tili expected resistance and anger from the warriors, he found only submission. They were allowing themselves to be brought. So, why had Vaqar targeted the colonel?

Negaer stalked past his men as they forced the Tahscans to their knees on the thick carpet. He nodded to Tili and offered the bloodied Tahscan scimitar. "The instrument, sir."

Tili studied Vaqar. Dark eyes swam with conviction but no regret. No apology. *Abiassa, guide me.*

Tili accepted the blade, rounded the table, placed the scimitar there, and his palms on either side as he slowly lifted his gaze to Vaqar. Not the one who'd posed as his leader. A tactic that likely served many purposes, two of which Tili understood: to protect Vaqar from an unexpected attack, and to allow Vaqar to witness how those they encountered treated the leader and the lessers. The lightning-fast strike of his blade was naught compared to the quiet, calm confidence lurking in his golden eyes. Vaqar Modia was not to be trifled with.

Tili had little doubt that Vaqar and his men could slaughter every Pathfinder and Jujak in this tent—Tili included—before anyone could act, should the leader deem it necessary.

But why? Why the charade? Why kill Chauld and not him?

Tili straightened. Folded his arms. Scruffed a hand over the beard he detested but wore for practicality. "Negaer, Rhaemos, Draorin, Tokar, remain. All else—dismissed."

The general jerked. "Sir? You cannot be—"

"I don't believe I stuttered." He coolly met Negaer's gaze. "Clear the tent." With a motion, he allowed the Tahscans to gain their feet. "Vaqar, choose one warrior to remain."

The Tahscan commander hesitated, wary. "I alone will stay," he said, his voice like rocks tumbling in a pot.

Though disconcerted and incensed expressions were tossed about, the men cleared out. Tili waited. Watched. Thought. Tokar drifted closer, along with Draorin, in whom he found strange comfort.

"Steward, I must—"

Tili raised a hand, silencing Negaer, then he paced to the far end of the tent and turned. Considered the Tahscan. "I will not pretend to understand yer customs or rituals, Vaqar. What ye did, killing the colonel assigned as my protector, is as much a threat against my person as if ye attacked me directly."

Vaqar stood silently, hands loose at his sides.

"Yet our men, clearly out-skilled"—Tili heard Negaer huff—"even to our own dismay and humiliation, were given no resistance when they dragged ye into this tent." He ventured closer. "This leads me to believe ye intend me no harm."

Vaqar's expression remained impassive.

"Come," Tili said. "I would have ye speak. Explain why ye killed the colonel."

Hesitation guarded Vaqar. He cast a look over his shoulder to the tent flap, before letting out a long sigh and pulling his gaze along the perimeter, eying Tokar and Draorin, on whom he lingered. "I made a vow." His gaze finally returned to Tili. "That my blade and my life would always belong to Aaesh. That where Her messenger willed me, I would go and deal violently with her enemies."

"Enemies!" Negaer objected. "He was an officer of the Fire King's Jujak. An elite fighter. Designated by Gwogh himself to protect the Steward."

The man's large frame remained unbending. His eyes firm but burdened. "Those names mean nothing to me. My men and I must fulfill Aaesh's call. It was the only way to find"—sweat beaded on his brow—"relief."

"Relief?" Tili asked.

"Sir," Draorin spoke quietly, moving from the Tahscan, who fixed his gaze on the tall man, "he does not look well."

Indeed, Tili noted the man's pallor. "Are ye ill, Vaqar?"

For a second, the warrior sagged. "A cloth, if you please, sir. A cloth"—his jaw muscle bounced—"to cover my face."

"I would have us be allies here," Tili said, motioning around them. "Ye have no need to fear us seeing yer face."

Vaqar breathed through a laugh weighted with pain. "It is not for you." He hesitated again, then—gaze locked with Tili's—a smile trembled on his lips as he lifted his tunic, revealing a glowing, marred mess of a scar on his side that almost matched the one on his face.

"Blazes," Tokar hissed. "That looks like Praegur's mark!"

"He gave it to me, said to follow the scent of evil." Vaqar breathed heavily. "It is our only relief, to end evil. To fight for Her. When we do—"

"But why the cloth?"

The man's brow furrowed deep. His nostrils flared. "You will think me mad."

Tili scruffed his beard. "Ye murdered my colonel before an entire contingent of Pathfinders. I think we are beyond mad."

Vaqar smirked. "We were marked. Each Tahscan here. Marked by him," his gaze lazily drooped, but seemed to reach toward Draorin. "When we accepted the mark, we were . . . changed."

"Changed?" Negaer snarled. "What the blazes—"

"We can smell it."

Tili scowled. "Smell what?"

"It. Them. The disloyal. The pungent stench of inflaming, jealousy, betrayal . . . The reek of the wicked is especially pungent." He breathed heavily. "We smell it all. Relief only comes when we deliver this world of it."

• • •

CASTLE KARITHIA, ITEVERIA

Every time he stepped from the Void, it seemed another piece of him stayed in the netherworld. A lie stole into his mind as he stood on the cold marble and scanned the room to figure out where he'd landed. Poired had told him to practice, to strengthen, so he worked on traversing the world via the Void. Diavel circled him as Drracien finally identified the location—the Infantessa's castle. He snorted. Wouldn't she throw a hissy to find him here?

Much had changed. *He* had changed. Like a creeping, darkening mist of night that consumed the light and joy of day, it swept over him. Thicker. Deeper. Summoning. Devouring. Until there was little of him left.

But there was enough. Enough that he was still Drracien. Enough that he fought to exert his will over the inky heaviness enveloping his soul. Gnawing at the barriers he'd erected as he struggled to keep himself together.

Diavel came to his haunches and snarled, looking into the hall of the Infantessa's castle. Drracien wanted to kick the foul beast for the bite that tethered them, burning, searing. What the beast felt, Drracien felt. What the beast wanted, Drracien wanted.

If he killed the blasted thing, would he be free?

There was only one way to know. But how did he kill a half-spirit, half-flesh beast? The stupid thing wisped in and out faster than Drracien could blink. Still, a well-placed bolt through its corporeal heart should work. If the thing had a heart.

But Drracien had a terrible feeling that whatever happened to the beast would happen to him. It was a crazed idea, borne of the way Diavel had forced a transference onto him. Forced him to embrace something that he'd probably known all along dwelled deep in his abiatasso: darkness.

And yet, somehow, he pitied the beast.

Because I am now that beast.

Traitor. Spawn of the Dark One.

Murdered his own mother.

She wasn't his mother. *She was a whore who took money and gave me over to depravity.*

Tingling wormed through his spine seconds before Diavel let out a low growl. Shadows moved in the long hall, pulling Drracien from the forechamber. He scanned the quiet, lonely—*desperate* halls. Feeling something. Bitter. Disgustingly sweet.

He let the scent draw him away from the stone table, following instinct and noting Diavel at his side, a low rumble stoking his fiery belly. Drracien's steps echoed in the vacuous emptiness. Was everything so blazing vacant here?

It was like he couldn't get away from it. He'd seen it in the village, in the shambles of a home his mother used. Anger churned through his chest again, knowing he'd crossed a line by killing her, but for the children—*because* of the children and what she'd done to them—he didn't care. He'd do it again. Except, maybe slower.

A woman's voice drifted closer, and Drracien drew himself deeper into the shadows, shielding himself as the Infantessa strode in the opposite direction. A good thing for the princeling, too.

Drracien slipped to the balustrade and squinted into the darkness below. Diavel's animalistic sight gave Drracien an advantage, revealing two faint forms skating through the inky halls.

Haegan.

Diavel growled and couched, then leapt over the balustrade. Down two levels. The blasted unearthly creature had an unfair advantage.

But I can traverse the Void.

Aye, and each time cost him a piece of his abiatasso. Each time ensured one day he would dwell there as a Void Walker. But if he allowed Diavel to alert Poired to Haegan's presence . . . Yet, if he hurt the beast, wouldn't he hurt himself?

But Haegan. The prince who wasn't a prince, who had been too good, too caring. His fear of rejection and failure had cost him everything.

Maybe the fool deserved—

Drracien's pulse sped as Diavel gained on the prince. There was only one who could stop him.

Grabbing the rail, he steeled himself. Then pitched over the balustrade and into the air. Into the Void.

• • •

Anger tightened. Churned. Wove deeper into the fabric of Haegan's soul as he moved through the icy palace. Where were the gilded accouterments he recalled as he sat at the table with Trale? The feasts fit for kings? Where had the deep black chill of night come from? The heaviness that weighted his very abiatasso?

"Wait," he said, still aching from the words he'd burned into his flesh. His thoughts tumbled into one another, tangling. Disorienting.

What had he been thinking about?

A boy. No . . . not a boy. A man, his age.

"Trale." Haegan glanced at the manservant. "Where is Trale?"

Thomannon shook his head, flinging tears in desperation. "Please, sire."

"You call me sire. You know. You know who I am."

Thomannon ignored the statement, instead pushing his gaze to the upper levels they'd just fled. "He's there. But if you go back up, you'll die. He'll die."

Indecision gripped Haegan, fanning into righteous anger as he stood in the grand foyer, lights dead. Plants dead. Hope dead. No. No longer. "You."

"Sire?"

"You," Haegan said, grabbing at the man. "Free Trale and bring him to me, or I will send you to the Flames myself!"

"But he won't come, sire," Thomannon choked out. "He's . . . he's like you were. Lost to his doubts and fears. But more so. It's too late."

Frustration seeped into Haegan again. He fisted his hands. Light haloed around them, shoving back the thick veil of darkness.

"You cannot free them both, Prince," Thomannon warned.

No. There must be a way. He would not abandon one to save the other.

Abiassa . . . Aaesh . . . Speak to me. Show me. I beg Your mercy for my failure, my selfishness. Lead. Lead the way.

His arms glowed, the marks he'd seared into his flesh illuminating. Where he expected pain from the burns, he found only strength. Shards of heat brought confidence and courage not his own.

His mind drifted back to one particular nightmare. To the one where his father screamed for help, but shoved Haegan away.

A dungeon. Below.

"If I go back," the manservant warned, "you are alone with no one to guide you, to see to you."

"I am not alone, Thomannon." Haegan stared through still-wet hair dangling in his face. "You know this, yes? That with me are Abiassa's Deliverers." He thought of the mighty men standing guard on the perimeter. They'd been but a whisper of a thought, a glimpse of what was there, yet wasn't. He felt mad for speaking it.

You're crazy, Haegan. It's why your father shut you away.

Falling . . . falling . . . his courage was falling.

No, not falling. Pulling—being *pulled* from him.

Inflaming.

Manipulated again. Anger rearing, he gritted his teeth. "Augh!"

Thomannon yelped and threw himself backward.

At first, it seemed the manservant acted in fear of Haegan's gift, but then he stared at something in the gloom of the hall. When Haegan shifted, shadows danced beneath the tease of moonslight.

No. The moons have no entrance here since the ceiling forbids it. So what then?

Darkness seemed to pour more of itself from the shadows.

A creature! Haegan's gaze fastened on the body slinking toward him.

Yellow eyes blinked. Another form coalesced from nothing. Not there one second, then there the next. How? Quicker than mist darkening a wool coat, the figure appeared.

Haegan started. "Drracien."

"Hello, Princeling." Drracien gave him a wicked grin. "Like my new trick? I can disappear"—he was gone, then there again but on the other side—"and reappear."

Haegan jerked. "How . . . ?"

Drracien laughed. "I'm not sure, actually."

"A-are you dead?"

"No. Not yet, but I will be if I keep dancing across the Void."

"Then don't. Come with me." He indicated the doors.

Drracien's gaze tightened. "Not this time, Princeling. I fear my path is less . . . hopeful."

"Leave them. I'll protec—"

The beast leapt into the air from the left. A blur of razor-edged teeth, long and needlelike.

Thomannon shrieked.

Haegan threw out a hand to defend himself, but before the Flames even left him, the beast howled and thudded to the ground. Confused, dumbfounded, Haegan watched the incorporeal body of the beast solidify.

"My lord, run!" Thomannon shouted. "They're both down. Run!"

Haegan glanced to his friend now slumped on the floor. "Drracien!" Who had struck him?

"No, my lord. You must—"

"What was that noise?" came a shrill voice far above. "Guards!"

"Go!" Thomannon yanked Haegan around. Pointed to a door beneath the stairs. "Your father is there, sire! Hurry before—" The manservant's head snapped back and struck the wall with a sickening crack. He crumpled in a heap.

Haegan spun. His heart pounded at the sight of Nydelia scuttling down the staircase, shouting to the guards rushing ahead.

With his goal yet in reach, Haegan bolted for the door and dove through, careening into a vacuous darkness. Fear choked him; he realized as he went airborne that he could not see ahead. He braced. His shoulder hit first. Jarring pain rattled his teeth. He tumbled backward, expecting to meet another wall. Instead, there was nothingness. He was falling . . . farther. Something whacked his head. A metallic tinge glanced across his tongue—blood. His cheek stung. Jagged steps pounded him, pitching him in a spiraling tumble. Stairs.

He landed with a bone-cracking punch to his back. Air punched from him. Haegan arched his spine, writhing against the torturous lack of oxygen and the inability to take a breath. He squeezed his eyes, straining. Feeling every pinch, cut, and ache in his body, but none more than the greedy demand of his lungs for relief.

Get up!

Nydelia—no, *Father!*

Groaning through the agony, Haegan flopped over, face in muck and dirt. Fingernails dug in the earth. Struggling for a breath that did not sear, he fought for bearings. Saw dots of light . . . dots that slowly glowed brighter.

Clawing the ground, he hauled himself onto all fours. Pain stabbed his side, and Haegan gripped it as he lumbered to his feet.

Clanking drew his gaze to nearby cells. Dingy, smudged faces pressed to the iron. A wail went up, then a repetitive thud. The noise came from a dark corner of the dungeon. Haegan cast a dull glow in that direction. As the embers spread, he barely made out a huddled shape pressed to the far side, rocking. Banging his head on the wall with each rock.

"Oy!"

Haegan shifted his attention. Through damp curls grown too long, he stared at the far end of the passage, where a large man emerged from a room leaking light down the dark corridor.

Ugh! What was that smell? Shielding his mouth and nose, Haegan took a step forward.

"You are?" Jangling preceded a man who came into the light of the lone torch.

"Your end," Haegan gritted out.

The man's jowls jiggled. Then his eyes bugged. "You again!" He lunged, keys forgotten and a dagger suddenly in hand.

Perhaps the anger is not yours alone.

Flames roiled true and hot with a will all their own. No, *Her* own. Haegan pushed into the wielding, funneling every ounce of anger he felt into vanquishing this jailor, whose scream died with him. Accosted at the loss of life, Haegan was bolstered by the influx of righteous anger. Emboldened by Abiassa's strength, Haegan stepped into his purpose.

• • •

Baen's Six stand as faithful sentries, jubilant in the victory of the Fierian. They exist in two worlds—Haegan's and Abiassa's. They serve one will—Hers. And now, Her will is exacted.

"He is free!"

Exultation rushed through the air of both worlds. Desecrators shrieked in mad fury, their defeat already whispered on the wielding of the Fierian. Baen shouts, his voice rattling the heavens, "Prepare the warriors. Send the Guardian and position the Paladin."

"The Guardian is coming," promises Draorin.

"The Paladin is ready," Medric vows.

"Ensnare the witch. Her hour is come!"

13

"Fool!"

A wash of heat much like a shove rushed over Drracien's shoulders. Annoyed, he brought his gaze to the Infantessa marching toward him.

"Why didn't you stop him?" she shrilled.

The Infantessa was not worth the fight. She'd played a game with Haegan's life, and lost. Drracien didn't care that he'd angered her.

Nydelia sent a spark toward him.

With a snort, he caught it, rolled it around his fingers, amused as he watched the flame dance. Then he lifted his gaze to her and crushed the spark in his palm.

It wasn't true that he didn't care. He did—the witch had imprisoned his friend. And that irked him.

Confusion and indignation combusted in her expression. "How dare you!" She shoved with both palms, flames convulsing from her hands.

Sidestepping her efforts proved easy. Drracien reached back and siphoned the heat and embers she'd thrown. He brought them around, hyperfocused the energy, and whipped it back at her. "You're predictable." He sneered. "And slow."

The bolt hit true and hard. She stumbled backward, her head jerking. When she straightened, shock riddling a face that looked like his hands after he'd been too long in the water, she gasped. "You impudent brat!" Even as she trained her wielding on him again, she froze. Her hand gnarled and extended. Mouth gaping like a part of the black void. Empty eyes bulging in shock and disbelief.

Should he kill her? And betray to Poired that he had come here? He really didn't need any more headaches or lectures. "I should end you." Diavel was there, snarling, rippling through mist and flesh, begging to carry out Drracien's thoughts. "But I want to see you fail." Drracien seeped into the Void, the pain numbing yet not as excruciating as before. Yet before he lost his grip on the Infantessa's palace, he heard the howl of anger.

Though his legs moved, Drracien felt air snatching at him, as if he was falling, flying.. Something unnatural that thrust him away. A strange white-blue light tore at his eyes. He squinted and shielded himself. "What is that?" he wondered aloud.

"A Deliverer."

Drracien tried to hide his flinch from the Dark One, whose presence he'd stepped into from the Void. "A Deliverer—you're sure? Where?"

"Just outside Unelithia. With the steward." Poired stood staring at the city, as he often did. How he could tell one point in the Void from another was beyond Drracien. "I want you to go there," he instructed. "They don't yet know of your new loyalties. Rout the Deliverer."

"Rout the—" Shock choked Drracien's words. "Have you lost your blazing mind?"

His head severed from his body. His abiatasso hovered over the split pieces, a searing, excruciating pain unlike anything he'd experienced tore at every fragment of him. A shriek rent the air—his own agonized scream. He writhed within his body, without his body. Confusion clamored and beat his mind. Focus lost, he thrashed, feeling as if his flesh burned off his bones.

And then he collapsed in torturous defeat on the cold marble floor, sobbing.

"Think not to question me or my orders. You may bleed my blood, but you *do* bleed."

Shuddering whimpers rolled through Drracien as he clawed onto all fours. That pain . . . His limbs. His mind. All wisps of smoke from the searing, crushing agony.

"Go to the steward," Poired ordered. "Find out what they're doing. Locate the Deliverer. When you've found him, come to me."

He *had* lost his mind! Cradling his body, Drracien dared not lift his head. Dared not look at the Dark One.

"I am not fool enough to think you've been cleansed of weakness. Not until I see the fire in your eyes, Drracien. You have an inordinate gift, but when you are fully immersed, you will be guarded. Diavel is never far. Neither are the Desecrators."

Something steeled in Drracien. Desecrators. He'd heard of them but relegated them to myth. Of course, he'd done that with the Drigovudd, and Haegan had awoken those giants with a few words. Who had awakened the Desecrators? Or had they always perverted and plundered, unseen?

"They do my bidding, as I am bid by Sirdar. You are not the only one tethered to the will of someone you detest, but until your sister is returned to me, I will play at this thing he has forced."

"Sister?" Drracien hissed, struggling to his feet. "Dati?"

Poired barked a laugh. "I would no more claim that weakling than her brother." He nodded. "Now do as I said, and you will live another day."

This was living? This half death, this torture? For that is all he felt now. Pain. Distracting, tearing pain that plied at his thoughts. Refused to leave him alone.

Alone.

Yes . . . alone. He was alone, but for the pain. What friends he'd had for a short time would no sooner accept him now than they would Poired.

There would always be pain. There would always be loneliness. He was accepted neither by the good nor the bad. Light nor darkness. His gaze traveled the twitching fabric of the Void and realized this was the best place for him, straddling two worlds. Two versions of himself. Here, he did no harm.

• • •

NORTH OF LITTLE HALL

"They do not trust us," Adassi said as they guided their horses into the long queue behind the Westerners. Dust from the supply wagons gave double purpose to their veils, though it did little to mask the bitter scents rolling off the steward's contingent. Even the wagon drivers seemed determined to mistrust Vaqar and his people.

"I would not have it any other way." Vaqar sought the young steward, who rode safely protected by a dozen in front and more white riders in the rear.

"What sort of man believes a story like ours with such ease?" Dwaith grumbled from behind.

"One who has seen much," Vaqar answered, his gaze flitting for the thousandth time to the two specks soaring high above the crawling snake of soldiers and camp followers. Raqine. Who knew what else the steward had seen? What drove him on his ever-northward journey?

"Remind me why we're joining them, delving deeper into the Nine? Shouldn't we be going south? Or to the mountains—maybe frozen lands won't reek so much."

It was a possibility. The warmer the region, the more amplified the scents. And they were continually battling incipients, which meant the stench could be intolerable.

"They may not trust us, but do you trust them?" Haandra asked from beside her brother, who had spoken little since they'd broken camp two rises past.

Trust? It was an embodied word, built of experiences and relationship. He had neither of those with the steward. And yet . . . "Her Messenger rides with him." That was enough, watching the Messenger remain with the steward, always protecting. If the Messenger was him, there was no choice. "We follow."

"So you *don't* trust him," Haandra said, always one to put the truth between them, regardless of courtesy or propriety. Had Vaqar still been commander, she never would have spoken to him so boldly. And he was glad for it. She was a friend. A wise woman, despite her youth and beauty.

"When I trust him, you will know," Vaqar acquiesced. "For now, we follow."

"How long?" Dwaith demanded.

Again, Vaqar eyed the Messenger, trotting so causally between the steward and a younger soldier. "Until He tells me otherwise."

Quiet fell among his people as the band struggled beneath the searing heat of the sun. His headache worsened with each league they covered. A tight pressure between his eyes and pulsing at his temples. Though he wore the cloth, the scents still proved difficult.

Why? Why had Aaesh chosen him? To burden them with this curse.

To bring to ruin fragrances he once savored. The smell of sowaoli petals. The sweetness of a cordi.

"Smell it?" Haandra whispered, her voice alight. "Water."

It was one positive that came with the curse—they could scout water long before they could see it.

"But where?" Adassi asked, squinting to the west where the sun settled into the horizon of a burned field.

Too dry. Vaqar scanned northeast, noting the way land fell away. He closed his eyes. Took a breath and tugged down his cloth. Braced, he inhaled. Held the scents in his mouth and nostrils, then processed them. Grass. Trees. Flowers. "There. Beyond the rise." He repositioned the cloth, relaxing at its protection.

"Should we tell them?" Adassi asked, then shrugged. "It'll show we have purpose."

"You mean it'll show that we're not out of our skulls," Dwaith groused.

Vaqar didn't want to flaunt their abilities, yet, Adassi had a point. With a sigh, he slowed his mount. What if the steward didn't believe him? He'd sensed as much when he'd explained the curse, though there had been a measure of reluctance in the steward's disbelief. If Vaqar had told his people that, they would have insisted upon departing to find their own way. And in truth, why remain among the Westerners fighting a battle not their own when they could find fewer people in the Northlands, therefore fewer smells?

At once, Vaqar felt a strange, heady warmth pulse and realized he was locked in the steady gaze of the Messenger. A remonstration seared the air between them, in spite of the distance.

Wordless, the Messenger said plenty. Vaqar experienced it. *He has me here for a purpose.* And it did not necessarily follow that the purpose was to benefit Vaqar. "We will tell them of the water," he said to his men.

He and Adassi jabbed their heels into their mounts and trotted up the line to the steward. But as they neared the front, the white riders closed ranks around the steward.

"Easy," coaxed the steward.

The gray-haired general broke rank and met them. "What do you want, Tahscan?"

The line slowed to a stop. Adassi slanted a wary, angry gaze to Vaqar.

The insult of being stopped like an intruder did not sit well. Vaqar clenched his jaw and forced himself to nod to his man.

Adassi's eyes narrowed as he turned to the general. "We thought you might want to refresh your horses at the spring."

"Spring?" The general barked a laugh. "Maybe you've been too long in the sun, Tahscan."

Vaqar tightened a fist in his horse's mane. But he detected something in the air. A bit sweet, a bit . . . burnt. Desperate hope. It was then he felt the gaze of the steward on him, but Vaqar kept his focus on Adassi. The one actually speaking to the general. The one ready to abandon the Westerners to their scorched lands and sniggering superiority.

Soft and discordant fluttered another scent. Vaqar stilled, isolating the smell from the ones of disbelief. Did it annoy the Westerners so much that Tahscans were able to smell better? That they would feel vindictive?

No, not vindictive. It was something . . . more. More desperate. Chin down, he angled to his right. Thinking, sorting, pushing his gaze to search for the source.

"Where?" The steward nudged through the wall of white cloaks and green uniforms toward Adassi and Vaqar. "Where is there water?"

The question, spoken in earnest and without ridicule, drew Vaqar's gaze back.

"Sire, there isn't water for leagues," a young white rider said around a laugh.

"Please," the steward insisted, pulling up alongside Adassi. "We are all tired and thirsty. Show us the water."

Without breaking eye contact, Adassi nodded to the east. "Beyond the knoll behind you."

"Captain Rhaemos," barked the general.

The burly soldier surged from the pack and galloped toward the knoll.

Vaqar and Adassi guided their horses around and returned to the Tahscans at the rear of the column.

"Maybe now they'll trust us," Adassi said in Tahsci.

"I would not be so sure," Vaqar countered gravely.

"They are not worth our time," Dwaith mumbled.

"Perhaps not." Vaqar sighed as he led the Tahscans toward the spring, looking for a decent place to camp.

"It's here!" the captain called.

Shouts sped through the column as Vaqar crested the knoll and rode down to the small pond ringed by stunted trees. Removing his veil, he slid from his mount. He walked the horse to water, where it drank greedily. As he crouched to cup some of the cool liquid to his own lips, he detected it again. That discordant scent. Sweet desperation. His gaze tracked across the surface of the water to a small cluster of trees.

"This comes in from the Bay of Winds," Dwaith suggested.

"Nay," Haandra argued. "It's too far north for that. This is a spring."

"Doesn't matter where it comes from as long as we can soak our cloths, fill our skins and bladders, and refresh." Jadrile bent and cupped his hand in the pool.

Wind drifted across the water and carried that scent again. Vaqar let his fingers dangle on the surface as he probed the dark trees. It was a small copse, but enough to hide someone. Warning prickled the back of his neck.

"You feel it, too," Haandra said. "Something's not right."

"Mm." As Pathfinders and soldiers clogged the pond's tiny banks, Vaqar stood. Smoothed a hand along the flank of his horse. "Wait here," he ordered the others, who responded with not even a note of stiffening or surprise, though he smelled their alarm. If he met with trouble, they would be at his back in an instant.

Staying close to the horses and revelry that pervaded the Westerners, Vaqar made his way around the pond toward the trees. In a flash, he broke away from the horde and sprinted to the copse, where he slid up along a trunk, giving his eyes time to adjust to the protective darkness.

Then another smell hit his nostrils—blood. A smattering of dark spots on the leaves caught his attention. Scanning the foliage, Vaqar squatted. He reached for a stained leaf, not taking his gaze from his surroundings. Crouched there for the better part of an hour convinced him of two things—the quarry with the desperate scent was female, and though he could not isolate her location, she would eventually betray her position. This was another benefit of the gift: No need to race and panic through the hunt. Simply wait.

A scent stabbed at him.

He latched onto it. Even as his left hand moved toward the blood, his right freed the dagger from his boot. He threw it. The blade landed with a decidedly loud thunk. "I will not miss next time," he warned as he pushed to his feet. "You are injured."

"It's not my blood," came a voice. Female. As he'd predicted.

He lifted his fingertips to his nose and checked the blood with a sniff. Then grunted. It *wasn't* human. And he hated that he could tell the difference. No man should have the ability to discern human blood from animal blood. "What do you want?"

"Is the steward with you?"

Why did she care about the steward? To kill him? Vaqar stared into the shadows, barely able to decipher her shape. But the way she stood. It was odd. "Why should I answer? If he were, I would place him and myself in danger."

"I just"—she grunted—"tell me if he's here!"

Vaqar said nothing, only drew in a deep breath to better isolate the scent of her threat.

"I'll release my bow," she said in warning. "Then my dagger."

Another heavy draught. Anger. Fear. But mostly pain. "A bow," he said, walking to the side, eyes on the foliage, not to see it, but to better work out what lay within the darker shadows. Looking straight on, he could not see her. A type of night blindness. But from his periphery, his eyes sorted more. "A recurve bow. Fifty pounds of draw weight."

"Sixty," she gritted out.

A smile pushed into his assessment. "You are leaning against a tree. Which tells me something I already know—you *are* injured—"

"I said the blood wasn't mine."

"Agreed." He smirked. "But I smell the pain on you, the sweat, the desperation. The way you lean against that tree, the bow unsteady in your hands."

"Are you going to talk me to death?"

"To death?" He snorted, paced a little more, then wagged his head. "No." Again he paced back to the other side. Wagged his head. "But exhaustion?" He nodded. "Your balance is compromised, little bird."

"You know nothing," she said with another grunt.

An arrow spiraled from of the darkness and landed clumsily at his feet. Seeing her crumbling, Vaqar rushed in. Sliding down the tree. He reached for her. Though she shoved at him, her limbs failed, and he caught her. "Easy." Held her firm. "They have a physician with them—"

"No." Her eyes widened in wild panic. "No, they can't know I'm here. They'll kill me." She gripped his collar tight and twisted it across his neck in a choke hold.

Surprise lit through Vaqar as his breath broke off. The strength that wasn't there suddenly was, lit by her determination. And skill. She'd used his concern over her injuries against him. A blow to her temple would settle this now, but that blasted scent enveloping the girl stopped him. Instead, he shoved a hand up between her arms and broke her grip. She grunt-yelped and clawed away from him. Stumbled to her feet.

"If you had strength, little bird, you might have a chance against me."

Sweat beaded dark brown hair that framed a pretty face—well, maybe. Once the bruises and cuts were healed, she might be pretty. "I'll kill you."

Vaqar smiled down at her. "When you are better, perhaps."

Her eyebrow arched as she produced a scimitar. Not just a scimitar. *His* scimitar.

"Impressive," Vaqar muttered, ashamed and fascinated at the same time.

"The steward."

"I will not give him to you."

"Then he's here."

Vaqar tensed. "What do you want with him?"

"'Tis none of your concern." The blade wobbled in her hand.

"My scimitar. My business, little bird."

His blade flew into the air and Vaqar instinctively reached for the hilt. Arm up, he saw her tactic in the split-second before he felt the blinding pain stab through his ribs. Stars sprinkled his vision. Daylight blurred as he struggled to keep eyes on her. Where had she gone?

He whirled, feeling himself going down. But not before he spotted her speeding through the copse as he lost the battle for consciousness.

• • •

Dusk brushed its long hazy fingers along the horizon. Tili pulled himself off his cot and peered out the thick wedge of the tent flap. He smiled at the sight of the small lake, the double moons peeking down on their watery reflections. With a sigh, he made his way to the wash basin and splashed his face. When he looked up, he stilled, surprised at his haggard appearance in the shaving mirror affixed to a tent pole, and at his great similarity in appearance to his mountain-dwelling brother, Elan. The beard. It was the beard. And it must go.

He reached for the razor set, then hesitated. Glanced again in the mirror as he swiped a hand over the thick, soft beard.

It wasn't just the beard. The eyes. He'd changed.

Who hadn't in the fight for survival? Who was he anymore? Tili, son of Thurig the Formidable? Commander of the Nivari? Brother? Son?

"Steward?"

That, too. Tili lowered his gaze at the voice of the general outside the tent. "Enter."

The tent flap thwapped back and the general ducked in. "Sir."

"The camp is quiet," Tili noted.

"Aye," Negaer said as he stood at attention. "Many bathed, all have eaten and imbibed of the water."

Considering his beard once more, Tili debated hacking the thing off. He hated it. Made his face itch.

"If you shave now, you'll only have to do it again on the morrow."

Tili snorted. "Aye." He grabbed a towel from the stand and dried his hands. "What brings ye, General?"

"I think we should break camp and continue north."

Concern weighed heavily. "Yer scouts picked up something?"

Negaer hesitated.

"It can get no worse than facing down the Sirdarians."

"Not just Sirdarians, but Poired himself. Desecrators."

"Poired." Tili shook his head, feeling the punch of that revelation. He pointed to the chairs set up near the front. "What business has he this far east? I thought he'd be breaking for my father's kingdom or—"

"You," Negaer said firmly. "You are his business."

"Me?" Tili scoffed. "I am a steward."

"Aye, *the* steward leading the remnant, maintaining the Nine's foothold. If they can wipe you out and destroy what remains of the Council, the Nine will cease to exist."

"Not as long as Haegan lives and breathes."

"We have no proof that he does."

Tili snapped a look at the general, who raised his hands.

"I mean no disrespect or treason. My objective is to keep you safe. The men and I will do everything to ensure you reach Molian when the Council summons you, but before that happens, we track down the prince as Gwogh instructed. We must be strategic and swift. There can be no hesitation in our movements, or the enemy will seize upon them. Make hesitation weakness. Weakness failure."

"Ye've given this thought," Tili said, realizing there was much more behind what the general had spoken. "What plan do ye suggest?"

"Start for Ironhall."

Folding his arms over his chest, Tili frowned. "Ironhall. Why there— we need to find a way to reach Haegan in Unelithia. Besides, isn't Ironhall abandoned and its walls broken or missing?"

"Only just," Negaer said. "Ironhall is a solid base option. We can set up camp there and dispatch scouts to find a way into Iteveria to see what we will face there. Eventually, we will need to go north to Molian."

Vid's capital. It made sense.

"Ironhall is a midpoint too convenient to ignore."

That the general tried to convince Tili to make for Ironhall warned him. Something had pushed the general to call for such an action. "General, ye are not just the commander of the Pathfinders, ye *are* the Pathfinders. Yer skill is tracking, ranging, and yet, ye counsel me to hole up in a defunct fortress."

Negaer held his gaze.

"What have ye learned that ye come to me and advise we break camp as night approaches?"

"My scouts have tracked the movement of packs."

"Packs?" Tili frowned. "Men or animals?"

"Little difference with these—Maereni. I've scouts several leagues out in all directions. One hasn't reported back since the last moonslight. Another had a harrowing encounter. The savages are hunting."

"Hunting what?"

"You. I told you—they want the Steward dead." Negaer nodded. "The land is pocked by the beasts. But if we make for Ironhall"—he dipped his head, acknowledging his own point—"we will have a place to fortify and operate from, better to figure out a plan to retrieve the prince."

Was there a choice? "Sit here and wait to be killed in our sleep . . ."

"Or ride hard and fast to Ironhall."

"Gather your captains, as well as Draorin, Tokar, and Praegur." Tili pushed to his feet. "The command tent in fifteen."

"Sir." Negaer strode out, and Tili took a minute to capture his thoughts.

Ye didn't expect to draw out the beast, riding up and down the Nine like a beacon?

"Fool." Tili grabbed his official overcloak and sash, then left. He stalked toward the largest tent, noting the quiet sentries and crackling fires.

A shadow came from his right. Tili's heart jammed into his throat, and he hopped sideways. When he saw the face, he breathed out. "Blazes, Vaqar. Give care who ye frighten."

"I must speak with you, Steward." Touching the back of his head, Vaqar stalked toward him.

"I beg yer mercy," Tili said, continuing toward the command tent. "We're busy—"

"Am I to be only a weapon in your hand? Or will I also have a voice?"

Slowing, Tili rubbed his forehead. Too many people demanding his time and energy. Is this what Father dealt with? Why had he not paid more attention to the way his father had managed these things? But of course, his father was not in the middle of the Nine, running from blood-thirsty Desecrators. He turned to the Tahscan. "Fair enough."

The great warrior, who stood at least a few inches taller and several handspans wider than Tili, inclined his head. For a savage, he was considerably more refined than even Negaer. "When we first scouted the water, I encountered a girl asking about you."

Frustration choked Tili. "Vaqar, I have no interest in females—"

"She was skilled in combat, Steward. I am concerned for your safety."

Tili hesitated, considering the large man. "Ye think her a threat?"

"She is injured and half my size, but that did not stop her from attempting to strangle me. I would have reported sooner, but she knocked me unconscious with a blow."

Tili blinked. A female. Knocked the Tahscan out.

"It would serve you well to be alert." Vaqar nodded to Rhaemos and a guard, who lingered nearby. "Keep them close. I will not be far either."

Exhaustion and urgency severed Tili's irritation. None else had seen this woman. Nor had they detected any threat. He needed Vaqar more than ever. "My men are meeting. Would ye join us or—"

"Tili!" A shout, a surprising one using his given name, pulled him around, where he found Tokar and Praegur rushing at him.

"Blazes and mercies, can no one function for one spark without me?" he hissed, waiting as the two skidded up. Tokar nodded to Praegur, who seemed to blanch beneath the glow of the firelight. But the man didn't speak, so Tili glowered. "I have a meeting."

"You must save her." Praegur's words were rigid, coiled with ferocity. Tenored with authority. Filled with rumble.

"He speaks Her words," Vaqar said in a whisper of awe.

"Whose words?"

"Aaesh."

Tili's gut tightened as he refocused on the two friends. "Who am I to save?"

A scream raked the camp.

Praegur grunted and took off running.

"Blazes and bolts," Tili muttered, hopping into a sprint behind the dark-skinned youth.

As they ran, Tokar said, "They found a girl at the edge of the camp."

The same girl Vaqar mentioned? Tili sped up, his mind at war with the idea. What was a girl doing out this far, alone? And why—*how*—did she knock out Vaqar? A refugee come to steal from the soldiers? Then why not join his contingent along with the others? There were always a few dozen displaced villagers tagging along with the soldiers, until they came across locales that could take them in. Tili had given instructions that no one was to be turned away.

When they rounded a tent near the edge of camp, Tili slowed as he spotted the cluster of Pathfinders huddled near the trees. Some laughing. Others cheering. Two held a girl stretched out on the ground. Another leered down at her as he reached for his belt.

Fury erupted through Tili. A bolt shot from his hand before he could think. It split and knocked backward the two holding the girl. Even as she scrambled onto her feet, Tili launched himself at the Pathfinder standing over her. Slammed his fist into the soldier's face and, for good measure, sent a shockwave of heat through it as well.

The Pathfinder fell.

Breathing hard, disgusted, Tili turned a slow circle, glowering through a thick brow at the others. Rage colored his vision, choked his words. He felt like Chima when she prowled a kill. "Return to yer tents. Or I will sear each of ye with a mark to brand ye for the cowards ye are!" He held out a hand to the girl and waited, eyes locked on the impudent Pathfinders. "And pray I do not seek yer white cloaks as recompense." He wagged her closer, impatient to deliver her from the men.

Tentative fingers touched his.

Tili gripped them tight and pulled her forward. She wobbled and grimaced—injured. Glaring at the men who backed away, he nudged the girl to Tokar. "See her to pharmakeia so he may tend her wounds."

The girl hesitated, glancing back to Tili.

"You are safe here," Vaqar said as he stepped near. "No need to run. Again."

Tokar and Praegur nodded, their expressions tight as they led her away.

One Pathfinder stood his ground. "She's mark—"

"Silence!" Tili barked, noting Rhaemos and Negaer running up behind the man. "General, I want each of those men arrested and held." Embers roiled through him and around his hands. "This is *not* how we treat anyone. Ever! And if this happens again, I will strip each one of ye of yer white cloaks."

Negaer looked ready to explode, but he turned his ferocious glare to Rhaemos. "Captain, you heard Steward Tili. Put them in stocks while this is sorted."

The addendum was not lost on Tili. When he turned, his gaze collided with Vaqar's, and the Tahscan warrior gave him a solemn nod, then stalked away. Ragged and trembling from the adrenaline rush, Tili stormed toward the command tent.

"What was that?" Negaer hissed as he came alongside. "Nobody orders my men—"

"Would ye speak such to Prince Haegan? Or the Fire King?"

"You are neither."

"Yet I am both!" Till drew up and pushed into the general's space. "I am their representative. There is no higher authority than me in the land at the moment. Regardless how ye or I feel, I *am* the crown." His chest hurt from the frenetic pounding, borne of rage and futility. "And I will never stand by while men beat and rape a woman."

"Rape? She is an assassin!"

"They had her stretched on the ground. The captain was dropping his trousers! And think ye I am so ignorant I cannot read her marks?"

Negaer drew up straight.

"And even if I had not found him so near the act, I would have beaten him senseless for abusing *anyone.*" He pushed into the general's space. "We face an enemy cruel and wicked, one who takes pleasure in hurting, maiming, and killing. We will *not* become that, we will *not* abuse the power given us by Abiassa. We will be better."

14

NORTH OF LITTLE HALL

Bent forward on the chair, Tili gripped his head. Grief plied at him. Would that this war were over. That the weariness seeping into his bones would heal. That the land and people would heal.

Coming up on that scene vaulted him back to Kiethiel when she was young and snatched from the hold in the dead of night. He would never forget the way she'd looked when she'd finally been returned. Brutalized. Broken. He'd needed a moment alone.

It was too much to think of it happening again. To another innocent.

Innocent. He snorted. What innocent girl wandered the woods alone at a time like this with the mark of an assassin? *Innocent* was certainly not a word they could place on her.

Oh that he had his father's ear to bend. That he had a friend to share the journey and battle. Sailing through life with a shrug and a sarcastic comment, he'd never been one to need a friend. But life . . . war . . . "I am not fit to be their leader," he muttered.

"She does not agree."

The rumbling voice startled him, and Tili jerked up, looking across the table to Praegur. He frowned. Where had he come from? "I thought ye didn't talk to anyone. That's twice ye've loosed yer tongue in my presence."

Praegur shrugged. "I speak when She gives me something to say. Most often with Haegan. But you are her steward."

"Steward." He slumped against the chair, rapping his knuckles on the wood. "Her fool is more like."

"She has allowed me to speak to you, so I do not believe you can be a fool." Dark eyes sparked with wisdom and laughter. "You saved the girl, and that is what Abiassa wanted."

"She's an assassin."

"She is marked, but are not we all, in one way or another?"

"She has killed. Done the work of the Dark One."

"Have not we all?" Praegur said. "Lies and selfishness are not relegated to Sirdarians alone. The land has prostituted itself to selfish desires and, ultimately, Sirdar."

Tili hauled himself out of the chair and discussion. "I have no strength to debate philosophy or theology with ye, Praegur." At the stand, he poured a cup of cordi and lifted it in offering to the young man.

Praegur shook his head.

Tili dumped back the juice, feeling the vitality it provided, then poured more. "Where is the girl?" He took another drink.

"Tokar guards her at your tent."

He sucked in a breath, juice flooding his lungs. He cough-choked. Thumping his chest, he strained through watery eyes to look at the Kergulian. "*My* tent? What madness is that? Ye realize the implication." Blazes and bolts! What were they doing to him?

Praegur nodded again. "That she is under your protection."

Snorting and shaking his head in disbelief, Tili abandoned the juice and dropped in the chair again, cradling his head once more. "Mercies, Abiassa, why do Ye torment me with such glee?" He pressed the heel of his hand against his forehead. "Bring her here."

Praegur frowned.

"Bring her," Tili growled. "She must stand before the . . ." What did he call the men who counseled him?

"I beg your mercy, but she is not . . . appropriate for public."

What in blazes does that mean? But as soon as he asked, he recalled her torn clothes. Her cut and bruised face. "Have the tailor make her new clothes. Is there another woman to tend her?" He snapped his fingers, remembering. "That Tahscan has a female warrior. Have her help the girl."

Praegur inclined his head, acquiescing, then bowed and left.

Tili snorted again. It figures. He protected a woman from being raped, and the men stuff her in his tent. Which would lead most, if not all, to assume he claimed her.

Mercies, he wanted no female. Tili growled and left for the command tent. As he entered, Negaer, Draorin, and Rhaemos ducked into the tent.

"Good news," Rhaemos announced, indicating a fourth man. "Major Grinda arrived with another dozen Pathfinders."

Tili eyed the younger Grinda—Graem. Saw the worn clothing and expression, and chose to spare him an interrogation. "Well met, Major. I am glad ye are well and safe."

"It's good to be with the men again, sir. Thank you."

He nodded as they seated themselves at the table. "First, I would apologize to General Negaer, who feels I overstepped by threatening to strip his men of their white cloaks." He could understand the revered man feeling threatened. "While I may attempt to make greater efforts to consider and counsel with those at this table, I will not hesitate to act swiftly when I deem it necessary. Rape of a woman—whether a criminal or not—is criminal in itself. I will tolerate no abuse from any man."

"What of the men you had me put in stocks?" Negaer asked, challenge in his question and expression.

"General, I will leave that in yer—"

"Might I make a suggestion?"

The half-dozen men turned to the one lurking at the tent opening.

"Vaqar, please," Tili said, motioning to the warrior. "Join us." As the Tahscan stalked to the table, Tili explained, "I have invited Vaqar to sit at the council table with us."

"Not to be impudent," Rhaemos said, "but what right has he to speak regarding the Nine's affairs?"

"'Tis a good question," Tili said. "Vaqar, would ye speak?"

The man half sat, then came back to his feet, knuckles on the table. "I have no desire to overtake your lands or systems. I was sent here—"

"By whom?" Tili asked.

Vaqar hesitated. "Aaesh's Messenger."

Tingling buzzed through Tili as Vaqar's eyes flicked toward Draorin, much as they had that first meeting. He'd long assumed Draorin simply shared the name of one of Baen's Six. The realm was notorious for naming its children after Baen's famous captains, men who were made immortal for their sacrifice and valiant fighting centuries ago. Was it possible . . . ?

Tili scoffed at himself.

Yet why not? It felt like a mockery, but what if one of Baen's Six sat among them? A Deliverer at their table. Heat shot through him at the thought.

Almost without his willing it, Tili's attention shifted to Draorin. "What would ye have us do?"

Shoulders square, hair untouched with gray despite his apparent age, Draorin seemed to grow—taller, bigger, fiercer—and when Tili met his eyes, he found himself staring into the eyes of eternity.

Sharp gasps filled the air as the others came to the same realization.

"Ask the one called Astadia," Draorin said. "Let Her guide the Guardian and the Paladin."

15

NORTH OF LITTLE HALL

"I will be no man's prisoner," she spat.

As he entered his tent with the others of his council, Tili started at the fair-cheeked, dark-haired girl. The borrowed pale blue tunic and trousers lent her a deceptive softness, but Tili had only to look at her face to see the ferocity of her spirit.

"That is good," he shot back, "because I have no time for prisoners."

"Neither will I warm your bed," she snapped, looking at the others over her hands anchored to the tent post.

"'Twould take more than slip of a girl like ye to warm that cot," Tili groused, then tipped his head toward her jailor. "Why is she chained?"

"It seemed safest, considering her mark," Tokar answered.

Ah yes, the mark of the assassin. "Show it to me," he ordered.

But the girl, her face far too abused for one so small and young, jutted her jaw.

"Is this where ye choose to stay chained to a post and gawked at?" Tili shook his head, realizing she was as defiant and obstinate as his sister. "Fine. When—"

Using her teeth, she yanked up her sleeve, eyes ablaze. And yet there was something in her expression, her posture, that spoke of brokenness. Subservience.

Still, that mark . . .

"The upside-down eye," someone whispered in terror.

"Ye bear the mark of the Devoted, Poired's assassins," Tili said, strangely disappointed to have found her in so deep with the Dark One.

Her eyes blazed. "Can I help it if the only way men find to get their way is to tie me down and leave their mark?"

Something in Tili went sideways. "Then ye denounce the Devoted?"

"How can I denounce what I never chose?"

"Denounce it or we—"

"Flames and blazes," she hissed. "Yes, I denounce them! How long are we to dance around this brand before we get to the crux of why I'm here?"

"You're here, witch of a girl, because you were caught sneaking into the camp," Rhaemos snarled.

"I'm one girl."

"You're an assassin—a Devoted. Better dead than breathing."

"Then kill me," she snarled, straining at her chains. She seemed ambivalent—no, oblivious to the raw marks where her wrists had been rubbed bloody.

But Tili wasn't. A girl who could ignore that kind of pain . . . what had she been through? How much had she withstood that she could shirk off bleeding wrists? And the strangest of all—she didn't look one wit scared.

"Kill me and end this charade."

"Nothing would give me greater pleasure," Rhaemos said, stalking toward her.

"Ye're angry," Tili muttered.

Her eyes, green and wide, flashed to him. "Of course, I'm angry. Have you looked around this tent? You're a bunch of male chauvinist—"

And in that second, Tili saw her fold the fat part of her thumb inward and slide her wrist free. Amused, he flicked a spark at her in the same moment the shock of the Pathfinders registered. But, in spite of the close quarters, the spark went wide and singed a hole in the canvas tent.

She dropped to the ground to avoid his shot, and for a moment seemed as surprised as he at his poor aim. Then she pulled to her knees, one arm still tethered to the pole, and growled as he closed in. "Release me, you foul—"

"Foul? I'm not the one who reeks of sewers and—"

In a flash, she swept her leg at his feet. Tili hopped over it, smirking.

Intrigued and yet annoyed, he stepped out of reach. "What do ye want, assassin? I am told ye asked after me. To what end? My end?"

A muscle in her cheek twitched as she stared up at him. Defiance. Annoyance. Defeat. They cloyed for cover beneath her fiery disposition.

Mercies, she was so like Kiethiel 'twasn't funny.

"You're the steward."

"Give her marks for intelligence," someone muttered.

When anger flared through her expression, Tili quieted the others. "I am."

"I saw you—in the Citadel. You were part of the Contending."

A heat simmered in his gut, one that said this girl was way more trouble than they could afford. Yet he crouched before her on the ground, remembering Draorin's words. But he put the pieces together, her words, her memories, her fire. "You're the assassin who took Prince Haegan."

Her face went white. Green eyes, like moss on Caorian wood, lit and darted over his shoulder. She wet her lips. "I . . ." She was looking at the others, who came alive at the revelation.

"Blazes—she took the prince!"

"Where is he? Did you kill him?"

"No." Her panic roiled out of control. "Blazes, what is with men? I'm here to help you. I can take you to your blasted prince."

Hope pushed Tili to his feet. Finally, after weeks of setbacks, a step toward Haegan.

"On one condition," she amended.

He watched, irritated and bemused. Did she realize the tenuous ground on which she sat?

"That you free my brother, too." She blew dark strands from her face. "He's being held with the prince."

"Who is your brother, and where are they being held?"

"My brother is Trale Kath. And they're in Karithia, Infantessa Shavaussia's palace. She's using inflaming to keep them as willing hostages."

"Willing hostages?" Major Grinda scoffed. "The prince would not be willing—"

The girl leveled a level look on the young officer. "You don't know. I do! I was there. Saw it. She twisted their minds—took every doubt and turned it against them."

If she was there . . . "Then why are ye here, free?"

She swallowed, guilt evident in her posture. "I . . . I don't know. The inflaming doesn't work on me, for some reason."

"She's a witch!"

Green eyes narrowed as she glowered at Rhaemos. "Come closer, and I'll show you how true that is."

Tili scratched his beard, thinking. If she was telling the truth, they were faced with penetrating a palace in an enemy land . . . "Can ye get us into Karithia?"

"Nay," Negaer said. "Do not believe her."

"She's an assassin. She lies."

But Tili stared at the face too small, eyes too large. Too innocent for the profession she carried.

She ignored the others and spoke to Tili. "Yes." The spitfire disposition dimmed, became tinged by something that hinted at vulnerability. "Then you trust me?"

"Trust ye?" Tili snorted. "Not a breath. But we were told ye could tell us where our prince was, and ye have."

Wariness crowded her expression. "Who said I could help?"

"You were with Haegan?" Tokar edged forward, eying her.

Inappropriate as the intrusion was, Tili found himself grateful for it. She considered Tokar for several long seconds, then gave a faint nod.

"He's still alive then?" Tokar pivoted, glancing between the girl and Tili.

"I . . . I've been gone awhile." Hesitation colored her answer. She batted back her brown hair with a huff. "But when I left, she was still controlling him like a puppet, so yeah—alive. If you can call it that."

Tokar frowned. "What does that mean?"

"It means I've seen what her inflaming did to my brother, and if Haegan is there much longer . . ."

When grumbling filtered through the tent, Tili held a hand to the others and eyed the girl. "That the Infantessa toys with him works to our benefit."

"How?" someone asked.

"Because it means there's a chance he's still alive"—he nodded to her—"as the girl insinuates."

"It's a long shot," Tokar muttered.

"The only one we have," Tili reminded them.

"If Draorin said to ask her, then he is alive," Praegur rumbled. "We must leave now."

"He's right," she said, her brown eyes enlivened. "My brother and Haegan were both in bad shape. You shouldn't leave them there."

"You did," Negaer accused.

Glowering, the girl rolled her gaze to the general. "She was going to kill me because she couldn't control me. So, yes—I left. But not because I wanted to. I was no good to my brother dead."

"We should ride," Tokar suggested. "If we abandon the supply wagons, it's but two hours' hard ride east."

"Aye," Tili said, "but we can't afford to abandon our supplies. Once we get Haegan, we still have a war to fight." He paused, mentally going over the map, which was still spread on the table in his command tent. "The raqine." He looked to Praegur. "Ye and Tokar should go—"

"Me?" Tokar interrupted. "I'm not getting on the back of one of those things."

"You'll do what the Steward commands, Lieutenant," Negaer barked, and the two fell into a silent duel before Tokar finally dropped his gaze and argument.

"Her castle is atop a mountain," the girl said. "There's only one way in—Karithia Road."

"Unless the raqine sets them over the wall."

"She has trebuchets," the girl said. "I saw them as I was swimming out of the gorge."

"Then I'm not taking a raqine," Tokar said. "It gets killed—"

"The Deliverers will not allow them to be harmed," came Draorin's gravelly voice.

"There are Deliverers there?" Tili barely stopped himself from adding "too." "Why do they not smite her, end this now, and free the Fierian?"

Draorin held his gaze firmly. "It is not their task."

"Of course we will use the raqine to scout ahead and gather intelligence," Tili said.

"Agreed," Negaer said.

"Rhaemos, Praegur, and Tokar, gather yer gear and meet me by the raqine." Tili turned to Negaer. "The raqine can only handle a few at a time. Ready the Pathfinders and Jujak to mount up with all haste. We'll rendezvous there."

Negaer's tight expression held. He nodded in deference. "Aye, sire."

Tili breathed a little easier as he focused on the Tahscans. "I'm certain we are outnumbered, whether with yer band or not, but perhaps with ye, we might withstand the onslaught. Will ye continue to ride with us?"

The great warrior behind Negaer bowed. Extended a scimitar. "The battle for the Fierian is not of the Nine alone, as you know better than anyone. My blade is at your service." He backed out of the tent.

"What of you, Steward?" The female voice cut through the murmur of male-dominated din like the whistle of a blackbird through the burr of bullfrogs. "Will you ride or fly?"

Tili considered her, wondering why she asked. Wondering if Negaer was right about not trusting her. 'Twas ludicrous to trust one who killed for a living. But there was this . . . innocence about her that would not leave him. "What do they call ye, girl?"

"Assassin. Whore." Again that defiance flared. *"Girl."*

He would not allow his anger to be aroused so easily, but his pity flared without his consent, especially because he could see past the hissed names to the hurt behind each one. "Fair enough. What is yer name, then? Or do ye prefer I continue calling ye 'girl'?"

Her chin lifted. Green eyes flashed. "Astadia."

With a nod, he turned the name in his mind. It was pretty, like her. "I will fly, Astadia. I have been sharing the air with raqine since I was but a lad."

"Good, it's faster," she said, thoughts churning behind those woodsy eyes. "We can get there—"

"I beg yer mercy, Astadia," Tili said. "But ye will not be riding with me. Ye will ride with the army."

She started, then scowled. "You need me."

"That I do not." Tili nodded to the guards as he left the tent. "Give care. She's quick and vicious. But every hurt done her will be answered tenfold."

16

Haegan stared at the seared body of the dungeon master. Grieved yet relieved. Also disbelieving. He hardly knew whether to trust what his eyes told him. So much of late had been untruth and dreams.

Voices skated from the main hall, mingling with shouts and scant torchlight. Swiping away a stream of blood from his lip, Haegan looked up the stairs he'd tumbled down. Saw dancing torchlight drawing closer.

Adrenaline shot through his veins, hot and demanding. *No*, whispered through his mind.

Wham!

Dank air gusted against his face as his wielding slammed the door and melted the hinges to immobile slag.

More voices came, but they were weak, frail. Agonized. Darkness concealed the evil perpetrated in this wretched place. He strained to see through the passage. "Father?"

Several doors clanked on this level. Haegan shifted closer, peering into the cells. A face shot toward him, shrieking. Banging against the iron bars. Hard. Hard. Again and again.

"Stop, stop," Haegan pleaded with the person. Woman or man he could not tell for the wildness of their unkempt hair and appearance But no beard, so perhaps a woman? But this . . . this didn't look like a woman. Or even a human. The creature grabbed her head. Tore at her hair. Shrieked again, piercing his eardrums. Then she fell still on the ground.

Haegan swallowed. Hard. What happened?

"Carved One," a man growled. Snarled. Hissed. "You've come too late."

Carved One? Did the man refer to the words Haegan had seared into his flesh? For a second, he wondered if he belonged in the cages down here, too. Had he lost his faculties to commit such an atrocity and carve his body?

I could not risk forgetting again.

If he'd forgotten—for the thousandth time—he would not be here. Would not be . . .

What am I doing here?

Clarity strained at the edges of his mind. Demanded attention. Demanded focus.

"Haegan."

He flinched and jerked around.

A hazy face appeared in a small square opening of iron bars. Bearded. Disheveled. "Haegan, hurry or she'll kill you."

His mind chugged to understand what he saw. He drew closer, afraid this person might start wailing and shrieking as well. "Who . . . ?" No—he knew this one. He'd come to the castle with him. But not as a friend. As an . . . "Assassin."

"Forget me. I am lost. Go! Before it's too late."

"Trale." But they said he was upstairs! Lies, lies, lies! Haegan sent a bolt of embers through the lock.

Trale jumped back, eyes wide enough to be seen. He yelped and lunged at the door, ripping it open. "Haegan—why? This . . . this is my fault."

"Nay," Haegan said, truth clanging like bells in his soul. "'Tis my own fault." Hollowness tugged at him, chastising him, accusing him.

You're weak, just like your father.

The words hammered home.

But the smell . . . Not just the stench of the dungeon, but something more familiar. It hurt his head. Hurt . . .

"They're not my thoughts." In truth, they *were* his thoughts, but they were . . . inflamed. Worse—a massive thudding drowned him in confusion. "Why am I here?"

"Your father," Trale said. "Hurry! Go before she breaks through."

Haegan blinked. Looked at the stairs again, only then realizing the thudding he thought to be in his head truly came from the locked door.

Anger jolted him.

Enough! Enough of this! He had been reduced to a sniveling, confused rat far too long. "Where is my father?" he asked, then turned in a direction that he somehow knew was right.

His dream. In his dreams, he'd walked this passage. Seen it. Smelled it. Heard his father's howls.

Only, there weren't any howls now. Prisoners murmuring. Whining. Squeaking rats. "Father!" Haegan shouted, stalking into the darkness with Trale at his side. Urgency sped through him with every step. But each cell they checked, each passage they entered, grew darker.

"It's no good," Trale complained. "It's too dark."

Darkness would rule no more. Haegan flexed his thoughts toward the black curtain and extended his hand. He pushed, sending a warm-blue glow into the passage, scattering the black void.

Murmurs grew louder and awed as prisoners came to the cell doors.

Haegan walked with hands extended to the sides, sparking locks and flipping them open.

"Uh, I'm not sure that's a good idea," Trale said warily. "They're all mad."

"The king, the king, the king is gone," sang a young girl of no more than twelve. Clothes hung on her, several sizes too large for her emaciated frame. Eyes hollow and sunken in gray circles, she danced—wobbled—toward him. "The king, the king, he's ever so empty. Fire and embers, toiling to remember, but the king, the king, is desperately vacant." Her cackling voice echoed through the corridor.

The king! Embers! Haegan gripped her. "Where is he? The Fire King?"

Her eyes widened. "Oh." Then her shoulders caved as she fell into a fit of hysterical laughter. "Come to free the empty king, the son will kill the queen."

The queen? "My mother . . ."

"I think she means the Infantessa," Trale said.

Right. Maybe. But what if . . . what if his mother was alive, too? And the Infantessa held her captive. Twisted her mind as she had Haegan's. "Father!" Haegan shouted. "Father, I am here. Speak, Father. Call to me!"

But only his voice reverberated through the dungeon.

"There," came a mousy voice. "There, two rights and a left. Last door to the Fires."

Haegan looked at the man who had a semblance of sanity, but only by a hair.

Thud! Crack!

Trale grabbed Haegan's tunic. "C'mon! She's coming!"

Together, they ran the passages, making the two rights and a left. When they turned the final corner, Haegan skidded to a stop at a brick wall. "No no no." He circled the juncture and shook his head. Desperate. Frantic. "Father?"

"Maybe the fool mixed it up. Maybe it should've been two lefts and a right."

"There weren't two lefts," Haegan said, his mind gaining clarity.

Then something reached out to him. He drew in a breath, closed his eyes, and froze. "What was that?" He gaped, turning, turning. Searching the walls. But it was gone. Emptiness clawed at him now.

"It's brick," Trale said. "I think insanity is closer than either of us would admit."

"Father!" Again Haegan shouted, ignoring Trale's taunt. "Father, can you hear me? I'm here! I'm finally here. Call to me."

Something whispered through the air.

Haegan tensed. "Father?"

Haegan.

It wasn't a voice. It was . . .

"Abiatasso." The fire of his father reaching through the barrier to him.

Why save him when he left you to rot in a tower?

Haegan shouldered against the doubt.

Even if you save him, he will not love you as he should.

No. He would no longer listen to the doubts, let them control how this ended. Haegan focused on the brick before him. Noticed the discoloration. "Look."

Trale frowned warily at the wall. Stepped away. "I don't think—"

"Two different kinds of bricks." Haegan ran his hands along them, detecting a noticeable variation in the temperatures of the two. "Stand back," Haegan warned as he grabbed the embers of heat—what little existed—and pulled it from the bricks.

Pulled.

"Haegan, stop." Trale whipped toward the passage, tugging at him. "Don't do this."

PULLED.

Mortar loosened.

Trale cried out. "Here!" he hollered. "Haegan's here!" He barreled forward, knocking him into the stone wall. "I'm sorry, but she swore to kill me if I let you find him."

• • •

NORTH OF LITTLE HALL

"I'm not getting on that thing," Tokar growled.

Draed growled right back, eying Tokar's gear on the ground.

Tili approached Umoni respectfully, asking permission with an outstretched palm. She settled her belly on the earth with a satisfied moan and allowed him and Praegur to mount.

Draed circled Tokar with a curled lip.

"Tili?"

"Don't move," Tili warned. "Give him time—No!"

Lunging, Draed snatched Tokar's gear in his teeth and shook it until bits of clothing, food, weapons, and more littered the ground.

Hands on his head, Tokar groaned. "Are you kidding me?"

Laughter rippled through the waiting Pathfinders.

"Make peace, Tokar. We need to ride."

"*I* have to make peace?" Tokar whirled, his brown eyes wild beneath his short-cropped hair. "*I? He's* the one! Tell that beast—"

"His name is Draed."

"More like Dread. Or Dead," Tokar muttered.

The raqine hunkered closer to the ground—not lying prone as Umoni had—barely enough that Tokar could climb aboard.

"Now," Tili ordered. "And with respect."

Expelling a huffed breath, Tokar tentatively gripped the raqine's neck and pulled himself up. Draed shook his shoulders back and forth, making it difficult for the young officer to swing his leg over.

"Freeze the flames!" Tokar groused, then hauled himself onto the spine.

Rhaemos then joined him—and Draed crouched still as a sleeping cat. Negaer and Vaqar were mounted and ready to lead the army to the palace. In one of the wagons, Astadia glared from within a constructed cage. Regret tugged at him, but she had given them no choice with her cynical, caustic words.

Umoni shot into the sky with an effortless leap that reminded Tili why he so loved the great winged beasts. He leaned into her, trusting her to sense where to go and allowing him to help guide. It took a mere twenty minutes to cross into Iteveria and catch first sight of Karithia, glittering in the morning sun. Tili aimed Umoni toward it, but the raqine defied his efforts to circle in on the castle.

The Deliverers. It had to be why Umoni wouldn't veer closer. The thought was heady as they scouted the outer perimeter and saw throngs in the street. Riots. Chaos. People shouting. Hurtling weapons and rocks and anything else within reach at each other. Tili's heart clenched at the violence. What kind of ruler sat in her castle while her people tore the realm apart?

For another half hour they circled and scouted the best routes, the paths of least resistance. Where they could gather supplies if needed. And how best to infiltrate the castle walls. As the girl had said—there was but one gate. Mountain and cliffs protected it on three sides. Options were limited. Supplies scarce. Defeat almost guaranteed.

He signaled Tokar to make for a clearing about a half league from the city, at the foot of the great mountain that bore Karithia on its heights.

Though he dispatched scouts, all returned in defeat. The assassin had been right—only one way to the castle. So, they waited for their army to arrive, allowing the raqine to rest and hunt and the officers gathered to make a war plan, which was as simple as possible—march up Karithia Road and break down the gate, using the raqine to push back resistance if they must.

• • •

Anger shot through Haegan. But he remembered. He focused. Father! He angled toward the bricks again and harnessed his abilities. Thanked Abiassa for helping him.

"Haegan, you stupid little puppet," Nydelia shrilled.

Fury ignited. He snapped his hands at the wall. Yanked.

PULLED!

Heat wakes roiled through the bricks. They rattled and crumbled to the ground in a heap. Just like the glass in the shower. Darkness threatened again but Haegan threw a ball of light into the void beyond the opening and climbed through.

His heart wrenched at the sight. The chasm. Just as in his dream, a chasm separated him from where a pile of tattered blankets lay huddled in the corner. Haegan moved to the edge, searching for his father. He aimed light down into the void that blocked him. But no sign of the Fire King.

This made no sense. Why create this chasm if his father wasn't here? Why lure him down here? Was it a trap? Had Trale helped with that, too?

Laughter rippled, bringing with it that bitter stench.

Haegan shifted to find himself facing the Infantessa. "Where is my father?"

She cackled, her mirage of beauty pointless. "Do you not recognize him, my pet prince? Are you so lost, so weak, that you cannot see the likeness between you?"

Frowning, Haegan looked over his shoulder, searching the shadows. Hauled into the past, into that wretched nightmare where the world fell away and took his father with it. Where fire claimed life and limb. Scourged. Scorched. "I don't . . ."

The blankets shifted.

As a moan seeped from the rags, Haegan's breath caught. "No," he whispered.

The pile moved again.

He thought to illuminate the area more, but he feared what he would find.

Leave him. He's weak. A failure. Ruination. He never loved you well anyway.

At the inflaming thoughts, Haegan grunted and shoved a blast of heat at the Infantessa. But it was diluted. With selfishness. With pride. With the piece of him that still clung to those childish thoughts and fears.

"See?" she crooned from the rubble. "Is this really worth turning against me? Is it worth sacrificing everything for such a despicable waste? Remember, he left you in that tower. *He* ignored you. *He* didn't care. *He* was humiliated by you—and you should be of him now. Why is a Fire King cowering beneath the palace of his enemy?"

Before he could fail himself and his father again, Haegan threw himself across the chasm.

"No!" the Infantessa gasped.

Haegan rolled out of the landing and shuffled over to the pile. The smell was abhorrent. The sight . . . hideous. He wanted to tame the light, but the embers roiled through him in a miserable fury. Glowing, growing out of indignation, his rage at the sight before him. What the witch had done . . .

Gray-blond hair matted, face swollen and bruised, burned. Pocked with boils. Beard long and gnarled, soiled with food and dirt that stuck to the wiry strands. Clothes sizes too large. But even as Haegan thought that, he noted the grayish tunic bore the tri-tipped flame. House Celahar. The Fire King's royal tunic. The one he'd worn the day he fought Poired. The day Haegan flew away, leaving him on the steps of Seultrie.

And it hung on him as if he were a child wearing his father's tunic.

Empty, vacant eyes staggered up Haegan's body, finally finding his gaze. "Oh," came a wheeze, foul and crude. "I . . ." His father's head wagged, too heavy for his neck, it seemed. "I . . . do I know you?" asked the weak voice, fragile.

"Father," Haegan said, tears blurring his vision. His hands trembled beneath grief and shock.

Bobbing began, then his father's gaze fell away. His arms went limp.

Haegan rushed to him and knelt. "Father—please. It's me, Haegan."

"Hae—" Eyes once an icy blue were now crowded with an empty gray. They seemed to search for sight, then drifted away. "No . . ." He shook his head. "No . . . who is Haegan?"

"Is it worth it, Haegan?" Nydelia taunted from the other side. "Look at him. This—*this* is what you are going to destroy everything for?"

Anger churned. Roiled. Thickened. But he pushed it away. Angry. He was always so angry. And that meant people got hurt. He wouldn't do that. Wouldn't be that scourge.

"Father, please!" Haegan pleaded, gripping his father's face. Ignoring the slime and mats and clumps pressing into his palms.

Gray eyes met his once more.

"Yes," Haegan urged him to remember. Willed him. "It's me. Haegan—your son. You watched me sleep every night. Remember?"

The thick, dirty brow knotted beneath the clumped strands of hair. But he hung his head. "No. No, I just want to be alone. No more pain. No more daggers in the head." He slapped at his temples. "No more. No more more more."

"Haegan—"

Whirling to Nydelia, he lunged to his feet. Fists balled. "What. Have. You. Done?"

She faltered, her confidence shifting as light rushed through the cavern.

"Release my father!"

Arrogance lifted her craggy chin. "Your father is in a prison of his own making, Prince." She shrugged, taking a step back, as if to feign confidence. But that was just it—it was false. Her face had gone pale. "I only helped him embrace what he believed."

"*Release* him!" Haegan shouted.

She groaned and rolled her eyes. "You're as pathetic as those blasted Deliverers, chanting, 'Release him, release him!' Night and day. You think *this* is cruel torture? Try living with their grating voices."

"I did! I lived with your voice scraping away at my soul."

She shook her head. "You're truly as pathetic as him, aren't you?" She sniffed. "You've been here weeks, putrid prince. You've eaten my words as if they were sweeties, and you—like that sizzled-out ember of a Fire King—have left your precious kingdom unguarded. Now it's ours."

"You will never have the Nine."

"We already have it." She smirked, stepping out of the cavern, back into the passage. "And now, I have snuffed out the Fierian."

The floor closest the opening dropped away in a gaping yawn of terror.

17

"And down comes the Fire King, son and all." Nydelia stalked back through the dungeon passages, a hand raised to any breathers hovering near the doors. She heat-smacked them and seared their faces. They fell away, screaming.

Paung rushed down the steps from the main level.

"What are you doing?" she demanded. "Get back up there—"

"Invaders, my queen! Sentries spotted them just inside the walls."

"Who? None would dare come against me!" She stomped up the stairs, secured the door, then headed upstairs to the observatory. From there she could see down the side of the slope Karithia had been built upon. She let out a frustrated growl at the tunics slipping unheeded through her city—white, gold, and green. "Fools," she hissed. "Why does no one stop them?"

But the answer was apparent. The people ignored the invaders sneaking past them because they were too busy venting their rage on each other. Nydelia pushed their thoughts into submission, gripping their doubts. Twisting them into sheer panic.

Instead of attacking the soldiers, however, the people turned from their bickering and began to shove and trample each other, desperate to flee. The soldiers' destriers shifted at the thrumming agitation, but still they pressed on.

She pushed harder, twisted more. Reached for the thoughts of the soldiers . . .

"My lady!" Paung cried.

"What?"

"The soldiers!"

Glancing down at the army forming columns, she saw the officers. Saw the raqine, which made her blood cool.

"You should leave, my lady. Before they arrive."

She narrowed her eyes. "I do *not* run."

"I would call it a *strategic repositioning*," Paung said. "They are many, and we are but two."

"Two? I have—"

"But you don't! They've left, one by one since they"—he nodded to the pillars of men around the city—"arrived."

She huffed, fidgeting beneath the apparent defeat. "Bring my carriage. At once!" She stalked down to the foyer and hurried to the front door, irritated at how slowly Paung moved for the carriage. Worry chased her, the disbelief of her failure—No, this wasn't failure. She hadn't failed. She'd succeeded. Not only had she destroyed the Fire King, but she'd also taken care of the Fierian. They would never emerge from that pit.

Sirdar should be proud.

Bah! She didn't care if the old Desecrator was proud. *She* was proud. *She* had done what she set out to do. But in that instant, a great chill seeped through her. Stumbling, she reached for the floor, confused—and froze at the sight of her hand. Parchment-thin skin. Shriveled flesh. Veins protruding.

"What is this?" she gasped, glancing up her arm—the same. She reached for the embers . . . and found . . . "No," she breathed. Panic thrummed at the emptiness growing within her. She threw a bolt. But didn't. "Nooo!" The embers were gone. "Impossible!" she cried out. Growled, reached again for the embers. Nothing.

A dark voice spoke, "Perhaps you now care what Sirdar thinks. I leave you to your end, Nydelia."

• • •

He hated his anger. Hated hating.

But Aaesh had told him that sometimes his anger wasn't merely his own. As he stared at his father's limp form, a burning wrath rose through

Haegan. He thought of the prisoners ensnared within their own doubts. Ghosts of themselves.

Making war on enemies of Aaesh and freeing enslaved minds;
releasing from prisons of their own making,
and then he finds himself standing obediently
and violently between life and death,
living and dead
first and last
then and now.

"Freeing enslaved minds," he whispered, glancing at the words carved in his flesh. "Releasing from prisons of their own making." The dozens of cells he'd passed. "Standing obediently," Haegan paused. Thinking. Tasting. Testing the next word. "*Violently* between life and death. Living and dead. First and last. Then and now."

Violently.

Between life and death.

She had robbed them—his father, himself, Trale—of their dignity. Of their will. Relegated them to puppets.

The glare in the cavern grew brighter.

"Standing obediently . . ." He stared at his hands. Remembered the night he'd been told his destiny. How he'd fled into the darkness. He breathed a laugh. He had fled again into the dark months later. Trapped himself. Lost himself. Selfishly. Only caring what it cost him to be the Fierian. Not considering that his disobedience cost thousands of lives.

He lifted his head. Spoke clearer. Louder. "Standing—I stand obediently."

Violently. The word nudged his will. He winced.

Think not of yourself, Haegan, heir of Zireli.

Zireli. His father. Haegan again knelt at his father's side. Touched the man's shoulder. His father cried out with a shriek that terrified Haegan, watching the man who'd been the strongest accelerant in the Nine since Zaelero cower and scrabble to the wall, clawing stones. Fingers bloodied. Bony shoulders bouncing.

How often had his father done that? Had she taunted him so that he feared touch?

"Father," Haegan croaked. "Please—"

"Go away! I won't do it. I won't touch the Flames again. I promise. Please. Just stop." His father wagged a bony hand, face pressed to stone.

Teeth gritted, lips trembling with restrained fury, Haegan rose. "I stand here," he shouted to the stone ceiling, to Abiassa, "obediently and violently between life and death. Living and dead. First and last. Then and now."

Heat spiraled. Bubbled. Roiled.

His father howled. Curled into a ball, his back to Haegan. "It's not me. No no no. I didn't touch the Flames!"

"Abiassa!" Haegan called. "I am here. I beg Your mercy—thank You for choosing me, not for the sake of being chosen, but that Your people will be freed by Your hand in Your hour! Thank You for this gift to avenge Your name, Your people!" he shouted, turning a circle and staring past the ceiling, up through the palace, into the clear skies where freedom waited. Where—

Haegan gasped.

He saw them. Saw through stone and dirt. Saw the Deliverers standing guard over Karithia. Although they were taller than buildings and mountains, Haegan somehow stood eye to eye with them. Their strength, fed by the purity of Abiassa and their vow to Her, blew through him. Their swords, stabbing the earth, lifted with their fiery gazes and extended toward Haegan.

No, not Haegan.

The Infantessa. Who looked a thousand years old, trembling on a withered frame. She stumbled from the palace toward a gilded carriage. The same carriage she'd used to draw Haegan into her net. She had tormented him. Toyed with him. Humiliated him. Not just him, but his father-king. The people. Before his mind's eye flashed thousands who had given her their will, imprisoned forever. And thousands more who had been unwitting prisoners.

"Nydelia!" Though Haegan called to her through time and walls, he hesitated. Could he do this? Kill her? The thought—

Release them, Fhuriætyr, Aaesh's words whispered through his soul. *It is time. She is only a symptom, but the end must start with her.*

Bolstered by Her words and the fleeing queen, he shouted, "NYDELIA!"

The wretched creature skidded to a stop, staring around. Startled. Terrified. She could not see him. She did, however, see the Deliverers. Noticed their swords had been extended. "No! You can't do this—"

"ENOUGH!" Eyes on Abiassa, Haegan crossed his arms, fisted his hands, and drew in. "THEN. NOW. FOREVER!"

Instantly, he stood in the cave again. White-blue heat roiled through the cavern like a smoke-demon seeking freedom. It grew thicker. Brighter until the white of it seared his eyes. But no pain came. Only fury. Only the righteous anger of Abiassa for Her children drawn away, imprisoned in their pain, doubts, and fears.

It grew so large, Haegan feared its unleash. He braced himself and . . . surrendered. It was not his to say what She did with his life, this gift, but to surrender to whatever Her will may be. He threw open his arms and embraced his role as Fierian.

The earth and everything in it belonged to Abiassa and succumbed to Her will. Bowed to Her touch. So it should not have surprised Haegan when the ground rumbled and rocks began falling like rain.

He extended a shielding hand toward his father and trusted that Abiassa would not let them get hurt. Fear squirreled in, and he felt the event lessening.

Haegan closed his eyes to his surroundings. Closed his mind to his fears and doubts, reaching for the Flames. A deafening roar engulfed them. Haegan pushed, wielding the pure source of Abiassa's righteous anger.

But a pressure pushed back. Resisting. Haegan stumbled and went to a knee.

18

Shouts snapped Thiel awake. She stopped short, feeling aches through-out her body. Her *naked* body. She grabbed the blanket as it slid away. She clutched it to her throat, watching Cadeif's bare back duck through the tent flap and vanish.

Choked at the realization of what'd happened, she whimpered. "No no no." Her head ached. Everything ached. Why? Why had he done this? They were . . . Why could she recall nothing?

Clothes. She needed clothes. She glanced around and spotted her belongings in a pile on the floor. Thiel yanked them on, wincing and grimacing. Hating Cadeif. Hating their blasted barbaric ways. Disgusted he would do this. Grief clawed her at what he'd stolen.

"We were friends!" she shouted. Her head pulsed with an agonizing pain. She hunched beneath it, then pushed herself out of the tent.

Ematahri darted in and out of dwellings.

Crack!

Chortling throttled the air.

Crack! Crack!

Thiel's mind caught up with the confusion in the camp. "Chima." She rushed in the direction of the cage. She'd passed between two trees when a peeled shaft whirled at her. Ducking, she barely avoided the rogue bar.

"Kill it," someone shouted.

"Before it kills us," another hollered.

Ematahri surrounded Chima's makeshift prison, some trying to hold the cage together, but most using spears and jav-rods to poke and prod the mighty raqine into submission. The fools were poking her into fury.

"Oy! Leave her alone. Yous what's the beasts!" Laertes growled from another cage.

Eyes red and roiling in the dull morning, Chima shook her shoulders. Snarled. The noise emanated through her throat and rumbled the ground. Using her forepaws, she cracked two more bars. Chima rolled her shoulders again, then lowered her snout, only to lift it and let out a mournful yet fierce howl.

The sound, one Thiel had never heard before, froze her. Scared her. What was she doing? "Chima!" Thiel called to the great beast. "Chima! Easy, girl."

The raqine's spine had risen. Hackles.

"What's wrong with her?" Raleng demanded. "One minute she is fine, the next—this!"

"I'm sure spears aren't helping." Thiel glowered at the Ematahri sliding the tips into the pen again. But Chima's behavior *was* unusual.

Another howl-shriek blasted. Chima shook not just her shoulders but her entire body.

"Something's wrong," Thiel said, half to herself.

"I don't need you to tell me that," Raleng said.

"Let her out," Thiel said as she hurried to the gate.

Ruldan stepped before her. "Not on your life."

Crack! Thunk!

They both ducked, looking over to find Chima snapping her wings against at the wood bars.

"Don't think this will hold her—and she resents it. They aren't meant to be caged. They come and go at the will of Abiassa."

"You might believe in some god, but we don't."

"Everyone believes in something, and right now—you'd better believe Chima will break free." *But what had set her off? Why was she so upset?* "What did they do to her?"

"Nothing, she was sound asleep—curled like a cat—when suddenly she comes up with a roar. Or whatever that thing does. Next thing, she's pawing the cage and screaming."

She wants something.

To be free.

"Free her."

"I want my clan alive, thank you very much."

"Keep poking her and they won't be."

More saplings splintered. A piece nicked Raleng's cheek. The warrior growled and wiped at the trickling blood.

Chima backed onto her hind legs, then lurched at the rods above her, howling, chortling.

"Archon!"

Thiel whirled and spotted a runner sidling up to Cadeif, who stood in the shadows behind her. How long had he been there?

"Another Sirdarian contingent arrived. Now they're all packing up."

Cadeif scowled, shot a look at Thiel, then stormed toward the main hub of the camp. The Sirdarians' departure was apparently unexpected.

Thiel hurried after him to find out what was going on, calling back to Raleng, "Free her or she will free herself."

Cadeif spoke before he halted beside a cluster of red-and-black clad officers. "We have not settled all our terms, General."

General? But Jepravia was a colonel.

The camp swarmed with activity as the Sirdarians hoisted packs and loads onto their horses. The large man Cadeif confronted turned toward him, and Thiel took a step back, recognizing General Onerid. Poiréd's right hand.

But he had been part of the attack on and razing of Hetaera. Did this mean they had been routed? Or were they moving on to fresh prey?

Lazy, apathetic eyes shifted to Cadeif. "Our schedule is not determined by the ineffectiveness of the Ematahri." Onerid nodded to Jepravia, who strode away, shouting orders.

Cadeif grabbed the general's arm and hauled him around. "We had a deal. You agreed—"

No swords had been drawn, but Cadeif pulled up straight. And only then did Thiel see the red dagger of angry fire pressed against his neck.

"Release me, you savage," Onerid snarled as he wielded, "or this will end what little life you have left."

Furious, Cadeif complied, skating a look around, his warriors watching. "Why are you leaving?"

"Plans change," the general said, stalking away.

"I heard you are going east." Cadeif strode along at the man's elbow, Thiel an unnoticed third.

"Not that it is your business, but the petulant boy you failed to subdue is proving difficult to kill." The general huffed. "And we are not going alone—the Ematahri are coming."

Cadcif slowed. Then stopped. "No. We remain here. That is not our fight."

"Oh, you will fight, or every last one of you will fertilize this ground with your blood." Onerid stared daggers at him. "Had you completed your task then, we would not be dealing with this trouble now."

Why did they care about Praegur?

"We thought him contained, but he has grown stronger and is a very real threat."

Thiel swallowed, a bitter truth dawning. Haegan. Her own loss, her own despair was not important. "Haegan," she repeated out loud, turning back toward the pen where Chima's chortling reached a fevered pitch.

Another truth punched her in the stomach. Chima had bonded with Haegan. Chima answered the summons of no man—save one: the Fierian. Haegan.

"Haegan needs her," Thiel whispered, now running toward the cage. And she saw that Chima's anger had unwittingly shifted the cage that held Laertes to an awkward angle, which afforded the quick-as-a-mouse boy an exit. He took it as Thiel sprinted past an Ematahri, freeing him of his dagger, then dove into the gate of the pen. She hacked at the lock mechanism.

Chima rammed her head into the gate, pitching Thiel back. She stumbled, landing hard on the ground. She pushed the hair from her face and huffed. On her feet, she again worked at the lock, but Chima barreled at her *again*.

Thiel was shoved back, but this time, managed to keep her feet. She glowered at the raqine. "Do ye want out or not?" She sawed, noting Chima rearing. "No no no," Thiel said, sawing faster.

"What are you doing?" Raleng demanded, charging her.

Unbelievable. She'd be slammed flat between the two beasts—the raqine and the Ematahri.

Chima struck first. With a blow that lifted Thiel off her feet, thrust backward, but she'd grabbed the cage door. It snapped outward, but the upper hinge caught and yanked Thiel to a stop, jarring her shoulder. Even as the pain registered, she felt the incredible heat of anger roiling off Chima, who leapt free with that terrifying howl. She shrieked at the warriors and soldiers who rushed her, rods and spears extended. She swiveled her head, screaming and rustling her fur. Then with a finality that startled even Thiel, Chima's wings snapped out with a crisp *thwap*.

Heat wakes tossed the men aside.

That's new.

Laertes ran to Chima, who—surprisingly—shouldered him onto her spine. Thiel staggered toward her, knowing where Chima was headed. To whom she was headed. She climbed on even as the raqine crouched to shove off.

"Stop her," came Cadeif's booming order.

Thiel steeled herself, afraid to look back. Afraid to see the fury that had turned the man she once cared about into the savage his reputation dictated.

Chima flapped hard, the weight of Thiel and Laertes slowing her.

• • •

"Am I right that inflaming does not affect ye?" Tili asked the Tahscan, as their column of men and horses approached the gate to Iteveria. Vaqar started to answer with a wry expression, but Tili cut him off. "Beyond the stench."

Vaqar inclined his head. "We are not influenced, not as most are, but it does feel as acid in the nose."

Tili gritted his teeth. "Then I must beg yer mercy."

Vaqar looked to the general then back to Tili.

"I need ye to place yer people throughout the column as we advance. The city is in disarray. If the Infantessa is inflaming her own people, we cannot expect ours to remain unaffected."

The warrior's eyes widened marginally. "As I said, you have my blade—and that of my people."

"Thank ye." He looked to Negaer. "Warn them. We need to keep our minds sharp." Tili nudged his destrier and galloped to the front of the column, where Tokar and Praegur waited with the raqine. "We need them to tear down the castle gate." With a lifted arm, he started up the cobbled road.

Amazingly, the chaos Tili had noted in flight carried on as they rode through the city at a steady clip—not so fast they'd trample people, but not slow enough to be targeted either. They advanced unhindered, pockets of bickering and fighting civilians moving aside to clear the way, like water parting around a boulder in a stream. Unease squirmed through Tili as he shifted beneath his armor. Not one person had looked at him.

"Blazes," a Pathfinder muttered. "They're like walking dead."

"The Infantessa has their minds," Draorin said.

Tili wasn't sure whether to take that literally or figuratively. He glanced back down the steep hillside with its switchbacks to where the last of the column entered the road.

Above them, green bounty stuffed up against a lush mountainside. A waterfall crashed violently down the slope and plunged into a vast sea. Incredible. Beautiful.

Yet . . . it delivered a prick of dread.

"Is anyone bothered that we've encountered no Sirdarians or combatants?" Tokar growled.

"Aye," Tili said.

"Sir!" A rider clopped toward them from the rear.

Tili glanced toward the voice, wondering what trouble sent a scout up the line.

"Sir, it's the girl."

Scowling at the red welt on the Pathfinder's cheek, Tili had another bad feeling hit him and skipped his gaze toward the center of the column, where he'd placed Astadia with her hands tied and four Jujak. "What of her?"

The man's face reddened. "She's demanding to see you, sir. Or she'll start killing people."

Tili's gaze shifted to Vaqar, who—as always—watched him. "I'll deal with her after we reach—"

A shout went up, followed by another. Whispers rippled from the rear, and Tili knew there would be no "after" if he did not deal with this—her—now. With a huff, he turned his horse and plowed through the column.

He found her in a small square, the line of his soldiers' progress broken and halted beside the tableau she had created, arms hooked around the throat of a Jujak, as she held him tight against her, a shiv pressed to his throat. Incredibly, her bound wrists had not hindered her in the least. Her gaze connected with Tili's and heated. "I will *not* be tied and led like an animal."

Tili steeled his temper. "Then stop behaving like one."

Anger flashed. "My brother is in there. I came to your camp for help."

"And ye are interfering with that help—we are preparing to breach the gates."

"I want to go in."

Rejection on the tip of his tongue, Tili hesitated. His gaze wandered to the palace. Why was *he* even here? *This isn't my battle. I wanted none of this.*

And yet here he stood on the precipice of war. None had forced him. *Someone else's fight. Go home, Tili.*

He should.

"A moment ago," boomed the firm voice of Vaqar, "you wondered why we have encountered no resistance."

Tili started, looked to the towering warrior. "Aye."

"She fights, but not with swords. Perhaps with Flames, but mostly"— he tapped his temple—"she fights with thoughts."

"She has their minds," Draorin's words returned.

Tili's heart thudded. "Inflaming." His own doubts and longing to return to Nivar.

"So I tell you and you don't listen," Astadia bit out. "But he tells you—"

"Aye," Tili barked, snapping his gaze to hers. "He doesn't hold shivs to our throats to make his point."

Without blinking, she shoved the Pathfinder forward and dropped the weapon to the ground.

He gestured to the Jujak she released. "Cut her loose."

A look of incredulity crossed the man's face, but he obeyed.

"Let's go," he ordered and drew his mount around, but not before he saw the shock ripping through her young face.

But she didn't hesitate for long. Astadia seized her chance. Jogged toward Tili. Caught his arm and hauled up behind him, stifling a small cry.

"Give me trouble," he tossed over his shoulder as her arms circled his waist, "and I will deal with ye myself."

"What is he?" Astadia asked, ignoring his threat and thrusting her chin at Vaqar.

"Tahscan."

"No dung, Steward." She huffed, and he glanced back at her, surprised at her impudence. "You forget—these are *my* people."

"Then why did ye ask?"

"The mask—"

"Oh. It's a cloth," another Tahscan said as their progress was slowed. "Used to block the stench."

She sniffed. "What stench?"

"Inflaming."

She made a skeptical noise, then paused, silent for a moment. "Is he earnest? They can smell it?"

"He has no reason to lie." Tili considered her. "I trust ye to help us so we can find yer brother, but have I cause to be concerned for my men regarding ye?"

"Only if they try to assault me again." She shifted closer, her curves pressed to his spine, and he really wished she wouldn't. "Trust me to find my brother—and I assure you, he will be with your petulant prince."

He glanced to the side, surprised to find her green eyes so close. "Yer eager words betray ye." Once they reached the top of the column, Tili eyed the main gate. No sentries. But surely it was protected. Warily, he dismounted.

She scowled. "If you expect me to pretend to care for your prince, then your overblown ego and muscles have guided you wrong."

He grinned up at her. "Overblown muscles?"

"That's not what I meant." Her cheeks pinked. "Just let me get into the palace. I can bring them both out."

Tili smirked, glad to have her off kilter for a second. But the truth remained. "Ye stay here." He nodded to Negaer, who stalked toward him.

Her expression darkened. Body tensing, she jumped down beside him. "Have you been inside that palace, Steward?" She had a point, but he had a war. "Do you even know what my brother looks like?"

"Haggard, dangerous?" When he saw her anger flare again, Tili opted not to test her abilities further. "Ye stay here. We will not risk yer life—"

"Don't you dare say because I'm a girl."

"Then ye're not a girl?" he asked, skating a look teasingly at her borrowed clothing. The air changed. And with it, Tili saw her move, but not soon enough.

Her forehead rammed into his face. Pain exploded through his skull, but he had long ago learned to respond regardless of pain. He caught her arm. Twisted it at the same time he gripped her nape and rolled her neck, forcing her head down and around, so that she faced away from him. He wrenched her arm back tightly against his chest and pinned her to the nearby wall.

She cried out.

"Try that again." Guilt gripped Tili. He guessed she'd injured herself. Knew her shoulder needed ministrations. And used it against her. But he'd have done it with any enemy. "Ye want me to treat ye as I would my men?" He pressed her to the plaster. "This is what I'd do to a disrespectful soldier."

He released her arm enough that she wouldn't will him to kill her to escape the agony. But the pain twisting through her pretty features nearly undid him. He sighed. Eased off. "Blazes, girl." As he shuffled back, hating what he'd had to do, he shook his head.

She spun around, cradling her arm tightly, eyes wet with tears and fury. Her scowl was as rabid as a hound's.

"Ye are worse than Thiel."

"Steward," Negaer said as he and Rhaemos joined them.

Tili shot a warning look to Astadia, and she jerked her gaze down. Enough submissiveness for him to trust she would not try to flee. Or was that a ruse?

The ground beneath his feet rattled. Vibrated so hard that Tili reached for the wall to stay upright "What's happening?"

Draorin now stood with Negaer and Vaqar.

"The walls." Negaer pointed to the castle. "They're coming down."

"It's time, Steward," Draorin spoke firmly, his voice . . . odd. Hypnotizing. "Minds will be freed and the Dark One will not be pleased. My time to leave has come."

"Leave?" Tili frowned.

"Your task is before you. Fight true, fight hard, Guardian." Even as he spoke the words, Draorin took two steps backward and vanished.

Shock gripped Tili in a fist-hold.

"Blazes," Tokar muttered, nodding past Tili. *"Look!"*

Tili glanced over his shoulder and saw what his eyes would not grasp before—men standing like mountains at the four corners of the great city. "Steady," he murmured, staring disbelieving into the face of the one on the east. Draorin. Sword held high. Cascades of light rushing off him the way water leaps from a cliff to the pool below. Arms taut with muscles.

"Their swords are raised," Vaqar spoke softly. "It is a sign of war."

Tili pried his gaze from the glowing Deliverers. Looked back to the castle. A roar from somewhere within rattled the ground again, as if some creature was trying to escape.

The thick walls of the castle began crumbling—including the one he'd just pinned Astadia to. She yelped, wobbling over the precipice. Tili lunged and pulled her to himself. Shouts and shocks rippled through the street. The Jujak and Pathfinders closest to the gate shifted uneasily. Around them, the people of Iteveria screamed in terror and ran down the curved road, still giving his men wide berth.

"The castle!" Tokar shouted.

With the wall gone, Tili could see across the courtyard to the inner gate that barred entrance. He swung back onto his horse and urged the destrier forward.

A hand, firm but gentle, slapped across his leg. Instinctively, Tili hefted his sword, but stayed the response when he met Astadia's urgent expression.

"You promised."

"I gave no promise," he countered.

Her eyes went soft. She leaned against the horse. "Please."

A thunderous roar writhed through the ground. Shook the mountain. Startled the waterfall beyond the castle, shifting the course for a fraction.

Astadia seized his confusion and vaulted onto the back of his horse. Tili huffed, but could not focus on her impertinence.

The road canted. Horses reared, frantic neighs mingled with the cries of the earth.

"What's happening?" Tokar asked.

"We must advance now," Negaer said. "Use the chaos to our advantage."

Tili looked to the courtyard again, noting a carriage racing around from behind the house. A flood of Silvers spilled out of the castle's main entrance.

Negaer's gaze snapped to Tili. "The gate then?" he called, his mount stamping the cobbled road.

Tili gave a sharp nod. "Tokar—the gate!"

But even as Tokar took flight with Draed, the great beast banked west and sailed out of sight, Tokar's objections and anger fading with them. Futility strangled Tili.

"Advance!" Negaer shouted.

Astadia's arms encircled Tili's waist as his horse reared again.

Tili dug in with his knees, keeping them mounted. When the horse released the panicked state and landed, Tili jabbed his legs into the destrier's flanks. They lurched toward the gate. He threw the strongest bolt he could muster at the golden barrier.

19

Flames leapt and danced along the crevices of the dungeon. Haegan curled his lip, anger churning as the wall the Infantessa created slid to the ground in a pool of slag.

Exhaustion struck him, sending him to a knee. He hung his head, panting, sweat dripping from his hair and brow. Sliding down his back. When he opened his eyes, he found himself staring at his father's curled figure, dark strands concealing his eyes.

"Father?" Haegan reached toward him.

"She's getting away!" a voice shouted into the cavern.

Haegan looked there and found Trale where the Infantessa had last stood. "You betrayed me," he said around a weak breath.

"If you want to be technical, yes. But I also saved my sister's life." Trale nodded to him. "And you're still alive, so I'm not seeing the point of arguing the finer points of betrayal. Let me redeem a little of my dignity—she's escaping. You're not." He jerked his head toward the dungeon corridor. "Hurry. For some reason, the walls are coming down."

Haegan's gaze flicked to the stones in the dungeon. Had his wielding destabilized the rest of the castle? Was it possible?

"Did you miss the part where I said it's coming down? As in falling apart!"

Could he take it down from within? The thought brought Haegan to his feet as he stared at the ceiling.

"Hey, Princeling!"

Crossing his splayed palms, Haegan guided the Flames up the wall. They licked the mortar until it began to sag in defeat.

"Haegan, c'mon." Trale slipped into the dungeon. Took a running start and leapt across the chasm. Another piece of the ledge broke away. Then another. And another. The gap widening. "Um, that's not good."

Haegan glanced to the side, seeing the impossible distance. "It was of no use regardless. I could not jump with him in my arms."

Trale quirked an eyebrow. "You couldn't mention that before I came to rescue you?"

"You're an assassin. You should've figured it out."

Trale muttered something, but Haegan focused on wielding.

"Planning to keep us warm until death, Fierian?"

"Bundle my father," Haegan said, concentrating on his work. Fingers and thoughts raking at the mortar, digging it out. Forcing it free. Never had he experienced this much control. This much intensity. But the Flames seemed to listen to his thoughts, obey his will.

Think not for a moment this is about you.

It was about the people. The ones trapped in the cages of their own minds. His father, who lay at his feet, catatonic. Haegan looked to Trale, who had gathered the scraps of cloth. "Give care—that's the Fire King you touch."

Shouts rose from the passage.

"I've got this," Trale said, pushing to his feet. "You"—he wagged a hand at the wall—"do what you do. I'll do what I do." A dagger appeared in his hand.

Light blinked at the opening.

A red glow grew into a rage.

"Incipient," Haegan growled, turning, his anger tumbling through him at the sight of an agent of Sirdar. "Enemy of Abiassa and the Nine." Fingers clawed, he held out his left and drew the right below and under it, tracing the underside of his arm, then shot the bolt across the chasm. Pure. Lightning fast.

It struck the incipient in the temple. He flipped backward and collapsed.

"Blazes. He didn't have a chance," Trale mumbled, looking at Haegan with both awe and dread.

"He had a chance. He chose darkness." Refocused, Haegan shifted back to the ceiling. He scraped away the stone. But as he did, he detected something . . . something violently wrong.

His gaze rose, and he hauled in a long breath. The stench that had packed his sinuses . . . he'd nearly forgotten that. But it was there. Above.

Realization dropped into his stomach like lead bricks. It was her. The Infantessa. He could sense her—the heat, the stench of her wielding.

Right above me.

Escaping.

She'd get away. All the people she'd injured. The humiliation she'd put him through. The degrading treatment of his father. Once mighty. Fierce. Now a pitiful lump of whimpering flesh. Legs like sticks, not strong and muscular. Arms with more bone than strength. The face, gaunt and bony-angular.

And she thought she'd get away with it. Her arrogance betrayed her belief that she was better, stronger.

Haegan stepped back with his right leg. Braced. Drew both hands to his sides. Hauled in a hard breath and drove his gaze up.

"Wha . . . what're you doing?"

Ignoring the assassin, Haegan slowly curled in his fingers, luring the heat from every inch of this cell and the surrounding dungeons, even from Trale, whose teeth began to chatter as Haegan pulled . . . pulled . . .

Light to the left changed.

Haegan mentally shoved it aside, guessing a torch had gone out, surrendering its heat to him. No longer would he be a prisoner. No longer would he live in darkness, clinging to selfish purposes. Enough.

Enough.

"No!" Trale shouted.

In his periphery, a second too late, Haegan saw a red bolt slinging toward him.

Trale was there the next instant, his body sailing in front of Haegan. The light deflected. With a strong gust, Trale flew backward. He hit the ground. Slid into the wall with a thick thud.

Haegan blinked, staring at his friend. The bolt had seared his chest.

The moment powered down to terrifying milliseconds. Trale had jumped in front of him. Taken the bolt in the chest. Died.

"NOOOOOO!" The intense heat Haegan had gathered began to slip.

His panic tripped his focus. He stumbled in his wielding. Then caught himself. *"ENOUGH!"* he roared. Rolled the intensity back to himself, crouched, and shoved outward. Upward.

• • •

A sea of red flooded the courtyard. Negaer and the Pathfinders rushed into the fray against incipients and Silvers. Though but a small unit of Sirdarians, it was challenge enough for a rag-tag band of soldiers who had journeyed hard, eaten little, and slept less.

Tili rode through the gate, all too aware of Astadia at his back. Over his shoulder, he ordered, "Stay clo—"

She slipped from the mount gracefully and bled into the sea of bodies.

"Hiel-touck," he muttered, noting his belt hung lighter. He cursed his own distracted mind. She had relieved him of the need to worry about her welfare. And his dagger. At least she hadn't buried it in his back.

Scanning the commotion, Tili assessed the battle. It was crowded and navigating on horseback proved difficult. He dismounted and pulled his blade from its scabbard. Nearby, Rhaemos engaged a Silver in fierce fighting. Even as he did, Tili spotted Vaqar moving—no, *gliding* through the Infantessa's guards. His scimitar and another blade moved too fast to see, glittering in the sun, flinging the blood of their enemies over the castle, Pathfinders, and cobbled stones. It seemed so effortless. So . . . natural.

"Steward!"

Even as he heard the warning shout, Tili detected movement to his right. He swung sideways, a sword tsinging barely an inch from his chest. Adrenaline jumping, he used the attacker's momentum. Shoved his arm aside and drove the man's own blade into his gut. The Silver gasped. Stood in frozen shock, as if he disbelieved Tili had run him through.

Steel sang through the air. And with a *phlat*, the Silver's head rolled from his body.

Startled, Tili gaped at the Tahscan grinning baldly at him, directly where the Silver's head had been. How he'd come up behind the enemy so swiftly that even Tili had not seen him was anyone's guess. "Ye could've taken my head as well."

"Next time," the Tahscan promised, then whirled and merged into another fray.

A blade shoved at Tili. He thrust away the shock and parried, but another Silver rushed him, red plume bristling. Two to one. He feinted left, drawing the Sirdarian with him, forcing the Silver to extend too far. Tili seized the mistake and arced his blade, catching the man along the belly.

He bellowed and threw himself at Tili.

The Sirdarian lunged as well. Tumbled. No. Wait. *What?* The man flipped onto his back, and a sprite of a girl landed on him, ending him.

Tili fought the Silver, his mind ringing with the swiftness of Astadia's moves, and somehow felt a challenge rise that he could not die at this one's hands if she'd freed him of the second.

Tili let him come again, this time, deflecting the blade to the left, leaving the Silver wide open. Tili ran him through. When he pivoted, he saw two men fighting. Ruthlessly, but only as his mind tripped over the details did he realize the wrongness of it. It wasn't a Jujak and a Silver. It was two Jujak. Negaer and Rhaemos. "No!" He lunged toward the two fighting each other.

"Inflaming!" Vaqar bellowed, tucking Tili back.

Tili held his breath as the two officers fought. As swords nearly swiped away limbs. Skilled fighters, but with bald rage in their eyes, this would not end well. "Negaer!" he shouted and started forward.

A Sirdarian surged at Tili. He crashed against the man, eyes still on the officers. "Rhaemos, cease!" Futility struggled with him, the Sirdarian annoyingly good. Focus. He had to focus. Tili thrust a bolt at the Sirdarian, who deftly avoided it—only to slide right into Tili's long blade. Freed of the battle, Tili pivoted.

Just in time to see Rhaemos and Negaer drive swords through each other.

"No!" Tili roared. But it was too late. And there were too many. "Where are they coming from?"

Even as another attacked, Tili sent a blast against the Sirdarian's chest. The man clutched at his uniform, no doubt trying to free the frozen stance of his heart. As Tili fended off another Silver, he spotted a red tunic blur into a tight cluster of fighters. Astadia.

A Sirdarian managed to hook an arm around her from behind. But she was quick. And had no bones apparently, for she slithered free of his grasp, grabbing the man's arm. Wrenching it as she whirled away and to the side. Even from fifty paces off, Tili heard the distinctive crack. The man's howl of pain was silenced by Vaqar, who cut him down. Toeing a dagger that had dropped from the man's grasp, Vaqar flipped it in the air. Caught and slid it into his belt with at least a dozen others.

Astadia spun to the next attacker and engaged.

An incipient stepped toward her, hand curled as if holding a ball. In the split-second that Astadia saw it, she was too late.

Instinct had Tili shove a bolt at the incipient. Though he'd aimed at the man, the wielding split like arrows, but unevenly. The first and larger struck the incipient. The second, thin and reedy, hit Astadia's arm.

The incipient stumbled but caught Tili's volley. He grinned, though Astadia's quick work with her street-fighting skills distracted him.

"Augh!"

The shout brought Tili around. He ducked at the wide, angry swing of the Sirdarian's sword. The man was panicked. Uncontrolled. Tili swiped his foot out from under him—and as he did, the entirety of the earth there fell way.

Two more Jujak, locked in battle with one another, vanished.

Not again.

Tokar and a Pathfinder were at blows, evenly matched both in agility and anger, unleashed on each other.

"No!" Tili yelled at them.

The ground collapsed. Tili yelped and scrambled backward, watching the earth yawn wide, as if bored with the battle taking place on its shoulders. Dark soil roiled and rattled. Rocks churned violently as if by the ministrations of a plow within the darkening chasm.

Alarm speared Tili as he took in the courtyard. The scrambling Pathfinders. Bodies disappearing into the opening chasm. "Back! Back!"

Blinking, Tokar turned. Bricks beneath his feet shifted. Canted down. His eyes bulged. Arms fanned out as the ground shifted again. He would fall into the emptiness!

Tili vaulted forward, grabbing for Tokar's arm. The boy's fingers grazed his, but slid. Abandoning his sword, Tili used his other hand to tighten the grip, stopping Tokar's descent.

Astadia was at his side, pawing to help bring the boy up.

Tokar scrabbled to safety, his face white and sweaty. A nervous laugh bubbled up his throat as he clasped arms with Tili in thanks.

Back on his feet, Tili saw his sword dangling from Astadia's hand. He met her gaze.

She smirked and extended the hilt.

Accepting his sword, Tili nodded at her. Then called to the army, "Move back to the road!" He waved them toward safety.

Astadia trotted with him. "I have to get in there to find my brother."

"And I the prince," he said, grim faced, monitoring the relocation to the road.

"What of the Infantessa?" Grinda asked as they regrouped at the gate.

"No sight of her since we stormed in."

Tili's gaze went to the castle. But even as he did, the earth slid from the side of the mountain, sloughing away the darkness. Skies blackened abruptly, bringing an ominous chill as clouds unleashed a deluge of rain. Cracking and popping threatened a mudslide.

"Farther back!" he commanded as screams went up. Disbelieving as people fell with the bricks and the south side of the castle, which plummeted down into the sea, he grabbed Astadia by the shoulders, pulling her with him.

She hauled in a ragged breath. "That's where Haegan's room was."

Tili frowned, not wanting to believe her. "Ye are sure?"

"It was from his balcony I jumped to escape the witch."

Disbelief choked Tili choked. "From that height?" He glanced at the roiling chaos of the churning sea, hungrily devouring the collapsing castle. "Into that?"

"Steward!"

A horrendous roar rushed through the sky. The ground rumbled, angry, furious, pitching them this way and that. Astadia started for the palace doors.

"Nay!" Tili grabbed her, but she wrestled against him. "'Tis not safe," he shouted over the raging din of the skies.

"My brother is there!"

"To the—" Grinda's voice was lost to the deafening howl of the earth's agony.

Strangely, Tili rose, the ground shoving him upward, over Astadia. It went down just as fast, then pitched Astadia. Eyes wide, she groped for purchase. Still, she stumbled.

This was worse than trying to break a wild horse. They tripped, pain scoring his leg as cobbled bricks seemed intent on punishing him for spilling blood on them.

Astadia reached for him and hauled herself up, glints of gold in her hair sparking. But even as he noticed, an entire shelf of earth rose behind her. Over her. Towered.

Pulse pounding in his ears, Tili caught Astadia. Yanked her into his arms, and launched them backward, spiraling through empty air. Bracing as his shoulder collided with the writhing ground. His ears ached from the din.

Pale blue, a shaft of light—so bright, so searing—shot into the sky and divested its path of debris, sending detritus spewing in all directions.

Covering Astadia with his body, Tili tensed at the expulsion of brick and earth that rained down. Pelted them. Popped him in the head.

An explosion of heat unlike anything he'd experienced blasted his spine. The backs of his legs. His head. Its force shoved him. Lifted him. Astadia's fingers dug into his side as they were flipped over and tossed away from the castle.

In the split-second he faced the direction of the blast, Tili saw something he couldn't believe. A raqine within the shaft.

Dirt peppered and scraped. Astadia bucked beneath his bulk. But he dared not move, dared not look. Whatever was happening, they might not survive it. The rage seemed to continue forever, until finally, all fell quiet.

Tili relaxed a little. He lifted his head and peered back—but rock again showered them. Muttering an oath, he jerked his head down. Covered their heads with his arm. The world seemed intent in its rage. Astadia tensed in his grasp again with a yelp, her breath skating along his neck, frantic.

A shriek rent the air, followed by a massive *whoosh*.

Then quiet fell. Deathly. Haunting.

Tili waited. Waited . . . waited as the quiet grew deeper. Slowly, he slid his arm from his head. Looked at Astadia beneath him. Her gold-green eyes were rimmed with terror. He breathed a smile, trying to reassure her, but failed. "Ye well?"

She gave a shaken nod but didn't move.

"Injuries?" He let himself touch her cool cheek. It warmed at his touch, which lingered a little longer than proper.

A slight shake was all she offered, her breathing coming in jagged spurts.

"Steward!" came a shout.

Tili peeled off Astadia, folding back on his haunches and extending her a hand.

Her gaze skidded around as she ignored his help.

"Blazes and fury," someone muttered. "Look!"

Tili rose and turned to the castle.

Correction. To the mountain that had shed itself of the monstrosity once called a castle. A hole gaped where Castle Karithia once stood. But the winding curve of the courtyard remained, holding in protective custody the one who had wreaked this havoc on her own people and city. The Infantessa stood there, her face death white. Hair disheveled.

"How in blazes did *she* survive?" a Pathfinder said, hefting his sword, his intent clear and probably mirrored in the heart of every remaining fighter.

"Why isn't she running?" Astadia asked.

"Can you not smell it?" Vaqar said with a half laugh. "Fear. She is afraid."

"Of what?"

"Them," Vaqar replied, nodding toward the enormous beings who remained in a wide arc around the castle ruins. Massive and terrifying, the Deliverers gripped their swords between both hands, tips aimed at the Infantessa. Steel threatening her with death.

"They're not striking," Tili noted.

Slowly, Astadia skulked forward. "Why aren't they killing her?"

"More like, why are they letting her live?" Tili said, catching Astadia's hand so she didn't move closer and draw the Infantessa's attention.

"Leaving her to us?" a Pathfinder suggested.

"Aye," another said. "Payback for what she did to us."

After a breath, a shout vaulted as they rushed the Infantessa, who looked as defiant as ever. And old. So old her skin might fall off. Even Tili found himself closing in.

"She is mine!" roared someone.

Tili searched for the voice.

A shadow fell on them.

He looked up, as did the rest of the contingent, and a familiar beast filled his field of vision. "Chima," he whispered in disbelief. It was her he'd seen in the blast of light. How had she gotten into that . . . dungeon? She'd been in the den at Nivar.

Hackles raised, eyes fiery red, Chima hovered over them. Stationary, she flapped twice then angled her shoulder to the right and a form slid from her back.

Two more solid thwacks of those wings thrust Chima upward.

Tili focused on the man she'd deposited. Tattered clothes. Tall. Shoulders square. Head inclined.

"Prince Haegan."

"*King* Haegan," someone corrected.

Haegan's clothes may be tattered and his appearance haggard, but there was a vicious intent in his bearing and gaze. This was not a prince or king come to face an enemy. This was the Hand of Abiassa. Her warrior, foretold through the ages. Hoped for by some. Doubted by more, including himself.

"The Fierian," Tili said.

Praegur was at his side now. "He has embraced his role."

Haegan strode through the crowd, his beggar clothes too small. Reeking. Torn. Several Pathfinders wrinkled their noses and pulled away.

"Come to face me, Fierian?" the Infantessa shrieked, her face red as she glowered wildly.

The expression Haegan wore was not fury. Or indifference. Or frustration. This was raw focus. Determination. *Intent.* As he made his way to her, he paused beside Vaqar, watching the Infantessa, who hadn't budged. Perhaps unwilling or unable to move. She trembled with rage. With terror.

It did not seem fair that the Deliverers would restrain her.

Haegan looked to Vaqar, spoke quietly with him before the Tahscan handed him a blade. With a nod of thanks, the Fierian turned to the Infantessa. His fingers fluttered.

The Infantessa released a gasp and collapsed to her knees in a fit of exhausted torture.

Only then did Tili realize it was not the Deliverers who held her in the halo. It'd been Haegan. New respect spread through Tili at that realization. When had Haegan stepped so resolutely into his abilities? It had not been so long ago he was a blaze waiting to happen.

The Infantessa shook her head. "If you think you can kill me—"

"Too long," Haegan's voice boomed, "have you held people trapped in their doubts and fears. Too long have you crushed hopes and dreams."

"You were *weak*!" she spat, her lip curling. "Look at you now. I made you strong!"

The prince seemed not to hear. "Because of your cruelty, because of the great harm delivered against so many, against me, against my father . . ." His voice sounded so unlike him, so deep. Fierce. "*You* have decided your fate, Nydelia."

"My fate—yes, my fate. Do not think for one minute you control it, Fierian," she snarled. "I kept you here, wrapped up in your own selfish desires—"

"Desires?"

"Yes, your desire to have it your way, to run from a path that didn't make you happy, afraid it would disrupt your plan to be liked by all." She snorted. "It's disgusting how easy it was to keep you here, to distract you, and hold your thoughts hostage!"

Broad shoulders and muscles seemed barely restrained. When had Haegan grown into such a man? He stepped back as silence reigned, lifted his chin. His dark-blond hair curled past his shoulders and tussled by the hot wind. "I will show you the same mercy you gave to those who could do nothing for you, Nydelia."

"Try."

It happened in a flash. So lightning-fast, Tili wasn't wholly sure what happened. Whether it was the blade that cut the life from her. Or the hyper-focused blast of Flames that seared her heart. Mayhap both. Which one killed her first, he could not tell. He did not care. One minute she was there, defiant and snarling like a rabid dog. The next she was but a lump on the ground.

Tili's gaze skidded back to Haegan, who hung his head. No exultation over killing his enemy who had enslaved so many. No victory shout. Just a heaving, exhausted breath beneath shoulders that lifted, then sagged. Grief played across his features as he dragged his gaze to the Pathfinders. To the Tahscans.

Finally, a victory cry rang among the people. But there was no victory here. And that shone in Haegan's eyes.

Chima returned, landing in the center of the courtyard. From her claw-like paws, she released a bundle, setting it down carefully and backing away, her white-hot eyes on Haegan. Her chortle warbled in a soft, pliant manner as she dipped her head. It amazed Tili to think Chima had finally chosen a rider. She had been obstinate for so long. Sitting, she drew in her wings, which crinkled softly as she folded them along her spine.

Haegan, sword in one hand, embers in the other, stared at what she'd delivered.

"What is it?" whispers quietly snaked through the contingent.

Revulsion heaved as he realized the truth of that bundle. By the prince's sagging shoulders and the droop of his head, the grief and exhaustion—

No. That wasn't exhaustion. "Defeat," Tili muttered.

Vaqar's sword clattered to the ground as Haegan swayed. Staggered closer, then dropped to a knee. The pale fire around his fingers snuffed out as he slumped amid the rubble.

A second later, a gut-wrenching shout snapped through the air. Legs bent beneath him, Haegan threw his head back, arms held out. Hands fisted. Face of fury and anguish. Strange and pure, glowing and glittering, a blue halo of light erupted around him. It arced into the heavens, then back down, billowing out at the gathered soldiers and citizens.

Startled by the wave of light and heat, Tili braced, expecting to be seared alive. Warmth rushed him. Invigorated him. Strength soaked into his muscles. Healing into his wounds. Peace into his mind. But even as his vitality grew, he watched in his periphery as men and women along the path collapsed. Standing, they were strong. Before their bodies could hit the ground, they were dust.

A panicked murmur ripped through the Pathfinders. Yelps rose as a few of their own met with the same deadly fate. Tili shifted, watching as the bow of the pale blue wave slid over the city, like water that climbs the shore, reaching . . . reaching . . . Down the hill. Across the lands.

"*What* was that?" Astadia asked, trembling, touching his arm.

Shaking his head, Tili turned back around. Disbelief and awe warred as he watched the Fierian stare at the pile. What was it?

Hacgan sobbed.

Pushing himself, Tili took the first step forward.

"Careful," came a low warning from Vaqar.

When he reached the prince, he staggered at what lay in the pile. "The Fire King," Tili said, closing the distance between them. His mind struggled with the sight. With the truth he'd spoken without realizing. The Fire King lived. A putrid odor so engulfed the air that Tili's exultation turned at once to grief. To smell so horrible, Zireli must have died days ago. Tili took a knee beside the prince.

Haegan didn't respond, his gaze so fixed on his father, on the tragedy of the death.

Tili touched his shoulder.

Still no reaction or hint of awareness that anyone else existed.

"Haegan."

The prince blinked. Lifted his gaze. In his pale blue eyes, the same color as the wave that glided through Iteveria, there hung a distance. As if Haegan were not here. His thoughts elsewhere.

"Prince," Tili said quietly, avoiding the corpse beside him, "we should get ye to safety."

"Safety." He grunted and looked to his father. "He . . ."

Squeezing Haegan's shoulder, Tili tried to reassure him that words were not necessary. "Losing a father—"

Haegan's fiery gaze crackled. "He's not dead."

Stunned at the vehemence, Tili frowned.

Haegan nodded. "Look—even unconscious, he draws the Flames from around him."

Surprised to see an ever-so-subtle dance of a heat wake around the tips of Zireli's fingers, Tili punched to his feet. "Bring a stretcher!"

20

Back at the wagons, Tili monitored the army as they tended the wounded, took a census, and enjoyed respite after the battle. That's when he saw him. Blond hair rustled on the hot wind. Light brown eyes stared back at Tili.

The first thread of hope sprouted in his chest at the sight of the lad. "Where is she, Laertes?" he asked, tempering his impatience.

The boy shrugged, his eyes wild and frantic. "She . . . We was going up and up, the wings flappin' so hard. Next fing what I know's, she's yanked backward."

"Chima?" Tokar asked, joining them.

"No, Thiel." He flashed his palms. "She right near took me, too."

"She fell?" Stomach clenching at the thought, Tili shook his head. "Nay, she was trained to ride from childhood."

Laertes' eyes filled. "They pulled her off."

"Who?" Tili asked, though he feared he knew the answer.

"Them monsters. The Ematahri."

Then Thiel remained a prisoner of the Ematahri. "Ye didn't go back for her?" Tili challenged.

"I couldn't! The beast wouldn't turn back. She flew and flew, not caring that I beat her or how I screamed." Tears broke free and trickled down his cheeks. "I tried! I tried, I did."

Grieved and confused, Tili wrapped an arm around the lad. "'Tis not yer fault. All will be well."

"How do you know?"

"She's too thickheaded to die," he said, pushing his thoughts to the two who had been recovered. He could not bear to consider how easily he might be wrong. "I must see the prince."

"Aye, you should tell the prince what happened to her—"

"Not yet," Tili snapped, then patted the boy's shoulder. "Not yet, Laertes. He needs rest. And peace."

• • •

Exhaustion tore at Haegan, yanking hard with each laborious breath as he stared at the young boy seated with him in the wagon. He knew him. Had known him once. But not so much now. Men were talking, hovering over him as he sat on a cot. How he'd gotten to the cot, he didn't know. Yet he was here. Sitting. Aching to lie down and rest until . . . eternity. But he wouldn't rest, not until—

"My father." He whipped his head up and looked around, dizzy and disoriented as he met unfamiliar faces.

A face wreathed in brown—hair, eyes, beard—broke into his visual field. "There beside you, Prince."

"Tili." The name came easy enough, but locating other pieces of information proved too difficult.

"Aye, Twig." There was a smile on his lips and in those words.

He looked where Tili nodded, another cot within reach, and found a bundle of blankets. A man hovered over a skeletal frame. The gaunt face. Haegan's grief collapsed, much like the cavern in that—"Dungeon."

"Ye are both safe now," Tili spoke softly but firmly. "Come, Laertes. Let him rest." He waited till the boy left, then nodded. "We are setting out north toward Dorcastle, then Ironhall. A long drive. Nothing for ye to do but rest."

"Nothing but . . . rest . . ."

"Aye." A hand guided him backward, and Haegan relented only because he had no strength to fight. And he didn't care. He just didn't care. His father was near death. And . . .

No, don't think. Don't remember. Just . . . sleep.

"My brother!"

Haegan flinched at loudness of the voice, a female voice. "Thiel?" He reached out and made contact with someone.

"Nay, 'tis not," Tili muttered. "Rest, Prince."

"I just want to know where my brother is!" she shouted. "Ask him!"

"Get back," Tili said, and his voice held warning.

"It's a simple question," the girl argued. "Just ask him where Trale is. I must know."

The only image that name conjured was searing. Death. Haegan curled away from the voices, away from the torment.

• • •

Catching Astadia by the shoulders, Tili whirled her around and nudged her from the wagon. "Leave off," he hissed.

Wild and angry, she stumbled back then lunged forward. Defiance etched into the soft contours of her face, hardening it. "We had a deal—my brother!" She slapped his chest. "Ask him!"

"He is half out of his mind with exhaustion and trauma."

"But you and your men are leaving Iteveria. Trale was in there"—she stabbed a hand at the ruins of Karithia. "And I'm going to find my brother with or without—"

"Without me? What would ye have me do?" he railed. "Karithia has fallen. Quite literally, if ye can't remember. 'Tis unstable and in ruins."

"So you're saying I should just give up on my brother."

"I'm saying"—*breathe, relax*—"we have no way of finding anyone in that rubble. 'Twould take months, which we do not have with the Dark One breathing down our necks."

She slapped his leather vest again and shoved hard.

Hands hauled her up and away from him, the Pathfinders taking her assault of his person none too lightly. She flailed like a fish out of water. "Let go! You can't stop me from going in there."

Tili's heart tripped at the thought of her actually trying to dig through that heap. "If yer brother was in there, though it pains me to say it—he's dead now."

"No!" she spat. "You can't know that. If you want to turn tail—"

"I'm not turning anything. Half the structure is gone. The other half is surrounded by a great chasm. 'Tis deadly." He willed her to understand the risk of even going near that place. "If ye go in there, ye'll die."

That hardheaded glint of hers returned. She lifted her chin. "Then let me die, but I won't leave—"

"He is dead." The words, spoken in a numb and dazed tone, came from behind.

Tili pivoted, glancing up into the wagon where Haegan sat, upright again and braced against one of the tarp supports that arched overhead to provide protection from the elements. He pushed to the edge of the cot, determination gouged into his bruised and cut face.

Tili hesitated, then looked at Astadia, who'd gone deathly still. And pale. His heart staggered at the sight of her so broken and undone.

"We were trapped in the dungeon," Haegan said, his gaze fixed on some point in the past. "He betrayed me to the Infantessa—he said it was to save you." His eyes flicked up, focusing on Astadia for the first time. "But then he came back to help me. An incipient tried to kill me. Trale . . ." Haegan heaved a sigh and let it out, his gaze unfocused once more. "Trale protected me from the strike. It killed him. Instantly."

Astadia gaped at Haegan, her young eyes that had weathered so much —too much—stared, disbelieving. Her mouth opened but nothing came out. Eyes watered to a muddy green. Her chin dimpled with restrained tears. Then that rage exploded. "He gave his life for you, a petulant prince who ran from his duty! If you'd been man enough to step into that, he never would've been there."

"Hey!" Tili snapped. "Enough, Astadia."

But she shouldered past him. "You took up with the very wretch who turned your mind against you." Her lip curled and she spat, "You weren't worth his life."

"Enough!" Tili barked, forcing her around.

Astadia slapped away his hand. "Beg off." She pivoted and stalked through the throng that had gathered.

Tili glanced up at the pharmakeia seated between the cots that bore the Celahars. "Give the prince herbs or something stronger. Just . . . make him rest." He released the wagon cover, concealing father and son. "Blazes."

"A lot like Thiel," Tokar lamented.

"Aye," Laertes muttered. "But iff'n you saw what she did to help free Chima—"

"Free her?" Tokar asked. "What do ye mean?"

"They'd caged us—me, Thiel, and Chima. An' Praegur," he added as an afterthought. "But he went off with them what came to rescue us. Thiel wouldn't go. She thought she could reason with them monsters."

Tokar pivoted to Tili. "We should go for her."

"Wouldn' do no good," Laertes said. "They was packing up camp and movin'. I don' know where to. Them whats beds with the enemy could be anywhere by now."

"An army doesn't move that fast," Tokar said, "or without leaving a trail. We could track them."

Tili roughed a hand over his face, hating the decision before him. "Aye, but we must needs set our path north. My sister is not a helpless child. She has relied on her wits before." He glanced around. "Any word on General Negaer?"

"Dead." Grim-faced, the younger Grinda approached. "He and Rhaemos—killed beneath that witch's inflaming."

Tili drew up, momentarily stunned. He had known his hope was futile—had seen the two run each other through. But the news still came as a blow. "Who's next in command?"

"Technically, a dozen of us," Grinda said. "We've been cobbled together from so many different forces that the chain of command is a mess."

"Fire and fury," Tili muttered. "We can't sort that now. We must ride."

"We're ready." Grinda fell into step with Tili.

"Good. We need to put as much distance between us and"—his gaze hit the rubble again, creating a new backdrop and violent end for the waterfall—"this."

"Many died here, and I'm not talking about the Silvers we killed in the courtyard."

"Matters not who you reference. Families lost loved ones." Tili cringed at the memories assailing him—people corporeal then wisps of dust. "We should ride out with all haste before they can stir a mob against us." But even as he turned, he spied Vaqar emerging from a crowd at the city's edge, determination lurking in his dark eyes. A determination that drew Tili toward him.

Vaqar cocked his head in the direction of those he'd just left. "The son of the mayor. His father vanished in the wave."

Vanished. That was a nice way of putting it. Tili again checked the crowd and tensed at the terse expressions and postures. "They're upset."

"Yes," Vaqar said.

"With me."

"With all—you, the soldiers, the Infantessa, the Fierian." Vaqar lifted his shoulders in a slow shrug. "I've given them distraction. Told the son to take a census, get the people organized." He sighed. "We should go."

"What the blazes happened in there?" Tokar asked. "How did he kill them? With a shout even. *How?*"

Tili jammed on his gloves. "'Twas not him but the Fire She gave him."

"So, you're saying Abiassa killed those people—innocent men and women lining the street. Fifteen Pathfinders," Tokar growled.

"I'm saying that none but Abiassa know the heart," Tili said, his breath short and his words more so. "Would ye challenge Her judgment?"

"Nay, but I—"

Tili jerked around. "This is what was written. This is what we are called to defend."

Tokar's jaw muscle bounced. "She could have stopped Sirdar."

"What ye should concern yerself with, Captain, is gathering yer men. Choosing yer five."

"My fi—" Tokar stopped short. "What? No!"

"The general and Rhaemos are dead."

"There are many more qualified—"

"Ye have a raqine. Ye have trained with Nivari and Jujak and Pathfinders. Ye will lead the air scouts. We will sort this more, but for now, we must ride." Tili took the reins of his mount from Laertes. "As for the Fierian . . . She sends one man with all of the fires of Her fury to deliver the lands, to separate the wheat from the chaff, and ye object?"

Face red, Tokar swallowed. "It's . . . violent."

"Aye," Tili said. "And our rebellious hearts need it."

• • •

Soaring through the air, wind rustling her hair from the thin band that held it back, Thiel savored the freedom as Chima climbed higher and higher. With Laertes tucked close, she relished the power of the great beast intent on her mission. They raced along the ravine, then Chima circled back, apparently to catch a wind current, but as she did, Thiel saw the Ematahri warriors galloping on their horses toward the great cliff.

If they beat her there . . .

Palm pressed to Chima's side, Thiel tried to both urge and warn the mighty raqine. The alarm must have rung through her loud and clear, because Chima tilted, angry and annoyed with the warriors trying to use slingshots and arrows to clip her wing, bring her down.

She barreled at one warrior—Raleng—and slapped him off his mount with a wing. Then she banked upward swiftly.

"Hang on!" Thiel shouted to Laertes, feeling the boy's small body tense with panic. "She won't let us fall." Which wasn't true. Chima had one mission—to save Haegan. And she would fight her way there, even if it meant she died doing it.

The people on her back? Fleas.

Chima banked right, chortling loudly at another warrior, who raced toward the highest cliff to stop them. But Chima's angle, Thiel's sweaty palms, the heights and dips and arrows tsinging past her compromised her grip. She slipped. Her leg dangled. A vise constricted around Thiel's ankle. Yanked. Her grip broke.

She slid sideways. A scream tore through her lungs. She was falling . . . falling . . .

Thiel jolted upright, her shriek still ringing in her ears. Instantly awake and painfully aware of the fire racing through her leg, she cried out. As the truth of her situation rushed upon her again, she fell against the pallet and fought tears.

"Get up. We ride!"

Thiel had barely lifted her gaze when something flew at her. She cringed and braced—only to be thumped in the head with a pile of material. It fell into her lap. She stared down at tunic and trousers. Then glowered at Ruldan. "I'm not going anywhere!"

He lunged and grabbed her hair, then jerked hard. "You ride when he says ride." With a shove, he sent her sprawling off the pallet.

Thiel caught herself, steeling against the pain rocking through her broken leg. The fire volleyed. Seized control of her stomach and catapulted its contents up her throat. She vomited onto the floor, crying. Agonizing.

"Leave!"

Ruldan jerked straight. "Archon."

"Out," Cadeif barked as he stormed in and yanked something from a basket. Not acknowledging her or Ruldan, he stuffed clothes into a pack.

Thiel spit out bile and wiped her lips, eying Ruldan as he exited. "Where are we going?"

Kneeling at the basket, spine arched as he worked, he said nothing. With no effort, he pushed to his feet and strode to the other side. There, he packed more items.

"My ankle is broken. I can't ride." True, but only then did she notice the splint and bindings someone had placed on her leg while she'd been unconscious. And the cup beside the pallet—herbs to stem infection and lessen the pain. "Why are ye doing this to me? Where is the man I knew?"

There was this muscle, right above his temple, that always twitched when he was angry. And it jounced now. Beautiful sun-darkened skin played with the flickering light of the fire pit. Muscles and power. Rage and fury. "You were not here long enough to know me, Etelide." He spun and left the tent. "Bring her."

Two Ematahri entered with severe expressions. Faces painted with blue and white streaks. Hunting. What were they hunting? Why were they taking her? They hauled Thiel upright and tugged her forward. She had to make quick work of figuring out how to hobble without pain stabbing her leg as they escorted her into the evening and . . . empty woods.

Surprise sliced through her as she darted a look around. Tents were gone. Structures torn down. They hurried her through a dense copse of firs and pines to a clearing. The scene stole her breath. She'd never journeyed with the Ematahri, but the sight of the warriors lined up with the Sirdarians nearly made her vomit again. These people were not like the bloodthirsty Sirdarians. They were stronger. Better.

A man in a blood-red uniform stalked toward her. "Where did it go?"

There was something about his demand that made Thiel refuse to answer.

A lasso of heat coiled around her neck and constricted. Heart thrumming, Thiel groped for air.

"Don't think I'm like the Ematahri," the Sirdarian sneered. "The only pleasure I'll take from you is inflicting scorch marks."

A large frame stepped between them, and the fire whip crackled and sizzled out. "Zorek, leave her."

Thiel wobbled, but the two warriors steadied her. She rubbed her throat, feeling the rising welts from the fire whip.

"You dare countermand me?" Zorek hissed.

Cadeif's thick arms drew back, ready for a fight. "We agreed to help in exchange for fertile lands, but my people are not yours to abuse."

"She is not one of you—"

"She is mine!" The veins along Cadeif's neck strained against his declaration.

Ripples of tension tightened the stances of the Ematahri around them.

"Think well your next move," Cadeif warned. "We may not have Flames to wield, but we have steel and iron, and knowledge of the forests." He looked to the trees, to the ridges of the gorge.

Zorek's eyes flared. "Think you can take us?"

"Have we not a task to carry out?" Cadeif sounded bored as he looked over his shoulder to the two guarding her. "Secure her on the horse."

Vises tightened on her arms as the warriors pulled her away from the two leaders. It was a deliberate move, she knew, to remind Zorek that she was not his to deal with. It made her feel protected. Which made no sense at all.

Raleng yanked her toward a horse. Without ceremony, he lifted Thiel off her feet.

She tensed and landed painfully on the horse's back. Indignation squirmed at his manhandling, but with a broken ankle, she probably couldn't have mounted the horse alone. "They are Sirdarians. Puppets of the Dark One. Why has Cadeif conspired with him—that man has no goal—"

Raleng tossed a sack at her. It thumped Thiel in the chest and unseated her balance. She grabbed the rein and the bag at the same time, struggling to stay astride. Hair dangling in her face, she steadied and only then noticed Raleng was gone.

She squinted across the distance to where Cadeif stood with Zoijan. Heads down as they secured packs did little to conceal the intense conversation happening between them. They weren't happy about something.

Zoijan thrust a hand to his left.

Cadeif snapped upright. He stepped into his first's personal space, nose pressed to the man's cheek as he said something, then turned and stalked straight toward Thiel.

She hesitated, breath caught at the darkness swarming his features. Cadeif had always possessed a raw presence. He lifted his gaze, striking hers for but a second. Long enough for her to detect something ominous. He reached his warhorse and swung effortlessly onto its back.

Even when she'd lived with the Ematahri, she had never wanted his anger turned on her. She'd known enough of him then to understand the mistake of that. Being his friend was one thing. Enjoying his laughter a pleasant surprise. Being on the wrong end of his anger—dreadful. He was, plain and simple, a warrior. True and brutal. And she was wilting beneath his wrath.

After looking around the mounted riders, he lifted a hand and let out a mournful call.

As if her horse had a will of its own, it started moving, nudged along by the advance of the clan. "Where are we going?" she asked, trying to reopen that broken bridge between them.

Hands relaxed, one on his leg, the other holding the reins, Cadeif gave her nothing but his silence.

The slow, arduous ride out of the pass took most of the day, and by the time the sun settled in the western horizon, Thiel's ankle throbbed in time with her horse's hoof beats.

When the warriors slowed, she let herself hope for a break. But as she took in the surroundings, that hope fell away. Something was off. The lands were too moist. Too green. This couldn't be the Outlands, which is where she'd assumed they were going. And it couldn't be the east—too few Sirdarians or ruined villages.

"Water," came a soft voice.

Distracted by the offer of friendship that came with that simple word, Thiel looked to the side and found a young Ematahri female. "Then a rest?"

The girl shook her head. "Not until after the moons rise."

"But surely ye need a rest as much as I do."

She shrugged. "It will be over soon enough."

"What will?"

"The wait."

"For what?"

"Fertile lands of our own. The general promised—"

"Thuli!"

Jerking at the bark of her name, the girl jabbed her horse's flanks and leapt ahead.

Thiel eyed Zoijan, who urged his mount alongside her, their legs nearly rubbing. "Is that why Cadeif is doing this?"

"You will call him archon."

"But surely he can't be fool enough to believe Onerid will grant you land—"

A gloved hand struck her face hard.

Nearly flipping off the horse, Thiel yelped. She caught herself, touching fingers to a throbbing and now-bleeding lip.

"Do not call him a fool! Not in front of others. Not ever!" Zoijan's ruddy face grew crimson. "You have no place here. Why he claimed you, I don't know. But you deserved whatever he did to you that night. Have you any idea what he has done to protect our people after you left?"

"Easy, Zoijan," came Cadeif's monotone voice. "She is not worth your anger."

The warrior nodded then drew his mount away, turning to ride with another group.

Thiel's thoughts tumbled and fell along the jagged cliffs of their rejection and remonstrations. "Cadeif," she said, keeping a pleading tone, "please—tell me ye do not believe the general. He's Sirdarian. He does the will of Sirdar. He's wicked, a spawn of Ederac."

His gaze remained ahead as they rode. "He has brought supplies my people needed and given us shelter when we were on the verge of starvation."

"Starvation?"

"After the Lucent Riders, a great fire destroyed the forests and animals along the Throne Road. We had nothing." He skated a sidelong glance at her. "I must do for my people what it takes to keep them alive."

As night fell on them, so did a daunting realization that she'd been right—they were not traveling west or east as she'd initially thought. They were traveling north. Toward Ybienn. Dread, insipid and cold, tightened around her courage.

The Ematahri were helping the Sirdarians attack her family.

21

Dressed in leathers and armor, Aselan rose from the den on Pharen's back and tested his injured leg. Hoeff's ministrations were helpful, but the calf still ached. Behind him came the Legiera, their raqine as fiercely annoyed as his own at the flushing out of the den.

Aselan watched the last raqine lumber from the dark cavern with its rider. Deep within the mountain, the women and children were making their way down a network of tunnels and passages that had long been closed. With them went his bound, the Mistress of the Heart. Kaelyria.

Pulling his gaze and thoughts from the sight, he turned to the battle at hand. To the north. To the skies where dozens of raqine circled. They flew high and hard, with intent to bring death to the enemy. The Rekken had come to decimate an innocent people. To make war and drive them from the home the Eilidan had claimed for a century. Aselan would not go quietly, nor would his men.

Twenty minutes into the ride, Aselan spotted the Rekken. Rarely one to call on Abiassa, he silently pleaded with Her to protect the women—Kaelyria. To bring them safely back together.

Using hand signals, he gave the order to begin the assault.

Byrin, Teelh, Bardin, and Caprit arched their raqine into a dive. Like arrows, they flew true and fast. Behind, Aselan guided Markoo and the other Legiera into a second barrage. Would that he could wield. That they had an accelerant among their number.

Pharen roared as they sped toward the mountain, trees growing larger.

The wind tore at their faces and armor, pushing them back. Threatening to pitch them off their raqine.

Arrows flew, tips glinting in the sun.

With expert precision, Aselan allowed Pharen to swerve to avoid being shot. The beast had barely recovered after the last arrow pierced his wing. They could not risk further injury. And yet, they must.

Aselan urged Pharen into another dive attack, this one so close, the Rekken threw themselves out of the path. Aselan swung his mace and landed a few strategic blows, felling several.

A rancid smell coated the air.

Banking up, Pharen shrieked.

Another raqine echoed the mournful sound.

And that's when Aselan realized the terrible truth. *They have an incipient!*

As if in response, a searing red blast struck Aselan. It snapped him backward, but thanks to the straps fastening his legs to Pharen's harness, he stayed mounted. Struggling against the pain that seared his right shoulder and the renewed throb in his leg, Aselan came up.

Straight into another blast. This one seemed to have a split nature. A larger one struck his shoulder numb. And a thinner, smaller one seared along the harness. His heart raced, watching in terror as the leather seared apart.

Cold air snatched him off Pharen. Flipped him through weightless nothingness. He plummeted toward the earth, wind tearing at his clothes and face. Death was seconds away. Tumbling, flipping, he was beat mercilessly by the air currents. Aselan struggled against the blinding fury in his shoulder. Against the panic that he would die and Kaelyria . . .

Thump!

The impact jolted him. He expected pain, but instead noticed a lifting sensation. It took a second to realize Pharen had come up under him. Fingers dug into the fur, Aselan struggled back to the riding position between Pharen's shoulders. Agony screamed through his arm and shoulder. Broken straps wrapped around his wrists, he pushed his face into the pelt and breathed deeply his thanks to Pharen for the rescue.

Aselan opened his eyes. Beyond Pharen's sleek skull, a plume of smoke billowed from the mountain.

The Heart!

As the black cloud belched ash and flames, women and children crawled free of the opening, a narrow cave that seemed to have collapsed, breaking a hole to the surface. Their small frames clambered over the rocky incline. Injured. Leaving crimson trails in the lingering snow. A larger cavity formed in the face of the Tooth. More dragged themselves out with another column of smoke.

But how?

The tunnels were solid rock. They were safe.

That's when he noticed the snow shimmering and tree limbs trembling. *Explosions.*

"No!" His word was swallowed as Pharen arced away, no doubt sensing the rumble of the mountain. The fire. The danger.

"No! No, back," he shouted, luring Pharen around, only to find the Rekken surging, falling upon the women and children. And there, among them was Teelh, who ran two Rekken through before a blast struck him down.

Incipient.

Aselan dove to attack.

A searing blanket of fire rushed at Aselan. It pelted him and Pharen, who howled. The earth and sunlight fell away.

• • •

Many peoples and brigands had been dubbed savages, but those herding Kaelyria, the women, and children of the Heart into a circle truly embodied that word with their abhorrent treatment and the ruthless way they'd cut down many, including Teelh.

"Circle up," demanded a large-bellied man who wielded a dagger. He poked it at a little girl and snarled.

The girl burst into tears, wetting herself.

The Rekken laughed cruelly.

"Leave her," Kaelyria shouted, pulling the child close.

The little one clung to her, arms tight around Kae's legs. She nearly pushed her over.

The savage now shoved a girl on the cusp of womanhood, then grabbed her hair and yanked her to his chest. "You of age?"

"The child is not," came Ingwait's soft, challenging tone as she stepped forward.

The man backhanded Ingwait, who stumbled into Kaelyria.

Bracing the woman and shielding the little girl, Kaelyria felt fury climbing through her. "Have you no honor?"

"Don't speak to me, wench!" His hand reared—but froze in midair, along with the collective breath of those from the Heart.

Three horses galloped into their midst. Riders dressed in black, their faces hidden beneath silver helms, inflicted fear upon the defenseless crowd. "Silvers," some whispered. It must be one of them who restrained the man from striking.

But these were not Silvers—the plumes did not arch in a single trail over their heads like a clipped mane. Instead, the plumes were black and red, stretching from ear to ear. One had a pure black plume. Capes black. Boots black, reaching to their knees, no doubt because of the cold. Not a single touch of silver on these. They wore bronze. The helmets. The buttons. The armor plating. The swords.

"Who are they?" Entwila hissed.

Kaelyria shook her head, having never seen these uniforms. A man in a navy longcoat with six bronze buttons and a high collar strode between the riders. His expression was impassive, but everything about him commanded obedience. "Where is the one called Kaelyria?"

Her heart flailed like an animal caught in a trap.

He turned, then drew in a breath. "The one called Kaelyria—step forth!"

About to respond, she felt a cold hand clamp around hers. Ingwait. The matron gave an almost imperceptible shake of her head.

"I will not ask again," the man barked as he paced their group the way wolves stalk their prey. He reached over and snatched a small boy. "I am told the Mistress of the Heart is compassionate. She would not want children to die."

Kaelyria swallowed.

The man rolled his fingers, a small but frightening display as a red flame skittered across his knuckles. Her father had done that many times. She had done that.

These men would no doubt end the child's life if she did not step forward. She would never be the cause of harm to an innocent. "I—"

"I am Kaelyria," came a voice.

Kae jerked, confused. Who had spoken? Her stomach plummeted when she saw Carilla from the cantina raise a hand.

"Bring her," the incipient snarled.

"No," Kae whispered.

"Quiet," Ingwait hissed.

Two black-clad Rekken stomped forward, cuffing Carilla by the arms. They dragged her to the tall incipient and thrust her at his feet. She yelped when her hands snapped forward, planting into the icy blanket of snow. A red halo encircling her wrists, she was held in place.

No. Kae couldn't let this happen.

The vise of Ingwait's grip tightened. "Don't be a fool. Ye tell them, and they'll kill her now."

"If I don't—they'll do it lat—"

Carilla cried out as her head popped up, straining so her face was bared to the incipient. A trail of red seared her chin. Tears slid down her cheeks, her skin mottling.

The girl wasn't straining. *She's burning!*

Kaelyria flipped her gaze to the incipient, who watched Carilla impassively. Only . . . *He's not wielding.*

It wasn't him. He wasn't the one hurting the girl.

A scream pierced her ears.

Carilla collapsed, the snow around her quickly turning red.

Cries and shouts erupted from the Eilidan.

"This," the tall incipient shouted, "is not Kaelyria. Or should I say—*was* not Kaelyria."

Heart hammering, Kaelyria looked to the two mounted incipients. The one with the black helm. Warbling heat snaked around his fingers.

"Would you like another demonstration, Mistress?" the incipient asked as he scanned over the crowd, his voice unnaturally calm. He adjusted his gloves.

She must do something.

"No," Ingwait hissed, tightening her grip on her hand.

"I must."

"They cannot kill us all," Ingwait said.

"If even one more dies because of—" Breath choked by searing heat, Kaelyria widened her eyes. Clawed at her throat. Felt the wielding dragging her forward. She fought, resisting. Stumbling. Angered to be treated this way. Terrified that they wanted her and would kill so needlessly to effect her capture.

Tears burned as she staggered. The edges of her vision closed in from air deprivation. The suffocation of heat. Her head tilted back of its own accord. Staring up . . . up . . . past the shifting horse. She gasped and wheezed, hands to her throat. Tears blurred what little of her vision remained.

The black-helmed rider stared her down. A vicious gleam hung in his dark eyes. Eyes that were strange. Familiar—distantly familiar. *I know him.*

Without a word, he brought his horse around.

The chokehold broke.

Kaelyria crumpled with a yelp, only to be seized by the Rekken, bound with ropes and chains, and placed on a sleigh. Four guards hopped into the back. Two facing her, hands on their swords. Two more watching the Eilidan, who were being herded away. They would not last long with winter biting their hands and feet.

The ride proved unrelenting as they made their way down the mountain. With each passing minute, the jounce of skids on the forbidding mountain terrain, Kaelyria felt her courage and strength leach from her. Why had she been targeted? And by an incipient? Was this an effort against Aselan? To force him to surrender the Heart?

Why would anyone want the mountain? There were no resources. Just rock, cold, and—*raqine*. Though the thought had merit, it also was foolhardy. Idiotic. Raqine could no more be controlled than the weather. Incipients should know that.

Rocking of the sleigh took a toll on her. Stomach roiling, head throbbing, she leaned back against the wood. "Please—can we stop for a moment? I'm going to be sick."

"Then be sick," one of the sentinels said indifferently.

Bile rose in her throat. She groaned and curled onto her side, sliding down on the floor of the sleigh. Which only agitated the nausea. She'd never had a strong constitution in carriages or buckboards. Give her a horse and she was fine. Pressed into the corner, she hugged herself, cold, wet, and shivering from the churning nausea. And then it was surging. Burning. Rushing up her throat.

Kaelyria lurched to the side and vomited over the edge. She sagged against the wood and spat. Her throat burned. Her eyes burned. Tears slipped down her face. She stayed there, expecting to throw up again. But her gaze slid to the mountain.

Where are you, Aselan? Would the others be killed? Would the Legiera return in time to save them? What if he was killed, too? Then . . . nobody would come for her.

Haegan.

She snorted, the sensation stinging. Haegan was lost to his own fears, she'd heard. So far from home and the path of Abiassa that even if he heard she was in danger, he probably wouldn't come.

The road flattened, affording the sleigh a smoother path. She closed her eyes, reaching for Abiassa. For some explanation of what was going on.

"Bring her!"

Kaelyria lifted her head, surprised to find an encampment spread around the sleigh. Tents, horses, fires—and many, many more Sirdarians. Where had they come from? How had nobody in the Nine seen this happening? Where were the Jujak, the Pathfinders? Were things so terrible in the kingdom that nobody remained to respond to such threats? She marveled that so great a number could gather unchallenged.

As the sleigh moved deeper in, she pulled herself onto the slatted seat. Before her in a tight circle around a larger, more forbidding tent stood several black-and-red tents of Poired's army.

Father . . . Grief struck anew as the guards ordered Kaelyria from the sleigh. They turned her toward that central canvas structure, which she now saw was marked with the upside-down eye of Sirdar. A chill swept her, and it was no longer because of the cold. Three men in black capes, including the black-helmed rider, stalked to the largest tent and ducked inside.

Guards ushered her across the open area. Fear washed through her as she neared the opening. A warm glow came from within, and only as the men pushed her inside did she see the flame.

The warmth was lovely. And terrible at the same time. Her gaze skimmed the interior, surprised at its luxury. At the pelts of great cats and icehounds. Cringing, she could not help but think of Duamauri and Sikir. She'd been separated from them when one of the walls collapsed, but she hoped the great beasts would find their way to safety.

The big tent had four openings into other, smaller spaces. Quarters, she guessed, save the middle, which held tables and chairs. At the far side, a shadow shifted, drawing her attention to the black-plumed rider who stood with his back to her at a credenza, removing his gloves.

A servant girl came forward, her face bruised and scarred—both healed and recent marks. She motioned Kaelyria closer. "Please," she whispered. "Don't make him angry."

Kaelyria frowned, a defiant streak coursing through her. She didn't care if she made the incipient angry. Whoever he was, he had attacked the Heart. He was responsible for the death of a child, for Carilla. And however many who died in the explosion that forced them from the ancient passages. Not to mention the Legiera—how many? For what? To capture her? Why?

The nasally incipient who'd addressed them on the mountain returned. He grabbed her arm and yanked her into the tent where the dark-plumed rider stood, unmoving.

"Go on, girl," the nasally one said, pointing to a chair. "Sit."

"I will not." Clenching her jaw, she steeled herself for punishment.

The rider tossed his winter cape on a wooden chair and moved to the fire pit, where he warmed his hands and glanced at her over his shoulder. Snorted.

"You may have to teach her a lesson, Master." The lesser seemed too eager.

Reaching up, the master lifted the helm from his head. With great ceremony, he set it on a pedestal. Ran his hand over the black feathers that glimmered like a dark halo.

"What do you want with me?" Kae asked through gritted teeth.

"What I have always wanted," he finally spoke and turned to face her. "You, broken."

Kaelyria gaped. Stumbled back. "Cilicien."

22

Farther from home, Tili and his contingent reached Dorcastle just before the high rise of the moons. They encamped on an open plain, where the approach of combatants could be easily spotted. As dawn cracked the night, Tili stood on the highest rise, assessing, thinking. Since departing Iteveria, they had gained followers long oppressed and now eagerly free. More stragglers from the north had swelled their numbers, which now sat near three hundred fighting men, let alone camp followers and refugees. Even now, two different groups approached. One from the northeast and one via the south, possibly from Luxlirien.

Peering through an eyeglass, Grinda studied the northeast group. "Jujak," he finally breathed with a smile. "I think that's Ghor."

Tili appraised him. "That sounds good."

With a sharp nod, Grinda grinned. "One of the best officers I've worked with, and a good friend." He returned the glass to his eye. "Not as sure about this other group. No weapons visible and clothing isn't such that they could easily hide them. They are weary."

"As are we all," Tili said, realizing the man beside him was one of the senior-most officers in their camp, though he was younger than the half-dozen arced behind them on the hillside. They had a recent shortage in the ranks. "Are ye prepared, Colonel?"

"*Major*, sir," Graem corrected, then nodded. "And aye—we stand ready."

Watching the incoming stragglers, noting the shorter, dark-haired man the others seemed to show deference to, Tili clasped his hands behind his back. "Think ye I became commander of the Nivari, the equivalent of the Pathfinders, by mistaking ranks?"

Though the young Grinda was no Aburas or Captain Etan, he was coming into his own and had held his own in the battle at the palace. The eagerness in his expression faltered. "I—No, sir."

Movement flickered among the blackened tree trunks that stood as burnt sentries, all that remained of the once-thriving area after Poired's scourge. Though Tili detected a form, he could not see who. He guessed one possibility—a certain female assassin, who'd been scarce since receiving news of her brother's death.

But he must redirect Grinda. "Would that war afforded us time to grieve, bury, and mourn the dead, but it does not. To my regret, Negaer and Rhaemos are gone. Both were exceptional leaders and irreplaceable, yet that is where we stand—needing those positions filled so we may continue the fight. It is given to the ruler of a land to promote on the battlefield as needed." Tili detected a subtle shift of the air nearby, and wondered if she'd left or merely advanced on them. "I believe ye are the senior-most officer, and what's more, yer competent in battle and well-liked among the men. As Steward of the Nine, I need ye in charge, Graem. Do I ask too much of ye?"

Grinda's spine pulled straight. "No, sir."

"Then, Colonel Grinda, I suggest ye get your men in order. I've promoted Tokar—"

"The boy? He's never been in an army. He has no official training. How can . . ." Grinda snapped him a look, though Tili kept his gaze forward, then inclined his head.

Tili had expected the objection. "We have two raqine," he went on as if he hadn't been questioned or interrupted. "If the prophecies are right—as they have been so far—more are coming. They will need a commander, or at least, someone to organize them. Since our young friend has been chosen by a raqine, untrained though he may be, he is the best we have for the job."

"Understood, sir."

"Now, do we have friend or foe here?"

"Coe and Laerian, with me," Grinda said as he stepped from the line of soldiers, hand on his hilt. "Who approaches?" he demanded as he joined the newcomers.

Tili waited patiently as the group talked, then Grinda alone returned.

"They have a hundred men and twice that in women and children."

Tili's gaze roamed the land beyond the remnants of the razed village. "Where are they holed up?"

"In caves in those hills," Grinda said, pointing. "They've been through much, and they ask permission to join our contingent."

The people no doubt needed provision and protection. "Granted." Tili turned, then hesitated. "Make sure they pass a Tahscan or two as they approach our camp. The last thing we need is an incipient among us."

• • •

"How is the prince?" Tokar asked.

Cradling a tin cup of lukewarm cordi as he mulled the state of the army and the two-hundred-plus mouths they must now also feed, Tili stared into the flames. "Still unconscious."

"Blazes, that doesn't help us if we find him what's got the bigger army coming at us," Laertes said.

"He wiped out hundreds of people with one shout," Colonel Grinda said, the words weighted with implication.

Laerian, a lanky soldier in his early thirties, nodded. "Decimated them without an effort. Just boom! And they're dust on my boots." He shook his head. "Scary that."

"It is as the prophecies foretold," Colonel Grinda said. "He's a scourge."

"He is yer future king," Tili reminded them, "and the Hand of Abiassa. As the colonel stated, he is able to destroy entire cities with a shout. 'Twould not question either, were I ye."

"How can you justify—"

"I justify nothing," Tili countered. "I recite facts only. We are sent to protect the Fierian, and that is what we will do."

"For how long?" Tokar asked. Then shrugged. "It's an honest question."

"We protect until we do as we agreed. To date, we have completed Gwogh's first mission—retrieve the prince. Now, we see Haegan to Vid," Tili said slowly, processing his own thoughts. In earnest, even he wasn't certain when it would end. When he would no longer shoulder the burden of steward. "Surely there will come a point when we know it is over. Then . . . She may release us."

A sharp whistle pierced the night.

Grinda shot to his feet and started running. "Enemy sighted."

Tili sprinted, overtaking the colonel shortly before the wagon perimeter blockade. "What is it?" he asked the sentries, who lay across the top of the wagon supports, scanning the surrounding area.

"Looks like a scouting party to the west," one said.

Another added, "And coming fast."

Tili glanced to Grinda, who handed him an eyeglass. He peered through it, but could not make out who rode at a breakneck pace.

"Refugees don't travel fast," Grinda offered.

"Unless they're being pursued."

For a moment, Grinda didn't respond. But then he shook his head. "Not enough thunder," he said, speaking of the telltale rumble of the earth beneath an army's approach.

Tili agreed.

"Silvers then," Tokar suggested, since Poired's elite branch traveled in small packs.

Silence smacked at the all-too-real possibility. "Think you they are fool enough to fall upon a camp the size of ours?" Grinda said, glancing at their surprisingly large cluster of tents.

"Arrogance is their hallmark." Tili locked in gazes with the colonel.

"Ready the men, Majors Laerian and Ghor!" Grinda shouted, eyes still on Tili. "Think you we have the accelerants to fend them off?"

Behind him, the camp buzzed in preparation and anxiousness. "We've picked up a few along the way—perhaps."

"Pathfinders, to your mounts!" Grinda commanded, then stormed to his horse.

Tili hustled toward his tent and removed his vest, dropping it at his feet. Quickly, he unbound it and made haste to don his leather armor.

"What is it?"

He startled to find that Astadia stood close. A dangerous gleam glinted in her eyes and made him hesitate. Her voice had been soft yet . . . excited. She'd made herself scarce for the last two days of journeying, and now that war breathed upon them, she appeared? Was it bloodlust in those wide eyes? "Riders fast approaching. Probably Silvers."

She grinned. Aye, bloodlust. She pivoted, her long, dark braid nearly smacking his face. In a sprint, she was quickly lost in the chaos as their contingent prepared for yet another fight.

Tili shook his head and slung the belt around his hips. He tucked the dagger into its sheath and shouldered into a boiled-leather vest as he stepped into the night. A commotion arose from the far end of the camp, where the wagon bearing the Fire King and Haegan rocked. Guards were there, reaching. Calling.

Laerian crossed his path.

"Major," Tili said. "We need a detail on the Fire King."

"He's half out of his mind—"

Angered, Tili flung a spark at him. "Ye will not speak of yer king as such. Remember who abused yer king. Hold fast to the man who stands for ye. Who bled, who fought. He is yer king. Forget it not!"

Laerian's jaw muscle twitched. "Aye . . . sir."

Weariness scratched at Tili. "Take Tokar and Praegur—they'll fight to the death for both the king and the prince. Nobody goes near the Celahars without my express permission."

Laerian gave a nod then trotted off to carry out the order.

"Hoa!" called the Pathfinder atop one of the wagons. "Sir—someone from our camp is going out to the enemy!"

Tili stilled, looking in that direction. "*What?* How close?"

"Half a league and closing." The man growled quietly. "Whoever that is, they're about to get themselves killed."

"Archers! Ready!" came the order from Grinda, who had lined up the Pathfinders.

Tili scrambled up to the sentry, took the monocle, and peered through it. He traced the striated land, searching the long shadows cast by the rising sun for whoever had broken rank. A traitor? A slight frame moved in synchronization with the horse that tore across the plain. Small build, hair bound in that whip-like braid. *"Hiel-touck."*

"Nock!" Grinda shouted down the line.

"What is it?" Laerian asked, returning from his errand.

"The assassin." Tili hopped off the wagon, his heart thudding hard at the thought of her getting speared by their own arrows, and hurried to the colonel.

"Draw!" Grinda continued.

"They'll kill her," Tili snarled. "Can ye . . ." There was naught to ask. He could not stop their defense for one assassin. One who may be a traitor. Why else would she run out to the enemy?

Yet . . . what if she was not? "Can ye protect her?" he asked Grinda.

The colonel glowered. "She's rogue!"

She's out there, alone. Tili swiped a hand over his face. Looked to the darkened field, where he could see naught but more of the same.

"I think . . ."

Tili glanced up at the sentry who'd spoken, this time with hesitation.

"This . . . I don't . . ."

"What?" Tili demanded, seizing hope.

"They keep vanishing," the sentry said.

Tili pivoted. Stared out across the open area. Only accelerants could make themselves invisible behind wakes that displaced light. "Incipients?"

"I think not," Vaqar said, his gravelly voice startling Tili. "There is none of their stench."

"Stand down! Stand down!" came the call from the top. "They're ours."

Tili looked west. "Ours?"

"Archers, hold!" Grinda ordered.

"They ride under the banner of the Fire King."

Tili's agitation hadn't waned. He stalked to the front of the line and strained into the distance. Who could—

But then he saw. The gray cloak and beard. Tili released the breath trapped in his throat. "'Tis Gwogh." He scowled. Gwogh rarely brought good news.

Ready for a confrontation, the Pathfinders stood tense and alert, their gazes sweeping not only the incoming party but the farther distance. They waited, painfully tense, as the group of six delivered Gwogh in a swirl of dust and irritation.

"Steward," boomed the throaty voice of the councilwoman who had pronounced him as steward in Hetaera and traveled with them a short while ago. "We are much relieved to see you alive."

"As we are ye, Councilwoman," Tili said, wondering if there was a penalty for lies when you were steward. "Welcome to Dorcastle, what is left of it. How came ye to find us here? As ye well know, this is not Vid."

"Chance, or Abiassa's hand. We have ridden far and wide in search of accelerants to add to your number." She considered the men gathered with Tili and settled on Graem. "Captain Grinda, I trust you are well."

"Councilwoman Kedulcya," Grinda greeted her with a curt nod.

"He is colonel, now," Tili amended.

"Is he?" She arched her eyebrow, silver-gray hair glinting the morning light. "Congratulations, Colonel. Where is General Negaer? I would have words with him."

"Fallen, Councilwoman—at the Battle at Karithia, along with Colonel Rhaemos."

Kedulcya jolted. "I . . . I am sorry, Graem. It must have been a sore blow after so recently losing your father."

The colonel's stiff façade faltered. "I thank you, ma'am." He nodded deeper this time. "My father died defending what he loved, as did General Negaer." He paused, glanced at Tili. "Be it known to you that we have recovered the Fire King?"

Surprise temporarily smoothed the woman's features. "I had not heard but guessed as much since you are traveling north," Kedulcya said with a smile. She slid from her mount and handed the reins to the young woman who had accompanied her before.

Tili cleared his throat. "Colonel Grinda, please escort the council-woman to the command tent."

As the young officer led her away, she put her hand on his arm in an almost maternal gesture. "Your father would be very proud of you, Graem."

"I believe he was, ma'am."

Their familiarity bespoke a relationship, a connection that awakened in Tili an awareness—nay, not awakened, but enlarged the awareness that he was an outsider. All of them belonged to the Nine. He did not.

"General Grinda and Kedulcya were long fierce allies." Gwogh's voice rumbled like rocks in a bowl. "I wondered for many years if they were not connected."

"Bloodlines?" Tili asked, surprised.

"Mm," Gwogh said. "So you got the Fierian *and* the Fire King." He clamped a hand on Tili's shoulder. "I had no doubt you were the right man for this," he said, as they walked after the others.

"You're a bleedin' blister," Tili muttered, shaking his head.

Gwogh's bushy brows rose into his wiry hair. "Blister?" he said, a laugh muddling his objection.

"Aye, ye show up when the work is done and annoy me with festering platitudes."

With a rueful smile, Gwogh patted his back. "I have heard through the rumblings how well you fare, Thurig as'Tili."

"Don't be usin' my surname to soften my anger, Gwogh."

"It was meant as a true and honest compliment of how you have defended—"

"I fought for a friend." Tili let out a heavy, anchoring breath. "'Tis all."

"It's more than enough. More than many would have done with the opposition you faced. The mantle of steward was not lightly placed on your shoulders, Tili."

"Aye, but 'twas *placed*." Why was he so annoyed? "Here I am, far from family, far from home. Fighting a bleedin' battle not my own." It mattered not. He must fight. He would fight. This was a war that went beyond borders. Still . . .

"Oh, I disagree. This battle belongs to every man, woman, and child on the planet."

Tili shifted to Gwogh. "The Fire King—"

"How is he?"

Heaving a sigh, Tili battled the weight that crowded between them. He nodded to the wagon where father and son rested. "Haven't seen anything like it. What is left of him is not enough to be called Zireli."

With a grave nod, Gwogh turned to a man who had ridden with him, and whose thinning, scraggly hair and face were carved in years. "Then it is good that I routed Pao'chk from the caves or Andouir."

"Good to see ye again," Tili greeted, recalling the healer had last tended Haegan when Thiel had delivered the unconscious prince to Nivar. It seemed so long ago.

Pao'chk gave a nod. "Also, we have the Drigo," he muttered, lifting his hand to something approaching across the plain.

Tili shifted a look over his shoulder and saw shapes emerge from a deep arroyo that cut through the land. To the unsuspecting, they would seem simply as very tall men. But Tili knew better. "Unauri!"

"Aye," Gwogh said, as one of the Drigo's great strides brought him near with astonishing speed. "Thankfully, they are not in their vudd state, which would draw attention and alarm. The band of seven caught up with us as we crossed through Luxlirien. This is Arnoff, a magnificent healer."

Black eyebrows that were more like forests bulged over Arnoff's thick brow. "Feel him," the giant mourned, his eyes sliding closed then open again.

"Come," Tili said, unsure what else to say to the giant and pharmakeia, or to Gwogh.

"Tell me of the battle at Karithia."

"'Twas bloody, frightening, and fierce." Tili stalked across the camp to the wagon and pointed to where two Pathfinders stood at attention. Their gazes shifted anxiously as the giant thudded closer. "The prince and king are there."

"Ye have no shelter other than the back of the wagon?" Pao'chk clucked his tongue.

"We found moving them to tents disturbed the Fire King's fragile equilibrium. It seemed best to change as little as possible as we journey."

"They need proper shelter," the old man insisted.

"I beg yer mercy," Tili snapped, growling at the absurdity of the comment. "Would ye like us to hew stone and build a fortress here? Think ye the Dark One and his incipients will sit idly by while we put the Celahars up in luxury?"

Gwogh's face tightened. "It was not meant as a slight. Traveling, the shifting of the wagon, and the constant motion could slow their healing."

"Had we a castle and peacetime to settle them, 'twould be done. But we have Sirdarians and Silvers tracking or attacking every other day, and that was before Karithia, not to mention the incipients inflaming, working our thoughts against us, the refugees needing food and provisions. Had not the Tahscans arrived—"

"Tahscans?" Gwogh scowled.

Tili slowed at the reaction. "Aye. And a good thing that."

Gwogh searched the camp with gray, probing eyes. "How many?"

"Nay," Tili said.

Gwogh's gaze flicked to his. "What do you mean nay?"

"What do ye mean how many?"

"I must know their number. Tahscans have never been allies of the Nine."

"Aye, and I fear 'tis still true, though these ride with us," Tili said with a sigh. "But we have a common enemy to defeat—Poired. Everyone is an ally when we have a common enemy."

"Trust them not," Gwogh said as he caught the iron handle and hauled himself into the wagon. "They have but one oath—to Tahsca and their steel."

"And we have our loyalties, but as ye said—I am the right man for this, and I chose to make allies rather than another war."

• • •

Storms tore through his mind. Fires leapt and danced to a virulent, poisonous song in his veins. Etching words and prophecies into his flesh. Haegan pushed away from the darkness. Reached toward the light. A sliver. A crack. He forced himself at it.

A shape loomed over him. Blurred, then came into focus. Eyes widened, then relaxed as the man smiled. "Good to have ye back, Fierian."

Memories, lopsided and faint, swirled the man's aged face. "I know you," Haegan rasped.

"That ye should," the old man said, lifting a cup of a warmed liquid, scented with tingling spices. "I tended ye after the Great Falls."

"At Nivar." Haegan sipped the concoction and felt a dart of energy at the same time a weird haze rushed his mind. He groaned and nudged it aside.

"Good, good," the healer said. "That tells me yer abilities are in full balance." He shifted to a table, mixed a few more bottles, then held out a new cup. "Yer weakness is temporary. Sip slowly, and yer strength will return."

"What's wrong with me?"

"Wrong?" the healer scoffed. "Absolutely nothing. But ye are a human harnessing the power of Abiassa and—well, that takes a toll on the body. Ye'll be back to full power in no time."

Alarm struck. "Full power?"

The healer nodded, then swiveled on a stool. He bent toward the other cot, lifting a wool blanket up to a bearded chin.

Haegan knew that face, too. "Father."

"Sadly, the Fire King is a very different story."

"What's wrong with him? Can you heal him?"

"What ails Zireli is deep in the abiatasso. For that," Pao'chk said, lowering his head, "I can but treat symptoms."

The wagon canted left. Then right.

Haegan braced, surprised to find a Drigo lumbering into the cramped space, oblivious to the tight quarters. Where would he sit or stand? He held a stone pestle and mortar as he went to a knee, the boards creaking and groaning violently beneath his weight. Then he lifted the mortar and a greenish-black concoction to the king's pale lips.

"What is he doing?"

"What only a Drigo healer can." Pao'chk shrugged. "I have studied for the last forty cycles, but I will never have an advantage over a Drigo youth who can heal."

Haegan liked the sound of that. He swung his legs over the edge of the cot. "Earlier, you said you can't treat what is wrong with my father—but I, too, was under her inflaming. Why am I healing and he's not?"

Grief scratched at the pharmakeia's bearded face. "Yer father . . . I fear he has too long been under her influence, her dark wielding."

"But the Drigo," Haegan said, clinging to a crackling hope that sparked in his chest, "can he heal him?"

"That is for Abiassa to answer. But"—Pao'chk shrugged again—"it would take a miracle."

"Then make a miracle!" Haegan hadn't meant to snap, and he felt marginally guilty as the Drigo's cautious gaze drifted to him.

When he pushed off the cot, Haegan marveled at the strength that filled his legs. He stood, relieved when a soft breeze drifted across his cheeks. He savored it as he stepped free of the wagon. With each step, he felt stronger, more focused. There was a thrumming in his veins he hadn't noticed before, one that buzzed and hummed, demanding attention.

But to what?

"Where be ya' going, Haegan?"

He stopped short, glancing down at the shaggy blond lad. "Laertes!" He pivoted, taking in the camp. "Where is Thiel?"

The boy's face twisted in pain. "I . . . I don' right know. We was with him whats got the muscles and blood-died cords."

Haegan started. "Cadeif? Why? And why are you here and she is not?"

"Aye. Sir Gwogh sent us there when you up and vanished. Then that raqine what helped you kill the Infantessa done brought me here."

"But Thiel! Why did you leave her?"

The boy's eyes grew large and wet with tears. "She fell. Fell from the beast." His hands fisted. "That blazin' raqine wouldn't go back neither. I tried to make her, I promise I did. What if she's dead?"

Haegan lifted his head. Looked to the west. To the skies. Anything but this blasted camp or the boy who had seen Thiel fall. "No, she's alive. She has to be." *Please* . . .

Only then did he see the way the camp watched him. Sidelong glances that held animosity. Fear.

They're afraid of me.

He caught sight of a barrel-chested man. A vague memory of him at Iteveria skidded through Haegan's mind, eluding him. He'd talked to him. Taken something—a sword. Yes. The sword. The man was too dark-skinned even for a Kergulian. Who was he?

When their gazes locked, the man slowly rose. Was the man angry? Something was . . . off. Haegan's mind buzzed.

The man came toward him, reaching behind himself.

Steel glinted.

Alarmed, Haegan palmed a halo with a warning shout, "Stop!" Focusing the Flames was infinitely easier and less taxing since he'd thrown open his arms to Abiassa's Fire in the dungeon. It surprised him, startled him. Pleased him.

"I beg your mercy, Fierian," the man said in a deep bass, "I but pull my sword—"

"No!"

He extended his hands—one of which held a long blade. "My sword is not against you, but *for* you." He laid it on the ground. Knelt. Lowered his head.

"He's telling the truth," came a soft voice.

Haegan glanced to the side. A girl with dark brown hair that dangled in a braid stood watching him. "Astadia."

A wry smile tugged at her lips. "Well, I see blowing up all of Karithia didn't fry *everything*—your brain is still intact." She lifted a shoulder. "What little of it you have." She nodded to the now-kneeling man. "That Tahscan is Vaqar Modia, one-time commander of the royal guard. Fierce but loyal. Saved my life more than once in Karithia's battle, and that's saying something."

Indeed.

"Fierian." Vaqar lowered his shorn head as he raised his sword. "My blade is yours."

Unsure what to say, Haegan nodded, only realizing then that the man wasn't looking. "Thank you. R-rise. Stand." He sidestepped, anxious to be away, alone. But as he did, a presence lingered behind him. A glance back confirmed his suspicions that Astadia was pacing him. "I thought you were done with me since your brother died."

"If you are only going to mock his death—"

Haegan stopped. "I mock nothing. Trale gave his life for me. *Never* will I forget nor take lightly that sacrifice." His heart pounded a death cadence. "In the end, he was the only friend I had."

Astadia gave a cockeyed nod. "Which is why I'm following you."

A Tahscan bowing to him, an assassin following him. Could things become more twisted? Haegan resumed course, but slowed as he searched the forest of small tents cluttering the field.

"Do you know where you're going?"

He sighed and shook his head, feeling the ache of loneliness and confusion. "I'm not sure I've known in a very long time."

Understanding flickered through her face as she indicated to a large black tent. "Command is there." She drew closer. "They are all gathered with the steward."

Haegan frowned, then looked at the assassin. "Steward? Steward of what?"

"The Nine."

Haegan faltered. They'd installed a steward. *Because I failed. Walked away.*

"You should talk to them."

Perhaps he should. Yet his feet seemed rooted, refusing another step. The thought of a steward being put in place angered him—not at the steward. At himself. Too long he'd been a prisoner. Too long feasted on his doubts and fears.

He started forward, then glanced back. "I could do with a friend."

Her eyes widened, but she fell in step with him. "I'm not sure you'd call me a friend, if you knew the truth."

"You wanted to kill me rather than bring me back to the Infantessa."

Astadia's breathing shifted, but she maintained pace. "You knew?"

"You kept it no secret."

She skidded him a glance as they covered the last dozen steps to the command tent. "I suppose I didn't."

"Then it follows that I owe Trale my life doubly, since he didn't let you end me."

"I'm not sure I'd go that far. She addled his brain with inflaming, made him her lapdog. Trale was smitten with the witch." Astadia's tone dropped to a growl. "If you hadn't killed her, I would have."

"Then we are of the same mind and freed of a problem." Haegan entered the command tent.

A table sat to the side, accommodating nearly a dozen men in heated conversation. They hadn't noticed him, and for that, Haegan was grateful. It afforded him time to gain his bearings, work out what they were discussing. They mentioned locations—the hall of iron, Vid, Unelithia—and urgency, time was short.

At the far end sat Tili—Thiel's brother—and Sir Gwogh. Near him was Kaelyria's boyfriend, Captain Grinda—nay, the cords indicated a rank of colonel. As Haegan's gaze continued its trek, he met familiar eyes. The sight of his friend allowed Haegan to breathe a laugh, feeling warmth and pleasure as he had not in a long while.

Praegur rose and the conversation din faded.

Next, Tili stood. "Haegan."

Wind rustled as others punched to their feet. Most bowed curtly. "Sire."

The recognition and respect they offered froze Haegan for a moment. When the silence hung heavy and cumbersome, he forced himself to speak. "The Fire King yet lives, so I am no sire. But I thank you for the deference." His considered the seat at the end of the table.

Praegur was already there, drawing out the chair. "My lord," he said, his voice rusty and catching.

Haegan smiled as he reached him. "'Tis good to see you." Seated, he looked to the others, still standing. Though he was no king or ruler, he realized he was the only able-bodied sovereign they had right now. Or was he? He motioned to the seats, and the men quickly resumed their positions. "I was told there is a steward." He settled his gaze on Gwogh. "You have set a steward in my place?"

His old tutor inclined his head. "A steward was chosen by the Council when we thought the king dead and the prince missing."

Interesting choice of words and lack of hesitation. "You mean, when I fled." Haegan swallowed, his gaze skipping around the table again. Who had they named in his stead? Was it Grinda? His youthful vigor and charm so easily swept Kaelyria from her good senses, so why not the Council? Was it Rhaemos? Or Negaer? Though neither was present at this meeting.

But as Haegan considered the possibilities, he grew convinced of the most unlikely suspect. The one person not of Nine blood. "Tili."

"Princeling," Tili said, acknowledging him with a slight smile. "Good to see ye on yer feet. We are all grateful for yer . . . work in dispatching the Infantessa."

The Infantessa. Yes. It seemed an eternity, and yet, he could still feel her talons raking his mind. Had Tili mentioned it to remind Haegan of his failure? To remind him he had walked from the Fire Throne straight into the hands of their powerful enemy?

"I have failed," Haegan admitted openly, his pride skewered on the table before them. "I chose a path that seemed right and best, but it was far from what Abiassa willed."

Quiet dripped like an annoying tap.

"I would beg your mercy. When I left the Citadel and journeyed east, I failed each of you." It no longer mattered—him, his pride, his insipid selfishness. "I failed Abiassa. I walked from the halls of safety and surety to a false sense of peace, sinking right into disaster."

The men shifted. Some looked down, away. Others held fast.

"I have seen my mistake and regret my actions." Haegan's throat grew raw. "We face a powerful enemy who knows how to enter our minds, how to ply our fears and weaknesses against us."

"But you killed her," someone countered.

"I killed Sirdar's pawn," he conceded. "The Infantessa was nothing more than a spoiled child playing in her father's water garden." He looked to Graem. "I heard you speak of the hall of iron."

"Aye, Ironhall is abandoned."

"Yet you mention it as a way station."

"Though in ruins, it *is* a fortress," Graem said. "Much to work with, unlike an open plain that leaves us exposed."

Gwogh cleared his throat. "But we have reinforcements in Vid, and it has been re—"

"No." Something stirred in Haegan. "Poired must march east, intersect with Ironhall, if I remember my Histories and its placement. Correct?" he asked the young colonel.

"Aye," Graem said warily, eyeing Gwogh and Tili. "But 'tis in ruins."

"We are all in ruins, Graem." As the idea took hold, Haegan grew convinced of its legitimacy. Of the opportunity to quicken his confrontation with the Dark One. He had a thirst, a hunger to deal with the darkness that had pervaded the lands for too long. "We make for Ironhall."

23

"You must stop him!"

Stuffing on his gauntlets, Tili glanced over his shoulder at the girl. "Why would I do that?"

Astadia pointed at the tent flap as if Haegan were standing on the other side. "He is bent on going after Poired. Nobody does that! It's a fool's errand—worse, it's idiotic."

Tili huffed and turned. "He is the Fierian. His purpose is Sirdar and Poired. He's seeing the end goal."

Wisps of brown hair flung her face as she moved forward, eyes brightened by an angry flush. "He is seeing *his* end. Period. He will die if he faces that monster!"

"Then he will die."

Jaw jutted, she spun around, defiant. "How can you stand by while the only man worth his salt is walking straight to his death?"

"Because the only man worth his salt is the one who might *not* die walking to his death."

"You're singewood, Tili Thurig."

A flare of amusement at her use of his names, though backward, glided over his annoyance, smoothing it. "'Tis Thurig as'Tili," he corrected. "And Haegan is powerful. Did ye not see him in the courtyard? He was designed for this war by the Lady."

She slapped his shoulder. "Bah!"

Disbelieving she'd struck him, he scowled. "Did ye—"

"I did," the little nymph said with another jut of her jaw, "and I'll do more if you don't grow a brain in that thick skull of yours. Haegan needs help. He's been through"—she shook her head—"I cannot describe what happened to him while in her grip, but I saw it. Gave witness to the cruelty he and my brother—weak-kneed males that they were—endured at her hand."

Curiosity got the better of him. "And what did ye see there?"

She stomped forward, eyes blazing. "They were changed. Tortured. You do not come away from that untouched. And now? Now he wants to face Poired!"

"Haegan is not weak-kneed. He is intelligent and—"

"He was a slobbering fool when he thought the Infantessa a young pretty thing. All men are!" she exclaimed. "We must be strong for him."

"But ye just said all men were weak."

"Because I know what Inflaming does and am not affected by it."

Curious. "And how is it ye are not infected by the inflaming?"

Astadia drew back an inch, but it felt like a mile. And another slap. "You accuse me?"

"I question ye, Astadia Kath."

"Kath." She snorted.

"'Tis not yer name?"

"I know not my name." Vulnerability skated through her knotted brow so quickly, it might have been a ruse. "I was an orphan, as was Trale, when we both took the name."

"Then he wasn't yer brother?"

"He was my brother—everything to me," she snarled, her eyes flaming and nostrils flaring. "Think not for one second I wouldn't gut you if I thought—"

"Gut me?" Tili's pride was tweaked. "Ye think ye can take me?"

Ire glinted in her large green eyes as she lifted that dimpled chin. "Before you knew what happened."

His eyebrow arched. He smirked. Then stepped back into a sparring stance.

Astadia started, glancing at the foot he'd planted for more control. "You think that foot makes you stronger."

"Aye." Talk was cheap and distracting. "Are ye all talk, Astadia? The men fear ye. Show me yer best." He raised his eyebrow again and motioned with his hands. "When yer ready."

"I kill men like you for a living."

"Well," he said with a grin that was far too cheeky, but her arrogance stamped his propriety into the ground, "show me. But I have an army to lead, so please—keep at least my foot on this side of the grave."

She eased back, defiance sparking. "By how much?"

Tili fought the laugh crawling through his chest. "I have to protect the prince and represent the Nine." He scratched his cheek. "Leave enough for that."

"Only that?" Astadia walked to the side basin and poured a glass of water. She sipped slowly, then poured another. "You know . . ." she began.

Tili detected the fabric of her trousers shift—she'd tightened her leg muscles.

"My brother and I had a routine," she said quietly, her voice almost grieved. "I distract the target—they'd see only a woman. With curves." She threw a sultry look over her shoulder.

Tili chuckled. "To see a woman, ye'd have to be one." This wasn't just a conversation. She was a vixen, a wench bent on winning, but he was ready. His hands twitched in anticipation. "I'm sorry ye lost yer brother."

Her gaze grew icy. She lifted the cup to her mouth.

Any reasonable person would think she was drinking, but she never swallowed, at least—not one big enough for imbibing.

She pivoted around, her heel snapping toward his head. He barked a laugh and ducked, surprised and impressed at the same time, but also expecting a punch or another kick.

Which came. She hopped, her other leg whipping up then slicing down in a chop. Narrowly missing his head and shoulder.

When she drove a fist at him, he deflected, shoving her off balance.

Astadia recovered and spun to face him, hands up and loosely held. Ready but not tense. She had confidence that she didn't need to attack violently. Quick, short strikes were more efficient, more deadly. And considering she knew that, Tili had better up his game or she'd knock him on his back. Though he might have started this sparring with amusement, he was dead serious now.

"What?" she taunted. "Too weak to attack?"

Try to draw him out, force him to attack. Tili bounced to the side, watching. "Show me."

Challenge lit her olive complexion.

Before Tili could process what happened, a flurry of hand strikes flew. He blocked and thwarted the first dozen, but she came on, relentless and furious. Her hands struck and punched and stabbed. It took every bit of training and experience to stop her from knocking the sparks out of him.

But as he palmed away one strike, she stabbed at his abdomen with her left. He also blocked that. But was too slow to see the round kick that nailed his temple.

Teeth clattered. Tili staggered, his vision blurring. Hands up, never backing from the fight. And she wasn't going to allow him. Two more kicks—deflected.

He responded with strikes of his own, which she deftly avoided and kept coming. Leaping aside, he tipped over a small table. It crashed, sending silver clattering across the ground. Tili backed up, not caring about the upended table or its contents. He wasn't going to lose. Or get his brains knocked out.

He punched, nailing her on the cheek.

She stumbled back, eyes wide—with surprise or fury, he wasn't sure. But when she lunged at him, he guessed the latter.

Anger. She was fighting out of anger now. Rabid. Uncontrolled. Dangerous. A line had been crossed somewhere. She wasn't playing to win now. She was playing to kill.

"Astadia," he said, parrying her strikes. Forcing himself not to punch again. Not to react. *Breathe. Breathe*, he told himself. *Easy.*

But she never slowed. Her kicks. Her punches. Her strikes. Faster. More furious. Fire in her eyes. Lips pulled into a thin, tight line.

"Astadia," he repeated more firmly.

Her fist struck his cheekbone. Pain shot through his skull. Head snapped back, but he cared not. He couldn't. Not with the way she was fighting. She was taking him to task. Venting, Punishing.

She growled, punching and kicking again. A jab. Right cross. Uppercut.

Enough. Tili monitored, caught her rhythm. Then her hand. Twisted it, down. Around and up. Pitched her around.

She dropped and broke his hold. Shot back up with a right cross. Tili deflected and shoved her backward. Pushed in. Pinned her against the post of the tent. "Astadia!" he hissed, desperate for her to regain her bearings.

"Augh!" She struggled with him.

"Astadia. Stop!" he barked, securing both hands and holding her in place. But she bucked. "Hey—*hey!* Look at me."

Green eyes blinked. Confusion mottled with sweat covered her brow. She peered at up him, her chest heaving. Each rise and fall pushed against him. Tili told himself not to think about it. Not to notice her body pressed to his. To focus instead on the eruption of anger and instinct that could have done serious injury or killed him.

But her curves were surprising against his chest. Her eyes liquid and searching. Strands of hair clung to her sweaty temples, giving her a wild, vicious look bathed in a beauty he had not seen in . . . ever.

She gulped a breath, her eyes widening ever so slightly. Her breathing slowed. The rigidity in her muscles softened. Everything softened. *She* was suddenly soft.

Soft. Beautiful. Fiery. A slip of a girl. Lips blushed with color that also filled her cheeks. He saw it, saw her reaction to being with him. Saw the same desire that made him ache squirm in her.

Tili uncoiled his fingers, one by one, from her hand . . . then gently brushed the hair from her face.

She responded, drawing up a little, her lips parting as she pulled in a quick breath. Her cheeks were bright from sparring, but more than exercise colored them now.

Something awakened in him at the realization he'd put that color there. He'd tripped up her icy assassin protective covering. Emboldened by that thought, he slipped a hand around her waist and drew her closer. Watching. Monitoring her every reaction.

It felt like approaching a viper. He half expected to get struck.

Her throat processed a nervous swallow. When she wet her lips, his gaze snagged on their fullness. He homed in on her mouth . . . But even as he did, even as she stood there frozen, he remembered. Remembered the men trying to rape her.

This time, Tili swallowed. She deserved better. And he wasn't going to take advantage of her. Blazes, he didn't even know her. But he wanted to.

"Steward?"

Startled by the intruding voice, Tili straightened. "Enter." He looked to the tent flap. Felt her pull away, and instantly sensed a cold distance grow between them.

Laerian ducked in, a furtive glance darting to Astadia as she silently hurried out. His attention moved to the overturned table. He met Tili's gaze with a smirk.

"Ye have need of me, Major?" Annoyance climbed Tili's veins, suddenly remembering when she'd punched him. The knot growing on his cheek probably gave the wrong impression, that he'd tried to make a play and she'd socked him. It was good—a bit of shame to remind him to take the higher road.

"The Fierian has ordered we break camp." He looked to the table again, then added the taunt, "If you have time."

• • •

Haegan stalked down the line toward Tili, one thought on his mind. One ache in his heart. He found him packing his horse. "Where is she?"

Tili frowned, skating a glance around the camp. "Where is who?"

"Thiel."

Tili almost seemed relieved, but then a cloud settled over his face. "I know not. Gwogh"—he nodded to the gray-bearded accelerant at the front of the column—"sent her . . . west."

The man who never hesitated was now hesitating. Which meant he was also withholding information. "What are you keeping from me?"

Tili's jaw tightened.

Haegan stepped in closer, surprised to find himself looking the Northlander in the eye. "What are you withholding about Thiel?"

Reticence held the Ybiennese prince. "She went west to seek help from the Ematahri." He now peered over Haegan's shoulder, forcing him to follow his gaze to where three raqine napped in the sunlight.

"Laertes said she fell from Chima."

"Aye," Tili conceded.

"Is she dead?" Haegan's voice pitched. "Tell me!"

"Gather yerself," Tili warned, shouldering in. "Ye are the Fierian and prince. Conduct yerself as such when people depend on ye for direction and leadership."

Haegan drew up, stealing glances at those who watched but didn't.

Tili tugged hard on a strap, then slid around his horse to test the other side.

"What do we do?" Haegan asked in a quiet, even voice. Authoritative enough to convey that he would not let this rest.

"We ride to Ironhall, as ye ordered."

"I should take Chima, search for her."

"Nay!" Tili growled. "Ye stay where ye are directed by Abiassa."

He should know that. But the panic over Thiel strangled his thoughts. Having so nearly died himself, he could not bear the thought . . . "If she's in hurt or in danger or d—"

"We are all in danger, Twig. And Kiethiel can handle herself."

"How can you be so calloused? She's your sister! What if she's broken and lying somewhere—"

"She made a choice to accept the mission Gwogh set before her." Tili moved with precision and intensity. "I trust her to the Lady, and ye should, too. Besides—forget ye that raqine are willed by Abiassa, not by whims of man?"

Haegan worried that Thiel had been with Chima in Ematahri territory and had plummeted from the raqine. If she survived the fall and was still with that muscled clan chief . . . "Chima wouldn't have left her—"

"Aye," Tili said. "She would. Chima is bonded to *ye*. She will abandon everyone and everything, even her own health and safety, to meet yer needs. Think not that she cares about anyone else. She is a raqine. They answer to Abiassa first, and second, their bonded."

"What about their mates?"

"She's like any other female—she tolerates her mate." Tili huffed then sighed. "Though I have no evidence, I do not believe Kiethiel is dead. Does her absence worry me? Aye. And if she is unharmed—if a miracle exists that protected her, then one thing I know: she'd give her right arm to be at yer side, not that it sits well with me." The words even bolstered him. "When she can be here, she will. Nothing will stop her."

Haegan frowned. "How can you be sure?"

"If ye don't know the answer, I won't tell ye."

Tokar joined them and the conversation. "And do you really want Thiel here when we are walking farther into the Desecrator's maw?"

Haegan considered him, surprised at how the friend he'd journeyed to the Falls with had somehow become a man. Behind Tokar, the Tahscans gathered with their leader, who gave instructions as they prepared for the march north. Haegan couldn't see their faces due to the cloths over their noses and mouths. They were all brawny and intent on the task at hand. Each time one bent to retrieve gear from the ground, the sun glinted off nearly bald heads. Why had they shorn their hair to the scalp?

His hand went to his own wavy, rumpled hair that had not been tended in . . . he knew not how long. He'd always worn his long because it was expected. It was a sign of his nobility. He was a Celahar, a royal, even locked in that tower.

Now who am I?

Something rattled deep within him, trembling until it violently seized him. He wasn't the petulant prince as Tili and the others had for so long accused him of being. He also wasn't the crippled teen who'd had his every whim catered to—save the attention of a father who saw only his own failure when he looked upon his son. He wasn't the coddled boy whose mother had conspired against him with an accelerant, unwittingly creating a torturous effect for Haegan.

No, he wasn't those people anymore.

He was . . . His gaze dropped to his hands, thoughts catapulting back to the courtyard of Karithia. To the moment he'd cut the breath from Nydelia's throat. And yet, he felt so disembodied. Separated from all he had known. All he wanted.

Dark eyes bored into his mind, and Haegan latched on, sensing both strength and belief. Focus and determination. He blinked, realizing the Tahscan had closed the distance between them. Why was he so close? What did he want? Haegan took a step back.

"How is your father, Prince?"

The question jolted him. Haegan turned his gaze to the healing wagon. "I . . . know not. The Drigo," he said, his breath and thoughts staggering, "is tending him."

The man nodded.

Haegan squinted. "What was your name again?"

"Vaqar."

A nod was all he could manage. Then, he frowned. "Why are you with the Pathfinders?"

Something in the man's gaze told Haegan he'd already explained, but the expression also said more. "We may not be allies, but we have a common enemy. Because you dealt with the Infantessa, I have committed my blade to you."

"Why?"

The man's cheek twitched. "She cost me much. Every person sent to intercede for Tahsca fell victim to her inflaming."

Shame squirreled through Haegan. But this wasn't about him. "Including you."

Vaqar inclined his head slightly. "For a time."

"There is no shame," Haegan said, though the lie sat as acid on his tongue, "in falling prey to her dark magic. What is important is that we continue to fight."

"Aye." Vaqar leaned his head forward. The sun shone on the sweaty scalp beneath a haze of black.

"I would ask a favor of you, Tahscan."

24

Flames grant him mercy, he would die in this Abiassa-forsaken land before he completed his task. And with Haegan returned and determined to make for Ironhall, not Vid, Tili was not sure what task remained for him, except the protection of the thinblood.

"Your thoughts are weighted," came the voice of Colonel Grinda as they led the column around an abandoned village.

Some structures stood defiant in the wake of Poired's attack, but most—like the people of the Nine—had crumbled. Lay broken, changed, if not shattered.

"There is much weighting them," Tili replied, his gaze on the horses lumbering through the hot, dry terrain.

"Have you see him?"

Tili frowned. "Who?"

"The prince—Haegan."

"I think we all saw him, Colonel."

"No, I mean . . ."

Tili shifted his full attention to Grinda now, surprised that he was at a loss for words. Then he followed the colonel's gaze to a cluster of riders. The Tahscans. They moved through this trial and land as if it hadn't fazed them.

"I don't understand."

"Aye, neither do I."

"No—" But then it struck Tili. The Tahscans numbered one too many. They were not simply riding in a band, they were following. Trailing one man. He'd missed it because all their heads were shaved. Including that of Haegan, who rode with Vaqar. Head now shaved.

Tili startled at the stark contrast. "Blazes." How had he missed Haegan shearing off his hair? What was the message in doing so? Among the Southlanders, it was a sign of nobility to wear the hair long. Was he shedding that persona? Rejecting one more piece of his identity?

"Steward," came a voice from the side—Gwogh, who rode a black horse alongside Kedulcya. "We ride to Vid and will bring the accelerants we have gathered."

"I am not sure I can afford an escort for ye."

"We would not ask it," Gwogh said. "The fewer our number, the less likely we'll attract attention."

Tili nodded, his gaze again drifting to Haegan. This was not the boy who'd stolen a kiss from Thiel, thinking none save the stars had been witness that night. Nor the boy who fled the gathering room when his destiny had been revealed.

Nay, this was a man. Not *just* a man. The Fierian. His back had broadened, shoulders filled out.

"He will need you, Steward," Gwogh said. "Stay with him, stay true to him."

The Fierian, the one who had blasted an entire city with a deadly wave of heat, would need Tili? He nearly scoffed out loud. But even he knew—felt—that the aged accelerant spoke true. "Fear not," he forced himself to say, "I will remain until he is safely upon the throne."

Grim faced, Gwogh heaved a sigh. "I fear that may not be the goal."

"'Tis my goal and all I promise." Tili swung his gaze again to the prince, who had turned to them. Strange, the Hand of Abiassa looked more a man than ever before, and yet . . . there was a glimmer of trepidation radiating through his face that was every bit the petulant twig who'd fled the great library at Nivar.

Gwogh rode away with Councilwoman Kedulcya, and Tili shook his head. Never had he seen a more splintered faction. One going here, another heading there. Different purposes. Different intents. And the remnant somehow finding him, joining so that now they numbered in the hundreds. *And this is how we defeat the most powerful accelerant known to man?*

"Where are they going?"

Tili slid his gaze to Haegan, who'd negotiated the column to gain his side. "They have an errand in Vid. They will join us at Ironhall in due course."

Haegan nodded but made no move to return to the Tahscans.

It was hard to miss his pinked scalp. "Lice? Chiggers?"

Haegan glared.

"No?" Tili shrugged. "Tried to cut yer own hair?"

Haegan's jaw muscle flexed, giving Tili entirely too much pleasure.

"Slept too close to the fire, then."

"I needed a change."

"A change," Tili said with a nod. "So blowing up a city and killing a queen wasn't enough change for ye." He grunted. "Change—in that ye have succeeded."

Haegan urged his horse away.

"You do remember," came Laerian's quiet, speculative tone, "that he's the one who singed hundreds of people to dust, don't you?"

"Someone needs to remind him he's human."

"Then let it be you, Northlander." He gave another snicker. "Me? I like my body parts in one piece, not a pile of ash."

"Hae—"

A whistle went up, one Tili recognized with the Pathfinders. His hackles rose. Beside him, Major Laerian had already swung around and jabbed his heels into his horse's flanks, aiming hard for the western scouts.

"What happened?" Haegan asked, having regrouped with Tili.

"Warning whistle. A scout spotted something," Tili said, watching as a lone figure grew smaller in the distance.

Grinda pushed up in the stirrups and gave his own whistle, ordering the remaining Pathfinders to form up.

"Go to the wagon," Tili said to Haegan.

"Nay," Haegan said. "I'll stay—"

"If they spotted incipients—"

"Then I will sense them and they me." Haegan squinted. "Hiding in a wagon with my unconscious father will not aid anyone in victory." He held up his hand and pure blue flames trickled along his fingers and knuckles. "She gave me a gift. I will use it."

Tokar came alongside Tili. "He's bringing someone."

They looked toward the plain, where Laerian was escorting a man toward the column. Something in Tili writhed as he realized who it was.

"Drracien," Haegan breathed around a laugh, then dropped from his mount and pushed through the Pathfinders. "Let me pass!"

This wasn't right.

"What's he doing north of Dorcastle?" Tokar asked, mirroring the questions tumbling around Tili's mind. "Last I knew, he was in Hetaera."

Tili frowned. "Hetaera? Ye're sure?"

"Aye, saw him climbing the walls. He visited Haegan." Tokar scratched his face. "Guess if we could get out before the city fell, he could as well."

Tili's eyebrow hitched. "Alone?"

"Traitor!" came a shout—from the Tahscans.

"Bleed him," another Tahscan growled. "He reeks of their stench."

"That's not good," Tokar whispered.

Tili urged his horse through the circle toward the front where Grinda, Laerian, Drracien, and Haegan stood. Confusion ran through the prince's sweaty face.

"Cut him down where he stands," Vaqar said. "He breathes the Void."

"Breathes the Void?" Haegan scoffed, but the laugh seemed forced. "You don't know of what you speak. Drracien is my friend. One of the truest."

Snatching the cloth from his face, Vaqar sneered. "I care not what he was. He is now what he is—and that stench is borne of the Dark One."

A strange flicker flashed through Drracien's eyes and then vanished. Lightning fast. "I've been accused of worse," came his familiar, arrogant taunt.

Vaqar drew his sword.

Haegan leapt in front of Drracien. "No!" He thrust out a hand, and that pale blue wave wafted to life.

With gasps and shouts, the crowd leapt back.

"Haegan," Tili warned, frowning, then turned his attention to the dark-haired accelerant. "From where have ye come?"

Drracien snorted. "West." Looked over his shoulder. "Thought you would've seen me coming."

Tili checked the boy's boots. Trousers. Dust. But enough?

"Leave off," Haegan said. "Drracien is here, safe. That is all that matters."

"It is strange, sire," Grinda said.

"No," Haegan growled. "It's not. He is my friend. Just like Tokar, Praegur, and Laertes. Drracien got me to the Falls. He protected me. Watched over me in Hetaera."

"Or did he lead the assassins to your door?" Tokar suggested.

"Why would I do that?" Drracien scowled. "He's my friend!"

"My brother and I needed no help from a slick snot like him," Astadia countered.

Tili shifted, unnerved he hadn't detected her coming up beside him. And that Drracien was taking this all calmly in stride.

"I smell the Dark One on him," Vaqar again warned. "The scent is never wrong."

"Where have you been?" Tokar demanded.

Drracien glanced at the Tahscan, then swallowed. "He's right."

Haegan stilled, uncertainty dancing over his face.

"I was caught by the Dark One," Drracien admitted, "but I managed to escape—perhaps that is why you think I was with him."

Tili glanced at the Tahscan, who seemed to waver in his determination. "Is that possible? To bear the stench of another?"

Vaqar frowned. "It's never been true before—"

Tili lifted a hand to the Pathfinders to secure Drracien.

"—but neither have I been very close to the Dark One, whose stench burns like no other."

"See?" Drracien laughed as he caught Haegan by the shoulder. "It's all—"

"Where were you when the Infantessa held Haegan?" Apparently, Tokar wasn't placated. "Where were you when the battle erupted and he needed assistance?"

Drracien shifted, his face blanching. A good look on the arrogant accelerant.

Truth be told, Tili would like to know as well. Was it too convenient that Drracien came upon them after the battle and before Ironhall? What was his purpose here? But what concerned him the most was Haegan's vapid defense of the absentee accelerant.

"Enough," Haegan snapped. "He stays. As my guest."

"Is that . . . wise?" Tokar glanced to Tili. "We know not where he's been nor where his loyalties rest."

"My loyalty," Drracien began, his expression a mask of indifference and apathy, "is with the only person who has ever truly cared about my well-being, and that would be me."

Tili gritted his teeth. There was a hesitance, a worry in those beady eyes. But there was something else that made Tili uncertain. Made his fingers itch.

"Why do you ask Tili's thoughts?" Haegan barked. "I said he stays."

"Aye, but you're half out of your mind," Tokar said, his dark hair adding to the levity of his tone. The smile fell away as his brows drew together. "And I am left to wonder: The half that remains—is it the part that wanted naught to do with your role and purpose, or is it the one that accepted the role as prince? Because in earnest, never have I laid eyes on that part." He nodded to Tili. "He's Steward of the Nine. Stepped into it, though he neither asked for nor liked it. But he thought of the people, of the realm, and owned up to his duty. So for now, I follow his orders."

The petulance of this conversation did no good, although Tili had to admit it was nice to have his position and authority recognized, accepted.

"I'm the Fierian!" Haegan growled.

"Easy, Princeling," Tili said gently. "We all acknowledge yer role as Abiassa's Hand. None question it."

"Not after seeing you demolish the Infantessa," Astadia added.

"Nay—it's questioned," Tokar barked. "By Haegan himself."

Though Tili didn't like the accelerant staying—or that he clung to Haegan—he relented because somehow, his presence was a comfort to Haegan, who'd been through enough. They could grant the prince this. But he not would let down his guard.

"We will respect yer request, Fierian," Tili said, intentionally using Haegan's role so there could be no doubt of whom he addressed. "There are enough divisions of late. But doubt this not: these Pathfinders, the Tahscans, are ready and willing to do violence on yer behalf should there be any"—he drilled holes with his eyes into Drracien—"need."

Haegan shifted. "That's not necessary."

"Aye, 'tis," Tili said. "Ye may be the highest ruling accelerant, but until the Council says otherwise, I am the highest authority over the armies, and I do not take that obligation lightly. Abiassa trumps even that."

"Abiassa?"

Tili smirked. "Much happened in yer absence. I was assigned the title of steward, the Pathfinders were brought south by a strange wind, joining forces with Tahscans, who have been imbued with a gift to hunt incipients."

Haegan hesitated, his gaze skipping around those gathered, then back to Tili.

"We are here to protect ye. And we will be faithful to our oath, to ye, but supremely to Abiassa." Tili pivoted and pushed through the thick crowd of bodies. His warning had been to Drracien, and the directive laid plain before the princeling. He must hope it was enough.

But why? Why was he so keenly rankled by that accelerant?

"Tili." Her soft, plaintive voice was tinged with urgency.

But he also felt urgency—to keep distance between them.

"Tili, wait. What did you mean back there?" she asked. "What wind?"

"Aye, Steward—what strange wind?" Laerian fell into step beside him. "There was none."

"Aye, but he needn't know that. Not now. He must believe this is bigger than himself or we are all singed."

25

Dread coiled in the pit of her stomach, bringing a cold, balmy sweat to her brow and the back of her shoulders. Kaelyria stared at the disgraced accelerant who, nearly a cycle past, had plied her will with smooth talk and perfectly placed words.

She wanted to claw out his eyes. Instead, she dug her fingernails into her palms and reminded herself she was above this slimy vermin.

"It is remarkable that, even when confined to a cage, you can keep that pert nose so high, Princess." His seedy laugh dripped with condescension. "Are you not happy? I mean, I do believe you owe me thanks."

"Retribution is all I owe you," she bit out, a tremor of fury rippling through her veins.

"For what?" Cilicien said with a deep chuckle. "For giving you what you desired?"

"You knew full well your suggestion regarding the transference was wrong."

"As did you, Princess." He stood smug and unrepentant. "You are not the whitewashed lamb you feign."

She inched forward. "Tell me, did you also know the truth of my brother?"

His thin eyebrow arched. "What would that be? A spoiled, arrogant pr—"

"Don't," she growled. It took every measure of willpower to restrain the vitriol she wanted to vomit on him. The hatred. The fury. "Did you know Haegan had the ability to wield as a boy?"

He widened his eyes and froze, mouth agape.

Then he hadn't known either.

His laugh cut short her meager hope. "Of course I knew. We are accelerants, Princess. We can detect each other by the heat we gather through the abiatasso."

It shamed her—she had never even thought to seek it with her brother. Or maybe she'd taken it to be her father's wake, since he was so much stronger. "You knew, and yet you let me go through with it, fully cognizant of what would happen to Haegan when he followed my instructions"—her voice strained against the anger rising through her breast—"*your* instructions to go to the Great Falls. It nearly killed him!"

He lifted a bejeweled cup to his lips and peered over the rim. Cilicien's fingers were so adorned with rings 'twas a wonder he could lift it. His amusement gleamed through his black eyes. "Nearly, but it didn't."

Kaelyria reached for the Flames to blast him with a bolt . . . but they were not there. Even after all these months, it was still instinct to wield. She swallowed, helpless. Useless. "Why did you bring me here?" Thoughts of the others—the girl, Carilla, the Legiera—rang through her mind. "What of the Eilidan?"

"What of them?" he asked, smacking his lips and setting down his cup.

Flames, the man was infuriating! He would force her to ask, to state outright what befouled her tongue. "Are they dead?"

His shoulders bounced in a shrug. "How am I to know? I am here. They are there."

"Nay, be not so cavalier. 'Twas you who attacked them. You singed the life from Carilla, the poor girl's only crime to protect those with her."

"No." Cilicien stabbed a finger in the air. "No, she *lied*. She claimed to be you. That is punishable by death."

"In what land?"

"My land!"

"*Your* land?" Kae scoffed. "Have you lost your faculties? You are naught but a disgraced and stripped accelerant!"

"And you are the princess to blame for her parents' deaths, her brother's wandering desperation, which"—he cocked his head and arched his eye-brow—"in turn left the entire Nine Kingdoms vulnerable." He marched around her prison, tracing the heavily carved Caorian wood chairs as he moved. "And that, my dear, opened the door for Poired's advance and attack." With a laugh, he shrugged. "It was most kind that you handed over the kingdom."

Enraged, Kaelyria threw herself at the bars, clawing for his face. Instead of finding flesh beneath her fingernails, she felt the searing heat of a wielding halo. The bubble was icy hot and taunting. She cried out, her nerves on fire.

"Gently," Cilicien chided the guards, who had haloed her.

Through tears and frustration, she felt the heat amplify, constricting her air. She drew up, breathing in tight against the draining oxygen, hissing.

"Easy!" Cilicien barked, extending a hand to the sentries. "You harm her and I will expel the life from you!"

Tears slipping free, Kaelyria closed her eyes, willing Abiassa to—just for a heartbeat—return her gift. Let her boil this incipient's breath from his lungs.

But this was her own doing. Kaelyria's. In truth, was not the downfall of Seultrie her fault as well? Just as he'd said. The futility of her hope that Abiassa would use her once more thrummed through her veins. Discouraged. Defeated.

"Tell me, my dear—who is the one disgraced?"

Suspended off the ground, halo pinning her, she tried to muster her courage.

"Be furious with me if it suits," Cilicien crooned, "but we both know who bears the blame for this fiasco. You were so desperate to defeat the Dark One, to throw your own brother into the vast, uncaring world, that you cared not the price. I told you that price, Kaelyria. If you think back." His smile was smarmy as he studied her. "I gave what you wanted. I supplied the ability to transfer your gifts."

"No, you *quenched* me," she said through gritted teeth.

He pursed his lips and bobbed his head side to side. "A technicality."

Whimpering against the heat that sent rivulets of sweat down her temples, Kaelyria knew to keep her anger in check. The halo seized upon the fire of hatred and constricted. The more she fought, the worse it would hurt.

She glowered through the warbling, crackling halo. Sparks danced and popped. One flicked her cheek, and she winced. His glee and arrogance reminded her of the dead of night. That was just it—*dead*. They were dead eyes. Creepy and bottomless. "If I ever get my gifts back," she said, trembling beneath the exertion it took to push out the words, "I will turn you to ash."

"I would very much like to see you try, Kaelyria. I always admired your wielding. It was so natural." He lifted a hand and waved it, the jewels catching torchlight. "Such beauty. Such elegance. Much like you, gliding through the gilded halls of Fieri Keep as if you owned the world." He sniffed. "In a way, I suppose you did. Perhaps that is why you were such a delicious target for the Dark One. Why he so desperately fought to get into your head."

Nausea rolled through her, the memories of the voice that nearly drove her to pitch herself into the Lakes of Fire.

"When I told him I could turn you faster, he did not believe me." Cilicien raised his chin. "I promised I could, because I knew how naïve and arrogant the daughter of the Fire King had become. So overconfident in your giftings, so haughty in your stature, wealth, and position, that you never once considered that you might not be dealing with someone who had the same goals."

"You're wrong," she said, wishing she could claw away the tears sliding down her face. "I knew you were not to be trusted."

"Ah, pet." He clicked his tongue three times. "And yet still you handed me the *key* to the kingdom."

Kaelyria went still, confused. A terrible dread stirring through the heat and her body. "What . . . what key?"

He sniffed a laugh. "Did you seriously think I gave your gifts to Haegan?"

She frowned. "He—he was healed. He walked."

Pursed lips and another shrug. "Easy enough for an accelerant with healing gifts. Drigo, for example, have near-miraculous abilities."

"But the Falls—"

"Ah, that was unfortunate." He held up his hands, as a superior talking to a subordinate. "Come, did nobody tell you there were rules to a trans-ference, most of which we broke, therefore it was not a transference." He inclined his head with a bounce of his shoulders again. "Not in the truest sense."

"Haegan went to the Falls. He was healed. He became the Fierian."

"All true." He smirked again. "But not of your doing. Well—" He clasped his hands, considering. "I suppose it *was* your doing. He was convinced to get to the Falls. Your doing. He was convinced he was healed. Your doing."

It made no sense. "But I was paralyzed."

"Of course—*think!*" He touched his temples. "I *quenched* you."

A deep chasm opened in Kaelyria, yawning greater and greater as she turned his words over. No, she refused to believe it. "I will never trust your words." She couldn't accept she had given her gift away to this . . . incipient. Cilicien had stolen it, gifted it to Poired. The very thing she fought. The very reason she'd made the sacrifice . . .

"Ah." He held up his bejeweled finger. "Probably your best decision, albeit a year too late."

"These are lies! You are wicked and cruel," she shouted, noticing the air thinning around her, the halo reacting to her distress. A constricting started around her throat, strangling.

Cilicien wagged his fingers to the halo. "Remember, your anger tightens the halo. Go easy."

Kae struggled for air. Tears squeezed past her clenched eyes. *Haegan . . . the kingdom . . . No no no.* Bereft, she felt her anger leak out as she deflated, tears streaming down her cheeks. *What have I done?*

"It was too delicious, really," he said with a rumble of laughter. "You were so adamant about stopping the Dark One from taking your gifts that"—a burst of laughter leapt from his snarling face—"you handed them right to him." He pressed his fingers to his chest. "Through me, of course." He gave a curt bow, casting torchlight over his oiled black hair. "And I thank you. Because of this gift of yours, I have been named one of his Three."

"I will kill you!" she cried, her throat hoarse and raw. "I will make sure you feel every—" She gasped. Groped for air.

"Princess, calm down or you'll strangle yourself right out of existence."

She couldn't breathe.

"Calm . . ." His words were growing more agitated.

Her pulse pounded in her temples. Strained against her throat. Her body went rigid. Even in her wild panic and raw anger, she saw the same mirrored in Cilicien. But that only fueled her determination. The singewood would never again control or manipulate her. Not if she was dead.

The edges of her vision ghosted. As she lost consciousness, the rage faded. Which opened her breathing. Gave her room within the halo.

"Better," Cilicien crooned.

Anger! She needed anger.

Focus.

Father. On the drawbridge of Seultrie. Burned alive by Poired.

The scene before her—Cilicien's dark, cruel face gripped in panic that she would die—blurred.

Anger. Haegan. Mother. The keep. Her friends.

Cilicien had kidnapped her. Now, she was not with Aselan—a true man, a man worthy of much more than he'd been given. Father would have appreciated him. Mother would have loved him. Mother . . . Mother! They were both dead. Because of Poired. Because of Cilicien. Because of herself!

"Kaelyria, stop!"

Darkness closed in. She welcomed it. Welcomed the—

"Stop or you'll ki—"

She glowered and saw him throw a blast at the halo.

Crack! Whorp!

Darkness snapped in. Kaelyria was falling . . .

• • •

"I must speak with you."

In the third day of the march to Ironhall, Tili glanced to the side at the large warrior. "I welcome the reprieve from boredom."

Vaqar slid a look around at the others. "Alone."

Tili didn't dare follow his gaze, but instead thought through who was nearby: Astadia, Tokar, the boy Laertes, Praegur, Haegan, Drra—

Ah. He understood. With a nod, Tili nudged his horse aside.

As the column moved past, he nodded to the refugees who had attached to the contingent for protection as much as to have a sense of purpose. They seemed worn of body and of spirit.

Vaqar's destrier stamped next to him. "The newcomer still reeks of the Dark One," he said. "He *is* aligned with the enemy."

Adjusting on his horse, Tili hesitated. Then leaned on the pommel with crossed wrists, affording him a moment to stretch his back. "What ye suggest is treason." He eyed the front of the line, where Drracien rode, chatting with Haegan. It was a good change to see the prince relaxed, merry. Not in torment or pain. Granted, Drracien was fractious and nervy, but . . .

"I only suggest the Fierian is not safe with him." Vaqar seemed to dwarf his own horse, his shoulders broad and his arm muscles taut. "Nor are any of us."

"Ye are sure? This stench ye detect—how is it ye know one from another, or a lingering one from one being held?"

"Scents are as unique as the people. And I may not know you, Steward, but I know your kind. Even you hesitate over this newcomer." He inclined his head. "You must intervene."

"Ye ask much to expect me to act when there is no proof," Tili said, scratching at his beard again.

Vaqar huffed. "It is difficult, I assume, to understand what we Tahscans are cursed with, but—"

"Ye say ye can detect not only hate from love, but my scent from another's." Tili surveyed the people as they continued, children scampering about, in and around parents' legs. "Aye, 'tis much."

It seemed Vaqar growled at him, but a quiet settled between them for several long minutes. "If I can smell the attraction of your woman from here, think you not that I can detect the stench of the purest evil?"

Tili jerked his gaze to him. "My *woman*?"

Though Vaqar's mouth was covered, it could not hide the mirth that glowed in his eyes, struck golden by the glare of the afternoon sun. "You hide it well, but not well enough, Steward."

"Hide *what*?" His voice pitched, and Tili fought the heat creeping through his neck. "In earnest, I—" He clamped his mouth. No, he would not dignify that with a remark. He focused on the only important topic.

"Ye believe the youth is serving Poired. What of his claim that he was merely held?"

After several long moments of silence, Vaqar spoke. "The scent is too strong for one simply being manipulated by the Dark One. I believe not only has the youth been in his presence for an extended period, but that he himself has wielded the dark flames."

Tili flinched, but then came a protective swell. "Do ye know the Guidings, Tahscan? The laws that bind the accelerants and their wielding?"

"I do not."

"If what ye speak is true . . ." Iron weights pressed Tili's stomach, nauseating him. As if this war was not enough. "If Drracien wields dark flames, then not only do we have a traitor, we have an enemy combatant—an incipient—in our camp." But the problems only started there. "The Guidings demand accelerants eliminate those who wield the dark flames."

"And yet he makes merry with the one person capable of preventing that very action," Vaqar noted.

"Shrewd, if he is indeed wielding them." Tili swiped a hand over his mouth. "We must take care with this, Vaqar. 'Tis not merely one man's reputation resting on that accusation."

"I do not speak in haste, Steward. I speak truth."

"Ye are Tahscan," Tili said, eyeing him. The plain words alluded to where Vaqar's loyalty rested—with another country. Not with those in this camp. He watched. Waited and assessed the man's reaction. "I've heard ye're the queen's brother."

Vaqar did not react, save the small twitch below his left eye, where those double wave tattoos danced over the scar.

"So why did ye leave? Why abandon country and the possibility of rule to come here?"

"I *was* her brother," Vaqar said. "When the queen turned from our traditions and people to embrace the Infantessa, I braved once to counter her. When she discovered the depth, the extent of our . . . *gift*, she crafted a writ of execution for all found to carry the mark."

"But ye were her brother!"

"I was a threat," Vaqar countered. "We fled, and she subjugated all of Tahsca to the will of the Dark One."

Tili straightened. "Yer tale is painful at best, but it does not answer my query—why here? Why ride with us?"

Keen, bright eyes locked onto Tili. "I would ask the same of you, Prince Thurig as'Tili. You were commander of your father's elite guards. Renowned for impartial and strategic dealings. And, according to the queen, you were much-sought after by the daughters of the North, were you not?"

He wasn't sure whether to be amused or embarrassed at that last point.

"And yet here you are, unbound and fighting for a prince not your own." Vaqar's gaze rose to the sun, then back to the people who now numbered in the hundreds. "We both have left our homes and followed the path of Aaesh, which has led us to this camp. To the protection of the Fierian, it would seem. Would you not agree?"

"Yer point is made, Tahscan."

"Is it?"

Was that a challenge? Or a true question?

"I bring you a legitimate concern and threat against the Fierian, and you stand here arguing politics."

"I argue nothing," Tili said. "My intent is to sort facts. To consider every possible angle to this threat, weigh it against machinations, designs, and the future of all Primar. While ye and I seek the same end for the same blessed Hand, we might have very different routes to that end."

"Like what?"

"Division—dividing me against the Fierian. Isolating him."

A storm rushed into the man's face. "Would not that serve the Dark One better than myself?" He shrugged, his large shoulders rippling. "I have no motive, other than to rid myself of the reek."

"Ye mean, the scent."

"Aye."

"When did ye"—how had he put it?—"get the mark?"

"He came to me three months hence. The Guardian."

A face flashed through Tili's thoughts. "Draorin."

"He gave no name," Vaqar said, "but his presence with you confirmed where I was to be. As I have done little that others cannot do, it seems probable that he led me here for this purpose—to rout the traitor."

Tili roughed a hand over his face, then slid it up and over his head.

The Tahscan had no reason to turn them against Drracien. Suddenly, a memory leapt to mind. Tili had heard while at Hetaera that Drracien had been accused of murdering a high lord at the Citadel. The youth had been hunted. Hid. Fled. Was he guilty? Had he been turned by the Dark One?

"Steward." Laerian galloped toward them. "The Fierian suggests we make camp."

After a quick survey of the land, Tili nodded. "Agreed."

The captain rode away, shouting the command to break and set up camp.

Tili turned back to Vaqar. "I weigh heavily yer words, Tahscan."

"Understood." The Tahscan snapped a nod and drew the reins away.

"Vaqar," Tili called, noting they were not fully alone—someone was lingering nearby, listening. "A favor."

Annoyance rippled through the man's dark skin.

"When we resume our march, I would like to travel with the people, know them. Settle disputes among some stragglers from Iteveria." He eyed the throngs pushing toward them to make camp on the plains. "Replace me at the front?"

Vaqar hesitated, but seemed to understand Tili's intent, that neither of them would leave Drracien unmonitored. He inclined his head. "Of course." His people joined him and Vaqar dismounted, the man like a great boulder, the people like a river crashing around him.

"Steward," called a Pathfinder. "Your tent is there at the front, sir."

As Tili dismounted and started for his tent, he could not help but wonder. Was he buying into paranoia? Overthinking things? Still, the eastern plains of the Nine were vast. Amazing how Drracien found them. *Father, would that ye rode with us . . .* What he wouldn't give for his father's sage wisdom. Would he see his family again?

With another look in the direction of Vaqar, Tili caught sight of Praegur, walking a horse and talking with the young girl Kedulcya had left behind. There seemed an affection between the two. And it stirred an ache in Tili.

"You look like you're in pain."

Tili's heart thudded at the sultry voice. "'Tis yer presence," he teased, glancing down at the spritely girl who'd joined him.

Taking the reins of his horse, she rolled her eyes, then swept her gaze over the busy camp. "The Tahscan's words have made the Pathfinders nervous."

How had anyone heard them? Or was this her way of saying Vaqar had unsettled *her*? "They make *me* nervous." In his periphery, he saw her almost jerk her gaze to his again.

She smoothed a hand over his mount's blaze. "Then you believe him?"

Believe was a strong word. "I weigh his concerns with care. He has no reason to begrudge the accelerant."

"Except that Drracien has a seat of position with the Fierian. A seat that might have been given to the Tahscan."

"'Tis no competition, and there are no seats here, Astadia."

She tilted her head, exposing her bare neck. "Aren't there?"

With a sigh, Tili sagged under her constant challenges to his thoughts. He was tired. He took back the reins and, leading his horse, started again for his tent.

"You ride with him, yet the Tahscans are at the rear."

Blazes, she would follow him. "Because they are not citizens of the Nine."

"Neither are you, from what I hear."

"As steward, I am a citizen." Not entirely true, but enough. "Beside the Fierian, I alone hold authority here."

"And in the Northlands?"

Tili twitched, frowning at her. He wished to see her eyes and angled to accommodate that. Considered the inquisitive, intelligent gaze that stared back unabashed. Wisps of hair dangled around a face smudged with dirt and sweat. "How long were ye listening?"

She lifted a shoulder casually. "As long as necessary."

He shook his head. "I have no time for this. I beg yer mercy." With a nod of acknowledgement, he handed off his horse to a waiting Jujak and stepped around her to enter his tent.

But Astadia shifted into his path.

Tili stumbled, caught her shoulders to avoid a collision. "Blazes, girl, what—"

"I did not mean to argue against the Tahscan." Her eyes were round, impossibly green as waning light speared the iris from the side.

"Do ye always change yer mind so quickly?"

"It's your presence," she said, a teasing grin playing at her pink lips.

Throwing his words back at him, was she? "Well," he said, ignoring the way his heart thudded as he peered down at her. Aware, but not caring that they were inappropriately close. "Is this how ye make all yer points—throwing yerself at men of power?"

"To include yourself, you'd have to actually have power."

26

"I followed you as far as Iteveria's border."

Haegan started, glancing at Drracien, who sat outside the tent pitched for the evening. "You followed me?"

Drracien nodded, hair dipping into his eyes as he built a fire using his wielding and kindling. "Saw you leave the Citadel and hike the woods."

Surprise twirled through Haegan as he considered that revelation. "'Tis a time I would rather not think on."

"Then you regret it?"

"Of course I regret it," Haegan bit out as he flung a wool blanket to the ground.

"Tell me of it."

"I'd rather not," Haegan said.

"And the scars?"

Haegan flinched at the reminder of the words he'd carved into his flesh. Resisted the urge to tug his sleeves lower. "I would have peace, Drracien. She has been in my head too long, and I savor the quiet."

"I beg your mercy. 'Twas naught but curiosity, and as you know, I'm not good at being reverent."

That could not be argued. "What of you?" Haegan said, turning the conversation back on his friend. "You followed me to Iteveria, so where were you that you came upon us from the west?"

"When I lost you . . ." Drracien hesitated, as if weighing whether to say something or not, ". . . there was nothing for me, so I followed the wakes. But it wasn't accelerants I stumbled across."

"Poired?"

"Of his sort—incipients cleaning out a village, looking for Haegan the Fierian." He tucked his hands beneath his armpits. "Have you not come upon them?"

"Nay," Haegan said, standing at the tent entrance and gazing across the camp. He noted the Tahscans had spread out nearby, and their leader, Vaqar, stared in their direction. "Negaer and Tili encountered them several times, including just north of Caori, where they were joined by the Tahscans."

"Those are some wicked fighters."

"Wicked? Nay—"

"I mean it only with great respect."

Haegan considered his friend, then sighed. "Were you with the Dark One?"

Drracien cast him a quick glance, then he, too, looked around the camp. "One of the encounters with the incipients put me face-to-face with him."

"And yet you live."

"Aye." The word was clipped and doused in anger. "And 'tis no coincidence. He bartered my life for the discovery of a woman."

"What woman?"

"I know not. Only that I am to find her." Drracien huffed. "He said I would sense it when I did."

"That's vague." Haegan scowled. "But in earnest—you will not do it, will you? How can you sell your life and soul to the Desecrator?"

"I did not say I was searching for her." Drracien slapped Haegan's shoulder. "Enough boring talk. I would eat. What say you?"

At the other fire, the Tahscan surged to his feet.

Something in Haegan twisted, seeing the way the great warrior stared at him. No . . . not at Haegan. At Drracien. "Not yet," he said to his friend. "Go ahead of me."

Drracien slid his attention to the Tahscan, and for several long seconds, the two seemed to have a silent duel before Drracien headed away.

Wariness crowded Haegan as the Tahscan crossed the camp.

"Fierian," the man said as he inclined his head. "A word?"

Arms folded over his chest, giving him tingling reminders of the words seared into his flesh, Haegan nodded. He briefly wondered why these scars hadn't healed when others had during his wielding. But now he had a more pressing concern. "I know you are not fond of my friend—"

"He is not to be trusted."

"I hear your concern, Vaqar." He nodded, so tired of every aspect of his life being a battle. "I take it Tili has set you as guard over me where my friend is concerned."

A slow nod.

"Then I will trust that and you. But most of all, Abiassa." It seemed too easy to say and yet much harder to do when he wanted to reject the idea of Drracien betraying him. "We both have paths before us that are not pleasant." Haegan eyed the warrior. "You can smell the wielding?"

He gave a small nod.

"A smell." Haegan remembered the bitter taste that had been on his tongue the entire trip to Iteveria with Trale and Astadia. "I think I am able to detect it as well. Trust me to know when I must act, though I will not do it lightly—or hastily—with regard to my friends."

27

On the fourth afternoon of their journey, Haegan retreated to the rear, where the wagon carrying his father lumbered. He slid off his mount, grateful when the wagon driver slowed so Haegan could tie his reins and climb aboard.

He met the heavy-lidded eyes of the Drigo and then the Northlands healer, Pao'chk. "How fares he?" Kneeling at his father's cot, Haegan took in the gaunt, sallow face, which had been shaved. Hair had been trimmed. Now a clean tunic squared bony shoulders.

"He sleeps," Pao'chk said without feeling.

Placing a hand on his father's chest, Haegan marveled at how their roles had reversed. How his father lay abed unmoving, and now Haegan hovered over him. He silently willed Abiassa to send a stream of pure fire through his hand—not to sear his father, but to infuse him with healing and strength. But nothing happened.

"Have you no hope for his recovery?" Blond hair curled around the square jaw, more protruding than normal because of the near emaciation.

"Abiassa is our hope," Pao'chk said. "If She wills that the Fire King resumes his throne, he will. Until then, we work and he sleeps."

Reluctant to accept an answer that was more platitude than help, Haegan nodded. He chose to remain with his father until the sun lowered into the caress of the horizon, then he rose. "Keep me informed."

"Of course, my prince."

He climbed down and untied his mount's reins.

Drracien was there, riding slowly. "How is the Fire King?"

Unwilling to face the dreadful truth that his father would probably never rule again, Haegan sighed. "Recovering," he managed, but said no more.

Was he recovering? No one could tell, so neither could they say he wasn't. It still grated that his father had been calling to him in a deep . . . otherworldly way and Haegan hadn't recognized it. To this moment, the sound haunted him.

"Your watchdogs are faithful," Drracien said, as Vaqar and the Tahscan woman approached from either side of the wagon. "I fear they don't like me."

Haegan pulled onto his horse. "Most of us don't."

Drracien smirked. "A bit of your old self returning, I see."

"I could say the same of you."

A shadow flickered across his friend's brow as he turned to the rocky road, their horses trotting at a begrudging pace. Or maybe that was Haegan's exhausted self talking. He *did* begrudge every minute, every league crossed. And yet, he savored the distraction. Anything that kept his mind from going back to the dungeon. From finding himself in that dark cave, realizing over and over, over and over, that the pile of bones was his father. And Trale, sacrificing himself for Haegan. He wanted no more of that. He would not allow it. No one should give their life for him. A sacrifice so great should be worth the cost.

He shook himself and brought his horse to a steady canter a short distance behind Laerian and Grinda. Tili was nowhere to be seen, but Praegur glanced back, though he made no move to interpose himself between Haegan and Drracien. Laertes, however, whose pony had wandered again and was placidly tearing tufts of grass that somehow survived alongside the margin of the road, alternately cajoled and threatened the beast until it meandered over to Haegan. The sight made Haegan smile, chased away some of the sorrow.

"I haven't wanted to ask . . ." Drracien said quietly. "Thiel?"

Blinking at the mention of her name, Haegan tried to harness the failing hope that spasmed through his veins. "Gwogh sent her to the Ematahri—"

"And you let her go?"

Haegan snapped a glare at his friend. "I didn't *let* her go. I wasn't . . . there."

"Aye," Laertes agreed. "We don' even know if she's alive."

Drracien jerked. "What? Why?"

"She done fell from the raqine what fled to save him," Laertes said. "That beast don' listen t' my screaming."

A shadow slid over them, and Haegan pulled his gaze to Chima, circling lazily in the sky with Draed and Umoni. "Give care, Laertes. She may not understand words, but she understands intent."

"Then why are we going north?" Drracien asked.

"Because there is nothing in the south worth considering," Haegan muttered, remembering all the times his father had said that.

"And there is in the north?"

"You seem overly curious about our journey." Haegan had a thought then. "Where were you headed that we crossed paths in the middle of the barren lands?"

"Anywhere that was not the Citadel," Drracien evaded again. He fell silent for a time, and Haegan hoped he had abandoned his questions. No such fortune. "I beg your mercy, Haegan, but why have you not done more to find Thiel?"

"I told you—"

"Aye, and the Haegan I knew would've ripped the world apart to find her."

"The Haegan you knew no longer exists." Keen awareness that things had changed rocked through him since he'd reduced Nydelia to ashes. Though a portion of him still wrestled with it, he had largely given up fighting it. "I have a purpose to fulfill. 'Tis better, safer, that she is not here."

Drracien nodded slowly, his expression a muddle of confusion, understanding, and uncertainty. "You don't want her hurt." He shrugged. "Makes sense."

"Does it? Because I fear every hour that the fall from Chima took her from me forever, and if it didn't, she remains with the Ematahri. According to Laertes, they hauled her away one day, and he didn't see her again until the morning Chima came to me. As I prepare to face Poired, what happens to her?"

"Then why not act? Take that raqine and go for her."

"You think I haven't considered it?" Haegan sighed and shook his head. "Much have I pondered on what I could do. But whatever power

Abiassa has given me, I cannot confront the enemy alone. It is the same reason I cannot fly off and find Poired, end this right now. This"—he gestured widely to the soldiers and wagons and civilian followers—"the long, agonizing road, is right. We fight together. The Nine, the North, Iteverians, even Tahscans. I know not when Poired will return, but I must be here. I must be ready."

"And if he goes after Thiel? Everyone knows she's important to you. A band of Sirdarians were marching west to join an Ematahri clan. What if she is with them?"

"How have you knowledge of this?"

"I told you," Drracien said with a smirk. "I've been traveling. And you know I can get in and out of places without anyone knowing."

"We are not even sure she's alive."

"You sound guilty now, Princeling."

"I am. Had we not argued, she might not have fled and taken Gwogh's treacherous mission."

Silence settled between them for a few minutes.

"Any more giants since Baen's Crossing?"

Haegan sighed. His friend had many questions. Too many? "Very few. They returned to the mountains, and as you can see, there are no mountains here." Only a carved road through two chunks of rock that jutted upward, defiant of the flat terrain. "A handful, not in their vudd state travel here, I've heard. I guess them only by the height."

"But what—"

"Enough," Haegan said around a half-hearted laugh. "The day is long and your queries longer." He cast his friend a sidelong glance, finding strange solace in the clopping hooves. "You are much changed since Hetaera."

Shorn hills rose steeply on either side, their shadows stretching deep and reminding him of the Throne Road. Of Thiel. Of the encounter with the Ematahri. Which again reminded him of Thiel. If only she traveled with him instead of Drracien or Laertes. Or anyone.

"Me?" Drracien laughed. "Speak for yourself. You go off with assassins, angry and weak wielding, yet here you are, roiling with Flames and a shaved head. How am I to taunt you about your pretty looks now?"

Though he chuckled, Haegan didn't feel the laughter. In truth, the words hurt. Shame that he had willingly fled the course Abiassa set left him irrevocably altered.

"I fear we are none the same." Even as he spoke, Haegan felt something shift in the air.

"Then you've accepted your role as Fierian?"

More like embraced—at least that's how he'd felt when he realized how widespread Nydelia's inflaming had become. When he saw strong people reduced to cowering in dark cages well below the surface. When he found his father . . . The foul stench. The sizzle that had prickled the hairs on his arm.

Haegan glanced there now, surprised to see the hairs standing on end again. Was the memory so virulent? Wait . . . *The air!*

Shouts rose ahead, and a steady din grew as scouts approached from the front and sides. They pulled up sharply beside Graem, and Tili came charging up from the rear of the column, three Tahscans with him. They converged in a cluster of agitation.

Haegan drew back the reins, slowing. What was it? Why did this feel familiar? It left a very bad taste in his mouth. So familiar. What . . . ? Homing in on what changed, Haegan's gaze settled on the road ahead. Then struck the walls of the crevasse.

Laerian galloped back to Haegan and pulled up alongside. The Tahscan approached. "Fierian, are you well?"

"Aye . . ." Haegan murmured, half distracted, tracing the terrain. Breathing the scent. "Nay."

A nervous chuckle came from Drracien. "Which is it?"

"This isn't right." Haegan studied the shale walls. Scanned the heights where hedges bordered—

"Aye, the steward is concerned as well," Laerian said as Tokar eased in, assuming the position on Haegan's left.

"Ambush! To arms!" In a flash, Tili barreled his horse between Haegan and Drracien. "Protect the Fierian!"

Bewildered, Haegan found himself swarmed by Pathfinders. Immersed in confusion, he then saw the hedges moving. They were not shrubs but people with sprigs of vegetation stuck to their clothing. "Incipients," he whispered, his gaze tracking the ridge.

"Get him back!" Tili shouted.

Tokar grabbed Haegan's bridle and pulled.

But even as he was led away, Haegan yanked back his reins. The road before him shifted. The air tingled, different. Strangely transformed from full rise to dusk. Bodies were strewn about, blood soaking heavily into the hard-packed earth. Defeat. There lay Laertes beneath Praegur, whose back had been flayed open as he protected the younger boy. Friends in a crimson river that filled the ravine. Utter defeat.

What is this? Grief curled around his throat and constricted.

He blinked and the sun once more burned bright. His friends remained mounted, watching him warily. And he knew—*knew* if he fled, if he was ruled by fear and shut off, their blood would be on his hands.

"Remove him," Tili ordered as he and Graem closed up ranks around Haegan.

"No!" Haegan attempted to wrest his horse free, but another grabbed the other side. Hemmed in, he could not break loose. "Release me!"

Unyielding, the Pathfinders led his horse toward the middle of the column.

He tried slipping a leg over the side, but there were too many riders. He glanced back to where a violent frenzy erupted—Pathfinders riding hard into the chokepoint, a horde of Sirdarians flooding out. Incipients blasted chunks of the cliff down on the Pathfinders. Steel glinted in the sky—the Tahscan swords sparking against rock and the Sirdarians' weapons.

Haegan gaped. There were many Sirdarians. So very many.

"Stop!" Haegan shouted to his protectors. "Stop or every one of our men who dies will be on your heads!"

But they continued, driving him to the rear. To where his father lay senseless. "No!" Haegan flexed his hand, sending a bubble of heat that nudged the nearby horses backward. His focused intent—distance and protection—ensured no harm would come to animal or man. Thrilled at the breathing room the wielding afforded, he pushed more . . . more . . . His mount shifted. He pitched himself down and wheeled around.

"Haegan, no!" Tokar shouted.

Heedless of the pleas, Haegan sprinted toward the battle, using a halo to protect himself. Determined he would not let another man die because of him. Determined the river of blood in the ravine would be the Sirdarians'.

A giant boulder rolled from the cliff's edge, plummeting toward the Pathfinders.

Haegan skidded to a stop, rolled his hands around each other, and shot a blast at the rock. The pale-blue volley catapulted through the air and shattered the boulder into a million tiny pieces. Another leapt from the cliff. He dealt with that as well.

They needed every accelerant they could get. Where was Drracien? And Tili? He advanced and found the Northlander wielding with one hand to hold back an incipient and slicing his sword at a Sirdarian with the other. Haegan marveled at Tili's skill, wondering how he'd perfected that when his ability to wield had only just come to light. But the Sirdarian seemed fueled by rage and pushed forward.

Haegan flicked a fiery dart into the Sirdarian's temple, crumpling him.

Tili shot him a surprised look, then nodded. "'Bout time ye showed up."

"You tried to lock me away, remember?"

"That was the petulant prince I protected." He drew back his arm and shoved a blast at the incipient, knocking back a dozen feet. It gave Tili time to send a hyperfocused shot that dropped the man for good. "Ye are the Fierian."

Haegan caught another large rock, feeling its weight press against his wielding, and obliterated it. "They intend to bury us."

And where was Drracien?

"Less talk, Twig." Tili gripped his sword with both hands, stepping into a deadly dance with a Sirdarian.

"Think you can send another blue wave and turn them to dust, too?" Tokar shouted from a dozen feet away.

Blue wave?

• • •

Amazement froze Tili as he watched Haegan rally and pick up his role as Fierian, wielding with that fierce, pale light. It was blazingly powerful and left him a little envious. Gone were the haphazard bolts that held as much danger for Haegan and those around him as the intended target. These were tight, focused. Obedient to Haegan's will. And Abiassa's.

Tili had been at the rear when Vaqar's people alerted them to the reek roiling through that canyon. Had their senses not been aroused, the Pathfinders and Haegan—even Tili—would've been ambushed. As Tili rode back to Haegan with the warning, Laerian sent twenty Tahscan fighters up around to flank the enemy. Where were those warriors?

Palms slick with blood, Tili struggled for a firm grip on his sword.

A Silver rushed him, the sun's glare on his helm excruciating. Blinded, Tili struggled not to lose sight of the enemy. He felt the air swirl and brought up his sword. Vibrations rang through the steel. His grip faltered. With the next blow, the sword rattled from his hand. Tili lunged away, but not soon enough. Fire seared his neck. He hissed through the pain. For his own survival, he thrust out a bolt but the distraction of the pain and blood running down his neck weakened his wielding.

Blazes! Is this where he would die? Far from home, family, and Ybienn? *Get yer head out of the grave, fool.* He braced, focused on forming a searing arrow to shoot—

The Silver lunged again, his blade swift and hungry for Tili's life. His sword raised for a killing strike.

Tili stepped back to thrust a blast, but his heel hit something hard. He pitched to the side. Stumbled, lost focus. His blast went far too wide. *Hiel-touck!* The Silver was coming. Right at him.

So. Death it was. Right here. Now.

Wind stirred and a meaty *thunk* sounded very close to his ear before Tili recognized its source—the hilt of a scimitar sticking from the Silver's chest. Shock widened eyes and mouth.

Stunned but not stupid, Tili leapt to his feet again, readying for another Silver or incipient. Cast a furtive glance around. One of Vaqar's men stomped forward with an angry, annoyed set to his mouth, pried his blade free from the Silver. Tili would have offered a nod of thanks, but the Tahscan lunged back into the fight.

A blur to his left. Astadia made for an incipient who'd targeted a Pathfinder. But even as the two engaged, Tili saw a third racing at her. Her blade was quick and the kill clean as she whirled to the newcomer before Tili could even sound a warning.

When a Silver swung his sword at her, Tili sucked in a breath, but Astadia ducked. Whirled around, lowering into a crouch. When she rose,

Astadia swept the man's feet out from under him. She was like a tornado of rage. He recalled being on the receiving end of that rage in his tent.

The Silver landed with a thud. Astadia leapt and drove her dagger into his chest.

A scream from the canyon snapped Tili back into action. Haegan was advancing, his shoulders squared, his confidence sure. Amazing. Blue light haloed as the Fierian moved with fury and determination that could only be called perfection. Every incipient that encountered the Fierian fell. Every Sirdarian who raised a blade vanished.

It was horrifying. Beautiful. Daunting. Exhilarating.

And that's when Tili realized what was happening in the canyon—Pathfinders and Tahscans were advancing, incredibly, and from the other side, the small band sent to flank and ambush were tightening the perimeter, forcing the Sirdarians and incipients into a state of panic.

• • •

The farther Haegan progressed, the more he sensed the pure fire of Abiassa. Felt Her anger over the Dark One sending so many to their deaths. These had chosen their own paths, but it still grieved Her that Primar's children were lost. The blood he'd seen in the vision had changed from that of his friends to that of Abiassa's enemies. To those who put no value on human life.

Tili took a serious hit, nearly decapitated. If the girl hadn't saved him . . . That even one Pathfinder had lost their life here was one too many.

Where was the Dark One? Was he hiding, sending minions to dispatch Haegan to the grave? The thought spun a web of anger and frustration through him. He'd been gifted, not to toil with these, but to cut the beast off at the knees. Send him back to the Void from which he'd crawled.

"Come out," Haegan shouted, his voice echoing beyond time. "Show yourself!"

The Pathfinders hesitated, unable to surrender the fight when there were those who still sought their lives.

"This is between you and me! Come out!" he bellowed.

Wrapping a cloth around his bloody neck, Tili stalked toward him. Not dead then. "What're ye doing? We've enough trouble as it is."

Though he heard and understood the concern, Haegan turned, shielding himself from the onslaught. Ignored Tili. Called again to his enemy. "This is not their war, Poired." Haegan sensed something pulling, tearing the air. As if the elements themselves agreed and sought to regurgitate the Dark One from their bowels. "'Tis yours—answer for what you have done!"

"Haegan," Tili barked. "No. 'Tis not done nor right. Leave—"

Though it was impossible, though his mind struggled and his eyes strained, night stretched its dark veil over the crevasse in which they stood and hazed the land. Heart in his throat, Haegan watched a dark form coalesce in the midst.

As if he had walked from behind a milky glass, Poired Dyrth emerged from the haze. Beneath his boots, the ground squished with the blood of one the Silvers.

Shouts went up. The Pathfinders and Jujak struggled against their own fear. They shifted back, yet did not flee, their training too ingrained. Their honor refusing a knee to this specter.

With Poired came a half-dozen others. Three robed in black. High collars. Red belts. Vacant eyes somehow filled with darkness and death. Slinking along the ground like a viper, a black raqine wisped in and out of sight. He was massive. Terrifying.

Shouts and cries went up.

"Stop, stop! Let them go," someone shouted.

Fear galloped across the battlefield, filling every pore and sinew of flesh and bone with terror. Palpable. The taste bitter on his tongue and familiar.

"We should leave now," another said.

"This is a lost cause," another declared.

"Fierian, we must go before we end up like your father."

I don't know what I'm doing.

I'll fail, just as I did at Fieri Keep.

Just as—

"He's inflaming," came a deep voice of warning from Vaqar.

The revelation cut Haegan free. The Tahscan was right. Poired and his legion were inflaming, working the fears of the Pathfinders, Jujak, and remnant against themselves.

"Shut out the thoughts," Haegan called to their people. "Focus on your purpose, on Abiassa." He hefted the sword, realizing that while he might be able to drag his mind from the grip of the Dark One, those he led were new to inflaming. They were weak, drenched in fears, prone to thoughts that grew and overtook them, convincing them they would fail.

"Release them," he demanded, feeling the heat of Abiassa's Fire roil through him. "Leave their minds."

"You do not control me, *Prince*," Poired sneered. "You are weak! Worse than your father—he was this great and mighty Fire King, and look how I reduced him!"

"You claim victory that is not yours," Haegan growled. "And my father is recovered and healing—evidence to the power of Abiassa!"

The Dark One's brow knotted and he lowered his chin. "Her power. How has *She* done in protecting Her own Hand—you? We shall see who is more powerful. Who is worth serving!" With each word, the Dark One advanced, his hands talon-like. Wrists turning. His left then his right. Drawing back. Pushing out.

As if tendrils of fire were connected to his very chest, Haegan felt the plying. Felt the pull on his gift. He braced himself and drew back his hand, holding his left in place—aimed at the Dark One. "I am no longer your puppet. She has not given us fear, but power!"

"What of this?" Poired tossed a volley at him as he would toss an apple. "Look what she allowed."

Haegan felt a strange, sticky warmth slide over him, peeling back the barrier of his mind. Past his father. Past his own shame. Across the lands. Hills. Right over a sea of Sirdarians and savages . . . right into a tent. And there, prostrate on a pallet, lay the archon. Cadeif. To what end was—

The archon stretched an arm over a thin frame. Dark hair spilled over a light-colored blanket. The woman rolled onto her back.

Haegan staggered at the familiar brown eyes. Thiel. "No," he breathed. The vision vanished. The excruciating image of Thiel abed with Cadeif pummeled him. Numb, he blinked. It wasn't possible.

"He inflames your fears, Fierian," Vaqar spoke firmly, quietly.

But it was so real. As if he stood amid their intimacy. The embers crackled and fell limp from his hands.

"Fierian, fight!" Tili's voice was a rescue net as he turned to Haegan, blood seeping through the cloth around his neck.

Haegan blinked again. Saw bodies dropping around him, dead. Pathfinders being cut down. The vision he'd had before the battle—it was true. It wasn't a pretense. It was real.

He would fail, as he always had.

"Bend not to the reek," Vaqar growled.

Defeated. By Poired. Taunted. By Poired. Ruined. By Poired. And all because Haegan called him from Void.

With a shout, he thrust out a bolt.

Poired met it, his expression one of condescension and taunting. "You are a pup," he said, advancing, his wielding strong and livid. His movements confident, swift. Skilled.

Haegan's feet slid in the muck and blood of the field.

"Thank you," Poired taunted, "for calling me out, for giving me your location so I could end this charade. Prophecies." He barked a laugh. "Abiassa's Hand—more like Abiassa's carnival."

What have I done?

A shriek went up. A commotion rose from his father's wagon. Haegan dared not look, but 'twas impossible to ignore the shrieking and shouts.

"Even your father is wise enough to know his time is at an end, his failure thorough," Poired said. "The sooner you realize that—"

A bolt exploded from the side.

Struck Haegan's temple. He stumbled backward.

One of Poired's three surged against the Pathfinders. Graem went to a knee, a current of heat running through him.

Poired advanced. "You are no match. You have no training."

Tokar struggled against a Silver nearby. Suffered a horrible blow to the arm.

Unrelenting, Poired stood mere yards away, his gaze one of red fury and delight—in tormenting. In defeating Haegan. He reached in. "Your thoughts are putty, melted and turned against you, Fierian. A futile hope for a failing civilization. End it now. End this and let—"

"Augh!" Haegan shouted, spittle foaming at his mouth as he threw both arms forward. Pushed back, shouldering into the wielding.

Where was it? Where was the blue halo? The light that severed darkness? *Have I truly failed?*

"Inflaming, Fierian," warned the Tahscan once more.

Haegan blinked. *Blazes.* He'd let it happen again. His knee buckled. The heat became overbearing, suffocating. Moans filtered around the camp, through his people.

"We're losing."

"Fierian, *fight* it," Vaqar said at his side.

Praegur was there, too, lifting him. Steadying him. "He's in your head, Haegan. Reach for Her. For Her truth."

On his right came Vaqar, who hoisted him full up. "*Fight.* You can do this. We are here. She is here."

On a knee, sweat dripping down his temples and neck, Haegan focused. *Truth. What truth?* More blasted inflaming. He glowered through his brow. Reached for the truth of Abiassa. *That's it.* He'd gotten off track. Locked his thoughts on anger. On vengeance. He must think of his friends. Of the wrong being done . . .

"Target the Tahscans," one of the black cloaks ordered.

Cries and shouts went up.

"The one with the Fierian!"

"He's protected!"

"I care not—kill them both!"

Abiassa, guide me.

Visions of the statues at Baen's Crossing leapt to mind. A memory glimmered within reach of what had happened there. What could happen here. He had but to ask. Hope lanced his fear and closed his eyes. *"Ïmnæh wæithe he-ahwl—"*

Poired's empty eyes snapped to Haegan. "He's summoning the giants. Stop him!"

"—abiałassø et Thræiho—" Haegan fought against the counter-wielding, the Dark One's fear tangible in the wake that slid over the shielding. Needled through like worms in the dirt. Chin to his chest, he stared through his brow at the Dark One, thinking of all he'd done. All he was willing to kill to accomplish Sirdar's will. *"Miembo Thræiho!"*

Concern tremored through Poired, his lips parting. As if he waited.

No, he wasn't waiting. He was searching the Void, searching the air for the thunder of giants. When the slow smile slid back into his smirk, Poired's arrogance returned. "Seems even they are no longer listening to you, Fierian."

The words had been strong, fierc. He would not accept defeat or rejection so readily. No longer. He'd played into that, conceding ground in this war that cost far too many lives and minds. Haegan muttered them again, caring not if the giants came, yet greedy for the strength that the words alone imbued. *"Ïmnæh wæithe he-ahwl abiałassø et Thræïho. Miembo Thræïho! Ïmnæh wæithe he-ahwl abiałassø et Thræïho. Miembo Thræïho!"* Again and again, he repeated phrase, his voice and their strength growing. But then the taste of those words changed. *"Raqerier he-awl abiałassø and the touqær dohn Abiassa."*

The ground trembled as if it, too, cowered at the ancient summons. Haegan worked to steady himself. Noted Pathfinders, Jujak, and Sirdarians stumbling, their swords canting awkwardly as they struggled for balance. Wary, frightened glances traced the world around them. The resonance continued until only thundering pervaded their existence, pounding ears, chests, and boots.

They're coming. A smile pushed into Haegan's exhaustion, like a lonely dog nudging its master. Sensing the change, the response, he continuously voiced the words, amazed when the nearby accelerants chanted with him. It pulled from something deep within him, something of Abiassa.

A great rumble shook the walls of the crevasse, pebbles and rocks rained down, and with it came a deep roar that pierced so painfully, Haegan thought his head might split.

Four Drigovudd, forms larger than the biggest of the trees, pounded into the fray. When they slid to a stop between Haegan and the Dark One, muddy earth sluiced up, slathering a dozen or more incipients.

But then came a keening so violent, so horrible that Haegan covered his ears. Men fell sobbing as blood dripped from their ears and noses.

Shadows flew across the field as great beasts descended. Raqine. Dozens of them, their wings stirring the rank air and snapping like a thunderous applause. Haegan marveled, only then noting the Deliverers encircling both him and the Dark One. Swords down but ready. Through the fabric of time, he felt their readiness for evil to fall. For this desecration to end. For all that Abiassa had designed and created to once again be beautiful.

Haegan refocused. "Poired," he called, observing how those around him writhed in pain from the shrieks of the raqine. "You must answer for your savagery, for your alliance with Sirdar."

Amusement turned to anger in a shift so swift and fierce, it rustled the air. "Try me," Poired challenged, the haze growing, encompassing.

"He's going to escape," Laerian said from the left.

The captain was right. If Poired slipped away, they'd have to do this all over again. Haegan pushed forward, greedily reaching for the embers. Desperation hauling him another step. Another.

"No," came the resonating boom of the Deliverer in his head. *"It is not yours to do."*

As if a whip had been snapped at him, Haegan felt in his veins a tinge of fire—and then nothing save a rush of cold. Frozen, unable to move, he stared at his hands and wondered at the words of the Deliverers. He glanced to them and found impassive expressions. How could they render him impotent with such little regard?

"Have you a problem?" Poired snickered. "Still can't bring yourself to fight me?" The man seethed, and just as fast, he was winding another volley.

From the side, Drracien crept toward the Dark One.

Haegan's heart hitched. He already lost Thiel. He did not want to lose Drracien as well. The brace released, and Haegan staggered a step. "No," he cried to the dark-haired accelerant, who'd been the closest thing to a brother he'd known.

"Fool and Failure shall be the only names you will know, Haegan of Seultrie!" Laughing, Poired stepped back, and as he did, day again yawned, revealing the haze that swallowed him and his entourage. He vanished behind the veil. "You could not win this battle, and you could not keep your friends."

Haegan frowned.

"Drracien."

Less than a dozen paces from the Dark One, Drracien drew up straight. Rage colored his face crimson. His hands fisted.

"What?" Poired taunted him. "Did you not tell them you are my son?"

Hauling in a breath did little to stem the burn that roiled through Haegan. Shock held him captive as Drracien went pale. Didn't argue or object.

"Drracien!" Haegan moved forward.

"Nay, my lord," Laerian said, stretching an arm before him. "'Tis surely a trap."

Haegan hesitated, glancing back to his friend. "No," he said. "Drr—"

But the blue eyes came to him. Forlorn. Apologetic. And then a wave of fury. With flared nostrils, Drracien stalked toward the tear crackling the air.

"No," Haegan grunted, as Poired's beast stalked into the chasm.

Expression strange, Drracien turned. Faced Haegan full on. Lifted a closed fist.

"Wielding!"

Drracien pressed it to his shoulder and inclined his head. A salute. "Mercy."

"No!" Haegan lunged forward, disbelieving as Drracien vanished with the Dark One. The truth collapsed in on him, proving what he had begun to suspect. What the Tahscan had warned. What he did not want to accept, even now. Drracien's endless questions were not merely inquisitiveness or caring. His sudden appearance no accident. Drracien had been sent. As Poired's spy.

Traitor.

28

Being betrayed had a certain look to it. And it was all over Haegan's face as he sat in the command tent. Shock. Grief. The way he ignored the angry conversations over what happened and what they'd do to Drracien when he appeared next.

Tili grew concerned for the Fierian. While he had no love for the smart-mouthed accelerant, he knew the boy to have been a friend to Haegan. Betrayal was not easily accepted, and 'twas much harder forgiven when delivered at the hands of a friend.

Outside, smoke filled the air as Pathfinders burned the dead. Wounded were queued for the pharmakeia and Drigo healer to patch up. Since Poired left, the Fire King had been strangely silent. At one time, Tili might have thought it a mercy. Now, he feared the silence. Naught but trouble would come from it.

Within the tent, Haegan refused anyone but Tili, Tokar, and Praegur. His friends. He only wanted his friends. Tili wondered that Haegan had not mentioned the assassin, though she'd slipped in as well. Somehow, he'd considered her a friend, though she had been responsible for delivering him to the Infantessa. There was an alliance, Tili supposed, that grew from enduring the wiles of the wicked.

How it must pain Astadia to see Haegan here, when her brother had not survived the Infantessa. Mayhap fighting for the Fierian was the outlet she needed for her grief before it destroyed her from the inside.

Strange that he understood her so well. An assassin. Even worse that he spent so much time thinking on her. Tili stood, unwilling to sit, lest he find his brain soggier than his tunic from the cut on his neck.

"He betrayed me," Haegan finally muttered, as if Tili moving roused his brain from slumber. He ran a hand over his head, apparently still not used to the stubble there. "How can he be working with Poired? How can he be his son?" Gripping his skull, he closed his eyes. "We were friends! I trusted him—called him a brother. He was trained at the Citadel!"

"Aye," Tokar said. "And he killed his mentor and master—he is still wanted for that murder."

There were no answers to assuage his brokenness, nor Tili's failure in not giving more credence to the Tahscan's complaint. It did, however, cement Tili's trust in the Tahscans. He would not question them again when they brought a concern.

"That Tahscan knew," Tokar said, holding a mug of warmed cordi between his hands. He pushed his gaze to Tili. "Pretty amazing."

"He warned me several times during the encounter that Poired worked my fears against me." Haegan frowned, his eyes darting back and forth. "I don't understand. How can they smell it?"

With a sigh, Tili shrugged. "They call it a curse, yet 'twas Abiassa's Deliverer, Draorin, who gifted them not three months past. The mark they bear came with a price. Vaqar and his band were exiled, their families murdered for their refusal to obey the queen, who was under the influence of the Infantessa. Vaqar said they welcomed the exile, came west searching to rout the true source of the stench. I think he seeks to destroy Poired as much as ye."

Haegan considered the story. "Perhaps *he* is the one to kill the Dark One."

"What?"

"The Deliverers won't let me kill him," Haegan said with a huff as he resumed his seat. "I tried at Fieri Keep and they twisted my hand. I lunged again this time, and they shackled me to my spot and quelled my wielding, said 'twas not for me to do."

Tili's head throbbed. He stretched his neck—and felt a bead of blood slide down his neck. He cringed, knowing it needed stitching.

"But still!" Haegan again punched to his feet, restless. And angry, most likely. "Drracien walked right through there. How did he do that? How . . . ?"

There were no answers. "Ye will drive yerself mad with those questions.

Just accept it. Realize he is as much our enemy as Poired." Should Tili drop root in Haegan's drink as Negaer had done to him weeks past?

"Nay!" Haegan growled. "I will accept that only when I accept each of you is an enemy."

"We haven't sided with Poired," Tokar objected.

Laerian heaved a sigh. "Drracien's heart is dark because he is borne of it—Poired said he was his son!"

"Aye," Praegur said. "He is not our concern, though. We must pursue Abiassa's will."

The room bounced violently and tilted. First to Tili's left. Then right. Slowly blurring in the middle. Tensing, Tili jerked his gaze down, rubbing his forehead. Air. He needed air.

"Tili, after we break our fast on the morrow, how many rises until we reach Ironhall?"

Focus, Tili. Ironhall. They were . . . where? West. No, north of . . . Dorcastle. That was it. "We should reach it by nightfall."

"Good." Haegan nodded. "We need shelter. We need to stop moving. Regroup. Get our feet under us."

Tili couldn't agree more, especially when his knee buckled.

Eyes turned to him, surprised.

"If ye'll excuse me," he nodded—a move that sent his head reeling. Though he stumbled out of the tent, he righted himself. Took a long draught of air, and nearly choked. In his hazy mind, he'd expected the cool, crisp air of a Ybiennese evening. Instead, he got the acrid stench and smoke of burning bodies and the hot air of the east.

"You are a fool," came a chiding voice.

Tili glanced to the side, cursing how much he enjoyed the sight of the slight frame that slipped up alongside him. "Ye would not be the first female to call me that."

Astadia arched her eyebrow. "Then maybe you need to start listening to us."

"Someday," he muttered and turned—his legs tangling.

She circled an arm around his waist, and he tensed, unused to being handled. "Say naught or I'll punch you," she warned as she draped his arm over her neck for leverage.

He looked down at her. "Ye're short."

"Aye, but fast. Now shut up and walk, you oaf." She urged him to the right.

His mind twisted again as her soft curves pressed against his side. She was not supposed to be soft. She was a hard assassin.

Nay, this was too . . . intimate. "Leave me," he said. "My tent is"—he nearly tripped trying to point toward his tent.

"You need the pharmakeia." She pushed him into the makeshift infirmary.

Shame rushed him. "Nay." Never had he visited the infirmary. Ever. "Others have more serious injuries. Tend them. I'm well."

"Right. 'Tis normal to walk like a drunk when you've had no cordi."

As they staggered into the tent, Tili tightened against the humiliation . . . until he saw that it was partitioned and this section empty, save a wounded, unconscious Pathfinder, whose head and shoulder were bandaged.

Astadia aimed him at a folding chair beside a nearby cot.

The relief of sitting proved immense. And almost immediately his head cleared. He dragged in a long breath and slowly released it. Something cold nudged his hand.

"Drink," Astadia ordered, tucking her long brown hair back, which exposed her neck and the first button of her tunic that was undone, which led—

The cup. Pay attention to the cup. He tilted it so he could see the murky contents. "What is it?"

"Poison. Extra heavy dose. Just for you." She dragged a tray toward them, scrubbed her hands in a bowl near the entrance. When she returned, Astadia bent before him and reached for the cloth around his neck.

His gut cinched when her cold fingers brushed his throat. He stilled, all too aware of the darts of heat that shot through his gut at her touch. When he spied the silver tools laid out, he scowled. "What're ye—"

"Finishing what the Silver started," she groused, unraveling the cloth with but a small dose of gentleness. "Now shut up." She eyed his injury, her gold-flecked irises assessing, wincing. Then she tossed the bloody cloth aside and lifted a bottle. After pouring its contents into a bowl, she grabbed a wad of clean cloth and bent toward him.

"Nay!" Tili caught her hand, leery. "Ye know what ye're doing?"

"Killing fools is my specialty." When he did not leave off his suspicions, she sighed, her gaze relenting. "Aye, I know what I'm doing."

"Ye're an assassin. Ye put cuts in people, ye don't stitch them. Just give me a hot blade—"

"That will mar your neck worse than it already is."

"'Twill be quick and efficient."

Astadia huffed. Tossed down her supplies. Glowering, she removed her belt and let it drop to the ground.

When she reached for the hem of her tunic, Tili surged to his feet. "Whoa!" Would she undress? To what end? He held a hand toward her. "Wh-what are ye doing?" The roar of his pulse made it difficult to hear.

Ye aren't that dull-witted, Thurig as'Tili.

"Look." She rolled her eyes and lifted her tunic, angling her stomach and hip toward him. "I stitched that myself. Trale was unconscious, and I was bleeding out."

Hesitation held him in place. He did not trust himself to look, but when he did, more than appreciation for her stitching rose through him. Seeing her hip bared, the skin smooth—save the crescent scar that grabbed the torchlight, amplifying the discolored flesh that ran across her abdomen and raced toward her hip bone. All very tidily stitched. He had not seen so fine a work in Nivar.

He traced it with his thumb.

Her stomach contracted beneath his touch, and he heard the quick intake of breath.

Tili drew back his fingers, both amused and chastising his stupidity for touching her. Yet a dart of surprise and attraction pushed his gaze to hers. Those green eyes were molten. Sultry. His thoughts careened from touch to reaction and back, eliciting a swell of desire.

Cheeks stained—embarrassment or attraction, mayhap both?—Astadia shoved down her tunic. "You pleased now?" At her ill-spoken words, she shot a look at him, her gaze indignant and brightened by the flush. "I—is that proof enough that I can do this?"

What was she like, when she did not kill or maim? When she did not feel the need to throw daggers, with her hands or her eyes? He wanted to see that side of her.

Her lips parted.

An ache wormed through Tili to know what this girl—for she could be no more than twenty cycles—tasted of. There was more of her he wanted to touch, which he shouldn't want. But he did. And it frustrated him. He knew not what she'd been through. Nor would he take advantage of her or sully his father's name or his own.

Bouncing his gaze between those wide eyes and her lips, Tili somehow managed to reseat himself, closing his mind to the way her belly had rolled at his touch. Contracted. Involuntary.

From his chair, he recalled how her throat processed the swallow that allowed her to resume her work. Gentle, more hesitant this time, she worked. Her fingers braced his head and adjusted the angle as she leaned in.

'Twas maddening the way she worked, her tongue caught between those pink lips. Her breath skating along his neck. Along his jaw as she stitched. Every once in a while, she'd crane closer, her breath a whisper along his cheek, driving him blazing mad. Loose strands of her hair brushed his chin, teasing him like that flash of flesh.

Tili fisted his hand, forcing his mind to better places.

Like death.

There were dead Pathfinders. Dead Silvers. Who'd cut him. And he needed her tender—*tending*.

She let out a huff, her breath tracing his neck and snaking down his shirt. He clenched his eyes. Opened and closed his fist. Open. Close. But it played, over and over in his head—touching her. Skin and muscle contracting.

Somehow, his gaze found her lips. Watched them. Though she lived on the land, her lips were not parched or cracked. They looked soft. And he would know the feel of them. Even as that thought slid through his mind and will, a shadow moved behind her.

Tensed, Tili realized it was the Tahscan whose scimitar throw had saved him in the battle. "Thank ye," he called, grateful—desperate—for the distraction.

The Tahscan stopped and stepped back into sight, frowning.

"For saving me. Earlier," Tili explained, pointing to the wound.

The man screwed up his brow and shook his head.

"When ye threw yer scimitar into the Silver's chest."

The gnarled, thick brow pushed into the man's eyes now. He pointed to Astadia. "Thank her."

Right. She was stitching him. "Aye, but ye—"

"She grabbed the bloody weapon out of my hand and threw it." He held up a meaty paw. "Never seen anything like it. The power that drove it—she might be a small thing, but she knows how to handle a blade."

Tili slid his gaze to Astadia.

Annoyance played through her pretty features. "Keep still or I'll drive this needle through your neck and bleed you." She gripped his chin and turned it back to the tent opening. "Last stitch." A moment later, she snipped the thread. Wrapped a clean cloth around his neck.

"Ye? Ye did that?"

"What? You think only men can?"

"Nay." He blinked. "I . . . 'Twas a Tahscan blade. I assumed—"

"Mm," she said, her breath teasing his neck again. "You did."

"I thank ye." Somehow, Tili's hand found her waist. His pulse roared at her response, the way she stilled, that belly muscle doing its dance again. The way her lips parted. The way her eyes drifted to his.

Tili rose, catching her other side and pulling her close. Surprise flicked through him again at her small stature, the top of her head barely reaching his chin. But there was more surprise that she wasn't pressing a blade to his throat as he took hold of her.

Dark brown hair framed her round face. Her lips were pink like the blush that filled her cheeks and played thief with his mind, his willpower.

Father would not approve. Tili wasn't even sure *he* approved. He cared not. She was beautiful. Amazing. So soft beneath his touch. Tili angled down for the kiss.

She curled into him

Blazes! Don't do it. Cross this line, there's no going back.

To temper the thunder of his pulse, he brushed back a strand caught on her lip. But the roar increased, especially when he traced her jaw and she shuddered and turned into his touch. Eyes closing. Then coming to his, their sultry message clear. She was ready. Willing. Very willing.

Just because ye can, doesn't mean ye should.

The voice of reason, his father, was right. Kissing her, taking this innocence—was there an ounce of innocence in this girl?—made him no different than any other man in the camp. He would not do that. He would be set apart. Hoist himself above the fray.

Tili lifted his head. Nudged her back. "Mercy," he tried, but it came out a croak. When he saw the surprise, the hurt, the embarrassment that flashed through her, he pushed himself past her, forcing himself to break free of the headiness before it was too late. Before he caved. "Thank ye for the ministra—"

Thunk! Something smacked the back of his head.

Tili spun, feeling the raw tug of the stitches along his throat. Feeling the coldness in the hot air, caused by the loss of her nearness. Holding the back of his head, he scowled at her. "What—"

"*What* is wrong with you?" Hands on those hips he'd held just a second ago, Astadia glowered. Her face was flushed, but no longer with attraction. With anger. Indignation.

"Naught, I—"

"Then is it me?" Her voice pitched, hurt playing along the piqued tones. "Am I not good enough for you?"

"*What?*" Tili scowled, hating the way her eyes seeped with anguish. "How could—"

"That's twice you stole that kiss from me."

Tili's eyes widened, stunned. It wasn't right for a woman to pursue him. He didn't want that. It'd been the way of life all these years. He didn't need another simpering . . .

She was not simpering. She was . . . *demanding*.

A new twist, that.

"Are you afraid of a woman? Of me?"

"Afraid—" Cocking his head, Tili bit off the phrase. "I'm afraid of nothing, save doing wrong by ye."

"Doing wrong?" Her expression, taut with surprise and hesitation, stood guard over her wounded heart. "How?"

"We are at war, Astadia." He motioned to the tent beyond, the chaos that had nearly decimated their numbers. "I have no idea if I will live to see the next rise, and if we do manage to survive this, what will be left of the kingdom I'm to rule."

"Rule?" She frowned, then lifted a hand. "Haegan is the prince."

"Of Seultrie, aye. I am—" Tili jerked straight, realization thudding against his supposition that she knew his identity. "Ye don't know."

She shifted, clearly uncomfortable that he had a point she didn't grasp. "What?"

Tili swallowed, her attraction to him taking on a new light. A new . . . newness. No female had come after him without wanting his crown—as well as one of her own—and the power that would be his as king. This sprig of a girl, fierce with a blade and lightning-fast, made no pretense of her attraction and yet had no awareness of whom she pursued.

Which made it all the more important that he refrain from indulgence. From compromising his integrity or hers. "Astadia, my father is Thurig, King of Ybienn and the Northlands. I am heir to the throne—if there is one left when I return."

Wide eyes bulged. Suddenly, she scoffed. "Then that's it." A shrug-nod-shake. "I'm *not* good enough. Because you're a . . . prince?"

"Blazes! Yer position has naught to do with my restraint." His head wobbled again. Blast, he was tired. "I care not—" The world tilted. Tili steadied himself by gripping the back of the chair, his vision swimming as he then moved to the tent post. *"Hiel-touck!"* He cursed his weakness. His inability to convey his thoughts plainly to her.

"Sit." Her word was tight as she pointed back to a chair. "Yer head is still thick from the blood loss."

Trust himself to stay so close to her still? "Nay, I go . . ." He held the post, bracing and mustering the courage to walk out. Find his own tent. Get a good night's rest. He clenched his eyes and pinched the bridge of his nose, willing the dizzies to flee.

The air shifted beneath him, swirling, sweet. He opened them to find its source, and discovered Astadia's wide, warm eyes glowing inches from his. She had ducked under his arm, her spine to the post he still gripped, and eased close. Very close. Strangely innocent despite her profession.

Aye, that would go over well with Father, bringing home an assassin as my intended. And yet, there was so much that drew him to this assassin like a sparker to the Flames. "Astadia . . ."

Touching his beard, she rose on tiptoes, gaze dipping to his mouth, and pressed her lips to his. Soft. Gentle. Inviting. Warm. Teasing.

Tili groaned at her plying, knowing he should step away.

He inched closer.

Shouldn't touch her.

Somehow, his hand came to her hip again. This time, when she drew back a fraction, desperation coiled through him. He tightened his hold, unwilling to lose this or her. Unwilling to listen to his good mind telling him to step off. A glimmer of a smile washed through her face before she angled in. Kissed him again, this time firmer, longer. More confidently.

Willpower collapsing, Tili returned the kiss. Slipped his hand around her waist and pulled her against himself. He dove headlong into what he'd resisted. Her arms slunk around his waist and reached up his back.

With a groan, Tili hooked an arm over her shoulder and crushed her into his hold. He deepened the kiss, alive with passion and urgency. Surprised by her willingness and softness. Her curves. Soft moans that rippled through her.

A fiery pain shot through his neck—her fingers catching on the stitches. Tili grunted and jerked back.

"Mercy, mercy," she said, her breath coming in heaves. "Please—"

Holding his neck, the fire excruciating, he let out a ragged breath. Shook his head and swallowed. "Blazes, girl."

She aimed again for another kiss, apparently as hungry as he was for what erupted between them. So sweet, so taunting was her kiss.

"Oy," Tili said, veering her back, cupping her face and tracing his thumb along her jaw.

A frown tightened her features. "What?"

"Enough," Tili said, still trying regulate his breathing and yet seeing the hurt in her gaze.

"You do not want me?"

"Oh, naught could be more a lie." And somehow, his lips were on hers again. Her face cradled in his hand, the other twisting into her hair and bracing the back of her head, holding her close. The kiss was instantly deep and passionate. He kissed a line along her jaw, relishing the moans that rumbled against his lips, fueling his passion. Knowing it would take little to cross the line. Knowing he wanted to.

With a growl, he buried his face in her neck. "Nay nay nay," he breathed hard. "This cannot be."

"Steward?"

Tili flinched and drew straight. Glanced over his shoulder to where Tokar stood, the young man's knowing gaze holding him hostage. Annoyance cloyed at Tili—both that he'd given in to his desires and that Tokar had discovered them. "Aye?" he snapped, refusing to step away from or release Astadia, to make himself look guilty.

Yet in that instant, he saw the truth of this situation. He was a prince, tethered to the throne of Nivar, to leadership of a country and people. And she . . . she was an assassin. A killer. Death in the shadows. No loyalty except to the blade.

She would never be accepted by the people. By his father. And therefore, no union would exist between them. 'Twas one thing to pursue someone not of noble blood, but to pursue someone covered in the blood of—the Lady only knew how many . . .

Folly. 'Twas naught but folly.

He angled more toward Tokar. *"What?!"*

Tokar slid a look—disapproving and disappointed—between them again, before he shifted away and threw over his shoulder. "The Fierian would see you."

Tili ran a hand through his hair and sighed. Turned back to Astadia—but instead found an empty tent. Light glared then snapped shut as the side slat closed.

"Hiel-touck," he muttered with a heavy exhale, swiping a hand over his mouth and face. He knew better. Knew better than to turn his attention to the fairer sex. Trouble. It was always trouble.

29

Strange how the air felt cooler with his hair gone. Haegan ran his hand over his shorn head and smiled, remembering the gaping expressions from the Pathfinders. From Tokar and Praegur. It had been oddly liberating.

His smile faded as the tormented murmurs from the healer's wagon broke out afresh. The plaintive cries made Haegan tilt his head to see past the canopy shielding the Drigo and his father. There had been no progress, no healing. Only moans and wails. Murmurings. Agonized.

Agonizing for not just his father, but for Haegan and those gathered. Those who had served and fought with the mighty Fire King. The mightiest in generations.

Haegan climbed into the wagon and knelt at the cot where his father twisted and twitched, brow bathed in sweat. He swallowed hard at the ragged appearance—even with a shave and sponge bath. "Father."

His father stilled, wild vacant eyes searching the air. What world he saw, Haegan knew not, but 'twasn't the one in which they stood.

"Father, 'tis me, Haegan—I'm here." He placed his hand over knobby fingers.

For a blink, his father remained still. "Not real," he whispered.

"Aye, real. I *am* real, my father-king." He squeezed his hand and edged closer. "I'm here. Haegan—your son. I'm here."

Frantic shakes of his father's head tossed wavy blond hair. "Nay." He groaned. "Nay, not real. Haegan . . ."

"Aye, Fa—"

"Haegan's in the tower. Can't walk." Grief churned through the sunken cheeks. "My fault. Should've . . . stopped."

"Father, I'm here. I was healed, remember? Abiassa chose me. I'm the Fierian."

A blood-curdling scream wrenched his father's spine upward. Contorted his face in rage and agony.

Startled, Haegan pitched backward. Stumbled. Felt himself falling.

A viselike grip clamped his wrist. Yanked him forward.

Haegan stared into the hooded eyes of the Drigo, his mind rattled and ears scorched from his father's wails, still shrieking through the day.

The Drigo nodded to Haegan, as if to be sure he was steady, then released and moved to his father. Administered medications, balms. The screams quieted but little before Haegan pushed out of the wagon. Landed with a thud, his heart pounding. When he looked up, he found several people staring. Apologetic. Sympathizing.

He shoved himself around, right into the broad chest of the Tahscan. "I beg your mercy—"

"You saved him, Fierian."

Haegan snorted at the Tahscan commander. "I'm not sure what I saved, but 'tis not my father."

"Give not the victory to the Desecrator."

"For my father, the work is done. He is lost to madness." Haegan ground his teeth, remembering well what it was like to be drowning in inflamed doubts and fears. "He was held too long, inflamed too . . . pervasively."

"You saved him. Freed him from—"

"*Freed* him?" Incredulous, Haegan shouted at the man, "Do you hear that?" He stabbed a hand toward the wagon. "Does *that* sound like freedom?"

"It sounds like pain," Praegur said, joining them.

"Aye." The Tahscan stayed calm, confident. "Freedom is never pain-less, Fierian."

Haegan sniffed and shook his head. Turned.

"Maybe you should have left him there, then?"

Stilled, Haegan closed his eyes. Told himself not to respond. Not to blast this warrior out of existence. Yet the words defied his will and escaped, "Left him there."

"You said he's not free. If you had left him, he would have died. Is that freedom of which you approve?"

Haegan swung around, a blue halo rushing out.

Vaqar smiled and lifted his chin. "Your anger is also born of pain, Fierian. The pain of seeing one you love hurting." He inclined his head. "He will heal. Perhaps not in total, but it will take awhile for the poison of her words to fade. While we wait, we fight—for those we love. We fight the Desecrator. We fight our frustration. Our weariness."

The words sunk in like a warm balm to his wounded soul. Haegan hesitated, lowering his wielding hand. Realized this warrior had probably lost someone he loved. "Was it a woman?"

Small and faint, a smile rose then fell through his earthy features. "They all were."

"All?"

"Sisters, friends, aunts."

"Why did you leave them?"

"They rest in Primar's embrace."

"They're dead."

Again, Vaqar inclined his head. "At the queen's hand. She punished them because of me, because I refused to bow to her will or the Infantessa's."

"I . . . I did not know."

We fight—for those we love.

Love.

Thiel.

He must find a remedy. Before it was too late. Before . . . Was it too late for her? Had Cadeif ravished her? If so, 'twould be the last thing he did.

• • •

Anger wove a thick cord through Thiel as they pressed across the Nine, now heading east, away from Ybienn, at least. But toward what? Haegan?

There had to be a way to escape, to warn whoever lay ahead.

Yet, if she did—where would she go? They were too far south for her to reach Nivar before being stopped. And she had no friends east of the Throne Road, despite travelling it more than once.

They'd been riding for days, her mount tied between the twins' as they followed their archon across the blackened terrain. Thiel would give no complaint. She would sit—endure the beating sun and the icy silence of the Ematahri. Though she had lived off the land for years, it had been awhile since she'd ridden so hard and long. Her legs and thighs were raw proof of just how long, worse because, with her broken ankle, she had not even the slight reprieve of stirrups. However, she would not complain about that either. Nothing to draw Cadeif's attention and anger.

Her gaze rose to the skies, searching for Chima. Many times she ached to call for her, to whisper into the wind her anger that Chima had obeyed Haegan's call and flown away. It was right. Chima bonded to Haegan. It was her job to protect him. And he had a greater purpose, and he was busy, so he wouldn't come for her either. He had a Desecrator to stop. Besides, he would not want her once he knew what Cadeif had stolen.

Me? What purpose have I? To what end did she now exist? She had no gift. No purpose. Frustration writhed through her. *What is the use of me?*

"Etelide."

At her Ematahri name, Thiel looked to where Ruldan glowered from the ground, holding out the wooden crutch she kept tied to her saddle during their ride. Impatiently, he waved her off the horse. Irritation skittered through her. She'd need help to dismount. The thought grated. With care, she caught the horse's mane and slid over the side, releasing herself at the last moment. Landed hard. She braced for a second, gritting through the jarring pain. Commotion swirled as the others swept into motion, setting up camp for the night.

Ruldan pulled her through the activity and straight toward a tent that snapped into order before them. Cadeif bent through the opening, sun glinting off his broad, bare back.

Sirdarians, Silvers, and the warriors leered as she was tugged onward like chattel. Ruldan shoved her inside. Darkness blinded her for a second, her foot catching on something and pitching her forward. Hands caught her shoulders. She came up, staring into Cadeif's dark eyes.

Momentary relief pulsed into anger. She wrenched out of his grasp. "Release me!"

"Etelide—"

"No," she heaved around a breath. "Ye have no right to use that name now."

He scowled. And mercy, he looked a fright. "I am archon!"

"Aye." Nerves squirming, she refused to show him weakness. "And a beast as well."

Rage turned his face deep red. "How can you say this of me?"

"Ye did to me the very thing the beast who sent me running into the desert all those years ago did—rape me!" Her voice broke. The tears broke.

Cadeif started. "Etelide." His gaze slipped over her shoulder. And in a split-second a hand flew. Struck her face.

Thiel fell, twisting over something. Landed hard. Her head struck a post. Her ankle screamed and pain scored her temple, plucking a cry from her. Vision blurry, she shook her head. It cleared. The skin over the spot tightened beneath a growing knot.

"Put her in the cage," someone growled.

Hands pulled Thiel to her feet, dragging her away. She glanced back to Cadeif, who was turning to talk with the Sirdarian general. There was something in his expression she could not read.

And she didn't care. It was time to leave. To escape. Somehow. She'd get back to Haegan, even if she had to swim the Lakes of Fire.

● ● ●

Agony pulsed through Kaelyria's veins, surging and roiling. Painful and yet—a release. She stood on the bridge of Fieri Keep, despite its ruination. Chunks were missing. The little that remained canted and rumbled beneath the storm in the skies overhead. She wore a pale blue dress, as she had before the attack on the keep. Before Poired destroyed her family. And a circlet weighted her long blonde hair, which danced beneath the cool breeze swirling around the Keep.

Cool? Never was there such a thing in Seultrie. Not with the Lakes of Fire. She turned to the near distance, to the molten pools. And gasped. Instead of hot embers and lava creeping from Mount Fieri, there streamed a glistening, frothy wake beneath a waterfall.

Where am I?

'Twas not Fieri Keep.

Vibrations tickled the bottoms of her slippered feet. She glanced aside and found a great drawbridge lowering. Slowly, the double-hung doors of the keep came into view. Instead of the Celahar emblem scorched into the wood, there blazed three interlocked triangles.

Definitely not Fieri Keep.

Groaning doors opened. Darkness shrouded all beyond. Slowly, sunlight caught the legs of someone coming into view. Then another pair of legs. And then the hem of a green organza gown.

Kaelyria held her breath as the three emerged from the darkness. "Haegan," she whispered, her gaze resting on her brother. He was much changed. In earnest, naught remained of the boy who'd spent all those years in the tower. This version stood strong, confident. Handsome and fierce. The woman at his side—auburn hair hanging in thick coils around her neck and down her spine, frame slight but sturdy, face rosy and filled with adoration for Haegan—held a small boy, whose mop of dark curls were a contrast to Haegan's golden hair. And even to the woman's.

Beside them appeared a man leaning heavily on a cane. His weathered face spoke of lifetimes of pain. Regret and defeat hung heavily on his shoulders—as if the twisting crown of flames atop his head pushed him down.

The Fire King.

Father!

Kaelyria threw herself down the hill toward them. But her journey persisted. Distance stretched on and on.

A red hue grew behind those gathered in the keep. Kae's heart staggered, breath trapped in her throat as the crimson glowed angrily, breathing into existence a creature, sliding closer and closer to the three.

A man rushed forward, ignorant of the flaming looming behind all.

Kae sucked in a hard breath. Then surged as his face came into view. "Aselan!" Elation warmed her.

But the distance was too great. They were distracted. Focused on each other. On the boy.

The creature was growing larger. More threatening. Breeding off their inattention.

"Haegan!" she shouted, but her words would not release. Her throat constricted. She tried again, yet it would not be birthed. Kae rushed forward.

Stones fell away beneath her feet. She slipped but caught herself and scrabbled backward. Again, she looked to the keep, where the group stood, oblivious to the threat. "Behind you! Haegan!"

Smiling, Aselan reached out. Took the child from the woman. Hefted the now-laughing boy into the air. Their faces were mirrored with delight. With laughter. Idyllic. Beautiful. A sight that enraptured her. Her attention snagged as realization washed over her: father and son. Aselan was the boy's father. That meant the boy was—

Mine!

At that instant, the creature lunged. Fire erupted as razor-sharp teeth clamped down over them. Haegan. Thiel. Her bound. Her son. Vanished. Devoured.

"Noooo!" Kaelyria jolted up, blinking rapidly in the dim light of the tent. Sweat plastered her clothes to her chest and arms. Bracing herself, she panted against the terror of the nightmare. Her arms trembled as the images came in crashing waves over her, again and again. Seeing them die. Burned alive.

She collapsed with a sob, grief pouring through her body.

"I tried to warn you," came the surly voice of Cilicien. "But you always were willful. Perhaps you understand now."

Kae shuddered through another sob. Recognized the acrid taste. Released the anguish of what she'd seen. And yet . . . couldn't. 'Twas too palpable. Too horrible. "You . . . *you* put those thoughts in my mind."

"I cannot put thoughts there. No accelerant can," Cilicien said as he circled the cage holding her. "We only inflame what is already there. Tease your doubts, fan your fears."

"The child." She shouldn't have mentioned him. Shouldn't have allowed herself to think of him.

Irritation scratched at his slick features. "The thought of that child was in your head already." He squinted at her. "Are you with child?"

Kae hesitated, then shook her head.

"Huh," Cilicien said, angling his head from one side to the other. "Your cycle then?"

Kaelyria glowered. As if she would speak of such things with the cur.

He smirked. "Indelicate, but necessary. I am surprised you aren't already sure." He rippled his fingers, an orange flame dancing over them as he pointed at her. "When I probed your thoughts, I sensed the child."

Kaelyria's heart skipped a beat. Her hand found her abdomen, mind reaching for the boy in the dream. A son? Was it true?

"It's disappointing, though no surprise, of course—what man in his right mind wouldn't take you to his bed?" His lecherous grin only wearied her. "But we will conceal it for now."

"Conceal it?" Confusion rattled her. Why did it matter? "What do you care if I carry his child?"

Scoffing, Cilicien pressed a hand to his chest. "Me? I give not two wits about your intimacy with that Eilidan chief." He tucked his hands behind his back and stood with his feet shoulder width apart. "However, when Poired's overturn of the kingdom is complete, I will need the daughter of the Fire King at my side to make the seizure of power legitimate." His eyes narrowed. A thought seemed to take root as he twisted his mouth and chewed the inside of his lip. He spun and stalked to the entrance of his tent. "Bring the pharmakeia!"

At his darkening expression, Kaelyria had no time to consider the wonder of carrying Aselan's child. Instead, deep dread washed over her shoulders and wrapped her throat. "What?" she asked, not sure she wanted to know. "What is your plan?"

He considered her again, silent and pensive, his gaze constantly bouncing to her belly.

Something about the way he studied her forced Kae to turn away, curl her back against the bars and to him. Protecting herself. Protecting—was it possible?—a babe. Could it be? Again, her palm went to her abdomen. She closed her eyes.

Is it true? Are you in there?

A subtle *thwap* of the tent flap came with a burst of light.

"My liege," came a gravelly voice. "How may I—"

"This woman—if she is pregnant, can you remove the child?"

30

The image would not leave his mind—Thiel with Cadeif.

It tormented him as much as the harm done his father. Unable to sleep, Haegan pried himself from the cot and moved into the balmy night. Stood beneath the waxy moons and lifted his face to their light. Willed it to burn away his memory of finding his father, of the moment Trale leapt into the blast meant for Haegan.

He deflated against the images, the stark reality of what happened. Grief and guilt weighted his limbs. He should've taken his father from the bridge, back at the Keep. Even when he believed him dead, he should have—

What? He could not have lifted both Kaelyria and Father. Or his mother. Had he the giants' strength, mayhap. But as one with a fledgling gift, it would have taken multiple trips. Poired would have blistered him into oblivion.

Had She not stopped him, he could have turned his anger, his vengeance against the Dark One. Why had She forbidden him? Why did She allow Thiel—

"Fierian." Though gentle and quiet, the voice exploded, awakening Haegan to the nearby shadow that was a man.

"Praegur."

A smile brightened his eyes. "Turn not your anger in the wrong direction, Haegan."

"You can say this after She has stolen your tongue?"

"What is given cannot be stolen."

Haegan frowned.

"Long ago, I gave my life for Her use. If She chooses to borrow my tongue to speak only Her truths, who am I to object?"

"But . . . why?" Haegan threw his hands up in emphasis. "Why has She done all this? She can send Her Guardians whenever She wills, yet She allowed this. Allowed my father to be tortured, my mother killed. Then She forbids me from killing Poired when She has made me Her Hand!" He hunched his shoulders, tightened by agony and grief. "Look at my father! *Why?*"

His friend watched, amusement in his eyes.

"You mock me. You think because I'm this"—he shook his head—"powerful Fierian, I should be grateful."

"Should you be grateful?"

Uncertain of his meaning—whether to mock or to chastise—Haegan cast him a furtive glance. He wanted neither instruction nor correction. The days had been hard enough without the burden of letting down yet another friend.

His gaze wandered the camp and came to the raqine nesting on the field. Soft moonlight caressed their overlarge bodies.

"Tell me of your father," Praegur said, dirt crunching quietly beneath his feet as he moved to stand shoulder to shoulder with Haegan. "Do you remember the moment you first saw him wield?"

'Twas a trap. Somehow, there would be a lesson here. Praegur had become as bad as Gwogh. And yet, his mind instantly conjured a memory. A smile pried at Haegan's unwilling mood. "I was little, no more than four or five, climbing the crags to see the Lakes of Fire." He swiped at his nose. "We weren't supposed to be there, but"—he snorted—"I never was much for the rules. My foot got stuck. When it went through, 'twas as if the rocks closed in, clenched tight against my ankle. I was trapped." Another shake of his head. He recalled all too well when he'd first seen the blond hair bouncing as his father climbed the ridge. Eyes that burned with admonishment and reprimand. "I expected him to discipline me, rail at me for being so foolish and disobedient."

"But he did not?"

"Nay, he did not," he said softly, remembering. "He knelt. Rustled my hair. Then smiled and looked down. His hands were glowing as he reached toward my trapped foot. Somehow . . . somehow, he freed it with the barest warmth. I was in awe." Haegan drew in a long breath. "I'm sure he'd wielded in front of me before then, but to see it, so perfectly controlled—to carve away stone and not cause injury to my leg . . . He was my hero." Swallowing, Haegan tried to reconcile that Zireli with the one who'd abandoned him. "We sat on the ledge until the sun was abed and the lakes glowed in the night." An ache tightened his throat. "He loved me . . . once."

"He has always loved you. As She has loved you." Praegur nodded. "In your story, when the king was able to free you, did you question Her gifts?"

Haegan frowned.

"When the gifts are to our benefit, we think naught of them and go on about our lives. When they interrupt our plans or take an unexpected route, we object. Because we understand not the purpose."

"Well put." Haegan nodded.

"Her gift is no less good now."

"'Tis less favorable."

"Perhaps inconvenient and uncomfortable—painful even—but the favor still remains." With a nod, Praegur wandered away, leaving Haegan to his thoughts, his grief.

Mumbling and groaning from the wagon battered his will. Would his father ever be free of the Infantessa's cruelty?

He rubbed his head, the stubble still a surprise, wondering what the Infantessa had done to him as well. Was there damage he hadn't yet detected? He didn't feel damaged.

Thiel. Lying beside that warrior.

Haegan stiffened. Nay, Thiel would not take to Cadeif's bed. She loved Haegan. Cadeif had been but a friend. Yet he would not put it past that savage to take what she refused. To conquer her. 'Twas their way, was it not?

Chortling and keening rippled on the warm night and drew him to the knoll where the raqine were resting. He stood, watching. They had not attacked Poired. Neither had the Deliverers.

They left it to me. Yet . . . stopped me.

"Never seen this before?"

Haegan flinched as Tili joined him. "Most of my friends haven't seen a raqine, let alone an entire herd." He recalled the nest in the Heart. A large number, yet he saw not Zicri or Pharen among these. Were there truly so many on Primar?

Hands tucked under his armpits, Tili jutted his jaw toward the beasts. "Convocation."

"What?"

"Like eagles, a group of raqine is called a convocation."

"Whatever 'tis called—never have I seen so many."

"Ye summoned them."

Haegan nodded his acknowledgement. The great beasts were sleeping, chortling their contentment.

Sleeping. Thiel. In Cadeif's bed. "During the battle, I saw a vision—something. Thiel." He eyed Chima, curled against a dark blue raqine.

"And it worries ye?"

"Aye." Haegan shifted. "I fear 'tis real, because all the weeks in Karithia, I heard my father calling me, even when I thought him dead. In my dreams, I saw him. Heard him when I was in the shower. That was real. Yet . . ." He rubbed the back of his neck. "I know not what is real and what is—"

"This vision during the battle, did it break yer concentration?"

"Aye."

"There's yer answer." Tili shrugged. "'Tis widely known yer feelings for my sister. They used her against ye." His eyebrow arched. "Won't be the last time, if ye let it work."

"But she was with Cadeif."

Tili flinched. "I am not one to play guessing games, Thinblood. Nor should ye at this point. War is upon us, and the enemy is high powerful, as ye've seen for yerself. Mayhap we should thank the Lady that Thiel is not here."

"How can you say that?" Haegan gaped. "She's your sister! Have you no care for her safety or—"

"Careful," Tili growled, his hands falling to his sides, as if readying for a sword hilt. "Ye know not my mind nor my concerns."

"She's your own blood, and you shrug off a threat against her. Would ye do the same were it Astadia?"

Tili jerked. "What has she to do with anything?"

"You were seen kissing her."

"Blazes," Tili hissed. Then he shook his head, lifting a palm. "The threat—that is where yer focus must be."

"Why?"

"Because!" Tili closed his eyes and lowered his chin, hand fisting. "The vision with Thiel, as I said"—his words were tight, controlled, edged in steel—"may not be real. May have been planted in yer mind. If it is a legitimate concern, Thiel is strong and smart. She needed not yer anger, nor yer lopsided wielding to protect her the years she journeyed to find herself. Give her credit. Trust her." He nodded to the field. "Train yer mind, Fierian, on the true battle—the one before ye, smiting the Dark One. Until ye can deliver us from this wickedness."

"The danger is real if she was with him. And it didn't look . . . contrived."

"And ye know the difference between contrived and real thoughts? Is that why ye so quickly escaped the Infantessa?" Tili used sarcasm the way some used a blade. Cut right to the heart of the matter. "We, all of us, are in danger, Fierian." He huffed. "But Thiel would not give herself to that savage willingly."

"Exactly!"

"Ye suggest he would ravish her."

"Aye!"

Tili scratched his jaw, then planted his hands on his hips. There had been a day not too far gone when he had towered over Haegan and seemed twice as big and strong. Now, they stood on even planes in height and breadth. Tili's cheek twitched as he stared at the convocation. "Though it pains me to say, ye cannot go after her."

The itch to send Chima was real, but Haegan knew raqine were not to be ordered about like beasts of burden.

"I know yer thoughts, Thinblood."

Haegan stilled at the words. "Everyone seems to know my thoughts but me." He huffed. "How is it I can summon giants and raqine and even battle Poired—"

"And fail."

"—but I cannot save the woman I love?"

"Love, is it?" Tili balked.

"I go," came a voice like thunder and rain.

Haegan shifted, finding a large shadow blotting out the campfires. He stepped back to look up into the timeless, somber face of a Drigo. Not in his vudd state, he was different, but the eyes, the tenor of his voice remained true. "Thelikor." His heart skipped a couple of beats—one for the sight of the overgrown man, one for the thought of sending help to Thiel. "I could not ask it of you."

A trilling breath rushed over Haegan's face. "Fierian not ask. I say go." He gave a hefty nod as if it were done.

"We need the Drigo," Tili argued, but not too ardently.

"The danger is great if you leave us and if you are alone in the scorched lands. If—"

A growl silenced his words. And the shadowed darkness around them grew. Or was the Drigo growing?

"I'm not sure I'd keep arguing," Tili said and started back to his tent. "Unless ye like sipping yer meals through a straw."

Aye, Thelikor was growing. As if need alone fueled. *Nay, the Fierian's will.* Should he release the giant? Allow him to find Thiel? A new grief tugged at Haegan. "I know not where she is."

"I go." Thelikor's chest rattled—a sigh, it seemed. He then pushed to his full height and started walking south.

Just like that. Haegan marveled that the Drigo made a decision and set out immediately to put it into action. But he had the power of Abiassa and superhuman strength to succeed.

I have both Abiassa's power and other-than-human giftings. Why then do I keep failing?

• • •

Coarse and thick, something dragged across his face. He could feel it through the layers of the mask.

Mask?

As consciousness struggled through his body, Aselan attempted to open his eyes. The pressure to his face persisted. He blinked. Blinding light stabbed his eyes. He groaned and fought to lift his head. *Where am I?*

A blast of hot, steamy breath washed over his nose.

Through narrow slits he peered out, blinking rapidly against the accursed brightness. As he pushed up, pain tore through him all at once. He collapsed, feeling the cold sting of the snow he lay upon. Panic rushed through him. *Why am I here?*

Something tugged at his shoulder with a growl. Duamauri. The shearing of fabric reached his ears. Another growl as powerful jaws pinched for hold once more. Aselan tensed, knowing he should feel pain but there was none.

Awareness flared as a furry white snout nudged his cheek. Sikir. The other pulled him onto his back. The move was torture, his limbs numb. Red stained the snow around him.

The hounds. His icehounds were here. Why were they not with—

"Kae!" Aselan surged, but fiery shards sliced his limbs. "Augh!" He threw himself back, only then feeling the strange, swollen weight of a broken arm. Cradling it did naught but stoke more pain. He hooked his hand to his shoulder, which provided a mediocre measure of relief. But what was that compared to the rampant pain searing his heart?

Sikir drew close again, her breath hot. She swiped at his face. Though he felt only pressure, he knew she licked him. With a trembling hand and great effort, he reached for her. Weakness, frostbite, wounds refused his attempt to find his feet. Nay, even to lift himself to a sitting position.

I must. I must find Kaelyria.

He strained forward, only to have the edges of his vision ghost. He dropped back, snow padding his fall.

Jagged pain exploded through his ankle. He felt warmth. But he should feel naught. He glanced down the length of his body and saw Duamauri take hold of his leg. It was not an attack. His hounds were doing what they knew to do—protecting him. He was one of their pack. But when his hound gave the first tug, a rush of black, violent and torturous, crashed over him.

• • •

Drip. Drip. Splat! Drip.

Clawing free, Aselan caught a tentative grip on consciousness. It'd winked in and out as Duamauri hauled him across the Tooth. Darkness, a greedy master, seized his vision and held it hostage. Surprising warmth cradled him in a soggy embrace. Something spat in his face. He flinched away, pulling himself erect. But pain coiled through his body, tensing like a viper ready to strike, and he slumped once more to the ground.

Panting came from his left and right, and only then did Aselan realized his hounds had packed him between their warmth. Relief and gratefulness coddled him. How long had he lay unconscious? Hours? Days?

Ye have to get up.

With a groan, he angled to the side, propping himself. Darkness still reigned. Aselan planted his gloved hands and hauled his aching body upright. Only as he took his full weight did he remember his injured arm. "Augh!" He dropped again to the frozen earth.

Hissing, he drew his hands close. Winter had bitten him cruelly. He knew better than to remove his gloves, but he ached to do so. To blow on them, but that would not help. It was too cold. His body too injured.

The priority was to determine where the hounds had hidden him. He strained to see. He had the sense of being closed in. Ahead. The hounds would face a possible threat. So . . . ahead must be his option. He felt along a furry spine, unsure which hound this was, and determined the entrance must be in the same direction his feet pointed. He squinted around a swollen shut left eye, part of the problem, but he detected a pinprick of light in the distance. He grunted. Though his aching limbs demanded rest, to do so would mean death.

Reaching out, he stretched and found a wall. Cold. Hard. A cave then. Using it for support, Aselan struggled to his feet. He groaned, each movement torture, but staggered forward, using the wall as a very awkward crutch.

Duamauri and Sikir were on their feet, ready.

Pain scorched as he forced his way toward the ever-widening circle of light, which fueled his determination. Drew him heedless of what his body screamed. By the time he reached the mouth of the cave, he once more cradled his throbbing arm to his chest. He stepped out and released an exhausted, relieved breath. His gaze locked on the sight in the distance. The last place he wanted to seek help, shelter, healing.

Nivar Hold.

Just beyond the cave mouth, he paused long enough to grab a thick

limb and use it for support. A sight he would be for the family. He knew
he was a fright—beard mottled with blood and ice. His eye swollen shut.
Clothes filthy, wet, and torn. On top of the broken leg that had barely
begun to heal, he had a frostbitten leg and now a wrenched arm. He
limped through the thick pines that skirted Nivar Hold. As he gained
the edge of the trees, he slumped against a trunk to rest, eyeing the high
walls surrounding the hold. It was not a great distance, but enough for
him to worry about making it.

Kaelyria. They took her. He *must* make his way.

He started forward, lumbering, the hounds at his sides. A dozen paces,
already having to talk himself into each step, to lift the leg. Plant the foot.
The staff cracked. He stiffened seconds before it snapped in half. Aselan
flopped into a bed of snow.

Hooves thundered closer . . . closer. Alarm speared him. *Hiel-touck!*
How had they found him so fast, the enemy constantly nipping at his
heels? Out of nowhere. Disoriented by the pain and the trauma, he hadn't
heard or seen the riders closing in. His hounds came alert, growling.

But when he saw the cloaks, Aselan sagged in relief. Nivari.

"Name yerself. What are ye doing on Ybiennese land?" barked one.

After pushing onto all fours, he brought up a knee, wobbling. "To
see the king," he growled, his swollen lip muddling his words. Waves
of nausea and gray swept him. He swayed, but jerked himself upright.
Grabbed the tree.

"Not like that—"

"Stand down!" came a familiar bark. "Lower yer weapons!" A great
black horse barreled into the group. The thick, muscular bulk of the king
dropped to the ground with a quiet thud. Cheeks red and face wrought,
his father stalked forward, lips set in a grim line amid his beard.

Aselan set eyes on his father, saw him hesitate a yard from him.
"Father. I beg yer mercy . . ." His lids drooped. "I . . . I need . . ." Could
he remain on his feet much longer?

"Assist me," the king barked to the men. "Get him to the hold. Aburas,
go for the pharmakeia." An icy storm blazed through his father's brown
eyes as his gaze traced Aselan, and he closed the last few feet. "What in
blazes happened?"

Surprise and relief warred. "The Sirdarians," he managed. "Incipients—on the . . . Tooth."

"Aye, we've just returned from an encounter." His father's gaze rose in the direction of the Heart. "They hit ye?"

Aselan gave a weary nod, feeling the world whirl and tilt. "They . . ." Everything spun. Upended. The blur of his father's rich fur cloak rushed at him. Caught Aselan, who thudded into his father's shoulder. "Mercy . . ." The edges of his vision drew shut.

"Naudus, help him onto my horse," his father said. "We've got to get him to the hold."

Aselan gripped his father's pelt cloak, caring not of the pain in his fingers. The pain in his heart was much greater. "They took her." Anguish squirmed violently through his chest. "They took her!"

"All right, son." He set his grim face on one of the men. "Naudus, on three. Watch his leg and that arm. One . . . two . . . three." Hands shoved and pulled, and Aselan cried out as his bad arm wedged against the saddle.

He drifted in and out as the horse carried him the distance to the hold. After they passed under the gates, a half-dozen men lurched into action, lifting Aselan from the ground and ferrying him through the stable yard and into the side entrance of the house. The door he had passed through every day as a boy. Chased Tili. And even a toddling Thiel. As the day folded shut on him again, he fought to stay coherent. But he floated . . .

• • •

"Elan," came a voice from a dark chasm.

He shifted and blinked, light flashing across his eyes with ferocity.

"That's it, m'boy. Wake. We must talk."

He knew that voice. Loved it as a child, the rumbling of it. The deepness. "Father."

"Aye. Look at me, boy."

Aselan blinked again. Cleared his vision and swung his gaze around until it rested on the broad shoulders of the man towering over his bedside in his old room. It would do no good to remain here. He must get on his way. Borrow a horse. Beg for provisions. Set out. Track down the vile men who stole Kae.

The thought of her in their hands, after watching the way they'd incinerated the girl—

Aselan hoisted himself up. Pain exploded, blinding and agonizing.

"Easy," his father said, a hand weighting Aselan's shoulder. "Don't be so stubborn. Pharmakeia says ye broke a few ribs. Rest."

"They have her—" Pain chomped into his side. He clamped a hand over his ribs and dropped against the mattress, biting back an epithet.

"Breathe through it," his father coaxed, hand extended. Warmth radiated from his fingertips, sailing across the gap between them and heating the tissue around the injury.

Surprise spiraled through Aselan, glancing at the Flames roiling from his father's hand. "'Tis true," he croaked in amazement, easing back slightly. "Ye can wield."

"The heat will do naught but ease the sting of pain. I am no Drigo or pharmakeia, but it should help a little." His father lowered himself into a nearby chair.

"He's better than the other one," a burly voice spoke.

His father grunted.

Aselan forced himself to search out the other person and spied Aburas hovering to the side. His uniform crisp and clean, but his flesh swollen with fresh cuts and bruises.

"What other?" Tili asked.

"Tell me of the attack," his father insisted.

Disconcerted when his father did not answer, Aselan hesitated, but surrendered the fight. Closed his eyes again, relaxing against the pillows. "I was on Pharen. We went out to confront the Rekken. There . . . there were too many. They had incipients."

"Aye, we faced the same. Drove them back, but not for long. They have reinforcements," his father said. "My sentries found your men in a ravine. Most were dead. A few were not."

A few. Grief wracked him, unable to fathom the loss. "By the Lady . . ." Swiping a hand over his beard, Aselan could only imagine what they'd do to Kaelyria.

"Aburas was witness to the attack from a ridge. Too far to be of help, but close enough to see what happened." His father's expression went grave. "They wanted none of the Legiera or the people. They only wanted her."

Stilled at that pronouncement, Aselan gritted his teeth. "So they did take her."

"Aye," Aburas said. "There was an incipient I've never seen before. He and a handful routed the girl and then left."

"The Eilidan?"

"Those not killed we brought here," Thurig said. "They're in stables and barns for now."

Aselan looked at the man who had ruled a kingdom with resolute confidence and resolve. If Relig knew he had taken Kae as bound, then surely his father knew as well. But he gave no indication either way. And that somehow angered him.

He would not believe his father did not know. This was a power play. Just as it had been during Aselan's youth, when his father forced him into confession.

"Ye took Zireli's daughter, the heir to the Fire Throne."

So no entrapment. Just bald truth. Apparently, he was not the only one who had changed. "Nay," Aselan said around a laugh. "Forget ye how things be in the Heart? *She* took me. Chose my dagger from the table. Came to me. And Kaelyria is no longer the heir."

"Yer a fool if ye believe that, Elan."

"She relinquished all rights to her brother. Kae has no gifts—her wielding is gone." There was no time for games, for explanations. She was out there, with those brigands. He again worked to peel himself off the bed, fighting the pain. "I must—" Agony choked the words from his lips.

"Will ye rest, ye thickheaded—"

"I won't rest." He pushed to a sitting position. "Not while they have her. I won't lose her."

"Ye may have already—"

"No!" Aselan's bark rattled his skull. He groaned and braced his temple. "I won't accept that. If Aburas is right and they took her, then they had a purpose. It means they didn't want her dead." He frowned at his father, shaking his head. "I must believe that means she is alive still."

His father grunted, nodding and pursing his lips beneath his thick, bushy beard. "Now that I have the full of it, I'm inclined to agree that she may yet live. But why? Why take her?"

Aselan sighed, propped on the edge of the bed. "I know not. She has no ability to wield. She can do no harm or good."

Something flicked through his father's ruddy complexion.

"What are ye thinking?"

His father, the mighty Thurig the Formidable, heaved a great sigh. "She *can* do them great harm or great good."

"She can't wield!"

"Aye, but her brother can."

31

Twisting the reins of his mount did nothing to ease the tension roiling through Haegan as he stared at the fortress roughly a half league from the knoll he waited upon with Graem. Between them and the outlying village flooded in another two hundred people.

"Are they mad?" Haegan muttered, shaking his head as he watched a mother and three children scurry across the road to the rear, taking shelter between the Pathfinders.

"Mad? They have hope for the first time in ages," Graem said.

"What hope?"

"You. The army."

Haegan sighed. "Do they not realize the worst is yet to come? Any with me are square in the path of this storm."

"Some may come to hide, but many are here to fight. They are tired of being carpets for the Sirdarians to walk upon."

Haegan pushed his gaze again to the fortress in the distance. Something in him swelled as he considered what was left of the flanking towers and curtain wall of Ironhall. 'Twas not made of mud and plaster but hewn from ironstone, the hardest rock and similar to the steel used for Tahscan blades. Builders used the same for Fieri Keep by the Lakes of Fire. And yet, the keep had taken hard hits.

Graem looked there, too. "Not much of a castle for a Fire King, but—"

"'Tis enough." Haegan shifted. "The Fire King should be secreted into the fortress. None should see him. Not like this."

"Understood. Our number is too great now to house them all within the walls. But the other streets close to the keep will serve well."

"See that it's done," Haegan said.

"Aye, sire." Two hand signals had a Pathfinder heading to the wagon, where the Drigo tended his father.

Haegan had never been so glad for crumbling walls and unfeeling piles of rock. The curtain wall gaped in some places, lifted its hem in others. One flanking tower had been obliterated, and a large section of another was missing. The pinnacle of the keep's tower had sustained significant damage, as had the footbridge, barbican, and drawbridge. But still—'twould work. He was sure of it.

"Rider," Captain Laerian called, urging his horse forward to meet the messenger.

Haegan's heart lurched as he locked onto the rider—one of their own, Glomain—in the distance, where Laerian met him. The captain came round, rode hard and fast back to Haegan. Was that an urgent stride? Or a jubilant one?

Laerian drew his horse to a stop. "Glomain reports several hundred refugees within the fortress, encamped in the bailey. The castle itself is now kept by a score of Viddan fighters!"

Relief struck Haegan as he scanned Ironhall. Their contingent was in much need of rest and stability. A place to organize. 'Twas required they recover in a defensible position, and he could not imagine a better location.

"Clear the keep," Graem ordered Laerian. "Make ready for the Fierian and the Fire King!"

"Aye, sir."

Like a flood, Pathfinders cantered down the knoll and spread over the scorched fields that had once been lush grass waving beside a wide moat. As he followed at a more sedate trot, Haegan eyed the people spilling out of the bailey with naught but the clothes on their back. They cheered him as they vacated the fortress. He spied men hefting sections of wood—remnants of the portcullis—over the remaining sludge of the moat for the safer crossing of Haegan's men.

Once through the gate and past the guardhouse, Graem, Tokar, and Laerian swept around the smaller campsites to the far side of the bailey, where the entrance to the battered castle waited. A man stood in the doorway, hands fisted at his side and shoulders squared. His clothes hung crisply, in sharp contrast to the decay surrounding him. Dozens had made this bailey their home yet apparently received naught but walls for provision.

Haegan dismounted and started for the man.

Bodies swarmed him, clamoring and clawing. "Prince Haegan!" someone called.

Haegan stiffened.

"Fierian!" another shouted.

He refused to shield himself from the desperation clinging to their beings. They were his people, Abiassa's people. They were the reason he existed.

"Stand clear!" came Graem's booming voice.

"Help us," a woman cried.

"Save us," another moaned.

"Children are dying. Many are sick," a man shouted. He looked like he'd been recently beaten, with bruises around both eyes and one ear swollen shapeless.

Haegan met his gaze. "I am no healer."

The man snorted, revealing a line of white teeth marred by the black hole of one missing. "Healer? We need no healer. We need a deliverer!"

The very word made Haegan hesitate. His gaze rose overhead to the covered parapet walk with its large gaps, looking for the Deliverers. Draorin. Medric. Kaiade. Onaven. Zaethien. Bremar. "Be careful the wishes you make," Haegan warned. "With a Deliverer comes great trouble."

"Trouble is already here," the man retorted.

"Then pray—"

"We prayed and you came," a young man said.

Haegan stared at the man, then considered the crowded bailey. What was—

"Something is not right here," came Vaqar's voice.

"Aye," Haegan muttered, sensing . . . something.

"We should get you inside," Graem muttered, nudging Haegan's shoulder and directing him into the castle.

The well-dressed man at the entry clapped his shoes together and bowed low with a flourish. "Your highness, I am Drumon Ro'Stu," he announced, gaze still on his feet. Which seemed crowded into a pair of leather tips. And his breeches seemed a bit long . . . "I thank you," Haegan said quietly. "Please—be at ease. I am—"

Air whooshed around Haegan. He started, stepping back as the very large frame of Vaqar broke past him. In a blink, he had Drumon pinned to the wall by the throat.

"Vaq—"

Metal clanged against the stones, silencing Haegan's remonstration as his gaze struck a dagger on the floor. Haegan eyed the man struggling beneath the iron grip of the Tahscan. He writhed, his actions violent. Not out of fear for his life. But rage.

"That's not Drumon," someone in the bailey shouted, and the gap-toothed man slid forward, his bruised face pained. "I am. I beg your mercy, Prince Haegan. He threatened my family and life if I spoke up."

Haegan eased back, swallowing.

"Get the prince to safety," Graem barked to his men, who ushered Haegan into the castle.

"Go," Tili said fervently. "We'll deal with this then join ye."

Numb, startled, Haegan paused just inside, hearing Graem order the Pathfinders and Tahscans to protect the doors and passages, forming a blockade.

"Blazes," Laertes murmured as they climbed the steps. "Was him what had the dagger going to cut you? Why? I fought this place was loyal to the Fire King."

"The peace was tenuous even before Poired." The truth slowed Haegan as he realized the man not only intended to kill him, but he'd seized the castle. How many more in the bailey were disloyal? He turned back to the Pathfinders. "Warn your men, Colonel. He probably did not act alone. We need to rout the rebels."

"I'll stay with him. An accelerant would be of use," Tili said. "And a Tahscan."

"Agreed."

Nape prickling, Haegan scanned the shadows, tapestries, and corridors as his guard led him deeper into the cold halls. Only one had detected the threat, and he had already made himself scarce. "Vaqar," he said slowly, then repeated it more assuredly. "I need Vaqar."

"I'll retrieve him," Tokar said and turned back.

"No." Haegan caught his arm. "You stay." Meeting his gaze, he tried to silently communicate his concern. He knew not whom to trust, save Tili and the four who journeyed with him in the Nine when he'd been known as naught but Rigar.

Tokar faced the Pathfinders. "Bring Vaqar to him."

"In the library." Haegan pulled on what felt like ancient memories from his childhood as he studied the landing above. "Second level, second door on the right." His eyes searched that route even now. His father—

"The Fire King," he muttered, shaking his head as he took the stairs to the damp and musty passage.

"That's you now, Haegan," Tokar said.

He slid a look to his friend and kept climbing. As they approached the room, Tokar held out a staying hand. Nodded to Praegur, who sidled up next to Haegan, then eased open the door.

Tokar and the remaining Pathfinder vanished inside.

Haegan moved to follow them, but Praegur stopped him and shook his head, his scowl quite loud.

"I liked it better when you could talk. You said less."

A grin tugged at his friend's ebony features.

Light bloomed and spread out of the room, inviting them in. "Clear," Tokar called.

Entering, Haegan was surprised to find much of the room undisturbed. Sunlight struggled through dirty windows, lighting the dance of dust motes stirred when the curtains had been opened. He dragged his finger across the round table adorned by a single vase filled with brittle blooms and stems. A layer of dust clung to his finger. Musty and dusty. Dingy sheets draped furniture, paintings, and fixtures.

"I'll have the housekeeper whipped," Tokar said, his sarcasm thick. "And maybe fired. This place hasn't been cleaned in months." He stalked from the room, returning a moment later with a torch, which he used to light the sconces.

Haegan paced to the window and tried to peer through the grime. Even with the blurred shapes below, he could make out the hundreds littering the fields. So many . . .

"Sire," came a stern voice.

Haegan pivoted to the doorway.

Laerian stood there, scowling. "They're bringing the Fire King through the rear. Drumon—the real one—suggested the councilman's solar, which has three bedrooms. Will that do?"

"Show me."

"Fierian!" Tokar snapped, coming swiftly to his side.

Haegan hesitated, surprised both at the use of his title and the tone coloring it.

His friend came to him. "You should remain here until the castle has been cleared."

"Where is Vaqar?"

"With the colonel and steward, I believe, my prince." Laerian fastened steady eyes on Haegan. "There was concern for incipients in the crowds."

He could not remain holed up while they tended to one thing after another. "All of you—with me." Haegan started for the door. "Let us see the Fire King to the chambers and verify they're safe—"

"But your safety—"

"I am the Fierian," he said wearily. "If I cannot defend myself against insurgents, we are in far more trouble than any of us expect." He nodded to the major, who bowed his head, then started for another flight of stairs. Even as Haegan took them, his mind climbed to Nydelia and Karithia. To the incredible sense of futility and powerlessness that had overtaken him. He had nearly lost himself like his father.

How easily and effortlessly the inflaming slid into his mind on the field with Poired. What if they got in his head again, and he lost the battle? Lost the Nine? Lost Primar?

Two Pathfinders waited in the chambers, overseeing a flurry of maids and servants, who pulled sheets from furnishings and laid out linens and thick quilts. The long, narrow space offered a table for six and additional high-backed cushioned chairs hugged the corners. A benched window overlooked the fields. Fireplaces at both ends warmed smaller, more comfortable seating areas. The farthest end boasted double doors, white with gilt trim, that no doubt led to the lord's chambers. To Haegan's left, two separate doors were open to smaller rooms.

Not as roomy as his father's chambers at Fieri Keep, but just as luxurious, with tapestries, thick rugs, and exquisite paintings. Haegan nodded as he walked to a nearby fireplace. A fire would be too much in this heat, but he ached for light.

"Blazes," Laertes muttered, his wide eyes taking in the rooms as he turned a circle.

Haegan stalked to the open double doors where maids were smoothing clean sheets and bedding onto the four-poster bed. They curtseyed before hurrying from the solar.

"Haegan," Tokar said under his breath.

The Drigo ducked and angled in, his large hands hoisting the stretcher that conveyed his father into the bedchamber. Pathfinders held the other end, followed by Pao'chk and a pharmakeia. Standing aside, Haegan watched as they relocated his father to the bed.

"Fire," the Drigo growled, nodding to the fireplace.

A servant had just placed three logs there and went for matches. "Here," Haegan said, reaching toward it, sending flames across the wood. When he saw the other servant staring at his father, Haegan groaned. "Enough" he said evenly. The staff rushed out, leaving him with friends.

Graem and Vaqar entered the solar, closing the doors as they departed. Haegan met them. "What of the imposter?"

"Dead," Vaqar said, his voice steady.

"Dead?" Haegan flinched. "But we—"

"He had one intent and mission and that was to kill you," Vaqar said. "He would not have stopped until he met with success."

Graem nodded. "What the Tahscan did might seem extreme—"

"Aye, I would say so."

"—but 'twas necessary," Graem finished. "There can be no mercy here. We are at war, not just for the Nine, but for all people, all of Primar."

"Our enemy," Vaqar said, his voice rumbling, "is not one who fights fair or obeys rules of battle. They are merciless and will kill any and all to accomplish their end."

"Then we are to become the monster we fight?"

"Become them?" Graem said. "Nay. But fight viciously, relentlessly? We must. They outnumber us and, as our friend here has stated, will not hesitate to annihilate us."

Haegan strolled to the long table and ran a hand along the carved winged fish that adorned the backs of the chairs. He dusted off his hands as the sound of approaching boots met his ears.

"Ah, Thinblood," came Tili's old taunt as he reached the table. "I see ye have the choicest accommodations."

"Had to make sure you didn't get them," Haegan teased, though a tremor of annoyance ran through his words. He had not even thought to look for his own room. But as they both stood there, he realized the potential problem—both held positions to rule the Nine. He as Fierian and prince of the sick Fire King. Tili as the Council of Nine's chosen steward.

"Leave us," he said, wandering to a rust-colored chair near the fire. When Tokar hesitated, Haegan nodded for him to leave.

As the entourage started out, Haegan locked on to two men. "Vaqar, Colonel. I would have you stay."

Tokar frowned as he and Praegur left with the Pathfinders and Captain Laerian, who closed the doors after barking orders for Pathfinders to stand guard and let none pass without consent from Haegan.

Alone with them, Haegan turned, not surprised to find the men watching him. Letting the fears fall away, he drew back his shoulders. "Vaqar, I would ask that you remain at my side until—"

"I will leave when he tells me to leave."

"Who? Tili?"

"No," Vaqar said, nodding toward the heavy curtains that shielded them from the morning light and prying eyes. "Him, the Guardian."

Confused, Haegan met Tili's gaze, which held fast.

"The Deliverer," Tili confirmed.

But Haegan knew. When he looked and saw nothing, he did not worry. In fact, he grew acutely aware that they were not alone, even if they could not see with their eyes. They must see with their hearts. The Deliverers.

"Draorin," Tili said, "was among those who escorted me from Hetaera under Gwogh's instruction, but he vanished after the Infantessa died."

Haegan nodded his understanding before returning his attention to the Tahscan. "I trusted you before we reached Ironhall," he said, "but your efficient detection of the traitor within the hall proved you are vital. At all times, I ask that you remain at my side. I will trust your word and counsel."

Vaqar gave a nod. "It is an honor, Fierian."

Haegan could only pray that Abiassa would allow the Tahscan to help him for the duration of this battle and even beyond. But the weightier matter. "Tili, I fear the men do not trust me, and the Jujak and Pathfinders discount me."

Tili shifted. "That might be an overstatement."

Haegan lifted his head. "I need no pandering."

"I have no ability to pander, Thinblood—not when it comes to ye," Tili said. "The men respect ye because of the blood in yer veins." He indicated to the door that hid the Fire King. "And out of respect for yer father."

"Aye, but I am the one to battle with them. And in that, I lack their confidence."

"And perhaps yer own."

Haegan considered the words, not meant to be sharp, but singing through the air like a blade. His heart thudded at the accusation. He wanted to argue. "You speak . . . truth." He managed a weak smile. "The Council chose you as steward—"

"I was expendable, not a citizen of the Nine. My mission imperative was to secure ye, and I have succeeded in that."

Temptation lurked in the shadows of this room to hide, to relieve himself of any more stress or potential to fail. But as he stared at Tili, he saw the warning in the Northlander's eyes. Not a threat, but . . . stiff encouragement.

"Abiassa knew this day was coming."

"Aye." The answer was tight. Controlled.

"Knew each of us"—Haegan glanced at the other men as well—"would have our own roles to fulfill."

Tili lifted his chin. "Aye," he said, more relaxed, confident.

"My role is to address Poired. Even if I am not allowed to finish him, I have to be the one to face him," Haegan said. "Which means I will need someone to head the army. You are much needed if you would remain, Steward."

"I will see this through to the end."

"Good." Haegan took a measuring breath. "Colonel, he is as my voice."

"You trust him that much, this Northlander?" 'Twas said in jest, but there was uncertainty in Graem's question as well.

"Aye. Like a brother."

Tili arched an eyebrow, surprise rippling through his face. Or was it question?

Mercies. Thiel. Tili thought Haegan made reference to taking Thiel as his bound, their families joining. He felt his cheeks heat. That was not his intention in what he spoke, but in truth—there were greater fights to be met. "We, none of us, can afford to be petty in our dealings. We face a foe intent—as you said, Graem—on our annihilation. We must be just as lethal. If we are divided, we fail." Haegan looked to Vaqar. "What you did with the imposter, smelling the . . ."

"The reek," Vaqar said with a slow nod.

"The others of your number can detect it as well?"

Another nod.

"Why did She not pick a warrior like you or Tili as Fierian?"

Tili sighed and shook his head, seemingly grieved. "She chose ye, because the weapon ye wield is unfathomable. She needed someone She could trust to use it wisely."

"Had I your gift," Vaqar added, "I would have wiped out anyone and everyone after the death of my family. No mercy, no restraint. My response would have been only anger and violence."

Something in Haegan trembled at the thought. A piece of him, tethered to the past. To the cripple who had lain in the tower. The teen who fled a father's rage. Was that only a cycle past?

"I fear we warriors are all the same," Graem acknowledged with a half smile. "Our hands are trained to war."

"Ye are not." Tili held his gaze and let the words sink in.

Haegan winced. "I've failed—I tried to kill Poired and couldn't. He nearly killed me. Twice."

"Ye said they forbid ye—that 'tis not for ye to do," Tili said. "Those incipients also used my sister against ye, to break yer thoughts, yer focus."

Aye. They had. And he must remedy that. "I have to learn to recognize the inflaming more quickly."

"That is my role, Fierian," Vaqar said. "That is why the Guardian sent me. And though I would as soon cut off my nose as take in that stench again, it is an honor to serve the Lady with you if it means we free our world of incipients."

32

Tahscan steel flashed in the midafternoon sun, delivering the land of one more Sirdarian. Cries of shock went up, but the crowd quickly stepped away. The people were as ready as he for the land to be rid of the vermin. They had been persecuted long enough by the darkness.

Had Haegan seen that deliverance?

Amid the people and routing trouble, Tili shifted his gaze up to the windows of the castle, searching for the prince. There, a curtain drifted closed. Just as well. Haegan was not a warrior, though he had been called to war. Truth be told, even Tili longed to leave this war behind, to sit by the fire for a few weeks and sip cordi. Laugh at Relig's humorless reports on the state of Ybienn, and perhaps even entertain the odd offer of marriage.

Entertain. But never take seriously.

He scanned the unit with him—his men, Tralak, Asokin, Crigor—for a smaller, rounder face. Soft, full lips. He'd angered her by taking the higher road. Acting with honor. Honor, however, would have been not taking that kiss from her in the first place.

"Sir," a lean Pathfinder approached Laerian. "Reports are coming in of a handful of Sirdarians slipping out through the woods."

Tili's gaze hit the blackened carcasses of the trees, their spindly arms stripped of leaves from a fire. No doubt incipient-incited. A thick haze still lingered.

"Steward," came a firm voice—a Tahscan. He nodded toward the northernmost edge.

Tili saw nothing at first. But then, the slightest flicker of movement. Darting in and out. Small, lithe. Lightning-fast.

Astadia.

She must've spotted the incipients. She'd get herself killed confronting incipients. But as an assassin, she would know when the odds were against her. That would temper her, would it not?

She's still angry about Trale.

"On me!" He threw himself up onto his horse, rammed his heels into the destrier's flanks, and gave pursuit. His men pounded across the field and into the trees, spreading out to avoid the trunks and fallen limbs.

Blinding light shot out. Trees cracked, thundered as they collapsed in exhausted defeat. Smoke billowed.

Another explosion, this one more southward. He redirected his horse, men shouting directions.

Crack! Boom!

Each explosion he took as a sign that she was alive, still tracking. Immersed in the blackened remains of the forest, Tili followed the telltale cracks of wielding.

It fell silent. Light surrendered to the smoky haze. Drawing his long blade, Tili slowed his destrier, listening. Readied for an attack. He slid his gaze to Adassi, the Tahscan, to see if he detected anything.

C'mon, Astadia . . . where are ye?

"The smoke is thick," Adassi said, shaking his head.

Was that impeding him? A potential weakness? If it was, then the incipients would exploit it.

"South," Adassi announced.

"Yah!" Even as his heels met meaty flanks, Tili saw a shadow spirit through the smoky haze to his right. Was that Astadia? He veered toward her. Heat sent rivers of sweat down his back and chest. He ignored the tickle, attuning his senses to the popping trees.

"There!" Tralak hissed.

"Careful," Tili warned. "Don't hit the assassin."

"One less killer," someone muttered.

Tili jerked his eyes toward the voice but could not discern who'd made the comment. "She dies, ye answer to me."

Marginally repentant gazes slid away with lowered heads.

As they rode, searching for incipients or Astadia, Tili grew convinced they were giving themselves away with the horses. He needed more stealth. Track the way Elan had taught him. He slid from the horse. Gave its flank a slap then scurried up to a tree. 'Twas quiet. Very easy to walk into an ambush.

Stalking, he put every ounce of training into play. Freshly broken branches. Subtle depressions in the ash-covered floor. Though he skated his gaze around, he paid more attention to what he heard.

The men moving farther off.

Something told Tili to wait. To hang back. As if a hand rested on his shoulder, staying him. He anticipated an ambush from the rear, so he let the others move ahead and pivoted, walking backward. When their noises grew faint, he lifted a foot to trail them.

Shapes peeled from the trees. Darker. Tall. His heart crashed against his ribs, watching them. Stealthy. Almost inhuman. Incipients.

Ambush.

Tili freed his dagger. Wished for the Nivari. For the seasoned fighters who knew the benefit of waiting. Listening. Even as he aimed at the closest attacker, he drew a second blade. Threw the first with a heated wake.

It thumped into a man's neck. He wilted to the ground with a soft thump. Dead. No crying out.

Eying the unaware incipients stealing through the trees, Tili balanced the second blade on his fingers.

Voices skated out, and he froze. One voice came from behind. *Her* voice. Astadia.

Never losing sight of the incipient following his men, he sidestepped. As he did, her voice grew louder. And another. A man's. Tili couldn't afford to betray his position but itched to alert the others to the ambush.

"You are mad."

"I assure you, I'm not."

At the lulled conversation, Tili slid up to a scorched tree and watched the two shapes in the gray veil. Astadia and . . . Drracien. *What* was she doing talking with the traitor? Is that why she'd come? Had she known? Was this a rendezvous?

"No. I won't go with you."

"You must have sensed you were not who they said," Drracien said. "Trale was not your brother."

"He was more brother than you will ever be. Even dead."

A subtle crackling noise thrummed through the woods.

"Release me," she hissed, "so I can drive my dagger into your black heart."

Halo. Tili inched forward, peering through gnarled branches. As expected, a faint blue glow surrounded her.

"Killing me won't end this," she gritted out.

"Killing you? I do that, and I lose my own life," Drracien said. "You have to come back. He wants you. He won't stop until he has his daughter."

What was this? Tili himself struggled to breathe—was the traitor insinuating Astadia was Poired's . . . daughter? And Drracien—her brother?

"I am *not* his daughter! I have no father." Her chin was tipped up, so completely that breathing had to be a chore.

This was absurd. Laughable. Ludicrous!

Why? Because you found her attractive? Kissed her?

He'd kissed the daughter of the Dark One. Something in him recoiled.

Inflaming. Had to be. Could be the only explanation for this. Drracien turning her will weak so she wouldn't fight him? She was an assassin and could easily end him before he would know her blade had flown.

And if Drracien's manipulation worked, she might drive that blade against Tili without meaning to or even realizing she had.

Tili gauged his options. Kill the traitor—would anything happen to Astadia in the halo if he did? Or would she turn on him, for killing this brother, too? He hadn't killed Trale with his own hands, but in her eyes, he'd done that very thing with inaction.

Why did he trust her or even care? If she was the Desecrator's spawn, he couldn't. She would try to stop Haegan from fulfilling his role.

Matters not. *Capture them both. Sort it out with the Fierian later.*

"Steward Tili!"

Tili jolted. In a heartbeat, both Astadia and Drracien homed in on him.

The traitor whipped back to Astadia. "Come with me." Drracien held out a hand, the air around him tearing open.

That black creature leapt from the space and sprinted at Tili. The terrifying, wispy raqine growl-chortled.

Heart in his throat, he threw himself to the side. He felt the threat sink into his bones. Twine around his throat and squeeze. In the same instant, he saw Drracien wielding fervently—restraining the beast but also controlling the tear in time's fabric.

The bubble around Astadia constricted. She cried out, the scream seemingly lodged in her throat. Drracien drew the halo toward the tear.

Wide green eyes came to Tili as he climbed to his feet again. Astadia hung in frozen terror, her mouth gaping. Body rigid. And yet everything about her seemed to beg for help.

"No!" Though breathing was nearly impossible and a raqine paced violently between Tili and the tear, Tili pitched himself straight at the bubble. There was naught else for him to do but try. Though it may kill him.

The shredded raqine shrieked. Claws lifted as he rippled into the air, jaw wisping open. It lunged at Tili.

Knocked him aside. Tili thudded against the ground. But his fingers grazed the halo, the heat searing. That slight touch, his vain attempt to save her, had nudged the halo farther into the tear that started closing.

He flipped onto his feet and again threw himself at the strange gap between worlds. The edges slid together, seams stitching tighter. As it snapped closed, Tili saw through the warping field Astadia collapsed on a black marble floor. At booted feet.

Poired.

Tili surged. "No!" He would not let them have her. He would not—

A bolt exploded out. Struck him in the chest. Knocked him backward. Flipped him over and over. His back struck a tree. *Crack!* He dropped into darkness.

• • •

NIVAR HOLD, YBIENN

Kaelyria was dead. Rotting and decaying, she lay on the cold slab of their bed. Her face as white as her hair. Gray lips. Blue fingers. Ethereally beautiful, she had been his but for a short time. Now, she remained in the eternal embrace of death.

Aselan howled.

He snapped awake. Drenched in a clammy sweat, he let out a gargled cry as he lurched from the bed and grabbed a chamber pot. He emptied his stomach, wishing he could empty the morbid images of her corpse from his mind. He spat and slumped back against the bed with a trembling cry. Agony tore at him, less from the wounds of the attack than from the hopelessness that grew each day without her. Arm propped on his knee, he ran his fingers through his hair, shaking. Pain flared through his fingertips. He glanced at them, cringing at the swollen remnants of Legier's bite. 'Twould take time to heal. More time, even, than the bones that, days after his fall, had barely begun to knit back together.

But he would never heal, not if she died. Not if he had to bury her.

He must do something. Get out there. Find her. Track down the vile creatures who'd ripped her from the Heart. His heart. After he washed his mouth and face, he dressed, cursing the plaster-and-bandage bulk on arm and leg that made every action a chore. When, at last, he had packed a satchel of clothes, he hobbled down to the kitchens. Cook was already preparing the morning meals to break fasts. Leaning his crutch against the wall, Aselan took a couple of loaves of bread and a slab of meat. He rolled them in cloths and stuffed them clumsily in his satchel.

"Does the king know ye be doing this?" Cook asked with a glare.

"The king is abed, as he should be."

"He won't be likin' this."

"Naught I do is to his likin'." Aselan slung the bag over his shoulder, grabbed the staff, and made his way out to the stable yard. 'Twas strange to think of Zicri and Chima not in their den. Everything had been upended in the last year. Why not the raqine as well? They were as tethered to this land as any other creature.

He grabbed a bridle and led a black destrier out.

"Stealing a horse of the royal guard holds stiff punishment," came a gentle, teasing voice. Mother.

Feeling a twinge of guilt at her presence, her awareness of what he intended, Aselan used his good arm to heave the saddle onto the horse's back. As the heavy equipment thumped into place, the animal skittered, unused to such careless treatment. Aselan stroked its neck and considered how he would buckle the girth with one hand.

His mother approached and ran her left hand down the horse's shoulder, reaching under with her right to grip the girth and bring it into place. "Your father will not be pleased." Using her toes for leverage, she pulled up on the straps to tighten the girth.

Surprise bled into his guilt as he watched her help. "Aye, but I must go," Aselan said. "I canno' sit in here and endure one more night of dreaming she is dead because I have no' come in time."

She glanced up at him, a hand still on the saddle. "Where will you search?"

"I'm a skilled tracker."

"And a man blinded by rage and love with a body broken by enemy attacks."

Aselan shoved his crutch into his armpit and limped out to the bailey, the destrier walking lightly alongside, his mother trailing.

"I thought I taught ye better'n this," came his father's gravelly voice.

Hesitating, Tili looked at the leather thong of the rein. "I must go."

"Aye, ye must, but—"

Warning bells screamed through the early morning.

Heart in his throat, Aselan pivoted toward the guardhouse. Glanced at the towers.

"Rekken! Rekken!"

Shouts and screams went up in the village just outside the gate, proof of what the guard warned.

He spun to his father.

"In the house," his father barked to his mother. "Gather the women and children into the passages."

Aselan thought of the way the Tooth had been attacked. "Nay—not the passages. They know about them. How, I know not, but they do. They'll throw clusters down there."

His mother's face went white.

"Dress the Nivari in peasant clothes. Send them with the women and children out the south gate. They must ride for all the world toward Baen's Crossing."

"They'll think—" His father's face brightened. He barked a laugh. "They'll ignore them, want to target soldiers. Might just work."

"Won't stop them, but could give the women and children necessary time."

His father slapped him on the back, then turned to his wife. "Do as he says." Proud eyes lit on him. "Aselan—will ye lead them?"

Aselan hesitated, looking to the Tooth. The mountain where she'd been stolen. The incipients would not keep her up there. They were not acclimated to the mountain. So they'd go down. South was the only option other than the Outlands. "Aye," he managed.

• • •

THE CITADEL, HETAERA

"I don't care what you do to me, I won't be your pawn."

Drracien couldn't help but stare over Poired's shoulder at the girl hanging in the halo. She had brown hair, not black like his. Green eyes, not blue. And yet, he saw it—saw the resemblance to his own features. His own fire. Not to mention the way she'd pitched herself at Poired as soon as the halo released her onto the floor. Her viciousness had forced them to restrain her again.

"Easy words hastily spoken," Poired said, hands behind his back. If Drracien hadn't spent the last month with the Dark One, he would have said the man preened. That he was proud. Proud of *her*.

"True words earnestly spoken." Hands out, Astadia worked to balance herself in the bubble, her adamancy undeterred. "What do you want with me?" She glowered at Poired, then Drracien. "I have no gifts, no abilities like you or your rogue of a son."

"Oh, you have them," Poired chuckled as he circled her. "They may be dormant, because of your unfortunate upbringing. But that . . . mistake has been answered."

She scoffed. "What? Are you going to tell me you killed someone because I was left in an orphanage?"

"Nay," he said plainly. "'Twas not I who killed her, but your brother."

Drracien lifted his head, squared his shoulders. Hated that she would know what he'd done. And hated even more the surprise in her eyes. He could not help but wonder why they had been split up. Was it another attempt by that woman to stop them from becoming like the Dark One? What motivated her? Money? Power?

"When someone steals from me, they pay," Poired continued. "If they only have flesh and blood, I take that."

Astadia's green eyes held Drracien. "You're a traitor," she snarled. "He called you friend."

So, emotions then. He was coldhearted and calculating like their father, so she must take after their mother. Whoever she was. "The Fierian does not know what a friend looks like," Drracien said, his voice quiet. "He's an impudent prince with a power he can't understand or control."

"Which we will use to our benefit," Poired said, standing at a window that overlooked all of Hetaera, the burned city.

Her face screwed into a mask of hatred. "Or maybe he'll fling one of those bolts at you and relieve your skull of that glob you call a brain."

Drracien arched an eyebrow. "You mean like I did to your lover?"

"I have no lover," Astadia said.

But he saw the widening of her eyes. Felt her body temperature rise, the halo constrict against her. So, he'd been right to think the Ybiennese prince meant something to her. A mistake to reveal that.

"Is that why your heart rate just rose?" Poired whirled and stalked toward her, the black raqine slinking at his side, slipping in and out of the field of time. Drracien's stomach churned at the thought of the girl being bitten as he had by the creature. The thing's presence still made his shoulder ache. It was a leash of pain.

"If you knew anything," Astadia said evenly, "you would know I am not good enough for him. I'm a killer, a murderer—just like you."

"It is true we both are killers," Drracien replied. "But the Nivari commander was quite full of himself. Arrogant."

Impassive eyes came to his. "Arrogance is often confused with confidence."

"All the same, he is very protective of his family and name," Drracien continued. "He'd never take a murderer as his bound, nor lower his standards to look twice on her." Although, why else would a man throw himself at the Void, which could kill him?

"Mm, true," Poired purred, nearly smiling at the girl. "Was he entertained by you? The man might not take you as his bound, but did he take something else from you?"

Astadia fumed.

Surely she could see that withholding anything from the Dark One only meant more excruciating means of drawing out the answer. When her gaze flicked again to Drracien, he gave her the barest of nods, warning her to comply. For her own well-being.

That glower seemed set in stone on her face. "He wouldn't look twice at me."

"He hurled himself at the Void to save you." Poired smiled. "That indicates he has feelings for you, which we can twist against him."

"It indicates he is a better man than you. He cares for those he commands."

Poired angled his head to the side. "You like this Northlander," he crooned.

"I like predictable men who make my job easy."

Poired sniffed. Then squared his shoulders. "What gifts have you?"

She scowled. "Are you deaf? Has Void walking addled your brain? I told you I don—" A cry squeaked through her throat, which she clutched, losing her balance and flipping. She was not one to cry or scream. But her face was turning colors. Astadia seemed to swim in the bubble. Nay—*drown* in that accursed thing. She was defiant enough to let herself die, too.

Drracien tensed, shifting his gaze from Poired, who stared intently at her, then back to the girl—his sister. He started forward.

"Have the Auspex brought in," Poired said, his voice even, cold as he shifted away, Astadia coughing and spinning in the halo.

"The Auspex?!" Drracien's voice pitched. "But—"

"Do it!"

Drracien considered defying him, concerned—no, scared what the Auspex would do to her. That thing was the eye of Sirdar. Which meant, Astadia would be exposed to him. And she was too good of a person to—

"Move! Now!"

A crack of heat smacked his head. Drracien stumbled back. Enraged, he fisted his hands and spun, but not before shooting another glance over his shoulder at the girl. His sister. It changed things. But Astadia had no gifts, so why allow Sirdar a look? Why risk her life?

Worry for her survival pushed him out the door. He stalked from the hall and narrowly avoided a snap of the black raqine's massive jaws. Anger surged, but he dared not wrestle that vicious thing. He delivered the summons to the guard, who jogged off. Moments later, two incipients escorted the sickly looking Auspex, and Drracien led them into the chamber.

"Stretch her over the rune," Poired ordered, pointing to the upside-down eye of gold inlaid in black marble.

Drracien watched, his stomach roiling as he remembered when he had been stretched out there. A part of him willed Astadia to discover a gift, break free. She did not deserve that agony, to have the blackness consume her soul as Sirdar violated her essence.

Lips pressed into a thin line, body trembling with barely controlled rage, Astadia shot daggers from her green eyes as the halo lessened, then closed.

In its place, a guard shoved her against the cold marble.

"Brilliant," Poired said. "She's absolutely brilliant. Rage roils off her, but she shows none of it."

So he *was* proud of her.

The Auspex lumbered toward Astadia's head, his milky white eyes turning a violent shade of purple as he reached her.

Drracien tensed.

With far too much pleasure and intrigue wafting through his face, Poired eased away from the tableau.

Why was he stepping back? Warning shot through Drracien. "Wha—" But the word died in his throat, and not of his own volition. He'd been silenced.

A black veil unfolded as the Auspex placed his hands on either side of Astadia's face and held her still. She groaned, her body thrashing—yet not. Spittle foamed at the corners of her mouth. Veins bulged in her forehead. Her face turned violet.

What was he doing? Why were they not sic'ing the black raqine on her?

Angling his head this way and that, the Auspex was completely focused. Determined. *Searching.*

But for what?

Poired stroked his chin, watching as one might a boiling pot.

A howl from Astadia sifted the air.

Drracien fought his own control. Why he cared about her, he couldn't explain, but he could not stand by while they tore her apart, ripped her identity from her, and replaced it with one that fit their agenda. Drracien knew a darkness dwelt in himself, but her . . . She might have been an assassin, but there was a goodness to her.

He started forward.

Poired swept him aside with a flick.

As soon as he detected the wielding restraint, Drracien yielded. It was the quickest way to get released. And almost immediately, the Dark One's attention returned to the strange proceeding. He stalked back and forth. Knelt before her.

Astadia's eyes rolled.

The Auspex began speaking in the ancient tongue. Chanting. A haunting sound from a creature who otherwise made little utterance. He shook his head right. Then left. Then back and forth.

A sharp whistle shot through the room.

Of a sudden, Drracien felt strange. Heaviness coated his limbs. A pervasive chill. His surroundings tilted and wobbled. Catching himself, he braced against the wall as a wave of dizziness crashed over him.

Poired gasped, staggered.

The Auspex shrieked. Threw himself back with a guttural cry. "Unnatural! *Unnatural!*" He pointed a twisted finger and bared crooked teeth at Astadia. "Kill the Unnatural!"

Astadia dropped with a heavy thud. Her head bounced.

Poired was still staring, gaping, his knees buckling. Silvers and guards rushed to aid their commander. Others moved toward the Auspex, but grew wary of his flailing limbs.

Through the chaos, Drracien saw Poired. Rage flashed through his face. The Auspex wailed as if he'd been mortally wounded.

Something was wrong. Terribly wrong.

Drracien looked to Astadia, unmoving on the floor. Her fingers twitched. Not dead—unconscious. But the two others in this room were wilting. Weakness sucked at his bones. Legs felt like pudding.

Struggling, Poired scowled. His expression shifted into a hastening storm that took hold, dark and ominous.

Foreboding wormed through Drracien. In the space of one breath, he knew if Poired recovered, he would kill Astadia. Whatever she had done, whatever she *was*, whatever threat she posed, he would not let her live.

With Poired crowded by guards trying to help him, Drracien exercised his newfound ability. He flung open a tear in the Void, feeling it pull at him as he lunged at his sister. Lifted her. Spun and pitched her at the tear. Driving her the last several feet with a concussion of heat, Drracien collapsed. Breathing grew labored.

"No!" Poired shouted.

Even as the tear stitched back together and closed them away from her, Drracien felt himself flying through the air. He braced—counter-wielding and protecting himself from hitting a column. Deftly, he landed on his feet, but felt his knees buckling. His wielding fizzled. Like a fire with water on it. He jerked toward the Dark One, staring at him through a knotted brow.

"*What* did you do?" Poired howled.

"I saved you," Drracien managed. Not a lie—he was shaken and thereby hoped his words held a glimmer of truth. "Could you not feel it?"

Chalky-white, Poired glowered, his chest rising and falling unevenly. "What?"

"The . . . the . . ." Drracien shook his head. "I don't know what it was. I just *felt* it. Tell me you felt it, too. You collapsed. The Auspex—"

"Out!" Poired shouted to the guards. "Leave us!" He stumbled to a table with a decanter, pouring himself a stiff drink. Without word or threats, he dumped it back. Poured more.

Interesting. "Was I wrong?" Drracien joined him. "I . . . whatever happened, whatever she opened up, terrified me. I've never felt so weak, so . . . wrong. I just reacted." If thinking, planning, and putting it into action counted as reacting. "I was afraid for myself. For you." He looked at the Auspex. "What did he mean *unnatural*?"

Poired spun to the windows. "It's not possible. She's *my* child. I was promised. He *promised*."

Drracien closed the space between them, knowing it was a dangerous move, but he must appear desperate. "What does it mean, Father?" The word was acid on his tongue.

Leaden eyes came to his. "That she must be destroyed."

Drracien jolted. "She's my sister, you said—"

"She's *nothing* to you. She's an Unnatural," he said, his lip curling.

He'd not heard that before. It hadn't been in the annals. "What does it mean?"

The Dark One's shoulders sagged for a second, then lifted, bringing up that dreadful gaze. "She can drain our abilities."

Realization dawned with terror. "That's why I felt so weak."

"And if she is allowed to live . . ." Poired stiffened, shook his head. "She must die."

33

Chest still aching, Tili lay abed, rubbing the spot where the bolt had struck. It'd seared, leaving a marred mess and a deep bruise on his breastbone. But none of that ached more than seeing Astadia snatched before his eyes and not being able to save her.

A shadow dropped over the window, subtle since dawn had yet to split the dark chill of night. But having grown up in Nivar Hold, Tili recognized a raqine's shadow when he saw one.

He pried himself from the bed and went to the window, watching as a raqine silently stole into the camp of Pathfinders. Odd. The beast alighted with stealth, then skulked toward a tent. Which raqine—

Draed.

He slid into the tent.

Tili held his breath as he watched.

From within, a startled shout went up.

Draed backed out, dragging Tokar into the open by his ankle. In his bedclothes.

The young captain shouted. "Release me! Stop!"

The Pathfinder camp roused to investigate the commotion, then broke into laughter as Draed deposited Tokar in a murky pond, splashing the muck.

With a roar of frustration and anger, Tokar slapped the murk. Shouted at the beast, at those still laughing at him. After another slap, he pulled himself up and slogged out, bedclothes clinging to his lanky frame. "You foul, accursed—"

"Oh, I wouldn't . . ." Tili murmured, knowing how Zicri responded to things like that.

Sure enough, Draed angled his wings, then tilted one and whooshed the muck, throwing it into Tokar's face. He then let out a deafening growl-howl, forcing Tokar back—stumbling. He plopped again into the mud.

Even Tili laughed this time. Why Draed had chosen Tokar, only Abiassa knew, but it seemed the two were well paired. Turning, Tili caught sight of movement on the far edge of the village, where the people had done their best with makeshift repairs of battered plaster structures and barns. A rider turned onto the main road, shouting.

Tili grabbed his trousers and donned them, then shoved his arms into his tunic. He snatched his long cloak and hurried from the room.

Graem was coming toward him but stopped. "Rider from Vid."

"Aye." Tili hustled down the stairs, and together they stormed to the main entrance. Gaining the doors, they heard the commotion in the bailey. The rider threw himself from the horse and jogged to meet them. "Sirs," he breathed. "The Council is en route."

Tili started at that. Why would they come here? "How long?"

"They should enter the gates by nightfall."

"What of Poired?" Tili asked.

"No sight of him."

With Drracien knowing their location, they could not go long without taking an attack by the Dark One.

• • •

Thiel used a small flint rock on the ropes that bound her feet together—aggravating her swollen ankle. She wondered now if it wasn't truly broken, but maybe badly sprained. Still, the pain was too much. And she was done being a prisoner, even in a comfortably furnished tent . . . *especially* there. Cadeif had not drugged her again since that first night, had not touched her except in anger. But she would not wait in dread for his appetites to return.

She worked feverishly, knowing they would soon come to tie her to the horse as they set out yet again for another day-long ride. If she could just get free, she could—

Steps approached, hurriedly.

Thiel sawed faster.

The pace quickened.

So did her motion.

Feet appeared at the tent flap.

Thiel slid her feet and the half-destroyed rope to the side, out of view.

Raleng entered and came to crouch beside her, his hands roughly tugging at the rope around her ankles. She watched in fear. Froze when he hesitated at the frayed threads. But he neither made a comment nor a strike. Just finished untying her and stood back, that ever-present scowl dark on his face. "Up. Privy."

"But I don't have to—"

He grabbed her arm and hauled her up. Thiel yelped at the pain stabbing into her foot. She stumbled but found purchase as he dragged her out. She started left as had been their habit since encamping last night, but she barreled into his chest. He muttered an oath and spun her around.

"I thought I was using—"

"Quiet!" He gripped her harder and veered around the north side of camp. He pushed her behind a rock. "Go."

Confused, Thiel stood there. Glanced around and stilled when she spied the nearly perfect path that wound through the wood away from the camp. *Escape path.* Straight to a dry riverbed. This was a trap. He wanted her to sprint away so he could put an arrow or two—or ten—into her back. Or he'd beat her till the sun went down, then drag her through camp behind a horse. She stumbled ahead, then paused. Anxiety wound through her. Thiel worried her lower lip, staring ahead, then looked behi—

A large frame filled her vision.

Thiel staggered. Her ankle wrenched again. She strangled a cry as she stumbled. A strong hand seized her. "Cadeif."

"Hurry," he growled.

"Leave me—"

He swung her toward himself, eyes fierce. "Listen to me," he said. "Run. Run or they will kill you."

Thiel drew in a thick breath, searching his sun-weathered face.

"They are breaking their word. So I will break mine before they can use you against me more," Cadeif whispered. "They threatened you and my people to force me into this war, to do their bidding. At the battle, they will dangle you before the Twig, then slit your throat."

Thiel widened her eyes.

"Now you understand." Cadeif pitched her away and stomped off.

Stunned, she stared after him.

"Go, Etelide," Cadeif urged, looking back. "Run." He gestured toward the path. "Run and do not stop. Save your life!"

His warning sent her stumbling, running, ignoring the pain in her ankle. Faster. Faster. Down the trail. Down the dusty, dried-up riverbed.

A bolt struck the sand. Glass shot up, daggers willing her to fall on their sharp edges.

Skidding to a halt, breath caught in her throat, she searched the trees for the wielding incipient.

Thiel spun and tried to run, but daggers thrust from the sand, forcing her into a frenetic, terrified dance to avoid being sliced. She twisted around, furious. "Cowards! Show yerselves!"

Instead of a black-cloaked incipient, a horse barreled into the riverbed. A sea of Sirdarians and incipients came wielding as they rode behind the Ematahri warrior. Her breath caught at the terrible face—Cadeif! Had he changed his mind?

He angled to the side, reaching for her.

She lunged at him, catching his arm and swinging up over the horse's back. They'd done it a thousand times, training in the meadows. Now, it was life or death. She clung to him. Glanced back as more bolts chased them.

Their pace was hard, relentless. The ground seemed to shake with the pursuit of Sirdarians. Yet it seemed too great a sound for the small contingent on their heels. As they skirted a small ravine, one second Thiel felt the pounding rhythm of the horse jarring her, the next—nothing. Weightlessness. Sailing through the air. The world blurring into colors and violence. Wind. Dirt. Rocks. Horse. Man. Bolts.

The ground leapt at her. She shielded her head and face, her shoulder taking the first impact. Pain shot down her back. Arching her spine, she cried out. Awareness flared through her of the danger which had not stopped. The Sirdarians.

Flipped onto all fours, she stared through the dust and debris. Hair tangled in her face, dancing with her labored breaths. Thiel's heart thundered as the dust settled at an agonizingly slow pace. The whinnying horse jerked itself back onto its hooves. Shot off in blind panic.

Cadeif. Where was Cadeif?

Thiel struggled to get a leg under her, blinking rapidly to find the enemy. Where were they? They'd be upon her any moment. On a knee, she eyed the mound to her right. The spot where the horse had landed. What she thought a mound was a body. Unmoving.

No! With a gasp, Thiel surged to her feet. "Cadeif!" She stumbled but finally got righted.

A spear of light shot in front of her. Narrowly missed him.

She snapped her gaze to where the day grew dark with the army of incipients. *Fire and blazes!* Those traitors were far more effective than she'd expected. As they closed in, bands of heat energy coiled around her. Thiel stiffened, remembering what it was like to be haloed. Remembered to temper her response.

A sound came from her right. Cadeif. A groan rolled through his body. When she fought to take another step—the incipients must be too far to wield with strength—another dagger singed her boots.

Halted, she glowered at the rancid betrayers, but another grunt, a shift of dirt, drew her attention. On all fours, blood dripping from his lips, Cadeif clawed to his feet. A shaft wavered, embedded in his back. Blood streamed down his bare chest, the tip protruding there in a gory declaration of victory. He held his arm close. Teeth bloodied, face dirtied, he straightened.

Though he squared his shoulders, Cadeif was injured—badly—or he would be throwing himself at the incipients. Shouting, trilling, and calling his warrior brothers. But he stood there.

Thiel realized with a start the incipients were wielding against him as well.

She whirled to face them. "Stop!" But instantly heat seared her, biting fire trickling across her flesh.

Disbelief froze her as the incipients halted. General Onerid stalked through the line, his blood-red cloak fluttering. "It seems the good archon here has a very bad weakness."

"Cadeif knows nothing of weakness," Thiel snapped. "Weak is preying on others, manipulating them and restraining free will."

"Weakness is anything that allows your enemy to win."

"Weakness—"

"Enough!"

A jolt of heat seared Thiel's body. She shuffled forward, nearly falling to the ground.

"No!" Cadeif said. "Leave her! We had a deal."

"Which you broke." Onerid looked around. "You freed this woman." His icy gaze struck her—and simultaneously, heat showered her again.

It grew so unbearable, she wavered. Dropped to a knee. Sweat poured from her temples and spine.

"Leave her," Cadeif growled.

But the fire intensified. Thiel refused to cry out, knowing Cadeif would put his life in danger. Knowing it would feed the frenzy of Onerid's insanity. But the heat . . . blessed Lady . . . No longer was there blood in her veins. Only fire. As if she lay in the Lakes of Fire.

The Lakes . . .

Haegan.

Thiel closed her eyes. Felt the dryness of her lids. Her swelling tongue.

Beneath her, a vibration wormed through her palms and knees. Thrumming. Pounding. Like the beat of death drums. Was someone already mourning her?

It was growing louder. Louder. LOUDER!

She eyed the ground. Saw pebbles vibrating so hard they seemed to hover above the earth.

Men shouted. The band pressing her down snapped free.

So weak, Thiel could only drag her gaze up. The incipients stared behind her and Cadeif. She pushed her gaze there.

A massive boulder barreled toward them. Darkness grew. Light faded, but a howl took its place and rattled through her chest. The shape soared into the air. Over her. Rocks dribbled down. The ground shook violently as the great creature landed.

A crack sluiced, like a dividing line. To her stunned amazement, between her and the Sirdarians stood a Drigo, his voice like a mighty wind.

Though bolts shot at him, the Drigo railed as they bounced, his skin unusually hard in his vudd state. Did his head touch the heavens? For his anger at the attacks so roused the righteousness in him that he grew and grew.

With a great swipe of his hand, he tossed the incipients across the riverbed. Bodies flew. Men shouted. Wailed.

"Get back!" Cadeif shouted. "I'll—"

"No. Stop," Thiel said, pitching herself toward the giant. "I know him." She craned her neck to look up. "Thelikor." But her voice was lost to his shouts. She cupped her hands over her mouth and shouted his name once more.

The Drigo purred a sigh, his great shoulders rising and falling, then he stepped back and went to a knee, resting a forearm there. "He call for you."

Thiel's heart lurched. When she breathed, "Haegan," the overgrown man gave a slow, pleased nod.

Thelikor's gaze shifted and a glint of searing white hit his irises. He shoved upward and his fist—big as a horse—pounded a wielding incipient to dust.

The earth rattled at the impact, as did Thiel. She swung out her hands and stared in wonder as Thelikor's pale eyes came to her again.

The large lines of his lips curled in disgust. "We go." He growled with ferocity at something over Thiel's head.

She spun and spied the general stalking back into the open. His cloak was torn. Blood seeped from a wound on his temple.

Cadeif was at her side. "You should go."

"Both of us—"

A deafening roar pierced their ears and defying his size and shape, Thelikor moved quickly. Grabbed the general. Flung him across the distance—incipients jerked up their hands to catch him, break his fall.

Thelikor lumbered to Thiel, shaking his shoulders as a dog might shake his pelt. "We go. Now."

Thiel spun to Cadeif. "Come with—"

His legs buckled. He went down hard.

"Cadeif!" At his side, she appraised the chest wound. So near his heart, blood squirting out like a bubbling spring. How had he not died already? "Cadeif, ye will be well. Thelikor—"

"Etelide." He sat back against the riverbank. Dragged eyes with hooded lids to hers. "It never happened."

"We'll go to Haegan." Thiel blinked, fighting tears, desperate to fix this. Save him. But the fight had gone out of Cadeif. He'd never looked this broken, this tired, this weak. "Get up and be the warrior—"

"I never touched you."

Her heart hitched, stealing her breath.

"I had to make them think . . ." He swallowed, shook his head, eyes closing beneath the weight of pain and the approach of death. "Etelide, you . . ."

She inched closer, looking to Thelikor. "Can ye help him?"

The giant swung his head wide and low. "Too much blood."

Pressure against her hand snagged her attention. She looked to Cadeif, into those brown irises that had held light and love for her. "If I did not become their pawn, they would have ruined my people. I . . . bartered. Bought time." He wagged his head again. "I beg . . . yer mercy. Never would I . . . hurt you."

His eyes slid closed.

"Hey." Thiel cupped his face. "Cadeif—ye're strong. Fight it."

"You . . . are . . ." His eyes shuttered open and locked onto her once more. ". . . mine."

Throat raw and tight, Thiel again fought the tears. Finally, fully seeing that the phrase was not one of ownership as she'd railed against, but one of belonging. It was his way of saying, I love you.

34

Kaelyria pressed her spine against the cage bars as two Sirdarians stalked toward it. She shoved her gaze to Cilicien. "Do not do this."

"I have no choice."

"It is your choice—this does not—"

"If you had not bedded that feckless mountain man—"

"He is twice the man you are!"

"He was enough, apparently, to get you with child, but where is this great bound of yours now? Why has he not come for you?" Dressed in his long, red-and-black cloak, edges trimmed in red silk, he epitomized the villain of every tale told to children in warning of being wicked.

Guards entered, their expressions masks of stone as they reached for her. "Get back, vermin!" She yanked her arms and wrenched away, scrambling to the side. "I would scald that smug look off your face if—"

"If what? You had not squandered your gifts?" His chuckle was vile and cruel.

The guards, patience thin, grabbed her. She threw herself back—and struck the bars. Her head and neck ached.

"Easy with her," Cilicien snarled. "She's to be unharmed."

Grips like shackles, the guards dragged her out. She fought every step, demanding to be released. Begging. Crying. "Abiassa, help me!"

"I'm afraid it's too late. You threw Her gift in Her face."

It was true. Horribly true. She sagged in their grip, refusing to walk. But they simply hoisted and hauled her from the cage and tent. Hot wind smacked her face as they stepped into the day. At once, she realized how far they'd traveled—this was closer to home, closer to the Lakes. She writhed, caring not for the gawking incipients and Sirdarians, who watched without a word or compunction to offer her aid.

They drew her into another tent, where a large wood table spanned the length of the space. Four more guards waited, along with a man in a gold tunic.

"Do not assist this incipient," she pleaded with the gold tunic.

The two nearest guards forced her onto the table, one stretching himself over her to keep her in place, the other shackling her wrist.

She squirmed and kicked. "Do not perform this abominable act!" She thrashed, wood biting into her shoulder. They secured her other hand, and she knew if they got her legs, there would be naught she could do. She kicked violently. Thrust her hips right and left.

Weight landed on her legs, forbidding her freedom. Leather straps secured to her legs, then a tightening slowly drew her legs apart. "No!" she screamed, tears streaming down her face and into her ears. "Please! You know this is evil. Abiassa gives life! It is for no man to take the life of an innocent!"

"Gag her," Cilicien said. "We do not need the Verses here."

"Please," Kae cried out again. "Your very teachings instruct you to heal and save, not murder!"

From behind, the nearest guard hooked an arm around her head, keeping her still as he worked a wood grit into her mouth. The piece bit into her lip, warm blood snaking down her chin as he tightened it around her head.

Blessed Lady, hear my silent cries and prayers. Save my child! Through blurring vision, she saw the pharmakeia hesitate.

"She is right," he said, his voice small, his face pale. "We are taught—"

Cilicien flared his nostrils. "Do what I say or die."

"But you are an incipient—you can burn the child—"

"I cannot kill the child without risking her womb," Cilicien snarled, "and I need her intact to secure allegiances." He nodded before he walked over to a chair and sat, producing a fruit and chomping it. "Get on with it."

The reluctant pharmakeia lifted a long metal tool and started toward Kaelyria's feet. She whimpered and tried to move, but it did no good. She shifted her hips as he lifted her skirts.

"Be still, child, or I could do permanent damage."

You already do. Yet she would not comply with them, she would not willingly allow them to rip her child from her. She squirmed, the only thing she could do to protect her child.

The pharmakeia huffed. "She will not keep still."

"Give her a sedative," Cilicien barked.

"No. It will countermand the herbs she'll need after." With a nod, he said, "Strap her hips down."

The guards did as instructed, wrapping a large strap around her hips, forbidding her from moving.

"Nooo," she moaned. Bereft, terrified, she clenched her eyes. Sobbed.

Abiassa, please! Save my baby! Her thoughts drifted to Aselan. To what he'd do to every man in this tent. To the grief he'd feel, knowing he had lost yet another heir. Tears streamed, running hot into her ears. Anger churned, mingling with her tears, rolling through her. Would that she could squeeze the heart of the murderer trying to kill her baby. Take his life for the life he attempted to take.

Someone sucked in a breath.

A weight fell against her ankles.

"Pharmakeia?" a guard to her left called, tentatively.

"What's wrong?" another asked.

"He okay?"

The air shifted. She blinked away tears and glanced down, confused to find the pharmakeia's bowed head on her leg. A guard nudged him backward, asking if he was okay.

Mouth agape, the pharmakeia stared with blank eyes. Then slid off the stool he'd been seated upon.

"Blazes, he's dead!"

Shocked relief swelled trough Kaelyria, bottoming out the terror she'd felt seconds earlier. More tears flooded her, her thoughts rife with gratefulness. Abiassa had saved her.

"Get the other pharmakeia."

Fear clawed her relief.

"Do not give in to false hope, Princess," Cilicien said. "He was an old man you scared the wits out of. His protégé will not be so easily frightened."

Would that she could speak, but she shot defiance through the most heated glare she could muster.

Cilicien glowered as the guards returned with a younger man. "Ah, see, Princess? Youthful vigor." With a wave, he motioned the pharmakeia toward her. "Relieve her of the child she carries."

The pharmakeia started, eyes wide. "'Tis forbid—"

"Dare you tell the Dark One you cannot obey his command?"

He paled.

"It must be done," Cilicien said, nodding to the body the other guards were removing. "And if you fail me, you will die like the one before you."

The pharmakeia finally turned his gaze to Kaelyria, and she saw the wavering devotion to the Guidings. He was young, he abided the dictates of his arts only in such that they provided a general foundation, but he thirsted for power and recognition.

She shook her head violently, pleading as loud as she could in her gagged silence.

He glanced over his shoulder to Cilicien and sighed. "If you promise the Dark One will hear that I have obeyed . . ."

"What else would he hear?" Cilicien crooned and regained his chair.

With a nod as if to reassure himself, the young pharmakeia lifted a long tool from the table. He squared his shoulders.

Kaelyria threw back her head. Cried out again to Abiassa.

"Oh." The pharmakeia's soft word sounded like an oath.

When she looked once more at him, she was stunned to find a greater, larger man standing before her. She felt his strength, his gift, rushing out in a pale blue stream. It infused her. Focused her. Their eyes were locked. He gave a slow nod. *She has heard your pleas. She has already given what you need.* The great man reached toward her face. The gag broke free.

Kae knew not what it meant. But when the pharmakeia's gaze slid to hers, fury erupted through her at his determination to do this wicked thing. "Touch me and you shall die, pharmakeia," she growled, beads of sweat drenching her scalp and back.

Surprise laced his features. He hesitated. But still he reached for her. For her child.

She envisioned his heart, like the pharmakeia before him, shriveling to the size of a prune. Envisioned the hand of judgment squeezing away his life as he intended to do to her babe.

The pharmakeia stepped back, grabbing his chest with a loud gasp.

She released him, staring boldly down the length of her body. "I warned you," she whispered, and released the clutch on his heart.

"What is wrong with you?" Cilicien demanded.

He hesitated.

Cilicien lifted his hand.

Kae felt a threatening waft of heat.

The pharmakeia shook his head and moved forward again. Greater this time, his expression more furious, the large man reappeared. A sword in one hand, the other extended toward Kaelyria. The world righted itself. To the healer whose heart had fouled, she growled, "You will not breathe your next."

The man's mouth opened in a silent scream. His eyes bulged.

"Finish it!" Cilicien shouted.

But Kae watched the larger man, his sword sparking as he lifted the great instrument with deftness and tipped the blade toward the pharmakeia.

He slid that tool between her legs. A burst of fury-red flashed, and he toppled, the tool clattering to the table.

Cilicien stood frozen, his face a mask of shock. He gaped at the now-dead pharmakeia. Then at Kaelyria. She knew exultation shone in her eyes and cared not. This was not her battle. It was Abiassa's, to protect life on this planet.

Cilicien shouted, "Get another!"

"We had but two," a guard said. "Nearest one is with Onerid's contingent."

"Then we ride for him." He glanced at Kaelyria. "Return her to the cage."

The guards removed the shackles. Kaelyria scrambled from the table. "How many lives will it take for you to realize Abiassa will not let you harm my child?"

Cilicien pivoted and struck her with a dark bolt. Kaelyria tumbled backward and collapsed.

35

On the plains overlooking Ironhall, Haegan stood strung up to a pyre to be burned at the stake by Sirdar's hand, Poired. The wood shifted. The sticks and branches beneath his feet morphed into limbs—arms and legs. Bodies.

They were the warriors. But he saw no tethers, no bindings that held them there, propping up the bier. "Get up! Free yourselves!" he cried.

Yet they remained.

"Accelerants and Pathfinders will burn for you, Fierian."

Haegan snapped his gaze to the dark figure looming before him on a giant black raqine. Poired. Fear writhed in Haegan's chest as he spotted Drracien and Astadia on another black raqine.

"Abandon this path, surrender your life, and they will be freed."

"Freedom is not decided by any but the one it involves," Haegan pronounced, and suddenly he was on a horse in the midst of a great plain full of soldiers. "If a man wants to be free, he finds a way. If an incipient wants captivity, he surrenders to it. I will not be that man."

"What say you of your father, prisoner in his own mind?" Poired taunted.

Haegan grew uncomfortable. He had no answer. No hope his father would be freed. His was now a physical condition, not a mental one alone. Damage of the brain, not the will.

"Look there! Even now your father exercises his will, Fierian." Poired pointed.

Haegan glanced back, peering over the thousands gathered, the army of Abiassa, to the great ironstone walls of Ironhall. Atop a parapet stood his father, precariously perched on the ledge.

Haegan's heart lurched. Even as he brought his horse around, his father spread wide his arms. Free. *And leapt.*

"No!" Haegan jolted upright, gulping frantic breaths. His heart faltered as he skated a look around. The dark tapestries. Musty, pervasive smell. Damp room. *Where am I?*

Ironhall.

Right. He'd bedded down shortly after the full rise of the twin moons in a room far removed from his father's. Thanks to his nightmares, Haegan was too familiar with his father's haunting screams, so he did not want the real ones crawling through walls.

He heard hurried steps in the hall.

Haegan glanced at the dance of torchlight on the floor, approaching his chamber. Not just one or two come to ascertain his well-being. There were a lot of guards. Too many for this late hour. He tossed back the coverlet and slid from the bed. Tunic sticking to his chest from the perspiration of the dream, he went to the door. Tugged it open.

Guards Faris and Gannel snapped to attention. "Sire."

Haegan drew open the door farther.

Four Pathfinders sprinted down the main hall, giving no heed or attention to his presence.

He frowned. "What is the roar over?"

Gannel straightened. "The Fire King, sire. He's missing from his room."

Alarm lanced through Haegan. "Why has nobody wakened me?"

"The Steward—"

Haegan ran after the Pathfinders, ignoring his guard's shouts as he raced up a spiraling staircase. He hurried, his heart anxious and thoughts burdened by the dream. Going up . . .

Nay, nay. It could not be.

Hand tracing the stones, he faltered when the stones gave way to a gaping hole. He jerked back. The missing wall tore at his thoughts—what if his father . . .

Haegan peered out and saw naught but scant torchlight. Immediately below was pitch dark.

"Here!"

"By all the Flames!"

"Call the accelerants!"

At the shouts from above, Haegan threw himself up the last dozen steps and broke out onto a flat, open terrace. Darkness hung its heavy blanket over the still-warm stone and land below.

Pathfinders twitched, surprised at his presence. "Prince Haegan—"

He gained a step. "My father—where?"

One pointed. And only then did he see his dream come to life. His father stood on a ledge of the turret.

Haegan flashed out both hands, encircling his father with a halo. While he could exert enough to keep his father in place, he found it next to impossible to draw him back to safe ground. Why? Was he too weak? Too inexperienced?

"Something . . ." He gritted his teeth, unwilling to lose his father due to lack of focus or training. Never again would he abandon his father, leave him, as he had at Fieri Keep.

Not for the first time, he wished for Drracien. That he had his friend here. "I need help," Haegan cried out. "Get Gwogh."

"My prince!" A guard lurched forward.

Haegan wavered as his father took a step and now stood suspended over nothing but wakes of heat. Arms trembling, Haegan clawed his fingers into the wielding. Holding with one hand. Drawing back with another. But it was like trying to pry ironstone from its bed with naught but fingernails. "I. Need. Help!"

"They're coming," shouted someone from behind.

"Father," Haegan growled, hoping to call to what was left of the man who raised him, the remnant of the Fire King. "Father, come in out of the cold." It was a bald-faced lie. A vain, raw hope that his father's mind would accept what was spoken.

Unbelievably, blue eyes, pale and bright, met his. "Haegan?" A flicker of confused hope. "Son?"

Haegan's heart beat faster. "Aye," he managed around a tight focus and quavering muscles. "Mother asks—" His throat caught but he cleared it. "She asks for you."

His father turned toward him, still cocooned in the halo.

One wrong thought, one wrong twitch, and his father would plummet.

Whispers of dread skated across the night as Pathfinders watched helplessly. In his periphery, Haegan noted Laerian slipping along the wall, crouched and hidden in shadows as he hurried to reach his king. From the other side, Graem did the same.

"Adrroania?" The tenderness with which his father spoke her name, gutted Haegan—that and the expression of joy, of hope that lit his eyes, bringing a familiarity and strength that brightened his bearded face, made the effort more painful. But then a hitch of doubt furrowed the blond brow. "She's . . . gone," he whispered, his voice hollow. "Dead. She's dead!"

O Abiassa, preserve me and my father!

Panic thrummed. "Nay," Haegan lied. "She waits in your chambers."

The Fire King stood, confusion tumbling through him like the crashing of waves. "And you . . ."

Oh no. Haegan knew. Knew his father's moment of clarity would destroy this effort.

". . . you're crippled."

"Father," Haegan huffed around the wielding, "please come down."

"Down?"

Haegan cursed his mistake. Saw the collapse of the ruse. "Come inside, Father." He felt as much as saw the lessening of the halo, the static crackling. His father wobbling. He growled, straining to hold it in place.

His father canted.

Rumbles of fear ripped through the Pathfinders. Graem and Laerian were nearly there, working hard not to draw the Fire King's attention. But 'twould not be soon enough.

The wielding waned. Strength faltered. "Augh!"

A white-hot blanket wrapped him, then extended to his father. Drew the king forward, as if someone had shoved him. Haegan's halo collapsed.

His father dropped—onto the wide wall—and tumbled onto the terrace, his feet unsteady.

Graem shot up and caught him. His task made easier when Laerian ensnared the king's legs and hauled him back to safety.

Seeing their arms around his father, Haegan went to a knee, heaving breaths. Even his knees did not want to hold him.

Pao'chk rushed forward and slid a needle into his father's arm, delivering what Haegan hoped was a powerful sedative. Pathfinders converged. Secured the railing Fire King and herded him below. As the sedative took hold, his father's shouts and complaints died before they were even out of sight.

With a howl of rage and fury, Haegan stalked up to the wall and shoved all his anger and frustration outward. A blinding white blanket drifted across the night, the wake glittering and crackling beneath the light of the twin moons. The last of his strength gone, Haegan collapsed against the wall his father had just walked. In the distance came a yelp, startling Haegan.

"Did you know?"

Haegan turned to Gwogh, both surprised and angered to see him there. "Where were you! He nearly died."

"But he did not."

Haegan palmed the cool stones and stared down. Naught but jagged rocks. His stomach churned. 'Twould have been certain death.

"You did well."

He spun. "Well? I couldn't even pull him back. He almost fell to his death!"

"Again, he did not," Gwogh said, a kindly smile tugging at his bearded face. "And you saved him."

"No, I nearly killed him. I couldn't hold the halo!"

"Because there was no anger."

"What?"

"Halos are most effective when the one held is embroiled in anger. Your father had no anger because he was not—"

"In his right mind?"

Thick brows bunched. "—standing on the wall in his thoughts. He was elsewhere." Gwogh inclined his head. "There is no need to challenge me, Haegan."

"Isn't there?"

"We have enemies aplenty without creating our own."

"You poisoned me."

Gwogh stared into night. "Can you feel it, Haegan?"

Frustrated, annoyed, exhausted, Haegan shoved his hands through his hair. But there was no hair. Only stubbly scalp. And again, it somehow freed him. Helped him loose the anger.

"Did you hear the scream in the distance?"

Haegan turned a wary look to his old tutor.

"You threw out the wake."

Guilt chugged through his veins as he scanned the trees just beyond the reach of the keep. "I was angry, scared."

"Righteous anger that found an unrighteous."

Haegan jerked his gaze there, remembering the scream he'd heard. "What are you saying?"

"You could not bring your father from the ledge because one out there"—he pointed to the trees—"wielded against you, inflamed your father's thoughts again, convincing him he was in no danger. Then when you stepped in, the one out there fought your attempt to save the king."

Haegan's stomach clenched. Only then did he notice the Tahscan standing by the door. Had he detected the inflaming? "Why did you not summon me?"

Vaqar cocked his head. "Your guards refused me entrance. So I searched for the steward, but could not find him."

"I will speak with them—you are to have unfettered access to me."

The Tahscan nodded.

"I fear it is too dangerous and open here," Gwogh said, taking in the fields and woods.

"We should go inside," Haegan agreed, but the flickering campfires caught his eye. *The people are tired. I am tired.* "How much longer until it is over?"

"I fear that the time is nigh upon us, Fierian."

"There is a prophecy—" a female voice began.

Gwogh snapped up a hand, silencing the woman who had come up behind him.

Haegan glanced to Kedulcya, then to his former tutor. "I know that look," he said. "What knowledge do you keep from me this time?"

Gwogh glowered at the councilwoman. "There is word about this place, what some"—his gaze hit Kedulcya—"call a curse. Ironhall is said to be a devourer of kings and rulers."

More prophecy. More doom. Could there not be a good word, a blessing rather than a curse? Palms again on the stones, he stared up at the twin moons. "Then it is all the better that I stay, because I am no king or ruler. Only a destroyer."

36

Straddling the middle of a large, empty receiving hall on the second level of the fortress, a dual-sided fireplace seemed to fight the vines digging through its mortar. Vaqar traced the vine to a crack in the outer wall, where the plant had forced its way between the stones. Much as they had done these last weeks, marching northward. The plant, it turned out, was hennidrile, a heavily fragrant flowering vine. His people had made quick work of cutting the vine and draping it over the doorways to shield them from the scents plaguing this ancient place.

Most of his people were stretched on pallets of blankets to catch the warmth. Faces uncovered, they enjoyed a reprieve, thanks to the hennidrile.

Perched in a window of the third-level balcony overlooking the hall, Vaqar noted that while Jadrile snored, his sister slipped out. Haandra was a fine fighter, but she had taken to the sword far too young. Why had she, alone of her warrior sisters, been cursed with the reek?

With a sigh, he turned back to the land, peering down on a brown swath. It must have at one time been a creek or small river that had wound through fields and trees.

A raucous noise below drew his gaze to a crowd in the bailey arguing with some of Grinda's men. The encounter grew lively, shouts and fists raised. The crowd then shifted, quieting, and broke apart as someone approached.

The steward joined them, resting a hand on the shoulder of the nearest angry local and nodded to the soldiers. Then he lifted a child into his arms.

A loud bark snatched his attention. 'Twas only laughter from his men.

In the bailey, the steward set down the child, so he could clasp arms with the man, then both went their way. Whatever the confrontation had been about, the steward had smoothed it. How blessed to be able to walk and enjoy the crowds, the people. Vaqar had been that man in Tahsca, before . . .

Now, he was homeless, a man who could no more endure the stench of crowds and their agitating emotions than a dog could endure being submerged in an ocean.

Why? Why had he been forced onto this path? Why had any of them? To serve a prince who was prone to allowing the enemy in his head? To watch a Northlands prince win the hearts of the people, priming them for a very effective coup of the lower kingdoms? Was that his intent? To steal the Nine?

With a grunt, Vaqar hopped down, since it did no good to sit and bemoan what he could not change, or see uprisings where none existed. Would he be useful or would he be dead? Because if he did not harness what had been forced upon him, then he would surely die. If not from the reek, then from the Dark One.

Remember what you lost.

Hustling down the grand staircase, he chose to make himself useful with one who already sought his help. He strode across the marble floor, keeping his steps quiet but not stealthy. When he slipped through the double doors, he was blasted with an unexpected scent. Almost immediately, shadows shifted. Quiet words carried.

Vaqar hesitated, drew back, remembering the last time he'd smelled that scent it had been with the steward and the assassin. But she was gone. So, who . . . ?

A giggle sailed out.

Surprise struck him to find Haandra in the shadows. With whom?

Boots scritched as the man adjusted his stance. Leaned in, the barest light tracing their faces as he bent to kiss Haandra. It was the young Pathfinder—Tokar, they called him. Indignation coiled through Vaqar. His hand went to his hilt.

But Haandra pulled away, as she should. 'Twas not the Tahscan way to so easily surrender modesty. The boy should be glad she saved him a painful lesson, for Vaqar would have surely delivered it had she not distanced herself.

Should he leave them, or make his presence known? Would Tokar press his desire on her? Surely naught more than a kiss would happen here in the open hall. And there had been much grief in their paths of late. Perhaps a kiss was not so egregious.

Air stirred behind him.

Vaqar tensed.

"What are you—" Jadrile sucked in a breath, too quickly sighting his sister and the Pathfinder. "Why I—"

"Leave them," Vaqar hissed.

"How can you say that?"

"We are too short on pleasures and laughter."

"But he's tasting her virtue."

"He's testing his curiosity. And she hers. Leave them." Vaqar patted his shoulder. "But later, feel free to deliver him a warning."

A gleam filled Jadrile's eyes. "With *pleasure*."

Vaqar started in the other direction, hearing the thump of doors. The severing of the attraction scent, and a quick gasp. Hasty footsteps quickly followed, the two parting ways it seemed. Probably best. Too long in shadows and they could become them.

He gained the main staircase, nodding to the Pathfinders who stood guard. As he turned for the third flight, he heard steps ahead and glanced up.

"Perfect." The steward stopped his descent. "The Fierian would speak with ye."

"Is something amiss?"

"Besides the Dark One scorching the Nine, his father nearly killing himself, and his blue wake of death?"

"There is that."

Tili chuckled as they hit the landing, but then faced him. "Do not mistake his youth and inexperience for lack of ability or desire."

"I would make no such mistake. He proved quite capable when he delivered us of the Infantessa, and for that, I owe him a life debt."

Tili nodded, eying him.

The inspection concerned him, so Vaqar braced before he allowed the scents to flood his senses. He took them in. Sorted them. Though he wasn't sure what to expect from the steward, he was surprised at what he detected: concern and the most peculiar—jealousy.

"This way," Tili said, motioning toward the double doors carved with the emblem of the house that had dwelt here. "He and the Council are waiting."

Vaqar slowed. "Council?"

Tili smirked. "Nervous?"

Holding the steward's gaze, Vaqar lifted his cloth and secured it to his left ear, grateful he'd washed and re-oiled it with hennidrile. "I have endured too many councils in the Tahscan court." Endured their logical but impractical decisions. Until Anithraenia exiled and murdered their families.

Doors clapped open beneath the guidance of sentries. A long table spread before him, where a half-dozen robed accelerants occupied the seats, along with a handful of men in suits that mirrored their wealth—noblemen.

"Vaqar," Prince Haegan greeted him with a smile that bespoke his relief. Candelabras threw light over the plain circlet sitting on his shaved head as he waved Vaqar to the table. 'Twas an odd sight to see a prince bald, but it fit. Fit who he had become. "Please, join me."

Clenching his teeth did not alleviate the strain his body took to protect his senses from the reek. Stiffly, he planted himself in the chair.

"Gwogh is explaining why we should advance north before our haggard little contingent encounters Poired again," Haegan said, nodding to the gray-haired man at the other end. "And Agremar has been sent on behalf of the Duke of Molian."

Vaqar inclined his head to the copper-skinned man.

"But strategically," Tili put in, joining the table, "Ironhall is the best position from which to defend. If we advance into Vid, we not only limit our options, we endanger the people."

"And then," Haegan continued, "you have Councilor Griese there, who would petition us to seek the safety of Vid's citadel."

Surprised, Vaqar noted the amusement coating Haegan.

A nobleman in a blue jerkin lifted his chin. "Next to Hetaera, Vid's citadel is the largest and most advanced—"

"Did it not take significant damage when Poired attacked eighteen months ago?" Major Laerian asked—no, challenged.

"It has been repaired." Griese sighed. "In earnest, Prince Haegan, you have no legitimate cause to remain here in the open. The Council has decided it is best to relocate you and the Fire King there where we can protect you."

"It is not wholly for the Council to decide," Colonel Grinda countered.

"Nor is it for the warring armies to discount the wisdom of the sages."

"Wisdom?" Laerian snickered. "Have you lessons on combat strategies? What of defense tactics?"

"We are accelerants and we—"

"*You* are accelerants," Grinda said, "but the thousands you protect within Vid are not. If we converge there, then we also lead the darkest wielders into the city. The people will have nowhere to go. Imagine the slaughter."

Picking olives from a tray, Haegan leaned to the side. "What say you, Vaqar?"

Startled at being singled out, Vaqar jerked his gaze to the Fierian. He frowned, glancing at the other dozen gathered, reminding him far too much of Anithraenia's council. That had not gone well, no matter his *say*. "I have no say in the matters of the Nine."

"As my . . . advocate"—the Fierian's eyebrows rose as he settled on the term—"you have a say." Haegan was still leaning back in his seat, eyeing him with discerning a smile. "I would hear your thoughts."

Straightening gave Vaqar a moment to gather and brace himself. Tenderly seek out the scents in the room. Annoyance from the councilors. Irritation from the Pathfinders—no doubt they did not appreciate being silenced in favor of him. Intrigue by the representative of Vid—but also, a heady scent. Desperation. Fear.

Should he call it? The Fierian had named him advocate. Vaqar held a young man's gaze. "What do you fear, representative?"

Shoulders stiffened. "I beg your mercy?"

"'Tis well, Agremar," the Fierian said with a nod. "Answer him."

"I do not see why I must answer to this Tahscan," he said, bristling, but then scoffed. "I fear nothing."

"That alone is a lie," the steward said. "We all fear something."

"Fear is nothing to be ashamed of," Vaqar said. "Fear saves lives, guides good men to better paths." No anger laced his scents, so what was it? "It can also lead to downfall, driving good men to treacherous paths."

Agremar's face reddened.

"You are wise, Vaqar of Tahsca," came the calm, strong voice of the female representative next to Agremar. "My brother and I *fear* what happened on Mount Medric and in Hetaera will be repeated in Vid. That our people, ready and willing to put their trust in us, will be disappointed or worse—killed." An attractive girl with not more than twenty summers, she looked to Grinda. "As the colonel suggested, slaughter."

He studied them both, breathing steadily. With a deep inhale, feigning resignation, he took in a deeper draught of her scent. Confidence tinged with fear, but a stronger scent he could not yet identify.

"Our fear," she continued, "is that our councilman is too afraid to go against his own order and do what he has trained for all his life—to protect."

"That his allegiance," Vaqar spoke for her, isolating the scent of betrayal, "is to the order, not to the people."

She inclined her head with a grateful smile. Her dark eyes glittered. Appreciation. Admiration.

"So, what say ye, Vaqar?" the steward repeated.

Prying his thoughts from the girl, Vaqar turned to Tili. "I say the Fierian touches the heart of Abiassa, and his instincts are to be trusted."

"That is a diplomatic answer if I've ever heard one," Tili chuckled.

"It is truth. Of all seated at this table," he confessed, "it is him alone I trust."

"I return that trust, Vaqar." The Fierian sat forward. "You have saved my life and my father's. What I owe you—"

"Is nothing. I serve," Vaqar said, giving a nod and keeping his gaze down.

"I ask one thing," the Fierian continued, "then consider your debt paid, Vaqar Modia."

Eyebrow arched, Vaqar glanced at the steward, who had repeated his words to the Fierian. "Name it."

"Remain with me until Abiassa finishes."

"Finishes what?"

"Me or this battle." The Fierian stood, fingertips on the table. "I have decided—we *will* remain at Ironhall. Poired will meet us here, and it will end here. Steward?"

Tili jerked to his feet.

"Your recruits need food and training."

Tili's jaw muscle flexed. "Aye, sir. They train even now in the fields." He thought of Tokar being dragged by Dracd and nearly smiled.

"Colonel, Major?"

The two to Vaqar's right stood.

"Prepare the armies. Recruit every able-bodied man. While Poired has his dark arts and minions, most Sirdarians rely on the blade. Train our army to confront that. Prepare them." The Fierian homed in on the councilmembers at the end of the table. "You are, Council of Nine, at the greatest battle of your gifting. 'Tis time to summon the rest of your brethren and as many accelerants as can be found to converge here."

Clanging rang through Ironhall, the sound vibrating the stones. Silence dropped on the meeting hall, the members staring.

Vaqar tucked his chin, closed his eyes, and reached for the scents beyond the doors.

"What do you detect?"

The Fierian's question drew his gaze. "Concern. Alarm."

"Terror?"

He probed, then shook his head.

Doors swung open and a Pathfinder appeared, rushing to colonel Grinda, who angled his head to receive the news. He came to his feet. "Sir, a great number coming from the western rise."

"How great?" Tili asked, his face a mask of concern.

"West?" Laerian stood. "That cannot be good—Poired was last seen there."

"What army?" Tili demanded, standing as well.

"No army. Well, not a whole one," the Pathfinder said. "The monocle shows Jujak escorting refugees. Hundreds of—"

"Refugees. That is no cause for alarm," Tili chided.

"Because among them are . . . others."

"Others?"

"Drigo. Raqine." His gaze hit Tili. "Northlanders."

The steward jolted. "Northlanders?" He started forward, then stopped. "Ye are sure?"

"I know the standard of Nivar when I see it."

"Nivar?" Tili jerked. "It canno—ye saw the standard?"

"Aye. Bold as brass with that gold raqine."

The steward sprinted out.

Vaqar frowned.

"The gold raqine," the Fierian explained, sporting the first genuine smile Vaqar had seen in some time, "is only flown when the king is in attendance."

37

Borrowing a horse already tacked up, Tili raced toward the western rise with a half-dozen Pathfinders. As they came upon the column, his heart stumbled at the sight of the people—haggard, drawn, some bloodied, all bone-weary. How long had they journeyed? How many injured, lost? Was his family well?

He slowed his horse to a trot, disbelieving the number as he worked his way down the column. Men, women, children. Though he searched for his family, he also recognized the need for order. The need to show care for all the remnant, not just his own. "Food and water await at the fortress. Keep moving. The Jujak will guide ye."

"Hundreds?" Tokar surveyed the masses with his mouth open. "More like thousands."

So many. Tili shifted to search out the banner. Though he found one, it bore the tri-tipped flame and crown—Zaethian, a Nines realm. There, the gold and black of Draedith. Even Kerral's orange. But where was his father's banner? Had the sentries seen it wrong?

"Who is he?" a little girl asked.

"The Steward of the Nine," someone responded.

Tili dropped his gaze to a man with a child on his shoulders.

"Thank ye, Steward!" He reached up and caught Tili's hand. "We thank ye!"

Seizing hope at the speech pattern, Tili searched again for the banners.

"For what?" Tokar asked the people.

"He saved the Fierian," the man said. "Then sent his father-king to our aid."

Tili's heart jumped. "Then ye've seen King Thurig?"

"Aye," the man said, turning. "At the rear with his fighters. They have fought off more than one unit of Sirdarians since joining us."

Tili snapped the rein at the horse's flank and surged around the people, galloping to the rear. As he hurried, he saw the subtle shift in attire that indicated the people were less Nine, more northern. Baen's Crossing, perhaps. Then he saw it—the first raqine, skulking across the land.

Zicri!

The raqine lifted his head and let out a chortle-growl, as if asking where Tili had been all this time. With a laugh, Tili hurried on.

"Prince Tili!"

"It's the prince!" A great cheer went up, hands reaching, people rushing, offering thanks and pleas. Tili raised a hand in acknowledgement. A black destrier parted the crowd and plowed toward him.

He laughed when he saw the rider. "Aburas!"

"My prince!" The barrel-chested commander came alongside and clasped arms with him. "By the Lady, ye are good sight for these tired eyes."

"And ye!" He glanced to where Aburas had come from. "My father?"

"Well. He rides with Elan."

"Elan, my brother? Ye jest!"

"Nay. He stumbled into Nivar, beaten bloody. Near death. He had barely recovered his senses when the Rekken came down from the Tooth. We tried to fight them off, but they were too numerous." He nodded to the rear. "The king ordered an evacuation, sent the queen and yer new sister to Baen's Crossing for safekeeping.

Too numerous? "The Rekken are but a clan."

"Aye, they were. Once. They been hiding their number, we fear. We have not seen them since the Crossing. After we regrouped there, we bedded down for but a night, then set out at first light. It's been a murderously slow pace."

"Tili?"

He shifted, spied familiar black hair. "Osman!" He clapped his brother's shoulder as he drew up beside him. "Ye are well?"

His brooding brother gave a curt nod, but in that small gesture, Tili saw he was shaken. Though his constitution was not made of steel like

Elan's or even his own, Osman was quietly strong. The boy—ten cycles younger than Tili—looked ready to crumble. He tugged Osman's rein, leading him back toward the Nivari colors. "And Mother?"

"Well. Mostly."

Concern blasted Tili. "Mostly? Do tell."

"The attack gave her a fright, and what with Peani's wailing and being with child—"

"With child? Already?" Tili laughed, an emotion he did not feel but needed to help deflect his brother's unsettled nerves. He realized how very long he'd been gone. How his brother, Relig, served to further the kingdom, a task once set at Tili's boots. "Relig must be a terror."

"Unbearable," Osman agreed.

Tili glanced at his brother, surprised at the fervency in his tone. They both hesitated, then laughed. "Not much has changed while I was gone."

"No. Much." Osman suddenly seemed thirteen again and on the cusp of whiskers and manhood. "Everything." He shook his head. "I would that ye had not left. 'Tis been . . . frustrating. They will not let me fight. At least ye gave me—"

"Be not eager to clash steel with the enemy, Osman." Gripping the back of his brother's neck, Tili squeezed. "Does me good to hear I am missed, brother. Does me good."

They trotted down the line of wagons and weary travelers, only to be met by two guards. "Zendric! Etan!" Forearms clasped, they both welcomed him. "'Tis good to see friendly faces."

"Aye. Glad ye are back where ye belong, rather than with the thinbloods," Zendric said.

A good laugh that. "I serve where the Lady calls," Tili said.

"The queen will be glad to see ye. She has inquired constantly after ye."

"I trust she is well."

"Aye."

He would go to her, eventually. "I must find my father."

• • •

"Who thought we would see the day Thurig as'Elan would ride again in the company of Thurig the Formidable?"

Moving stiffly from still-healing injuries, Aselan laughed as his younger brother rode toward them. "And who thought Tili, the champion of Nivar, would chase a petulant prince across the Nine to play pretender?"

Tili laughed as they gripped arms, leaning in for a shoulder-slapping hug. "'Tis good to see ye, brother."

"And ye," Aselan said. He shifted back and winced.

Tili looked him over more closely. "Are ye well?"

He let his expression sober. "Not since they took her."

"Her?" Tili darted a gaze from Aselan and over the crowds of Northlanders as he worked out the meaning. He considered his brother. "The princess."

Aselan bobbed his head, once more feeling the call of rage. "She is my bound now."

"Had to walk halfway across the Nine to find my long-lost son!"

Tili grinned as their father joined them. "I am glad to see ye well, Father. I'm sure the journey has been hard."

"It has. I'll be glad to have yer mother safe and resting."

"How is she?" he asked, looking to the large wagon lumbering across the parched land.

"Well, but the strains of war pull at her."

"I can well imagine. Ye can rest yer weary bones and find a warm meal soon."

"Speak for yerself, boy." His father scowled. "So, Ironhall. 'Twas lost a year past, right after Vid."

"Aye, but now the Fierian has established it as his stronghold for the great battle."

Aselan followed their father, guiding his horse through the scorched trees to the first sight of the fortress as they grew closer. His eyes narrowed as their mounts, detecting the excitement around them, trotted a little faster.

"Smart that," Father said.

The ride jarred Aselan's injuries, but he found he could endure it with the thought of a bed and warm food. But of more import—speaking to the prince. He knew Kae's brother would do whatever was necessary to find her, and Aselan must pull every cord to get her back.

It took them no time to reach the safety of the Jujak and Pathfinders. Curiosity drew the people to the roadsides as King Thurig and his queen rode in, followed by their Nivari. Into the bailey, which Tili commented had been cleared of those who'd encamped within its stone walls.

His father grunted yet again, peering up the heights of the parapets and keeping walls. "That needs repair."

"They are working on the southern walls first," Tili explained, his words quick and eager.

Little Brother wanted their father to approve his efforts as the steward. Did their father realize he was not assessing Haegan, but Tili's leadership?

Steel glinted in their father's eyes.

Aye, he knows.

"South," his father said, dismounting.

"Aye." Tili was met by a soldier as they entered the bailey. They spoke quietly, then his brother nodded. Looked to Father. "I would bring ye to the Fierian." He lifted his chin toward the officer. "Colonel Grinda will escort Mother and Osman to quarters."

"Good enough," Father said as they dismounted.

Aselan indicated their entourage to the doors. He spied four guards in black and white overcloaks. Pathfinders.

One with gold cords dangling from his epaulets stepped forward. "King Thurig," he said, his voice booming in the great passage and silencing those in attendance. "By the Fire King and Prince Haegan, heir of Seultrie and the Nine, and Abiassa's Fierian, you are welcomed to Ironhall."

His father swung out a hand, clamping Tili's shoulder. "Fire King." Eager eyes caught his. "Zireli be here? Alive?"

Tili breathed a laugh. "Aye. But . . . not well. Come." He nodded to the captain, who stepped aside, and with him, the line broke into halves, affording access to a grand staircase.

"I canna' believe he is alive."

Aselan noticed his brother's grim expression and feared what that might mean. Though a few tapestries hung as banners, Aselan saw the hall for what it was—a hastily arranged welcome for Thurig the Formidable.

Their father noticed as well. "A little musty," his father said.

"Be nice," Relig warned.

Father shrugged. "What? 'Tis."

Quick, confident approaching steps drew their gaze to the side of another staircase. Two men strode toward them in tunics and breeches, heads shaved. One moved a little swifter, more confidently, and as he came closer, Aselan spotted the gold circlet. "Prince Haegan," he muttered, marveling at the much-changed appearance.

His father started. "Nay," he said. "Aye, 'tis!" He barked a laugh. "Prince!"

"King Thurig," Haegan greeted him with a firm handshake, complete with back-slapping affirmation.

"M'boy, look at ye!" He rubbed his hand on Haegan's head. "Bad haircut?"

Haegan's smile barely passed his lips. "Bad life, it seems." He stepped aside, nodding to Relig, then hesitated. Faltered as he met Aselan's gaze. "Cacique."

"Thinblood," Aselan teased—and finally, Haegan smiled, but a flurry of questions met the boy's face. He gave a small shake of his head, warning they could talk later.

Haegan hesitated for a second, then turned. "Please—come. I've had a meal warmed. We have volunteers preparing rooms, so we shall sup while we wait."

"Ah, that's grand," Father said. "But I would see yer father first. Where is he?"

Haegan's smile fell. "A dozen different places in the same thought."

Aselan frowned. "Ye speak in riddles."

Haegan laughed, hollowly. "I wish I did." He angled to the officer who'd welcomed them. "Please take the guests into the dining hall." He focused on the king. "King Thurig, Cacique—if you would follow me."

38

Having dealt with the discovery of yet another incipient, Tili took the stairs to the grand hall two at a time, anxious to see his family. He nodded to the guards at the door, rapped twice, and stepped in. The apartment was not as lavish as the king's solar where the Fire King quartered, but 'twas comfortable—save the peeling wallpaper and broken chairs being removed by servants. An arrangement of chairs and couches clustered around an empty fireplace. Tili grinned. Haegan may crave the stifling heat, but Tili was beginning to think he'd never be comfortable again.

Dressed in greens and golds, his mother rose from the settee elegantly, hands clasped. Shoulders squared. Their eyes met. "O Lady beneficent!" A shudder rent her façade of courage and confidence. "Tili!"

He inclined his head. "My queen—"

"Do not!" she said with a groan, reaching for him.

He went into her arms, savoring the love that had guided him through unruly years and so many turmoils. After kissing her cheeks, he eased back, remembering Peani was with them. "Pray—are ye well?"

"As can be expected," she said, ever graceful and proper. She looked to Relig's bound. "Peani has not fared as well, considering the child—"

"Aye," Tili said, catching his new sister's hand and planting a kiss on her cheek. "Osman shared the news. Congratulations, sister."

She smiled, but truth had been spoken. The toll upon her was great. The battle had yet to begin and already she faltered. Was she so frail? He thanked the Lady he had not succumbed to the machination of his mother and taken Peani as his bound. She had been too pretty, too petty, and too pampered for his liking.

"Have ye word of Kiethiel?" Tili asked his mother. His heart ached to know the location of another, but his mother would hold no answer there.

"None," she breathed. "We had hoped to find her here with the prince."

"He has threatened to leave in search of her, but we have dissuaded him."

"*Dissuaded?* Why?"

Tili snorted. "The war, Mother. We all put aside our heart's wishes in this day. He is the Fierian and must remain here for the battle. As must I." He took her shoulders and looked into her eyes. "Kiethiel will be well. She is strong like ye."

His mother seemed ready to speak, then pressed her lips together and nodded.

Grateful for her silence, Tili released her. "I wanted to see how ye found the accommodations." He nodded around. "Where are Father and my brothers?"

"Your father and Aselan went with the prince, I am told. Relig and Osmon are on a tour of the grounds and armies with the young colonel. Aburas had much to say—"

Tili chuckled. "I imagine well he did." He considered his mother. "'Tis good ye are here. As ye are settling, I will beg yer mercy—"

"Mercy—no. Wait." Mother reached to him. "I think one would speak with ye."

Tili glanced to Peani "Aye?"

Startled, his sister straightened. Shook her head. Then rushed into an adjoining room, from where a servant girl in brown emerged.

He glanced at his mother for clarification. "I—" *The eyes.* He snapped his gaze back to the servant. Nay, no servant. *Astadia.* His pulse jammed. He started forward then thought better of himself. Of her. Of his mother. The queen.

Hiel-touck!

Fisting a hand, Tili swallowed, his mind taking a split-second assessment. When he'd last seen her, she wore trousers, leather armor, daggers, and braids. Now, she was all . . . softness and curves in skirts and coils. He had to admit, he liked this attire better, for her curves fit well the feminine cut. What he liked even more was the way the curves had fit against him when they had kissed.

Mercies . . .

Of note were the long sleeves that hid her mark. Was that her choosing? Or theirs?

"Two minutes, Thurig as'Tili," his mother said in clear warning as she left the receiving room and joined Peani.

With the adjoining door partially closed, he shifted. Faced Astadia again. Heat rolled up his shoulders, his hands itching to take her into his arms. *Think not with yer loins but yer brain!*

She was an assassin. Taken by Drracien. Poired. How was she here? What was her intent? Had she deliberately gone to his mother? To what end? Betray him? Hurt them? The thought sent a trill of rage through him.

"Til—"

"How?" The question barked past his barriers. Anger jolted him, realizing how easily she could ruin him, his family. "What are ye doing here? With *my* family?"

But her eyes. They were molten. Liquid. She looked ready to crumble. Nay! Astadia Kath did not crumble. She crumbled others.

Now her chin trembled. His instincts warred—one to strangle her, another to crush her into his arms. What had happened to effect this change in her? "Are ye well?" He hated that he cared. Not until he knew the full of what transpired, how she left with the Dark One, yet appeared here.

"Aye," she managed, softly. Brokenly.

And it undid him. "Blazes, Astadia. Ye had me worried," he confessed, running a hand through his hair. "How did ye come to be here? And why with *my* mother?"

Her eyes slitted. "You think I'm here for some dark purpose?"

"Nay," he said, drawing it out, stepping closer. "Aye," he conceded, seeing something new in her—brokenness. Raw hurt. Whatever happened, 'twasn't good. "Ye were fair angry when we last—"

"Think you I am so vengeful, I would harm them because you rejected me?"

He braved another step. "'Twas no rejection."

"Wasn't it?" Her chin lifted, her neck graceful and elegant—and bare right down to . . .

Eyes to her face, he chided himself. "'Twas merely an attempt to save ye injury—"

"So to save me injury, you inflict your own."

"I hurt ye?" Truly, someone had. They were inches apart, making it difficult for him to take a breath—so scared he would frighten her off. Which would manifest as a punch.

That blazing vulnerability appeared with the ripple of her throat as she swallowed. "I'm an assassin. How could you possibly hurt me?"

"Apparently with more ease than imagined." He reached for her.

Astadia slapped his hand away.

"What happened to ye?"

She glowered, and again he reached for her. Again she swatted. This time, he'd anticipated it. Countered by catching her wrist and securing it behind her. She struggled and jerked back, but he yanked her forward. Her other fist flew.

With a smile that fueled the fire in her eyes, Tili caught and drove it behind as well. Both hands at her back, he hauled her to himself. She was a wild thing of beauty. She stirred him and riled him as no other woman. Her beauty was not in coiled hair and rouge and low bodices—though hers at the moment certainly worsened his distraction—but of fire and courage.

Astadia's lips parted with a gasp, wariness in those liquid green eyes. But then she bucked. "Release me!"

"Never again."

She stilled, surprised by the words. Good. He'd intended that. Liked it that she now searched him, the truth of his words. What surprised him more was that he meant it. "Tili—"

"Never again," he whispered, releasing her hands and catching her lips in a soft, teasing kiss. "I'll never leave ye again."

Her hands slid up his chest.

Greedy to have her in his arms, he pressed her against himself, burying his face in her neck. But then . . . he felt it. Like a surf crashing against the rocks. Crying. Her sobs went violent and deep.

Astadia was . . . crying?

Tili strangled his desire. Chastised himself for not paying attention to the signals he'd seen then lost sight of as he held her. She tangled his mind. What had she gone through? He cupped her head and held her, enraged that anyone could cause her to cry. Whatever hurt they had perpetrated against her—"I'll kill them," he promised against her ear.

Her arms tightened around him, breath hot along his neck as her tears slowed raggedly.

No more could he take it. He eased back and framed her face in his hands. "What happened?"

She batted away her tears, shaking her head, but not enough to break free. Anguish roiled through her. "He—they—then he—" She clutched his tunic tightly in a fist until her trembling calmed. Then she shoved back without warning. Using the sleeves of her gown—his mother would rail at that—she smeared away the tears.

She glowered, shaking her head. Where grief and some very real terror had colored her cheeks a moment ago, now anger and that fiery spirit roared back to the surface. "I'll murder them. Both of them! All of them!"

Tili felt like he'd been struck with a sword hilt. "Astadia."

Her darting eyes locked onto him.

"Breathe."

She shuddered and turned away, swatting aside her skirts.

"What happened?" he managed around his traitorous thoughts.

"They held me prisoner. In the high tower of the Citadel, I think. Brought in that hideous creature-man . . ." Her thoughts sought purchase, gaze darting around the room, then back to his. "I don't know what he did to me." Again, her chin trembled. "But never—*never* have I felt such cold, horrifying darkness." She shuddered. "Then everything was sharp and torturous. Like shivs being drawn across every inch my flesh."

And she would know of that, being an assassin.

"That thing kept calling me *unnatural*, shrieking so that my ears bled. Next thing I know, Drracien is pitching me through"—she shrugged—"this space. Somehow, I ended up on the plains outside Hetaera. A day and a night alone before I found the remnant."

"Sounds like ye scared them." Tili liked that. She had certainly scared him when they first met. Or at least inspired a healthy respect. "What did he mean that ye were unnatural?" He reached for her, relieved when she did not push him away again. "I mean, I knew yer beauty is unnatural—"

She sniffed, rolling her eyes. "I know not what he meant, but the way that thing shrieked . . ." She covered her ears. "They all looked at me as if *I* were the monster."

"Ye are no monster, trust me. I'm an expert on them." The need to pull her into his arms tugged at him. "How did ye come to be here, with my mother?"

She lifted a shoulder in a lazy shrug, drawing his gaze to her bare clavicle that peeked out. "She had pity on me—my clothes were shredded. I was dehydrated and exhausted."

"Do they know—"

"We'll depart soon," came his mother's abnormally loud voice, warning of her return.

Astadia gave the barest shake of her head and stepped from his touch.

His mother entered with a bored, passive expression. "I trust you are reacquainted enough?"

Reacquainted? "How do ye know of Astadia?"

Regal in her bearing, his mother glided closer, a knowing smile on her refined features. "When we had her tale after discovering her on the road, 'twas her numerous mentions of the steward that alerted me." His mother was the most perceptive woman in the kingdom, and she knew it. "I see my intuition was right." She smiled at Astadia, considering her. Appraising her.

What did his mother think of her? Without knowledge of Astadia's profession, what *would* one think? He could not fathom, for to him she was the assassin and the beauty who had cut out his heart and made off with it.

"So, you are smitten with our Prince Tili." His mother seemed to preen. "You have chosen well, and a surprise at that. Not because of anything about you—after all, you are a comely little thing, but ask Peani—he is not easily snared."

Humiliated, and seeing his sister's face go crimson, Tili stepped forward. "Mother, enough."

Astadia twitched. The title. Their conversation. His words that it wouldn't work.

Blast, he just wanted out of here. Go fight an incipient—it'd be less humiliating.

"He's handsome enough," Astadia said quietly. "But a bit thickheaded."

Shock held him fast as his mother let out a peal of laughter. "Oh, I do like her, Tili. I'm so glad I convinced the king to take her under the Nivar banner."

"Took her—" Tili frowned, glancing again at Astadia, who stared back without a trace of humility or embarrassment.

"Aye," his mother said. "Is that a problem? Do you not trust us to look after her? She's safe here with us."

More a problem than either of them could ever know, since they didn't know they sheltered a murderer. The council at Nivar would not approve. However, it did solve one problem for Tili—making sure she was not far enough from his side to be snatched again. But that presented another problem: temptation.

"She is right," Astadia muttered, drawing closer. Too naïve, too unpracticed in matters of court to know how she stepped out of line just then. "I am well here. Your mother, the queen, has been more than gracious."

Where had this creature of diplomacy come from? Should he be concerned?

"The Nivari are at the door. Ye have only to call for me." He gave his mother a curt bow, then backed up, glancing again at Astadia. Something telling him he should not leave these two alone.

• • •

"King Thurig, I would have ye meet Vaqar."

"A Tahscan," Thurig said, a growl in his words and disgust on his lips. "Ye have Pathfinders and Jujak. Aye, even my own son. Why do ye need—"

"Where I go, he will go," Haegan said as he led them up the stairs to the king's solar. "I've asked that he not leave my side. As a warrior, he brings skills I am just learning, but also . . . Abiassa has gifted Vaqar with the ability to detect inflaming."

"How?" Thurig asked.

"Quite literally, he can *smell* the inflaming, the wielding. I do not want to end up like my father, yet nearly did." Shame seeped into him. "'Tis easy to miss the inflaming and embrace doubts. When Poired comes, I fully expect him to manipulate my will and doubts against me again, so he may gain the advantage and slaughter those I am tasked with protecting. Therefore, Vaqar or one of his people is with me. Night and day. When he detects dark wielding, he alerts me. Vaqar will be my shield."

Thurig answered only with a grunt as they trod the semi-darkened passages.

"What of my sister? And Thiel?" Haegan glanced to Aselan, quickly noting how their silence filled the hall. "Are they well? What word?"

"There has been no word of Kiethiel since Gwogh sent her out," Aselan said.

Haegan himself had news more recent than that, though it was of no comfort. "Chima came bearing Laertes but not her. Laertes said the Ematahri were keeping them in cages." He decided not to mention the fact that Thiel had been taken from the cage some time before Chima's escape, that she had almost escaped herself. "I've sent a Drigo to search for her."

"We thank ye," Aselan said. "She is strong."

As everyone said, yet it gave Haegan no relief. "And my sister?"

Aselan's face darkened.

Haegan stopped. "What?" Fisted his hands. "Is she . . . dead?"

"Nay," Aselan said, glancing at Haegan's hands, at the wakes roiling off them. "At least, not as far as I know. They snatched her—ambushed the Legiera as they fled the Tooth."

"Fled?"

"Aye."

"I would have this story."

"Prince Haegan," King Thurig broke into the conversation. "I would pay my respects to yer father, that I might sup before the moons rise."

"Of course," Haegan said as they climbed stairs and explained what had happened to both him and his father. "While I escaped mostly . . . unaffected, I am afraid the same cannot be said of my father, for he endured the inflaming of the Infantessa and the Dark One for much longer." He stopped before the doors, where two sentries stood faithfully.

"I . . . He will not know you." He thought to warn them, but what was there to say? No words could prepare a soul to see such degradation of a man.

He stepped aside and the sentries opened the doors. Mustering his courage, Haegan entered. Spotted his father sitting in a chair, staring blankly. Would he know *him* today? He'd known Haegan on the roof but for a second. "Father, I have brought guests."

No response. Haegan glanced back. And though Thurig hesitated for a second, he came forward. "Zireli, what are ye doing sitting about?"

More surprise spiraled through Haegan—that Thurig would address the Fire King so casually, but also that the query pulled his father from the stupor.

His father blinked. Looked at their guests. "Thurig?"

A bear-laugh boomed.

His father came to his feet.

Drawing in a breath, Haegan watched, marveled.

"What are you doing in Seultrie?"

The bubble of hope popped. Haegan's gut cinched. He feared Thurig would falter and then his father would grow agitated.

"Interrupting yer daydreams, it appears," Thurig said, never missing a beat. "Don't ye have a kingdom to rule? A nemesis to overthrow?"

They were the wrong words. His father shook his head. Slowly. Then frantically. He backed up, the chair clipping the backs of his legs, dropping him hard to the seat, which groaned beneath the impact. "No no no."

Haegan surged forward. Caught his father's hands. "Father, did you read mother's letter?"

Pale blue eyes met his, unfocused, confused. "Adrroania?"

"Aye," Haegan said softly, soothingly. "I'm told she sent another."

"I would like to read it," came his father's slurred words.

"I'll have it delivered at once." He patted his father's hands then rose and started for the others, motioning them out of the room. They complied, their expression hanging with the weight of what they'd seen.

As the doors closed, Haegan turned to Thurig. "I would have warned you, but there is naught to say to prepare one."

What he expected, he wasn't sure, but what happened never would have entered his mind. The burly, formidable king gathered Haegan into his arms. Patted his back. Breathed hard. "Ye have my sympathy, m'boy."

Something in Haegan broke. Shifted. Righted. Aligned. Stung his eyes.

"That should no' happen to anyone, especially no' Zireli."

Throat raw, Haegan nodded as the king gripped his neck and shook it—not meanly. But in affirmation. Solidarity.

"Why did ye show us?" he asked. "Ye could have hidden it, concealed—"

"I would have you know what we face." Haegan held their gazes, not so much for confidence, but because he was afraid of falling into the depths of darkness that held him.

"Will Zireli improve?" Aselan asked.

Haegan eyed the Drigo who lumbered back down the hall, giving them a long look before making his way to the king. "The answer is not known. He is vastly improved since I carried him from the dungeons, but . . ." Haegan shook his head. "The Drigo healer tends him, however, the damage to his mind—he is lost in his thoughts, as I was, but much worse."

"Yet, he called to ye," Aselan said. "Yer dreams—ye told me once a man called to ye in them. Yer father, aye?"

Smiling, Haegan nodded. "And that keeps my hope alive. Somehow, some crevice of his abiatasso harbors what remains of the man we once knew, and I believe that is what called to me, though I knew it not at the time." He indicated to Vaqar. "Once you have been the puppet of inflaming, the familiarity of it is welcomed by a brain and body tired of fighting. I am weary, which is why"—Haegan angled toward his advocate—"I have instituted safety measures."

"We will no' speak of it. 'Twill be carried to our graves."

Hide it? Conceal the truth? Haegan shook his head. "Nay, though I appreciate your willingness to protect me and my father, I would have you talk of it, have it always at the front of your minds."

"Why?" Aselan asked, bewildered.

"The people must know the danger. Even you are not immune," Haegan said. "And if 'tis forgotten, we are as well."

39

On the southern plains of Vid, Poired stalked the path with his black raqine, past incipients with knees pressed to the hard earth. None dared bring their eyes to the Dark One, dared tempt his patience. His anger.

Drracien knew that fear. He walked behind him, letting the anger and annoyance seep through his skin, sink deep into his bones.

A cluster of red tents emptied of Silvers, their gleaming helms hiding the darkness beneath. An impressive sight. All the same, he wondered if there was flesh there as well.

Resentment tightened his breath, his steps. He had not wanted this path. Aye, the enhancement of his abilities was nice. Though he'd always been strong in wielding, what he could do now . . . And tearing open the Void? Though it also tore at his abiatasso, he could not deny the glory of wielding such power.

"Commander ka'Dur," Poired said, met by the high-collared incipient who emerged from the main tent, flanked by four others.

"My lord," ka'Dur greeted as he bowed ridiculously low, his nose nearly touching the earth.

Impulse taunted Drracien to stomp his face into the ground he seemed so eager to eat. To dirty the well-oiled hair and the—was he wearing powders? Disgust flushed through Drracien, making him hate this man. He seized the anger, feeling it sizzle through his veins. Fuel his wielding. What had ka'Dur done to earn Poired's attention?

And why had he not invited his lord into the tent? A slight to be sure. As if the thought alone produced it, ka'Dur stumbled backward. Drracien smiled. Apparently Poired did not appreciate the slight either.

"What report have you?" Poired ducked inside.

"Mercy, my lord," whimpered ka'Dur, realizing his error too late.

"He wields not in mercy." Drracien bumped his shoulder against the lesser man as he moved past him.

The segmented interior had seating arrangements, lush sleeping quarters, gold decanters and plates . . . but it was the cage in the far corner that made Drracien's stomach tighten.

It held a beauty of a woman with white-gold tresses and a cobalt gown. Eyes the color of a pale sky. Princess Kaelyria. Drracien would know her anywhere.

"What is she doing in here?" Poired snapped.

When she did not shrink as Drracien expected, he was drawn to her. "Haegan's sister," he said, stalking the cage. Inspecting her.

"You promised she would be mine—"

Poired flicked his hand. The man staggered again. "Yes—after the battle. After this is done! Be rid of—"

"My father," Drracien said, his heart beating a little faster at the thought of her dying. Because he already knew the Dark One would never reward anyone for anything. He would kill her when he was done. "Such beauty should not be wasted."

Poired glared at Drracien. "You want this woman?"

"She's barely more than a girl," Drracien said, keeping his voice amused. Wondering why he would even answer the call within him. "But she looks . . . entertaining."

"I fear you will not want her, my lord, when you know," came ka'Dur's dull voice. "She's—"

Drracien pivoted. Thrust out a bolt and wrapped it tight around the man's voice. "Think not that you know anything of me or my wants." He had never been prone to bloodlust, but seeing this worm of an incipient squirm gave him delicious pleasure.

Poired smirked. "Leave him, Drracien."

Just a little more and there would be no breath . . .

"Son. I need him."

Hesitating just a few more beats, Drracien released the incipient with a huff. Dragged his hooded gaze back to the princess. Did Haegan know where his sister was? Drracien could not imagine—the princeling was far too concerned about her when last they met. If he knew, he'd have come.

And still, she did not tremble or cower. She was incredible. Regal. Proud. What iron did they breed at Seultrie, beside the Lakes of Fire? Truly, he would know.

"Sire, with all due respect," ka'Dur whined, "I—"

"When people say that, it really means with no respect," Drracien countered, pulling his gaze from the pale eyes that fastened onto him. "That you think my father too stupid to know something. Is that it?"

The incipient glowered as Drracien again swept past him with more condescension. Tendrils of hatred and embers reached after him. Drracien stopped. "You would test me?" He faced ka'Dur, relishing the fact he was several inches taller than the putrid one. Though the incipient held a high rank and had most likely wielded for decades, he was weak.

"Drracien, leave him," Poired said impatiently. "Cilicien, we must talk. What of the battle? The Fierian and our spies, our efforts to seize control?"

Face crimson and hands trembling, the incipient scurried to his master. "All is good, sire. Our spies report with regularity. Well, one or two are late, but there is no cause for alarm. We outnumber them three to one."

The Dark One unfolded himself and stood, hands behind his back, at the far end of the tent. "I would use Zireli's spawn."

"I—no!" Cilicien argued. "She is promised to me. You can't—"

Poired snapped up a hand, which smacked ka'Dur with an invisible punch. "You presumed to know my son's mind, do you dare suggest you know mine as well?" Warmth flared through the canvas walls, swelling from his anger.

Cilicien twitched and jerked his chin down. "No. Of course not, my lord."

Tossing back his overcloak, Drracien lifted a bronze censer by the handle from the trunk on which it sat, infusing the tent with a strong, spicy aroma. A memory clung to the wisps of smoke rising from the holes in the orb. "My tutor at the Citadel loved this smell," Drracien spoke. "Said it cleared his thoughts."

"Aye," Cilicien said. "It does the same for me."

Drracien pivoted. "Does it?" As he hefted the orb, tiny flecks of the smoking wad within flaked against his hand. "If it did, you would be aware that the Fierian has taken Ironhall and is amassing an army."

"Ironhall?" Cilicien scowled. "It's in ruins. What could he hope to gain by taking it?"

Working heat into the wad, Drracien started toward the incipient. "If your *clear senses* were on the mission the Dark One gave you and not distracted by"—he turned his gaze to the cage and the princess, who pressed her spine into the bars farther from him—"you would know he is fortifying it."

"I . . . I had not received word. As said, a scout is—"

Drracien pitched the censer at the man.

Ka'Dur caught it. Took a second—shrieked, dropping the orb and blowing on his scalded hands. "Fool!"

Darkness loomed and grew, flooding from Poired at the incipient.

Drracien held ka'Dur's gaze, loving the way he seemed to have forgotten so much—who was with him, who he was, who he was not.

"Take my son's warning and the pain in your hands as a reminder that your gifts are not permanent and are at my"—Poired cocked his head—"*mercy.*"

Pale and now trembling with both fury and terror, ka'Dur nodded.

"Pull up stakes and start north. We make for Ironhall and the Fierian."

"But—" Cilicien swallowed, lowered his head. Then swallowed again. "They have the advantage, if he is there. He's had time to refortify. He'll be prepared."

"*If* he's there?" Drracien drew up straight. "Are you yet again challenging the Dark One?"

Ka'Dur flinched. "Nay—I only meant . . . won't they be expecting us?"

"Aye." Poired nearly smiled. "But they won't see what's coming. He will see his sister, and that will be *our* advantage."

40

"I would ride with ye."

Tili glanced at his brother, one forearm heavily bandaged, the other hand holding reins. The lower part of his leg, which he favored heavily, was likewise wrapped in thick rags and plaster.

"The Drigo healer has seen to me. Ye know I have trained around worse injuries."

With a nod, Tili relented. "I could make use of yer tracking skills, brother."

Nearby Astadia checked her knives, head bent low, her brow surprisingly delicate. How had he not noticed that before? He slipped closer as she tucked a throwing knife into the sheath strapped to her thigh. "Stay close to me."

"I have not needed your protection before now—"

"I fear Poired will return for ye."

Shoulder to his arm, she brought those large green eyes to his, telegraphing her own fear of the same. With a sharp nod, she returned to checking her gear.

"Have ye no word of Kaelyria?" Elan asked as he secured a blanket. "Of her location?"

"Nay, nor of Kiethiel," Tili said. "But they will both be found. Alive." He met his brother's gaze. "I promise ye. Haegan will not give up on his sister or ours. He loves them both."

"From yer lips to Her ears." A knavish look crossed Elan's face. "What of yers?"

"Mine?"

Elan glanced over his shoulder to Astadia. "Has my warring brother traded his smelly stables and clanging swords for roses and sweet whispers?"

Tili glowered at the elder Thurig.

"Fresh-faced. Young. No blush, but there is an eager light in her eyes when she looks upon ye." Elan's teasing had always been relentless. "Mother says Father is not aware of yer affection—"

"There is no affection." He could not believe the lie so easily escaped his lips, even as his eyes sought their father, immersed in conversation with Colonel Grinda, then searched for Astadia, hoping she hadn't heard either.

She stood to the side, her foot propped on a crate as she tightened her greaves.

"'Tis not what Peani or Mother said—that ye could barely breathe in her presence."

"Me? Paralyzed by a woman? Ye know better, brother."

Concern darted through Elan's face. "Aye. But I've also heard of yer character from yer men, who give tale that ye were seen kissing the girl." Elan's dark eyes glinted. "What of her profession?"

Hesitating, Tili hated the truth of it. "Ye know of her?"

"Most here do and freely speak of it. Father will not approve."

Tili again looked to his father and prayed his hearing had turned as gray as his hair. "But neither did he approve when ye went to the Heart for Doskari."

"And ye saw how that ended. 'Twas painful. It tore at the family." He squinted at Tili. "And yet, ye are unaltered."

Tili stuffed on his gloves. "Never have I known a woman like her."

"Mayhap because most women do not run about killing people."

Annoyance turned Tili away, but Elan caught his arm. "Give care, brother. Assassins are trained on ripping out hearts and swaying men's attention. They are not trained to love."

"Does one need training for that?"

"Give care."

Tili tugged free. "Ye said that already."

"Could ye not choose one with softer means of breaking hearts?"

"What? As ye did?"

Elan's gaze faltered. "'Tis unfair."

"Exactly as I thought when ye left our home for her bed." Tili huffed, then ran a hand over his head. "I would not spar with ye, Elan. There is too much grief in this world already."

"Aye. It seems only right that all men should have their hearts shattered at least once."

Tili snorted, thoughts still heavily resting on the girl nearby, the one who'd donned leathers and daggers. The one who could hold her own against any Pathfinder.

'Twas strange to think of her—in truth, to have concern for any female. He was trained to protect. What was to be said of a woman better trained than her bound?

"The assassin rides with me," Grinda announced.

Heat shot across Tili's shoulders, praying in earnest his father had not heard. Praying Astadia did not go with the Pathfinder.

"Assassin?" Thurig asked, ears always too sharp. "Of whom do ye speak, Colonel?"

With his back to his father, Tili eyed Astadia, who slid two short swords into their sheaths crisscrossing her spine. She showed nothing that betrayed concern or annoyance regarding the question hanging over the bailey as she caught Grinda's hand and flew effortlessly up onto his mount. Nowhere except her eyes. Tili saw it. Hurt. Fear.

Anger snaked through him. He fisted a hand. Whether over the taunts or that she clung to another man, he could not discern. Mayhap both.

"Have ye not heard, King Thurig?" Grinda said, holding a gauntlet toward her. "We have the loyalty of a Devoted, one of Poired's assassins."

"Aye, she's also his daughter," Laerian chuckled, nodding to Aburas, who would join them on the patrol. "Dare you to spar with her."

His father's ruddy face neither colored nor paled. He simply measured the girl on the horse beside the colonel. "If ye trust her . . ."

"Aye," Grinda said, his hair bright in the afternoon sun. "As far as my blade extends."

"That close?" Astadia purred, her defiance a mask for the rejection inherent in their taunts. "You *are* a brave one."

Ripples of laughter sifted the tension that had built.

"Mount up!" Tili turned to his destrier and snagged on his mother's face in the door of the keep. Saw her remonstration. Her warning. Without acknowledging her silent signals, he hauled himself up. "We ride!"

"Tili!"

He glanced down as Haegan jogged over to him. "I did not want to give false hope, nor linger in it myself, but keep a weather eye out. Thelikor could return soon."

The Drigo who'd gone after Thiel. "We share reasonable hope for their quick return."

Haegan's expression softened. "Thank you."

Tili rode after the riders already trotting over the footbridge and banking southwest toward the copse of trees and dried-up riverbeds. He spurred his mount, trying to catch up with Astadia. When he realized his intent had been to apologize for the teasing, for the taunt by Grinda, Tili drew back. She was more used to that treatment than most. An apology or any reassurance would only annoy her, make her think he believed her soft or weak. How did one reach a woman like that? Tear down those barriers?

Not denying her to Elan is a good start.

Instead, he forced himself to stay near his father and spent the morning tracking, giving Grinda's men time to sketch maps for strategizing later, for weighing risks and advantages of various locations. But even as they considered the dried riverbed—clear line of sight that ran east-west . . . and more of a demarcation line than a route for attack—he noticed Astadia now riding with Tokar. Talking. Laughing.

What was that about? Those two had been near-enemies before. Need Tili be jealous—concerned?

"'Tis a good location," his father said in a deep voice that pulled Tili back to the mission. "He chose well."

Surprise tugged at him. "A compliment? For the son of Zireli?"

His father's eyes pinched beneath a smile. "'Tis a good man who can acknowledge the skill of another." He chuckled. "Even if begrudgingly." Thick fingers pointing, he went on. "The charred trees are helpful in hand-to-hand or sword fighting—even wielding—but they are also cover for advancing on us, especially as they are already burned." Then a shrug. "But 'tis better than being in a city with thousands and putting their lives at risk."

A ripple of laughter, then quiet conversation caught Tili's attention. No, it was her voice. Her voice drew him. Astadia. And that blasted thinblood. He was too young for her. Too scrawny. Not man enough.

They're very nearly the same age, aye?

And yet she was twice the man as the thinblood.

Spikes of fire peppered his arms, begging him to pull the reins in that direction. Twitched at his legs to quicken his horse.

"How long has the assassin been with ye?"

Tili jerked to his father, whose dark eyes monitored Astadia. "We discovered her before the battle at Iteveria."

"Discovered her?"

"The men . . . found her." Hands fisted, Tili fought the memory. "Praegur alerted me. They were intent on . . ."

"Ravishing her."

Tili gave a curt nod.

"And what did ye do?"

"Cold-cocked the one with his trousers undone."

"And held her prisoner?"

"Aye, until we could assess things."

"Why is she free now? She's not of the Nine, and she murders for hire."

"I beg yer mercy," Tili said, annoyed. "I forgot to check her papers and weapons."

His father scowled.

"Lest ye forget, Father, we are not of the Nine either, and we are not imprisoned." He nodded to Jadrile. "Neither are the Tahscans. We are in a war that defies political boundaries."

"But she's a murderer."

"Are not we all, when 'tis considered?"

"Ye defend an assassin?"

"I defend a woman who has saved my life and the Fierian's." Across the field, he saw Laerian lift a hand. "If ye will excuse me . . ." He rode through the group to the Pathfinder. "What it is?"

"Tracks," Laerian said, dismounting.

Tili joined him, crouching to better see and consider the imprint left in the dirt and ash. He rubbed his thumb over his lower lip, following the marks—several of them—northward.

"Villagers?" someone asked.

Tili shook his head. "Nay."

"Too small," Astadia's answer came at the same time as his. She met his gaze but forged ahead. "The shoe is wrong."

"Shoe?" a Jujak asked. "What shoe?"

"She's right," his father-king said.

Silence clamped the mockery that seemed all-too-ready to attack.

"Go on." His father yielded with a nod.

Astadia hesitated, her gaze hitting Tili—revealing surprise and uncertainty—as if expecting that his father waited for her to make a mistake, so he could ridicule her.

Wary of his father's motives, Tili gave her subtlest of nods.

"The shoe is tailored. Villagers wear sandals or boots they've made themselves or bought in a shop, if they can afford it," Astadia spoke softly. "See the way the top of the imprint is sharp? It's a tip."

"Incipients," said Laerian. "They're the only prigs who wear fancy shoes like that."

"Follow it," his father suggested. "Lead on, girl."

This time, Astadia never looked at him. She shoved off, her steps soft and lightning-fast as she rushed through the charred remains of the woods. It proved a challenge, following her over the rough terrain on their horses. More than once, they gained only to have her surge ahead and vanish.

"She toys with us," his father growled. "Trying to lose us."

"She need not try for that. Perhaps she slows at intervals so we can keep up," Tili offered.

"Here," came her voice, clear and steady.

Tili drew up short at a small trough of a dried creek bed and dismounted. He stalked toward her, marveling that she was not out of breath.

"What is it?" his father demanded.

But Tili saw it, a body—more a skeleton.

"Not twenty paces from the tree line," Laerian muttered. "Must've been here during the assault when Poired destroyed the fortress."

She held her arm straight out, pointing. "Look."

Tili stood beside her and glanced in the indicated direction. His breath backed up. A straight path gave a perfect line of sight on—"Ironhall."

"This doesn't make sense." Astadia's words were soft, confused.

"I beg yer—"

"The forest was burned during the last stand of the duke," she said quietly. "So why is the body atop the litter and ashes, not within?"

"Haegan," Tili said, his thoughts crashing in on one another. "When the Fire King nearly pitched himself off the terrace—"

"The wave," Laerian said.

"What wave?" Thurig demanded.

"Aye." Tili met his father's frustrated gaze. "When Haegan wields under Abiassa's guiding, it sends a sort of wave—combination of heat and shock—out."

"Killed half the population of Iteveria," Grinda said.

"The half that colluded with the Infantessa," Astadia added. "This—this could be the result of his wielding for his father."

"He wielded against Zireli?"

"Nay," Tili said. "Gwogh suggested someone inflamed his father's thoughts again, blurring reality and dreams . . . drawing him to the edge of the keep's tower to pitch himself down. It angered Haegan. He threw out the wave."

"Aye, we heard a scream in the distance—here." Laerian's gaze fell on the skeleton. "Think ye this is who wielded against him?"

"If it is," Thurig said, "for the first time, I have hope of surviving."

"But it still doesn't . . . match," Astadia countered. "When Haegan sends the wake, it disintegrates its victims. This skeleton is largely intact."

"This was an incipient and some distance from the castle," Tili observed. "Perhaps he had time to throw up a shield. Partially." He grunted. "Lot of good it did him."

Astadia looked up at him over her shoulder with those beautiful green eyes. Then she jerked around. Frozen save her gaze, which darted through the forest of charred trunks.

Tili felt the change. Sensed . . . something. He edged closer. "What is it?"

"Someone's coming," she whispered.

Silent signals by Grinda sent his Pathfinders scurrying into the trees. The stealth of their movements impressed Tili as the rest grouped up, hunkering along the dried streambed.

This was the perfect route into the fortress, just as the person who was now a skeleton must've thought. But to arrive amid Pathfinders, a Tahscan, and an assassin . . .

41

Though she had not been this far east before, Thiel knew the land. Sensed the thrum in the air as she and Thelikor—still quite tall but not the massive beast who'd fallen from the sky between her and Onerid—followed the Westerly, a river that had some spring source and circled a one-time great fortress, then trickled out of existence in the plains.

Feet blistered, lips cracked, she walked, hobbling along mile after mile. Because she must. Because if she stopped, the horrible truths might catch up. She'd cried nearly nonstop the first two days of their journey, unable to get the image of Cadeif's death out of her mind. She'd begged and begged Thelikor to knock her unconscious and carry her. To use Drigo healing—of which he claimed to have none—to take away the hurt.

She had never loved Cadeif, not the way she loved Haegan. But he was . . .

She hesitated.

Mine. He was mine.

"Close." Thelikor's voice hung like a hot, heavy mist over her as he motioned down the river, which also had been too afraid to remain alive in this dark time. She envied it, having vanished. Dried. Died.

The ache in her breast outweighed and distracted her from the ones in her body and head. Water. She needed water.

She stumbled, and Thelikor reached for her. She shook her head, not wanting his help. No longer caring.

"Mm, close," Thelikor said, his trunk-like arm motioning.

Thiel looked, and through the scarred, scraggly sentries, she saw the forbidding black stone in the distance.

Thiel sucked in a hard breath, seeing men bleed from the shadows. From the crevices. She backed up, choked with fear. No strength. She had no strength to fight. And even less to flee.

Why had Thelikor not warned her? Stopped her? Yet, something spiraled through her.

"Halt! Do not move or we'll bleed you where you stand."

Thiel fumed at the ambivalence with which Thelikor met the confrontation. "I am unarmed," she said, lifting her aching arms as she glanced at the giant—"well, unless ye count a Drigo."

One apparently not in the mood to fight. *That* she could understand.

"Thiel?"

She started, blinking. Shoved the strands from her face, searching the horde surrounding her. Then she saw him pushing through the small army. "Tili?" Exhaustion was the only thing that seeped through her, pushing tears to her eyes. Blurring her vision. A strangled laugh mingled with his name. She sagged, feeling every vestige of strength fail her as he rushed her. Her knees gave way.

Arms encircled her shoulders. Pulled her into safety. "Easy, sister," came his whisper.

"Don't pick me up," she muttered, sinking into his strength. "They'll laugh."

"Ever defiant."

"With my last breath."

"Aye, seems near."

With a near laugh, she shook her head, then rested against his chest. Hooked her arm around his neck—as much for the extra help in standing as to embrace him. "Yet too far."

"I carry," Thelikor said, shifting.

"Nay," Thiel objected again.

"Kiethiel!"

She jerked. Turned in her brother's hold, searching, wobbling. "It cannot be." She had yet to catch sight of his face.

"'Tis," Tili whispered.

"Father . . . ?"

Her father's broad shoulders broke through the gathered line. He stomped to her. Took her into his arms.

"Father," she said, fighting the tears. The relief. The joy. "Ye were so far away."

"Aye, but I'm here now."

"And I." A voice she had not heard for years but had not forgotten.

Thiel yanked round. "Elan!" She laughed. "Down from the Heart? How is it so? And to find ye—here, of all places?"

Elan hugged her, and she pressed into his shoulder. "A story for another time."

"We should get back to Ironhall," came a stern voice.

Tili took the reins of his horse and led her toward it. "Ride with me." He swung up into the saddle.

Thiel reached up, but before she could even try, Thelikor placed her behind Tili. She slumped against him, the act of holding him a trembling effort as the entourage picked their way through the dead woods.

"Are ye well?" Tili asked as they rode.

"I am now," she said, resting her cheek against his shoulder blade. She spotted a girl—*familiar*—riding, watching. Something in her expression . . .

"Yer words are weighted."

"Aye."

"Haegan will be pleased to see ye."

She lifted her head, leaning on his shoulder. "How is he?"

"Much changed."

"It seems everyone is. Father here. Elan down from the Tooth." She sighed and turned her head again . . . once more catching the girl watching. But not watching Thiel. Watching Tili. "How is Father come here?"

"Nivar was attacked by the Rekken."

"What?" She sat straight. "They are not large enough—"

"Allied with the Sirdarians, they were more than enough. Too much— the Heart evacuated, then marched here."

She was almost afraid to ask. She could not endure another loss, not so soon. "And Mother?"

"Here, in the fortress."

"Thank the Lady," Thiel whispered, relieved to know her family was here, safe. But her mind swung back to one face. Haegan. Tili said he was much changed. Though she itched to inquire further, she withheld her questions, too afraid of the answers. Of the reality. They had not parted on the best of terms. It was so long ago . . . She ached for him.

Over his shoulder, Tili turned concerned eyes to her.

"Ask not," she muttered, pressing her nose to his shoulder again.

"Open the gate for the steward," a shout went up.

"Oh, aye," she breathed around a laugh. "*Steward* Tili. Has the power gone to yer head yet? More ladies vying for your favor?"

"Shut it," he growled.

Thiel laughed, grateful for the familiarity, the laugh in her brother's tone. Her gaze drifted to the lone female among the warriors. No surprise the woman monitored Tili with a sidelong stare.

Who are ye that ye stare so openly at a prince? And travel with trackers, soldiers . . . ?

Hooves thunked against the boards of the footbridge as they trod into the bailey. The sound of sparring, swords clanging, and meaty grunts rushed out to greet them.

"They're at it again," one of the Pathfinders mumbled. "Start at first light and keep at it until well past dark."

"Never is there enough training and sparring," Tili responded. "The Dark One is at our door, and we have more greenies than soldiers. The sooner the villagers learn to fight, the better."

"Villagers?" someone snickered. "What of the Fierian?"

"Ye challenge him, after seeing that skeleton?" Another dark chuckle. "Make sure I'm standing far apart when ye do."

"What are they talking about?" Thiel asked as the horses were brought about.

But over his shoulder, she saw more than twenty men sparring with swords and jav-rods. Many missing tunics and pouring sweat in the midafternoon heat.

Two were going to blows, one far more ferocious than the other, but the less ardent moved swiftly. Deflected. Parried. Then attacked with lightning speed. His broad shoulders rippled with each strike, the muscles toned but not corded like her brother or Aburas. Intensity flowed through his moves. His profile was sharp and strong, too. Aye, a looker that one. His shorn hair added to his severity.

"Who is he?" she asked, not intending to say it out loud.

Tili glanced at her, then in the direction of her gaze.

Thiel chastised herself for being so distracted. "Nay. Forget I asked. I would see Haegan."

Exulted shouts went up as the two in the ring went rounds, drawing spectators and—once more—her attention. The handsome one had stealth, surprise, and speed. He was strong and determined. Quite impressive from this angle. She had to admit—the muscles were—

"Steward is returned!" someone shouted.

The men in the training yard yielded and spun to welcome their entourage back.

Thiel was struck silent when the warrior turned. Pale blue eyes hit hers. It took a second for the face to register. She forgot the air in her lungs. Then breathed, "Haegan."

"Must I chain ye up, sister?" Tili asked with laugh.

Haegan's eyes widened, and he tossed aside the sparring sword. "Thiel!"

She was off the mount, somehow—she knew not, cared not how—exhaustion and injured ankle forgotten. Amazed, mesmerized at the man rushing through the throng toward her.

Man. Gone was the *boy* who'd stolen her heart. Shoulders and jaw squared. Determination laced the ridge of his brow, which had deepened. How had these changes been wrought in so short a time? His blues fixed on her as he pressed aside beast and man to reach her, squeezing her belly tight with churning anticipation like a giddy cocktail.

In one fell swoop, she was in his arms, crushed to his chest. She tried to rein in her thoughts, but the muscular arms that encircled her were not the ones that had held her months past. The smell of sweat and combat clung to his skin, and somehow, she savored it.

"Months have I longed and prayed to Abiassa for this moment," he breathed against her neck, a thrill shooting down her spine. Released her and stepped back. His hands cupped her face as he stared. Those pale blue eyes, as always, undid her. Her stomach tightened. It had been so long . . . "Are you well? How do you fare?"

"Well," she managed. 'Twas a lie, but she would not voice complaints. "Better now."

His gaze pierced as he took in those words. He had no shirt on. She drew back, her hands running down his arms. The curve and swell of his muscles teased her fingers and mind—aye, in attraction but also alarm. There were ridges. Dozens of them. She looked down to see scars covering his arms. She started.

"No need for alarm. I did this."

"Why?"

"So I would not forget."

"Forget what?"

Tenderness glowed in his eyes. "Who I am. Who I fight for."

Her gaze spilled across his bulked, tanned chest.

"Mayhap ye could put a tunic on, Twig," Tili growled.

"And remove yer hands from our sister," Elan said.

Abashed, Thiel shifted aside—then grimaced as pain scored her ankle.

"Kiethiel, I believe ye should be tended by a pharmakeia within the keep, where there is shelter from the sun," Tili said.

"And bare-chested princes," Elan groused. "There is a Drigo healer here. He does fine work."

"Agreed." Haegan took her hand and helped her toward the great doors of the keep.

He was even a hand taller than before. How was so much change possible in such a short time? The reprieve from the heat was instantaneous as they entered the hall, and she sighed at the relief.

"Kiethiel!"

Thiel turned toward her mother's voice, disbelieving her ears. The surprise stole her breath, giving the older woman the seconds necessary to reach and embrace her.

"You look tired, but never more beautiful." Her mother stroked her hair.

"Ye lie," she whispered, ignoring the sting of tears, noting her throbbing lips and head.

"Come," her mother said, leading her, "we'll get you into a bath and clean clothes."

Thiel winced, her ankle again protesting. Tili was there and swung her into his arms, hustling her across the floor and up the stairs. This time, she would not object.

Thiel glanced over his shoulder to Haegan, who stood in the foyer.

But his expression, the fisted hands, warned he was not pleased that she was being stolen away from him. A conflagration of thoughts and feelings exploded in her chest, but none more fierce than the truth that *she* hated being torn from him again.

"Fierian, we would have a word with ye," Aburas said as he and a handful of Pathfinders darkened the door of the keep, stealing Haegan's attention. Though he turned to go, he glanced back to her. She was glad to see the same torment in his eyes as what beat in her breast.

• • •

Talk to him or gut him? She wasn't sure which would be less painful—for her. Was he done with her now? Is that why Tili had so easily discarded her when the beauty arrived? Astadia hadn't been able to endure it and fled to the stables as soon as they returned to the bailey. Everyone loved the girl, though Astadia could not discern who she was. That she had been delivered by a giant bespoke her importance.

A green cord of jealousy wrapped around her heart, reminding her of the anger she'd felt once when Trale had grown smitten with the Infantessa. But that was different.

Ah, Trale. How I miss you brother. What am I to do?

"Quit pining after a man and get to work," she hissed at herself and spun toward a horse, who lifted his broad skull at the swift move. That's when she saw Tili enter the stables. She bent close and feigned wiping down the horse. What was he doing out here? She glanced to the keep. Hadn't he gone in with the beauty?

Best to skip out before he noticed her. She drew the stall gate closed quietly, then slipped around the wall.

Tili was there, coming at her. Avoiding his gaze, she determined to bypass him. He swung her around until her back thudded against the dividing wall. His arm rested over her head as he leaned in on her. Eyes sparked with amusement. "Say it."

Blast, the man knew how to make her defiant streak rear to the fore. "What?"

He rolled his eyes.

She shoved him away.

He caught his balance and bounced back. "Ye've been brooding."

"A person *mourns* when their brother is killed."

"Is that why ye've been staring at me, yet avoiding me?"

"Might have more to do with your ill manners and distinct . . . smell." She let her lip curl.

"Smell?" He sniffed his underarm. "Powder fresh."

"Maybe powder keg, but not fresh that." She started away. "I have duties to tend."

"Did ye see her?"

How could she not? Astadia kept walking.

"It was wonderful to see her, hug and kiss her."

She whipped around, seething. Narrowed her eyes. "Ye are that free with yer favors. With yer kisses, aye?"

"So it does bother ye." Tili smirked, apparently enjoying this as he sauntered forward. "She is my sister, Astadia."

Stilled by his words, by the fact he knew her thoughts—nay, not all of them. Like why he'd said nothing to his father when they'd made comments about her. Or to the men who taunted her.

Her heart beat a little harder than normal when he came around in front of her again. The way his toned torso blocked her view. Voices from the bailey poked the semidarkness in which they stood. He stepped deeper into an open stall and drew her with him.

He's ashamed of me. The move riled her. Annoyed her. "Leave off," she spat and turned. "I have work to do, and you have a prince and family to tend."

"I would tend ye," he said, hooking an arm around her and drawing her back against his chest.

"Nay." Extricating herself, she jerked her tunic straight. "I will not be someone you steal kisses and virtue from while you play noble before your family and friends."

Though shadows shrouded most of his face, she saw his gaze darken. "Steal? Kisses and virtue?" His voice pitched on the last word. "Is that what ye think of me?"

"'Tis what you have shown me. You give no care that your men mock me, that your father glowers, and yet you are here, trying to seduce me."

"Seduce!" His eyes flamed. "Seduce." He nodded then shook his head.

"Seduce!" Shoving his hands through his hair, he turned a circle, muttering words she could not make out. "By the Flames, ye have judged me poorly." His lips pressed tight. "Yet if I recall, Astadia Kath, ye neither fought nor refused my kisses. Not here, not south of Dorcastle. 'Twas not I who cornered someone for *seduction*."

She smiled, her laugh hollow, her courage low. "Then you blame me." She lifted her chin. "I knew you not, Thurig as'Tili. I heard said once that the way a man treats his mother is the way he will treat the one he l—" She gulped back the word. "—likes. You have not treated me as well as you treated your mother or your *sister*."

He scowled.

She sounded petulant. But she cared not. Inched back.

He reached for her.

Astadia used a slicing motion to deflect his grab, then her other hand to shove the fist back at him, twisting and throwing him off balance. But for a second. He used her momentum and upended her grip. Spun her around.

She threw a punch, lightning fast. Nailed his side.

His breath exploded out of him, puffing the hair around her face, as he doubled with a grimace. She seized the distracting pain and hustled through the back of the stable yard, out the side foot gate, and hurried into the chaos of the villagers encamped about. Anything to put distance between them, between the vain hope that had spurted through her chest and the reality that bit her back.

Aiming around a small tent, she smacked away tears that blurred her vision.

You are not a weak, simpering female!

A tent flapped. She skittered aside—only to see something dark flying at her face. Her instincts blazed. She swept the leg of the attacker. Shoved out the heel of her hand for a nose strike. Heard the crack. Then heard another . . . seconds before her vision closed in, wrapping her in a terrifying cocoon.

42

Thiel had returned last eve, and he had yet to spend a moment alone with her.

The pain of that truth carved harsher words into his flesh than the words of the *Kinidd*—rejected. Failure. The words were not only on him but within. Haegan knelt before his bed, freshly bathed, and closed his senses to the world. The verses not branded on him were branded in his mind.

He uttered them as he had every day to keep them fresh.

> *Making war on enemies of Aaesh and freeing enslaved minds;*
> *releasing from prisons of their own making,*
> *and then he finds himself standing obediently*
> *and violently between life and death,*
> *living and dead*
> *first and last*
> *then and now.*

He knew them all now, the verses he'd branded on his flesh. But it was the final verse that called to him now. He traced his hand across the lines on his left arm and recited them. *"In the hall of iron and blood he takes his stand . . ."*

Was that why he'd felt it right to remain at Ironhall? The *Kinidd* writings?

"With races past and present to reclaim their land. | The people wandering and lost—" That certainly fit their circumstances, considering they had Northlanders, Tahscans, an Iteverian assassin, Drigo, raqine . . . *"Give*

witness as the one birthed from darkness | Decimates the poisoned and per-verted line of Tharqnis."

That hadn't happened yet, and it confused Haegan. Would they—

A knock came at the door. Haegan rose and reached for his robe. He rushed to the door, one person in mind. One hope thundering in his chest. "Enter!" When no one did, he opened the door. She stood in a green gown—clearly a reminder from whence she'd come. "Thiel." She, too, had bathed, though evidence of her trial remained—the cut lip, the staff she used. "How is your ankle?" he asked as he stepped aside to allow her entrance.

The fabric flared at her wrists and cinched at her small waist. Her brown hair, longer than when he'd last seen her, had been secured at her neck, coiling around and draping against her neck.

Mercy.

"We didn't get to talk—alone," she said.

She is nervous.

Strange that. She had been in his face and ordering him around since they'd first met in the tunnels of Seultrie. Though it had been but a few months since they'd seen each other, it felt as years.

"I'm glad you came," he said. Why did he feel awkward?

"Ye cut yer hair clean off."

His hand went to his stubbled scalp and he felt embarrassed, but only for a moment. Until he remembered why he'd done it. "It seemed necessary."

"Seems I have much to hear of yer time apart from me."

"Aye, as do I," he conceded and indicated the fireplace sitting area. "Would you like to sit?"

She managed a smile. "Thank ye."

When she slipped past him, Haegan caught her arm. Gently. Half telling himself to release her. But she froze, her lips parting as she stayed there.

Haegan touched her chin and drew her face around, but still she denied him her gaze. Mayhap it would be easier this way. "Harsh words were spoken when we were last together."

"Aye," she whispered, her gaze on his tunic as she turned to face him.

"They were the words of a scared, panicked boy."

Her hand lifted, she fingered his button, and a wave of heat crashed through him. "We were all scared." Again she wet her lips, her tongue tracing the cut at the corner of her lower lip. "But ye know, do ye not, that I . . . that we . . . nobody wanted to steal the throne."

Haegan sniffed and shook his head, rubbing a hand over his face as he remembered the night that felt a decade past. "I was a fool."

"Aye."

He grinned, peering down at her, noting the difference of the last few months—he taller, she curvier, her hair longer. His fingers itched for its softness. "When we met, your hair was shorter than mine." He gave himself permission to touch the silky strands and brush his hand along her collarbone to lift a coil.

Her lips parted with a quick intake as she shuddered at his touch. "Not quite."

He caressed the lock, amazed at the softness. Then smoothed a hand to the back of her neck and leaned in. Pressed a kiss to the satiny coif. Felt her lean in, too. Did she ache for this as much as he had, as he did?

But that vision. Her abed . . . "Speak to me of Cadeif."

Thiel started. The blush that crept into her cheek vanished. "He's— he's dead."

Haegan stilled. "Dead? How?"

"He set me free. Onerid, enraged, killed him."

Haegan considered her, their eyes silently locked. "Freed you. Then you were his prisoner."

She tensed beneath his hold. "I was." She swallowed. "But he never . . ."

Relief rushed through Haegan. "I am sorry he is dead, but selfishly, I am relieved he set you free."

Thiel wet her lips. Darted a gaze to his. "As am I."

Haegan inched closer. Bent in and allowed himself another kiss—this one against her ear. Then the lobe.

She drew in a labored breath as she rolled into his touch. Haegan caught her mouth. Kissed her, enlivened as her fingers trailed up his chest and around his neck. He tightened her in his arms, then broke the kiss and hugged her tight. "I have missed you. Needed you." He trailed kisses along her face, feeling a hunger.

"Ye are not so much a twig anymore," she said, running her hands along his biceps. "If my brothers find us, they'll murder ye." With that, she leaned up and kissed him, lingering as she sighed.

Haegan felt the smile that tore the veil on the shadows that had engulfed his life since Kaelyria tricked him into the transference. Stretching his arms behind Thiel, he tugged off his signet ring. The only piece of jewelry he had. The only representation of who he was.

"What are ye—" Thiel glanced over her shoulder to see what he was doing. She twisted sideways. Then went still. Snapped her gaze up to him.

Holding her, the scent of her clean hair teasing him, he pulled her back against his chest. Peering over her shoulder now, he lifted her hand. Slipped his ring on her finger. "Now they can no more prevent us from this path."

Her eyes flung wide. She smiled up at him.

Pleased with her delight, Haegan caught her mouth with his, brought her around. "When this is over, there will be no definable distance between us, aye?"

She smiled and melted in his arms. He lowered his mouth to hers again, this time deepening the kiss and promise to make her his.

43

Updates. Strategies. Reports. Contingencies. Suppositions. Propositions. It had been two rises since Thiel returned to him. Now, Haegan endured the singeing of his ears as the war council again convened. Pathfinders—Steward Tili included—gave reports of the outlying lands, the skeletal remains, the strategic layout. The good vantages. The weaknesses.

Haegan cared not, though he endured their discussions. During a break, he let his thoughts drift above to where Thiel was with her mother and ladies' maids, he guessed. He was tempted to order an accelerant to bind them now. Especially since she wore his ring. It was, in essence, as if they were bound. But even as he glanced at King Thurig, immersed in conversation with Colonel Grinda, Aburas, and a very moody, annoyed Prince Tili, Haegan knew better than to insist on that just yet. His attention fell on the older brother, Aselan.

Which flipped his mind to Kaelyria.

Where are you, sister?

Swiping a hand along his beard, the cacique came toward him. The man's expression always seemed terse and yet inscrutable. "I have seen Kiethiel."

Haegan's heart stammered. He swallowed.

Gaze sliding over Haegan's shoulder, he stretched his jaw. "She has new ornamentation."

"Aye." His voice caught, but he would not back down. "I love her and intend to take her as my bound."

Aselan squinted. "And ye think that's a good thing? Our houses joining?"

"I do it not for the house, but for my heart. Her heart. Yet, aye—the alliance would be prudent and bring a peace between the two that has long been missing."

Aselan nodded. "Then ye will grant yer mercy that by the laws of the Eilidan, yer sister claimed me as her bound."

Startled, Haegan considered that inscrutable face. "Ye jest?"

With a snort, Aselan met his gaze. "She chose my dagger, me, at Etaesian's Feast."

"That . . . that was months ago."

"Aye."

"And she is not here."

Aselan lowered his head, grief swirling through his eyes and face. "They attacked the Heart and stole her." Fiery eyes speared him. "My leg and arm were broken. When the Rekken attacked Nivar, I had to help the Ybiennese flee." Misery wreaked havoc on the man's confidence. "But I would ask—what of ye and Thiel? When did ye look for her?"

Haegan drew up. Then nodded. "You are right."

"War is unmerciful. Every breath I am not in war planning, I strategize how to find her."

"I have a feeling," Haegan said, a swirling fire deep in his abiatasso confirming what he was about to speak, "you will not have to look much longer. If Poired took her, he will come. They know I am here. They'll come."

• • •

Never had she felt so vulnerable, so . . . bare. Thiel smoothed a hand down her stomach, ignoring the flutterings. She stared at the ring he'd slipped on her finger two days past. Remembered his kisses.

Shouts from the window drew her to the shutters, which she eased back, hinges creaking noisily. Among the tents and shanties, Haegan strolled the paths. For hours he'd been locked in that council, and now he gave his time to the people, who clamored for his attention, his touch. The great warrior—the Tahscan was with him. Tili had mentioned that Haegan had taken the man as his bodyguard, something to do with him smelling fear or some such.

But the girls, the women of the villages, reached out to Haegan, too.

Patted his broad shoulders. He smiled and caught their hands. Touched their shoulders as well.

Why would he do that?

"What ails ye?"

Thiel whirled to find Elan standing in the solarium with her, his stance beleaguered. "I could ask the same of ye."

"'Tis no secret—my bound is missing."

Haegan's sister. It still surprised her, but she berated herself for being so self-absorbed. "I beg yer mercy, Elan," she said, rubbing her forehead. "I am not myself since returning . . ."

"Tili said Cadeif died."

She nodded, bracing against the memory. "He sacrificed himself to help me escape. They were going to kill me."

"'Twas the only honorable thing left for him after holding ye captive."

"Ye know not of what ye speak. He was in danger of losing his—"

"It does no' matter—if he cared for ye, he should have done all to protect ye, not hold ye prisoner."

She stuffed her arms over her chest. "Aye. As ye have for Kaelyria," she spat, instantly regretting the words. Wondering how her tongue had become so cruel and loosed.

Elan's face rippled with rage. But then he slumped. "She is as good as dead."

Surprise drew her head up. "How dare ye speak such a thing!"

"'Tis truth. She has been in his grasp nigh unto a month. I am no closer to finding her."

"Have ye even tried?" Thiel bit her tongue, hating the cruel words. It wasn't like her. "And why did neither ye nor Father come for me? Is this what strong men do? Play the victim when their women are taken?"

Quick strides brought him to tower over her.

"Does it make ye feel important? To think he wanted her just to take her from ye."

"Just as ye were held prisoner by that savage and ye expect us to believe he did no' take yer virtue. Think ye Father will be able to bribe any fool to take his harlot daughter—"

Her hand flew true and sharp. Connected a stinging smack against his cheek. "I have a fool already ensnared."

Elan surged.

"Enough!"

They both spun. Their father stood in the doorway, his face a mask of fury. Embers rippling off his hands. "'Tis no wonder Abiassa saw fit to take the Fire Throne from me. I canno' rule my own blood, let alone nine kingdoms!"

"There a problem?"

They all turned to where Tili stood at the top of the stairs, just outside the chamber.

Thiel felt idiotic for the fuss she'd started, but could neither bring herself to be contrite nor to answer.

"Very well," Tili said. "Thiel, ye might want to know Tokar is training a raqine. He could probably use help."

"My help?" She balked.

"It's Draed."

"Oh." Snickering, she left the keep and made her way out of the fortress to the training yard. It felt good to be out of the castle. Two days within those walls was almost enough to drive her mad, but here—the sun and wind made her heart light.

"Blazing pile of dung!"

Thiel laughed as she crossed to the field where Tokar threw down a singed sack.

In front of Tokar, an unrepentant raqine paced back and forth, chortling. She'd never seen her friend so angry nor a raqine so annoyed. "Have a problem?"

Tokar spun, hesitated, then flung his hands at the raqine. "This beast just burned all my gear."

"I might be wrong," Thiel said around a laugh, "but I don't think they spew fire."

"He dropped it in the campfire! Destroyed my greaves and gauntlets."

"Why?"

"Blazes if I know! The thing has had it in for me since day one."

"The *thing*?" Thiel wrinkled her nose. "Maybe I'm starting to see the problem."

He shook his finger. "Don't you start. I never asked for this raqine. I didn't do anything—it has blown snot all over me, dragged me from a dead sleep in my unmentionables, dunked me in a muck puddle, and now this!"

"Sounds like a crush," Thiel teased.

"Draed's a male."

"Ah." Thiel grinned. "Then he's jealous." She angled her head at him. "Have ye given a girl yer attention?"

Tokar twitched. His gaze flung across the field to a group of Tahscans and Pathfinders in the training yard. A girl there.

Thiel laughed. "This is delicious. Has my friend finally found a girlfriend?"

"I see you wear his ring."

"Don't change the subject."

"Aye, I will. I have enough trouble." He huffed and looked at the raqine. "I have to train on him, and he won't let me near."

"No," Thiel corrected. "Before that, ye have to bring something of hers so he'll accept her, accept the other scent. Raqine are as territorial as they are loyal." She casually made her way toward the raqine that so closely resembled Tili's Zicri, save the size. Draed was smaller, a runt. Which explained the attitude. "Hello." She held out her hand.

Draed tilted his head. Sniffed. Nosed her palm. With a lightning fast move, he flipped her hand so that she could run it along his broad skull.

"Unbelievable," Tokar said. "Every other unit captain is well into training, and I can't even get the thing to let me on."

"Silly captain," Thiel murmured to Draed, running her hand along his dense fur. "He thinks he's to be in charge."

Draed snorted.

Thiel laughed. "Exactly." She scruffed his jowl. "If he would just accept *ye*, then things might change."

"What does that mean?"

Thiel arched an eyebrow at Tokar. "He's in charge, Tokar. Not ye. They move at Her will. Not yers."

"But I need to train."

"And ye think She does not know that?"

"I don't understand."

Thiel jerked her heard toward Draed. "Come here."

Hesitantly—and with a huff—Tokar finally drew closer.

"Palm out."

"This is—"

"Palm."

He shook his head. "If that thing bites my hand off—"

"Ye will have deserved it. Accept Draed. Accept that he's the most magnificent of creatures and that he will carry ye where ye need to go. Naught else."

Palm out, Tokar waited. Thiel eased back, out of the way of the bonding. From a distance, she watched.

Draed swung his head toward Tokar. Warily considered him. Sniffed—hard, spraying a damp sheen over his palm. "Augh," Tokar groaned.

With a snap of his massive jowls, Draed lunged.

Tokar shouted.

The raqine barreled his powerful neck along Tokar's legs. Flipped him up. Onto his spine. Wings spread, Draed launched up before Tokar realized what was happening.

Thiel sucked in a breath. Covered her mouth.

Draed took flight with Tokar clinging hard. With a shrug, Draed nudged Tokar into position. Her friend seated himself. Held on. Then gave a victorious shout.

• • •

A raqine dropped from the heavens, diving toward the rooftop. Tili watched in amusement, though Haegan and the Tahscan cried out as the shadow slid over them.

"They are doing well," Tili said from the terrace of the solar apartment overlooking the training yards and outlying fields. To the south, raqine were allowing riders. Closer to the keep, Aburas and Grinda had broken the Pathfinders, Jujak, and Nivari into units to hone skills and allegiances. The Drigo were quartered within the bailey, but mostly they slept.

"Think you there will be enough time? It has been ten days." Haegan looked to the horizon, to the north. "Surely it will not be long now."

"Every minute our people get to train, the better. It's in Her hands now, Fierian."

And yet one thought plagued him. "I would bind with Thiel."

Tili's gaze lowered, then slowly slid to him. "Ye speak of facing the Dark One, of lives that are likely to be lost, and in the next breath ye speak of taking my sister?"

"I love her."

Tili snorted and turned away, then cast over his shoulder, "Ye should speak to the king—her father. His answer might have been more favorable had ye asked before marking her with yer ring." He started away. "I have men to train."

"What of Astadia?"

Tili hesitated, glanced at Haegan. "What of her?"

"Grinda said she hasn't been seen since Thiel returned."

A shadow passed through Tili's knotted brow. He glanced out, apparently thinking.

"Have you seen her since Thiel returned?"

"No."

"Think you she went to him?"

Glaring, Tili rounded.

"I agree," Haegan said quickly. "'Tis unlikely, yet . . . she is absent, so we must consider it."

Anger dug into Tili, but he said nothing, only spun away and disappeared back into the fortress.

Haegan leaned on the wall and peered past the parapets to the valleys below. Littered as far as the eye could see with people, tents, lean-tos, wagons, horses.

A sniffle drew his gaze to Vaqar, who stood with a cloth drenched in oils and spices, warmed by a fire just enough to create a soothing aroma.

"You should rest," Haegan said.

"When you rest, I will rest," Vaqar said, his words thick with the sinus problem that plagued him.

"The inflaming you sensed?"

"Still there," Vaqar muttered. "You should let me rout and bleed them."

Haegan started. "Have you bloodlust, Vaqar?"

The man steeled his gaze. Then slumped. "The reek."

Rest was not to be had. Not for him, not for his men.

Abiassa, be near. It was all Haegan could think to pray as he stood looking out at men who might soon die. Help never came in the form he expected. He knew better than to want all this to end now. Those prayers were selfish. And this was not about him. It was about the people. Her people.

If She was near, if She guided, he would be well. All would be well. Haegan did not trust himself to seek the right things, the right outcomes, because of his own innate self-centeredness. He would do as She asked. He had too long fought his role. Those days were over, and if he wanted the people of the Nine to find freedom and strength once more, he must step up to the fight.

But you are no leader. You fail in the simplest of tasks . . .

"The reek," Vaqar muttered without lifting his head.

Haegan blinked. "We all of us have doubts and fears, Vaqar. How is it you do not?"

Vaqar snorted. "I am well-equipped with doubts, Fierian." He stretched his neck and climbed to his feet. "But I do not linger on them."

"How can you not? They pummel my thoughts."

"Because you give them room, entertain them."

Haegan considered the man holding the cloth to his face, his gaze aimed south. "I suppose you are right."

"I am," Vaqar said with a hint of a smile. "When the doubts snake in, turn your thoughts immediately to the Lady. Ask Her to show you truth."

"And that works for you?"

"'Tis no charm or potion, but She will answer one way or another."

Abiassa . . . Aaesh . . . She had a name in each culture. And as he looked to the stars, he had the surprising notion that Her reach was not limited to this planet. *Show me. Help me defend them. Let me see—*

A shout went up. His gaze fell to the crowds. Men dove at one another.

"Another fight," Vaqar said.

"Aye, there have been many," Haegan agreed.

"Far too many."

"What drives the arguments? Fear?"

Vaqar nodded. "Doubts, too." His sinuses sounded clogged.

"Are they not bred on the same field of desperation?" His heart jolted, darting a gaze around the fields where it seemed a tide of resentment washed over the people. He thought back to the argument that broke out within the war council. And the argument he'd heard of between Thiel and Aselan yesterday.

Heat spiraled through his veins, spreading out from his arms, down his chest into his gut where it quaked. Stirred. Simmered. "Vaqar . . ."

The Tahscans had colds. Or was it something more sinister? Had someone somehow infected them—deliberately? That would be . . . convenient.

"Aye?"

His mind scrambled in the quagmire that encircled his feet. There was one person not affected by inflaming. "Have you seen Astadia Kath?" She could be of help, perhaps.

Vaqar stilled. "Nay, not since they returned with your woman."

Haegan dragged his gaze to the Tahscan. "The battle, Vaqar. The battle . . ." The bickering, the fears that bred discord and dissension in the ranks . . .

No. No no no.

As the idea took root, Haegan drove his gaze to the west. To the far reaches of the plains, dots of cities in leagues off. To the dull bleeding hues fading in the horizon. Not sunlight. "Blessed Lady! They are here! Incipients are within the fortress!"

44

"Have ye seen the assassin?"

Aburas's thick brows rose toward his short-cropped hairline. "Last with ye in the woods when we happened upon the skeleton."

Where was she? They'd had words, but not so bad for her to leave. Yet with each passing hour her departure seemed more likely. Otherwise, how could she avoid him so completely?

What did he care? She was an assassin, a blood-letter, and his father would never approve.

"Awful, that."

Tili twitched. "What?"

"Finding the poor person the Fierian singed to death."

"Ye should have seen what he did in Iteveria." Staying his anger proved unbelievably hard, and somehow he saw there was little merit it. "And 'twas an incipient!"

Aburas shrugged. "Still a might cruel way to die, burned alive."

"Would ye have him pampered and coddled until he breathed his last?" *Why am I arguing with my man?*

"Nay, but neither would I want to die as such. And *what* is with this?"

"With what?"

"Ye." Aburas scowled. "All riled and worrying over an assassin."

"Riled? And aye—I am concerned. Assassins are best kept where they can be seen."

"The closer the better, aye?" Aburas had a cheeky grin plastered on his face.

Tili glanced away, though he should give pretense that he still searched the people.

"Then 'tis true—ye do favor her."

He should not be surprised his man knew of his interest in Astadia, yet it shamed him all the same, allowing himself to be distracted by soft emotion when half the world was fighting for their lives.

"Aye," he finally managed. "But it will do no good nor come to anything."

Thurig the Formidable would show his dark side once he learned she had distracted his son. That mighty king would not lose another heir to the wiles of a woman. And to be with her, Tili would have to leave the throne. He'd been there as the family struggled with Elan's abdication. He could not fail his father like that.

"One war at a time, Commander."

The use of his former title drew his gaze up, and he silently wondered what his man meant.

"The darkness that has gathered may be the last we see," Aburas said softly, keenly. "If we survive this one, then brave the other."

"Facing my father, ye mean."

A slow nod.

"Were I to survive here, I would die there—at least where he is concerned." Tili shook his head. "I cannot do it." He looked away, running a hand over the stubble he'd let go too long.

"'Tis good. She only be a murderer. Ye wouldna' wan' that blood on yer hands."

Tili scowled, tried to give his man a warning that he was edging dangerously close—

"She'd probably kill ye in yer sleep, try to steal the throne."

Muscles tight, lips clamped, Tili drew back his hands, pulling on the embers. "Guard yer words."

"What?" Aburas shrugged. "Ye cast her off. Let it be done." He started past.

Tili slapped a hand on the Nivari's chest, heat sizzling against the fabric of his leathers.

Surprise widened the burly man's eyes, then laughter vibrated beneath

Tili's hand. "Ye might fool yerself, Commander, but no' me. When this is done, do not betray yerself or her. Fight for her."

Clanging bells silenced their argument. Tili spun, peering up at the guardhouse. "What cause for alarm?" he shouted.

Laerian looked over the wall. "The Fierian wants all the soldiers to the bailey."

A flood of Pathfinders, Jujak, and Nivari flooded into the bailey. A raqine deposited Tokar on the ground, then banked off.

Tili stalked toward the main house and found Haegan emerging. "What alarm?"

Haegan glanced at the gathering army. "I saw them." His chest heaved. "Poired's army is on the horizon."

Taking a step back did nothing to distance Tili from the revelation. "'Tis what, a day, two at the most?"

Haegan gave a firm nod.

"We'll need to gather supplies. Pull the people behind the walls."

"Aye," Haegan said. "I would give ye charge over organizing preparations."

"Of course," Tili said, then started away.

Haegan caught his arm. "There are incipients here."

"Here?" His mind struggled with what that meant. "The plain—"

"In the fortress."

"But yer Tahscan—"

"An infection has seized them, thwarting their ability to detect the inflaming."

Understanding lifted Tili's head. "The arguments. Irritation."

"Aye." The Fierian glanced at those gathered with ferocity. "They've worked us into a frenzy against each other, distracting from their approach."

"Aye," Tili said, glancing toward the bailey. He groaned. "I nearly took off Aburas's head."

"Scores," Tokar announced breathlessly as he jogged toward them. "Scores, if not hundreds south of the keeping wall."

"Accelerants?" Grinda asked.

"Incipients," a stern, shaky voice corrected as Gwogh and three mem-

bers of the Council approached from the lower stairs. "We are accelerants. Those who wield against Abiassa and Her chosen have taken a dark path."

"More like a dead path," Tili growled. He felt a twinge of resentment toward the Council. They had sent him here. They had . . .

Awareness erupted at being inflamed. Tili said naught, merely turned his gaze in search of the brown eyes, remembering what Astadia had said about her time with Drracien. Why had she not shown herself? This is what she lived for!

A throng gathered around them, all geared up and prepared, though jittery. Nervous. This was it. The final confrontation. He saw Nivari. Jujak. Pathfinders. Citizens.

"I must address the people," Haegan said as he moved out to the steps. His voice boomed as he explained their situation. Gave orders. Tili stood behind him, knowing that as steward and the one to organize their numbers, he should be present.

Just inside the great hall, he spied his father. But still no Astadia. Where was she? He met Relig, Osman, and Elan descending in armor and weaponry. "Have ye seen Astadia?" he asked his older brother.

"Nay," Elan said, his brow rippling, glancing about. "Seems this would be something she would enjoy."

"Keep a sharp eye out. Trust your instincts," Haegan was instructing. "They are here. But so are we. So are Abiassa and Her Deliverers. So are the Drigo and the raqine. Drown your doubts in truth as you prepare. Then fight hard. Fight true."

"Drown in truth," a shout went up from the back. The phrase was echoed, rippling out through the bailey. Eventually it roared from the crowds as the men filed out, searching. Hunting.

• • •

"Haegan," Tili said, sidling up to the Fierian. "Astadia is missing. After giving the captains their orders, I searched for the last hour. I thought at first she was just hiding. But now, with Poired on our doorstep . . ."

Haegan's brow furrowed as he took in those around them, as if he did not believe Tili's report. As if he, too, wanted to believe she was simply doing what an assassin did—blending into the crowds and shadows. "You think she's harmed?"

"I think she would not miss this fight were there breath in her lungs. She blames Poired for Trale's death." Tili knew something was wrong. "Remember, Fierian, she said they called her unnatural. That she—"

"*Unnatural?*" Kedulcya's question pitched as she hurried toward them, gray eyes tight. "You are certain of this?"

Tili nodded, watching as the councilwoman shared a long look with Gwogh and the other member. "Pray, speak. We are at war, in case ye missed it! Why do they think she's unnatural?"

"She's not unnatural, she's *an* Unnatural," Gwogh clarified. "They are few and far between. Histories record only two others."

"Two other what?" Haegan demanded.

"Unnaturals," Gwogh repeated. "It's not a word alone. It's a title, just as *Fierian*. If what you report is true—"

"'Tis."

"—then the assassin—"

"Astadia—"

"—can drain the embers of any who wield. That ability was long considered a perversion, an *unnatural* effect of someone not rightly aligned."

"Give care," Tili said. "She is the truest woman I've known."

Gwogh arched his eyebrows. "No offense meant, Steward. The Unnatural is viewed by some as a twisting of an accelerant's ability. But this . . . though she could do incredible harm to any accelerant here, including the Fierian, this eve it gives me hope."

"Why?"

His smile bloomed like the glow of embers. "Because she can strip Poired of his power."

Tili's heart thudded painfully, recalling the times his wielding had gone awry—when she was around. And the possibility of her making Poired impotent . . . "Think ye they killed her?"

My Lady, let it not be. Yet it made sense. Kill the one person who could unilaterally sap their power.

"When was the assassin—"

"Astadia!" His bark snapped through the great hall, silencing the quiet thrum that had engulfed it. Tili rubbed his forehead and slid his fingers along his stubble. "I beg yer mercy." He lowered his head, sensing his father's attention, surprise—nay, his glare. "'Tis the inflaming."

Questions hung in that formidable face.

Forcing himself to meet his father's gaze, he mustered what remained of his courage. "She has saved my life more than once, and many of the men in this hall as well." He shifted his gaze to the Council members. "A warrior like that should be mentioned by name, not—"

"We are all of us on edge," Haegan put in, clearly looking to help Tili save face. Which shamed him even more. "Vaqar says the scent of inflaming is heavy here, so we must be aware that they are plying our thoughts, turning us against one another."

"Of course," Gwogh said as Tokar entered the command room, his hair ruffled.

"Tokar, what learned ye from the scouting trip on Draed?" Tili asked, throwing off the questioning looks.

"It's bad," Tokar said, then pushed between Tili and Elan to use the map. "Poired and his Silvers are coming from the northwest." Tokar pointed to the area. "Spotted another army marching from the west—looked to be Onerid and those savages, the Ematahri."

"Kaelyria." Elan went tense, his expression tight.

Tili held up a hand. "Possibly. We will weigh it carefully. Let's plan."

"The people," Haegan said quietly. "We should relocate them. Move them east."

"There's a modest hill northeast," Tokar said. "We could push over it, have them continue north to Vid for shelter."

"Good," Gwogh said, nodding. "It would be better, and with a day to march, they would be far enough away that our armies could focus on the threat."

"We should send a unit of guards with them," Haegan said.

Tili stroked his beard, wondering about Astadia. Wondering about this battle. "Drigo, raqine, infantry, cavalry, and accelerants."

"Have our most powerful accelerants on the raqine," Thurig said. "Target the Silvers first—they're the strongest. They can inflame thoughts. Most accelerants can't. If we can eliminate that problem, we reduce the confusion in our own camp."

"Their gleaming helmets make perfect targets," Tili said with a grunt.

"After they are down, we volley the army to reduce numbers. Put them in disarray."

"Aye," Elan said. "Then have the accelerants before the archers and army."

"Nay," Tili countered, pointing to the flanks of the battlefield. "Line them up here. They can watch, monitor, and defend while our archers, cavalry, and infantry engage."

"This battle," Haegan said, his words quiet, hard, "is not about the cavalry or infantry. It's Poired. And me." He pointed directly west of the battlefield. "The woods are already scorched, so he can't hide. I'll use the wall, draw him through the woods, where the infantry and accelerants can divide them."

"I would like to know where Kaelyria is being held." Aselan pointed to the raqine nest on the map. "I'll take Zicri, do another pass, and see if I can spot her."

"Good," Thurig said. "What is yer plan if ye see her? How will ye get her out?"

Haegan considered father and son, agreeing with King Thurig that a plan was needed before rushing into the fray.

Aselan nodded. "If I see her, I'll drop in and sneak through the camp. Once I have her, I'll call Pharen."

"There's nowhere to hide," Tili countered. "Not for leagues. They'll see the raqine. And he'll expect this."

Frustration lifted the cacique's shoulders. "There is no foolproof plan. I worked it in my mind the entire march from Baen's Crossing. If they are alerted to my presence, I'll steal a horse. Ride hard."

"We can scout overhead," Tokar said. "Send volleys if you get in trouble."

Thurig grunted his agreement.

"Remember," Haegan said, "that those who follow the Dark One also follow the dark flames, so inflaming your thoughts is not forbidden them. Though we try to target the Silvers, any we miss will be in your minds. As most of you know after Iteveria, it's one of their favorite tactics. Doubt breeds fear. Fear breeds anger. Arguments and fights are earmarks of their touch."

"But not for all," Gwogh said. "Some are influenced toward depression, loneliness. I believe it was this that subdued the Fire King."

Haegan started, surprised at the possibility. "Regardless—be aware. Abandon doubts and fears. Drown in truth."

45

She would suck the life out of them. Gut them. Split them open and leave their entrails for the rats. Astadia paced the cell, fists and teeth clenched. Banging on the iron bars did no good. The lack of windows provided no escape and no way to mark time. From the scant meals she'd been offered, she guessed it had been three days. Cowards. Knocking her out and hiding her within the keep. Who would think to look for her belowground?

Heat and a bitter stench wafted into the cell. Astadia swung around, squinting into the darkness of the passage that led to freedom. "I know you're there," she said, her heart pounding a rapid beat, the way it had with Trale when they'd sprinted through deserts. Fleeing cougars.

Only, now . . . she was the cougar stalking prey. She nearly snorted. *Don't be ridiculous.* And yet, she felt it. Felt the heat wafting off him.

"Will not be long now." The man stepped into the stonelight with a toothy grin. A dull thud sounded from above, and dust sifted from the stone ceiling.

"Aye," she said, willing him closer. It wouldn't be much longer—for him. Just a few more steps. She could taste victory. Anxious, something pulsing in her, she reached for it.

He's an incipient. She could feel his embers. The heat. The undulating wake.

"You're a brave one," she purred, hoping to draw him in. "Haven't you heard? Your master is afraid of me."

He quirked an eyebrow and sauntered in closer. "Is he now?" He stretched his neck but never lost his bravado. Another *whump* from above. What was happening? She couldn't afford to wonder, not yet.

"Why else would he have you lock me here?" She coiled her fingers, narrowing her gaze. Though he wore villager's clothing, she detected the trill in the air about him. It called to her.

Nay, it *reached*. Reached for her. As she did for it. Like a babe desperate for its mother. It was odd, strange—beyond anything she could have fathomed. She could not see it, yet she sensed it. Felt his heat seep into her fingers.

Unnatural. Unnatural. The foul creature's words shrieked in her mind. What did it mean? How did it work? Could she summon it? Glancing at her hands, she searched for a way to make it . . . happen.

"You're locked in here, so you can't escape." He tugged at his collar.

She did not need any abilities, unnatural or otherwise. She had anger. It had been enough before. She tossed her chin at him. "Come near. I'll show you."

His gaze raked her, betraying his foul thoughts. Then he glanced at the lock.

"You're afraid? Of me?"

"You're an assassin with a reputation." The fool actually closed the gap. Stood within reach.

It served him right—and her well. "I am much more than that." She thrust her arm through the bars. Grabbed his tunic. Yanked him right into the bars. The move was so fast, so violent that he slammed into them. His head bounced back and his knees buckled. She fought to hold him as he went limp and slumped against the iron.

Astadia held fast. Closed her eyes.

How do I do this? Her time with that creature was a blur of pain and darkness, but she had seen how Poired weakened. *Can I drain this incipient's powers?* She had to before he recovered. Before someone noticed he was missing.

"Watrien?" came a shout from the end of the dark passage.

Blazes! Desperation spurred her on. She squeezed her eyes tight. Held tight. Tight. Tight. Tight.

She felt it. A trembling in the air—no, not the air. In the man. In his chest. She mentally pushed deeper, burrowing, willing to find it, his abiatasso. Extinguish it.

A dark void opened in her like a gaping maw. Like the canyons she'd trod from one mission to the next. Empty. Desolate. Chilling.

She shuddered and backed off, panting. Instantly, she felt the cold. The chill. The fear. With a yelp, she shoved away. Even as he fell, she realized her mistake. Snatched for him. Caught the jacket. Material ripped, a loud, shrieking noise it seemed in the dense quiet.

Whimpering, confused, Astadia noticed movement in the passage. She wasn't out. She hadn't gotten the keys. She hadn't broken free. She hadn't drained this one.

Arm hooked around the man's neck, she pulled him closer. Though she watched his comrade approach, she used her free hand to search for keys on the incipient and focused her Unnatural abilities through the hand around his neck.

"Release him!" The man surged into the open with a leap. His hands were a flurry of moves. Red wakes danced and built.

No no no. No keys. No freedom.

The newcomer pitched the volley at her, like a ball thrown across a pit.

Instinct shoved Astadia to her feet, releasing the first man, who groaned as he slid across the ground and deflated. She ducked the first volley, but a second was fast approaching. She braced herself. Threw out her palms. The wake hit them . . . and stuck.

Panic marched across her chest. She shook her hands, but it remained.

A strange sucking noise drew her attention to the incipient. Eyes wide, he stared at her, then at the band of Flames that stretched between them. He paled, mouth frozen in shock.

As if he can't breathe.

Astadia turned her hands over, watching the red meet her palms, burn to blue, then seep into her skin. She felt the strength. Felt the redemption of those dark embers. When she pulled her hands to herself, the Flames came.

And the man lurched.

As if drawing in a lassoed horse, she pulled again.

He stumbled forward, his face reddening. "No," he coughed.

She yanked. Hard. Then again. Harder.

Three steps forward and he was crushed against the bars with a clank, tears of pain running down his face. A twinge of regret squirted through her. Dust sifted over them both as the castle trembled. She knew now what was happening. It had begun.

Then she remembered Trale. Haegan. The Fire King. All good men. Like Tili. Above ground. Fighting for their lives.

With vengeance, she snapped both hands backward.

46

Air tore at Tokar as he rode Draed for yet another scouting run. They flew north to gain altitude, then circled back in a wide arc over the enemy camp. Surprise sluiced through him. It had been nearly a day since Haegan first sighted the enemy's approach. But instead of falling on Ironhall, Poired's army set up camp and left the incipients to tear the fortress apart from within.

It made no sense. As Draed locked his wings and circled far overhead, Tokar tugged out the pencil he'd tied to his wrist, and on the paper strapped to his other arm, sketched Poired's tent—as expected—situated center-back. But there were more guards and activity around a spot at the far rear of the camp. A tent he nearly missed because of its camouflage. They didn't want him to see or notice that one.

Draed shrieked and banked hard right.

Tokar grabbed the harness as the world tilted. Gravity clawed at him. He'd never been so grateful for the braces that locked him on Draed's back, but he still dropped a few inches, the harness straining against his weight. Only as he caught his senses and breath did he see the fire volleys flying at them.

Draed righted himself, zigzagging as he sped south again.

• • •

Dawn brought the enemy.

Aselan's skin crawled. His blade demanded blood. The wrong done him demanded justice. Tokar returned with no legitimate sighting of

Kaelyria, merely a strong guess that Poired had something of value in that semi-hidden tent. He would find her. And she would be alive. Or the person responsible would die.

"How do ye fare, brother?" Osman asked, drawing his horse from the stable yard.

"What?"

"Yer injuries—are ye well enough to ride?"

"Aye, well enough." Aselan skated a glance to their father, surprised to find him staring back. Hard. Cowering would serve no purpose. He had never been one to take that path. He would not start now.

"Flank him," Father said, slight hesitation in his voice.

"Aye."

Aselan lowered his head. Swallowed. Bit his tongue—literally. "I would have peace between us Father," he said. "Before I go, though I know I am not a son to ye—"

His father caught his good arm. Hauled him against his chest, startling Aselan into silence. "Ye have ever been my son." He clapped his shoulder, forcing Aselan to wince. "Always."

He hesitated, then embraced the burly man.

"And if yer bound is out there, find her. I would not have my new daughter sacrificed as bait to Zireli's son."

Aselan gulped the swell of emotion with a curt nod. "Thank ye, Father.

After another back slap, the riders mounted, and Thurig ordered them out of the bailey. Pharen met Aselan and alighted just beyond the bailey footbridge. Aselan climbed up, noting Tokar and several other riders doing the same as the army arrayed itself across the field, according to Tokar's intelligence report. Those would distract while he dropped behind the Sirdarian line.

The ride out was swift, despite the length. Each thwap of his raqine's wings beat air and pounded into Aselan the hope of Kaelyria's discovery. That she would be safe. The armies of the North would help rid the planet of a black scourge. At the woods, the infantry and cavalry advanced westward, following the streambed.

When he glided over the trees and caught his first glimpse of the Sirdarian army, Aselan tensed. His heart stuttered. So great a number? He'd known there were many, but this . . . ? The field bled with red uniforms, but there were also savages and regulars. Aselan saw the disparity of clothing. The variety of mounts. Where Sirdarians chose elegant horses bred for speed and endurance, the Ematahri preferred larger, more powerful draft-cross destriers. Not as fast, but lethal in a confrontation.

Four red streaks lit the sky. Pharen expertly navigated the wielding volleys with an annoyed growl that rumbled beneath Aselan's legs.

First wave. Tokar and the other raqine diverted north, allowing Aselan to slip into the low clouds and use that cover to fly up from the south. Clothes dampened by the atmosphere, Aselan guided Pharen down in a swoop.

They had no sooner left the clouds than fire roared in the distance, reaching toward the Sirdarian army. The Council and Haegan? For the moment they were stationed at the tower, the best vantage for the long-range effectiveness of their power. Were they burning back their enemies?

As accelerants collided with incipients in the first-wave attacks, Aselan saw the archers readying themselves. His father raised his arm in command. Then snapped it down. The archers released their arrows. As the arrows descended, Aselan guided Pharen down, down toward the black tent at the back of the field. Those left to guard it shouted and ducked as Pharen glided near. Aselan freed the straps and lifted his leg over the side. As Pharen skimmed the tents, Aselan slid off, landing awkwardly to favor his bad leg. He pulled his sword free.

A blade slashed from the left amid the hard slap of wings that raised his raqine back to the skies and safety.

Aselan narrowly avoided the sword by bending sideways. A horse whinnied and danced. Swinging around, Aselan brought down his blade on his enemy. Struck leathered armor.

The enemy thrust again.

Aselan repaid the favor with ferocity. Aimed for the soft spot beneath the man's ribs that would allow his blade entrance. A feint. Then a stab. Steel slid in and out.

The Silver arched his back. Aselan seized the chance and drove his dagger into his throat. Gurgling, drowning on his own blood, the enemy slumped away.

Turning his attention to the next—an Ematahri—Aselan tightened his gut. He hated fighting these ruthless savages. He continued to swing.

Strike. One after another. Ignoring the cuts and slices, struggling against the bulk of his injured leg and the pain as he strained barely knitted bone.

The very real awareness that he was severely outnumbered weighed on him. Distracted him. So that he saw the jav-rod too late. He angled away, but its iron tip lanced his shoulder. Knocked him backward. Though his left knee buckled and he went down, Aselan never took his gaze from the Ematahri warrior bearing down on him, dark eyes filled with bloodlust.

47

Cries and shouts went up, as did the death toll. The first wave cost a great many warriors on both sides, but the distance was too little for another wave from the raqine. The Nivari fought back the Sirdarians. Horses rammed one another. Swords sang through the air.

Crack! Boom!

Haegan steadied himself. The incipients had been sending what others called warning shots, but he knew the truth—with those flame balls, they were probing each location. Testing, searching for his signature.

"Incoming! Protect the Fierian!" Graem shouted and spun toward Haegan.

They ducked and braced. Haegan thrust out his hands and shielded the tower against the blast. Simultaneously, Gwogh shot a bolt right in the direction from which the wielding had come.

Alight with the way they worked together, one shielding, one aiming, Haegan felt a little giddy. The tower had not sustained a significant hit, and he could continue to target with the other accelerants.

"That won't do," Kedulcya snipped.

"What?" Haegan asked, annoyed with her superior airs.

"It is most certain he will now know where you are."

"I've been wielding the entire time—"

"Aye, but you have not used a shield until now, and that will—"

"Incoming!"

"Another one!"

"Three—no, five!"

Haegan stared in disbelief at the singularly focused assault, all too aware of the councilwoman's condescending nod. Disbelief turned to fear then outright panic when the blasts that had been on parallel arcs, drew together, as if someone had noosed them.

That's going to hurt.

"Shield!" Gwogh roared.

Before Haegan could process the command, four accelerants were in front of him. Hands stretching out directly in front, then spreading wide. He saw the rippling barrier of heat that surrounded them. Beyond it—the incoming barrage.

Would it hold? Protect them?

"Focus!" Gwogh commanded.

The convergence of the ball and the shield exploded with a deafening force. It held. Protected. But one did not defeat the other. Instead, they collided and rebounded with an enormous explosion of heat that threw Haegan. Slammed him against a wall. Creaks and pops rippled through his spine. His hearing hollowed.

"Get him out of here!" Gwogh shouted distantly.

Two accelerants reached for Haegan. Drew him to his feet. Cuffing his arms, they hurried him down the now-rickety stairs. At the bottom, they hesitated. "You need to be safe."

"Nay," Haegan protested. "I do not want safe. I want vantage!"

• • •

Crack! Boom!

Tili ducked as ironstone and debris fell from keep wall. Crouched, he scurried toward the guardhouse, where the Fierian stood with two accelerants. The Council members were hurrying down the wooden steps to join them.

Urgency bled into Haegan's features, an argument ensuing among the tightly huddled group. Jujak held close, tense and weapons ready. They were not ones to stand idly by in a battle, and he guessed they itched to defend their brothers-in-arms on the field.

Boom! Crack!

Ducking again, Tili gained them.

"—get to higher ground or closer," Haegan was saying, then his gaze lit on Tili. "What is the highest ground in the keep?"

Tili nodded to the north tower. "There, but it is also the most vulner—"

Boom-boom-boom!

As if to confirm Tili's assessment, the north tower took several hits. Stone dribbled down in defeat.

"Augh!" Haegan gripped his head. "I do no good behind this wall. I was gifted to end him. Let me out to finish this."

"Haegan," Thiel said, catching his hand. "You can do no good if ye are dead. I know ye would be out there—"

"I beg yer mercy, Haegan," Tili said, "but walls were no hindrance to ye in Iteveria. That heat wake rushed through every crack and crevice, seeking the darkness. 'Twould be no different here."

Haegan shifted. "I feel . . . useless."

Tili smirked. "Aye. I know the feeling with my father and brothers out there in the rage of battle, and me in here."

"Steward!" A Jujak indicated to something behind Tili.

A quick glance over his shoulder revealed nothing save missing sections of the keep wall and the heavily guarded fortress protecting the Fire King. He turned, but even as he did, something registered. A glint of faint color. Jerking back, he searched for whatever caught his attention.

Incipients, his mind growled. Embers leaped upon his hand, ready. There—a side entrance to the castle. Squeezing past two Jujak, a wisp of a person. Small. Much like . . .

His gaze rammed into hers. She had been standing there. As if waiting, uncertain. Why?

"Astadia!" Forgetting the others, he closed the distance and spied a red knot on her temple. The bruise beneath her cheek.

"No!" Her voice was fever-pitched, frantic. "Stop. Don't come closer!"

Tili slowed, stunned. Confused. Had he so wholly offended her? "Asta—"

"I . . . I do not want to hurt you."

"Hurt me?"

A Pathfinder guided Astadia forward, a hand span from her. "We found her coming up from the dungeon, sir. There were two incipients below . . ."

It was what they didn't say that gnawed at Tili. He waited for them to continue.

"Begging yer mercy, sire," the second said, nodding to Haegan, who had joined them, "but they were . . . No other way to say it but that they were sucked dry. Faces gray. Skin shriveled and leathery."

"Unnatural," Councilwoman Kedulcya pronounced. "You've found how—"

"Nay," Astadia said, her head down, eyes barely meeting theirs. Hair hung over the side of her face in frazzled curls. "I know not how to do it. I just . . . did. And it was dark. Terrifying." Her gaze grew distant. She licked her lips.

"The *how* is of little importance," Gwogh said. "What's important is that she *can*."

"Send her," Kiethiel said, though it looked like the words cost her dearly. "Send her out with Haegan. She can drain Poired of his powers and then the Fierian can kill him."

"Nay!" Haegan said. "The Deliverer said it was not for me to kill the Dark One, but perhaps 'tis for Tili."

He started at that. "Me?"

"Aye, kill the one who made her an Unnatural."

"I am not sure you can lay that blame on the shoulders of a man," Gwogh said, stroking his beard. "And I am of the mind that perhaps 'tis for the assassin to kill Poired."

"How—"

"If one of us tried to kill him," Gwogh said thoughtfully, his gaze never leaving Astadia, "he could step into the Void before it was done. But with her, with what she is said to have done to the guards . . ."

Kedulcya's eyes widened. "Poired could not open the Void if weakened enough."

Hope leapt anew in Haegan. "Would it be shut forever?"

"We are in untested times," Gwogh said. "It cannot be known until it is done."

"Then 'tis too dangerous," Tili argued. "If she goes out there, he would immediately target her. Then 'twould leave both of ye exposed."

"Not if he doesn't see me." Astadia stepped forward, chin raised. "I'm willing to risk it. Anything to be rid of this, of him."

"I am not sure you will be rid of the gift, child."

"But he will be gone." She nodded. "It is enough to be rid of him."

Tili hurt at those words, but knew she was right.

"I agree," Haegan said, smiling at her. "We'll go."

48

Hiel-touck!

The warrior went airborne.

Aselan could do little. He spiraled away, scrabbling for his dagger.

Weight slammed into him. Pain ruptured coherent thought, erupting through his shoulder and neck. The impact shoved his face into the ground. Rocks and singed earth scraped his cheek, the smell acrid. The taste worse.

He heard the unmistakable sound of steel against leather. A dagger or saber being drawn.

Panic ignited in his chest. He strained against the agony of his injured arm to reach his own dagger.

The warrior flipped Aselan onto his back. Raised a saber, the gleam of death in his eyes.

Aselan swung his legs to the side and lunged at the same time. Tossed off the savage. Before the man could right himself, Aselan pinned him. Snagged his dagger. Raised it.

The man sneered. "Kill me and you will never know where she is."

Aselan hesitated. "I thought Ematahri did not negotiate." He pressed the blade to the savage's neck. "Tell me."

The Ematahri hesitated. "Cadeif died for Etelide. Would you do the same for yours?"

Aselan recalled Tili saying that the Ematahri archon who'd claimed his sister had renamed her.

"Because that is what will happen if you go for her."

Aselan allowed a thin line of blood to appear. *"Where?"*

"Command tents. In a cage."

Easing away, Aselan released the man. Uncertain the warrior could not reach him, he walked backward, never once removing his gaze from the savage. They were branded as such for good reason. He could not die here. He must save Kae.

A thundering horse raced wildly toward him. No rider. Panicked. The scent of blood upsetting it. Aselan held up his arms to halt the animal.

An impact struck his shoulder. Reverberated through his spine, spewing with it fire and agony. Aselan pitched forward. Stumbled. Reaching back to feel the hilt of a dagger sticking out. He pivoted. Saw the mocking grin.

The savage suddenly arched his own back, eyes frozen in shock. Arms splayed wide. He staggered. Collapsed to the earth.

Another Ematahri stood behind his fallen brother with a dark expression. "He has no honor."

What was he to make of one savage turning against another? He cared not. With a growl of pain, Aselan snatched out the dagger embedded in his shoulder and half-ran, half-hobbled toward the tents, feeling blood sliding down his back.

A Silver rushed him.

Vicious and furious at the interruption, Aselan struck with ferocity. Surged, shoving the man back. Gaining ground and making it harder for him to use the blade. Drove his dagger into muscle and sinew. Pitched him aside.

Pressed on.

A man came alongside.

Aselan raised his dagger—

"Whoa, there!"

Startled, he recognized the face. "Byrin!" He choked beneath surprise and injury. "Where did ye come from?"

"Following this lot, certain they would lead us to adventure." He grinned. "Why are ye here and not with the others?"

"Kaelyria."

Byrin scowled. "They have her here?"

"Aye. In the tent."

Together, they broke into a run. The severity of his injuries seemed to lift as they ran toward the tents and slid up behind an overturned cart. Four Silvers lurked outside.

"Ye are wounded," came a familiar, quiet voice.

Aselan smiled at the red-bearded face. "Caprit."

"What adventure awaits us here?" the man asked.

"The Mistress," Byrin growled.

Caprit started. "She be alive?" He breathed relief. "After the Rekken attack, I had . . ." He swallowed his words, slanting a worried look at Aselan.

"Four out, how many in?" Byrin asked.

"The savage said death waited inside."

Feet hustled toward them. Aselan spun, sword raising. He was surprised to find yet another Legiera. Markoo.

"We must needs draw them out," Byrin said.

"Markoo and I will go first. Attack," Caprit suggested. "Ye and the cacique slip in the back."

The two men sprinted to carry out the plan. Byrin swatted his shoulder—eliciting a grunt from Aselan—then hurried around the back. Aselan trailed him, hustling the fifty paces to the rear, his leg screaming. Hunched low, they slid around until they found a loose stake.

Shouts and grunts from the other side—Markoo and Caprit engaging the Silvers—stirred voices inside.

Aselan hesitated, listening.

"Go. Check it out," a stern voice within the tent ordered.

A second later, "They're attacking."

"Kill her!"

Aselan sheered the tent wall with his sword, cutting an opening. Before he'd finished, Byrin lunged inside. Heat shot from the right. Aselan ducked to avoid the blast. He spun and arced his sword at a man in a long black tunic and with glowing red hand. The steel sliced clean through the incipient's neck. The red warbling vanished.

"Aselan!"

Her voice, drenched in fright and yet relief, yanked him around.

Byrin and Capit battled a man with slick-black hair and incredible powers. The incipient had his back to Aselan, who crouched as he rushed up behind him, fueled by Kae's voice.

Capit was thrown backward by an invisible punch. Byrin choked.

With violence, Aselan threw himself at the incipient and drove the sword right through his back. The man crumbled, the wake sliding away.

Byrin slumped to the ground, rubbing his neck. "Blasted incipients," he muttered.

Aselan pivoted to Kae. Met her eyes. "Ye are well?" Relief sped through him, then anger at seeing her caged.

"Aye," she breathed, reaching through the bars for him.

"How—"

"The keys are there," she said, pointing to a stand. "Hurry."

Byrin was on his feet, hurrying to the table.

Aselan touched her face. "Ye look . . ."

She pressed her cheek to his hand. "I care not how I look, as long as you are here." Her pale blue irises came to his—then widened.

Noise rent their reunion.

Kae's eyes went red. She growled.

A *thwump* from behind snapped him around to find the incipient he'd driven through crumpled at his feet. How . . . ? He jerked his attention back to Kae. She wavered. Swayed.

"Byrin!"

His man jammed the iron keys in the lock. He threw open the door. Aselan lunged, catching Kae before she struck the ground. He lifted her into his arms. Her eyes fluttered open. "I . . ."

"'Tis well." He could not sort what happened, nor would he attempt to—not now. She was alive. That was all he asked of the Lady. Outside, he stopped short. A large destrier blocked passage. Atop it, an Ematahri warrior watched them. Aselan's stomach clenched. They'd been so close. Almost free.

The warrior whistled, and another horse trotted up with no rider. The savage gestured to the animal. "Ride west a half league, follow the riverbed north. There aren't many forces there. You might make it."

Aselan hesitated only half a beat then nodded, shifting Kae into Byrin's arms before hauling himself onto the horse. Even as he gathered his bound to himself once more, he looked to the savage. "Why?"

The man pursed his lips. "You are the son of Thurig, are you not?" At Aselan's nod, he continued, "My archon gave his life for your sister.

Perhaps this is the beginning of a new era between our people." Turning, he spurred his horse, who leapt away from them. A trilling, shrieking call went out.

All across the field, Ematahri remounted and rode with all haste westward. Away from the battle.

49

Exhaustion clawed at Tili.

It's not worth it. Just give up. Go back to Nivar.

Shaking his head and the thoughts, Tili turned from the inflaming. A Tahscan nodded to him, eyes rife with amusement that Tili had recognized the wielding tactic. Many of their number surrendered. Dropped their weapons. Discouraged.

"Fail me not, Tili," Astadia whispered, her voice a rasp. "I can feel him clawing my mind."

"'Tis said the princess Kaelyria could feel the same."

"I'm afraid he'll use me against you."

"I'm here. I'll help ye."

She looked to him. "I would rather die than hurt you, Tili."

He reached for her face, only to reassure her. When she drew back again, he closed the gap. Cupped her face. "I care not if my wielding is lost—I have always been better with the sword anyway." He pressed his lips to hers. "I believe in ye, and no matter the outcome, I will never leave ye."

She closed her eyes. Then bucked. Drew in a breath. And spun.

An incipient appeared there, the fabric of the Void opened.

Growling, Astadia—unbelievably—caught the volley of fire. And yanked. Hauled the incipient from the Void, which snapped closed. With a thud, the incipient tumbled forward. Fell, joining the ash of the field.

"Accelerants, back!" Gwogh shouted, the circle around her widening.

Though he felt her draining ability, though it tickled and pinched the edges of his awareness, Tili did not move. He watched. Readied.

Astadia drew up her shoulders. Breathed a little deeper, as if she had dragged her gaze from the Void itself. A smile wavered. "I see them."

Tili glanced around, the Silvers, the Sirdarians, accelerants. Poired's army. "We all see them."

"No, the Deliverers," she breathed. "They're guarding the field."

With a deafening crack, Silvers rushed them. Struck. Sent jav-rods spiraling through their numbers. Tili swung his sword at a Silver who reached them. Swords clashed, a great reverberation of steel ringing through his arms. He flicked his fingers, sending a slash of heat through the steel.

The Sirdarian cried out, dropping his hilt in shock. Tili ended him. Another came from his right.

"Tili," Astadia said.

He maneuvered to see her and batted the Silver who moved with such speed and ferocity that Tili had to focus completely on the soldier. The man tried to close the space, limit options, but Tili maintained a safe distance. Countered the moves.

The Silver grew frustrated.

"Tili."

"Augh!" the Silver shouted, lunging forward.

Tili sidestepped, slipped behind his opponent. Arced his sword once more, but then flashed a bolt at the man's back. It bounced off the Silver.

"Astadia!" Gwogh hissed to Tili.

But the Silver was unrelenting. He spun, parried against Tili's strike. Then came up—and Tili caught him. Sent a hyperfocused dart into the man's neck.

The Silver gasped. His legs twisted and he went down.

"Steward, the assassin!"

Tili pivoted to Tokar, who pointed in the opposite direction. Toward Poired, Drracien, and two other incipients who wielded their dark flames on an ancient stone foundation.

And Astadia. Running with the Fierian straight at the enemy.

50

The time was now.

Haegan sprinted toward the raised foundation on which Poired stood, trusting the Council of Nine—what remained of them—to protect him and the assassin as they made for the stone. They did not need to reach it, but they must be closer.

The tension in the air went from taut to strained. He glanced up and saw those on the stone foundation shifting, coming around to focus against Haegan.

"Miembo Thræiho!" Haegan breathed over and over, never stopping. Next, he called the raqine.

A deafening roar shocked the air.

Haegan smiled, glancing at Astadia. But her eyes were wide, trained on their wielding enemy.

Seconds later, Drigovudd thundered across the battlefield. They leapt and dropped in front of Haegan and Astadia, the ground thundering beneath them.

The first hyperfocused barrage from the incipients shot out.

Shrieking filled the skies. The sun blinked and wavered, and Haegan knew raqine were answering his call as well. The great beasts dove in and out, capturing incipients, picking them up, and dropping them from great heights.

Together with the assassin and Drigovudd, he edged in farther. "Close enough?" Haegan asked, turning to Astadia, who hovered in the shelter of Thelikor.

She glanced to the stage. Closed her eyes. Stretched out her fingers. She twitched, then squared her shoulders.

Haegan started at the shadow that rippled through her face. Felt the chilled strain. Eased back. Looked past Thelikor's massive legs to where the nearest incipient swayed. Legs tangling. Went to a knee. "It's working!"

Astadia grunted.

The incipient fell aside.

Astadia reached, shook her head. "Too far. I can't . . ."

Haegan pushed his own wielding at the stone. It did little and was not powerful like the seeming bladed strikes of those who stood above this field.

"I can't reach," she said.

The closer they got, the greater the risk. But they were not here to play it safe. "Advance," he called to those protecting them. Gwogh, face as crimson as the embers roiling off the incipients, fought the current of wielding and pushed ahead.

Astadia stalked forward, head down as she tested her reach.

A howl stabbed the air. A Drigovudd stumbled. Tilted.

"They're targeting the Drigo," Tili shouted.

Haegan gaped in disbelief, in abject horror as the giant canted and fell. Drigo were fierce in their vudd states, but they were the gentlest beings on this field. Anger churned as the Drigo shrank to his normal size and death claimed him.

Fury raked Haegan's focus. "Protect the Drigo—counter the wielding against them!"

A swath of accelerants marched under Gwogh's command, their hands moving almost in cadence. Song, pure and quiet, rose over the din. Haegan blinked, realizing he was witnessing the demonstration teams, who had once seemed to him so useless. Now there, there was elegance in wielding. With a chanting shout, they advanced. Stomped. Shouted. Stomped. Blasts and bursts, arcs and arrows warred in a beautiful, unusual dance. 'Twas strange to think so in light of what they effected. Too, he could not help but notice the way the incipients slowed their attacks, distracted by the demonstration team.

"Move! Now," Haegan urged, pushing ahead, leaving less than a hundred paces between them and the stone foundation. The flurry of arcs and thrusts by Poired only intensified. The Dark One would never surrender or slow. Behind him was the deformed creature with opaque eyes, the one tethered to Sirdar himself.

"The Auspex," Haegan whispered. If they targeted him, would that lessen Poired . . . ? He bent to Astadia, who'd taken down another incipient. "Can you reach the Auspex?"

She shook her head. Frantically.

Haegan frowned, realizing she wasn't saying she couldn't but rather that she wouldn't. "You must! He is the tether."

"Incipients first," she said, her words a mere feather of breath before she was reaching again.

"Astadia—target him. Cut the cord."

"No."

Frustration grew in Haegan. "'Tis the quickest way—"

"No!" she shouted, chin trembling. "I can sense him from here. He is dark and fathomless. I will not touch that." Dark eyes darted to him then back. "I will lose myself."

"Lose yourself?"

Face sweating, she grimaced. "I feel it—each time I capture their embers, I feel the darkness that fed them."

He glanced at the etchings on his arm. Laughed. "It's you!" he cried. "You're the one borne of darkness—of Poired." He'd thought *he* was that one. Elation ruptured his haze. "Astadia, you're the one to bring him down."

Tears welled in her eyes. "I will not, cannot . . . Please. Haegan." Her voice cracked. "Don't ask me to—"

"Look out!"

Haegan glanced over his shoulder—and right into a focused arrow of flame. He sucked in a breath. Thrust out his hand. It snapped against his palm, searing. Shoving him back, his feet dragging in the dirt.

• • •

Tili gaped, seeing the collisions of red and blue. Watching Haegan pitched back twenty feet. Terrifying. Horrifying. And yet, he withstood the flames of Poired.

"Target the Dark One!" Tili commanded, ordering the Drigovudd to rush him. The accelerants to counter his wielding. He went to Astadia, whose face was ashen. "How close?"

She frowned up at him.

"How close do ye need to be to drain him?"

"I . . . I can't, Tili," she whimpered. "They're too dark."

He angled in. "If ye do not, we have lost. The Fierian is dead. People wiped out. Everything good will die."

"It is not my fault!" she strained, spittle at the corners of her mouth as tears shot rivulets down her dirty cheeks. "I did not bring this war—"

"Aye," he said with a growl, his heart aching and yet writhing that she would not see the truth. "Ye did. We all of us did. We have naught to blame but ourselves."

Tears welled, slipping over her round cheeks and streaking dark rivulets toward her lips. "Please . . ." She shook her head, then shuddered through a sigh.

Tili cupped the back of her head and kissed her ash-covered hair. "Ye must, Astadia. It was given for ye to do this—ye were in the prophecy."

A howl wormed through the air, forcing them to look. Haegan, both hands extended, pushed. But he was still losing ground. Though several Jujak braced him and Councilmembers wielded with him, they were all moving.

Tili glanced back to the stone. His gut cinched. Poired had Drracien. "They will obliterate him," he muttered. Glanced at the incipients and Silvers guarding the plinth.

"But why is the prince not wiping them out, like Iteveria?"

Tili monitored the confrontation, the prince's twisted expression. "Fear—he's immersed in fear. Not holy anger."

They needed to eliminate the experienced fighters. Which meant that Tili had to deal with Drracien. Cut the power in half.

Thelikor roared in fury. He moved to interrupt the Flames churning between Haegan and Poired. But the giant howled, yanking back his arm. Tough flesh singed black. He shook his head. Glanced at Haegan. Growled. Then—

Oh, no. No no no.

"Zicri!" Tili cupped a hand over his mouth and gave a trilling call.

From somewhere in the chaos came the raqine's response. A great dark shape rose in the smoke-riddled sky. "Thelikor," Tili shouted.

The giant heard nothing, for he had set his course to fulfill the purpose Abiassa gave him. With a shout, he lunged into the churning Flames. He howled. Smoke rose from his chest.

Poired's gaze darkened, his lips set in a grim line. But he did not yield. In fact, he shouldered into the Flaming. He would bore a hole straight through the Drigo!

Haegan broke off with a yelp. He sagged, held up by a Jujak. *"Thelikor!"* Zicri shrieked as he descended.

Tili sprinted to meet the beast on an open spot in the blood-drenched field. He swatted aside a sword with a blast of wielding. Then ducked as a jav-rod wobbled. Not a deft throw, that.

Then he caught Zicri's fur and hauled himself atop the beast's blue spine. Four great flaps vaulted them into the sky. As they banked around, Tili sighted the dais—and aye, the entire battlefield. Smoke billowed into the sky from several locations. Ironhall had sustained great damage, though it was still surprisingly intact. The west seemed to be slowing, the great number of green tunics giving witness to how they faired. Thank the Lady. Most of the fighting remained around the dais, between Poired— with the help of Drracien—and the Fierian. Between the Dark One and the Hand of Abiassa.

"Low and true, Zicri," he requested.

The raqine folded his wings and angled. Tili tightened his knees behind Zicri's shoulders and leaned into the dive. With each second, they cleared hundreds of feet. His eyes burned from the ash-coated air, but he would not break his lock. It was time to even things up. Drracien would meet his end.

51

The great giant fell backward, landing with a reverberating thud. Air and smoke plumed from his chest. He gave one last great exhale and began to shrink.

"No." Haegan rushed to him in gripping terror. *"Noooo!"*

They were servants, answering the call of Abiassa to help others. The brutality with which Poired killed him—

"Enough!" Haegan shouted.

But his shout was lost in the scream of a raqine, which pulled his gaze to the skies. Not just one raqine. Dozens. With Tili in the lead, his massive blue raqine diving in for the kill.

Poired sensed the change and glanced up. He shifted back. Drracien did the same, their wielding momentarily weakened.

Dive-bombing, the raqine carried Tili, who threw daggers of fire at the incipients. Each hit cracked the air.

Drracien stumbled, his expression terror-stricken as Tili flew, unheeding, straight at him. He threw out a bolt.

The raqine dodged. Then spiraled. Somehow—miraculously—Tili remained seated. But in the second corkscrew, he released. And dropped into Drracien.

Poired turned his attention to the two rolling on the stone plinth.

As the Dark One lifted a hand, Haegan's heart thudded. There was no way to aim and hit one but not the other. Surely he would not strike them both! Afraid Poired would unleash a bolt, Haegan flung one of his own. Silvers dove for cover, some hurrying to help Drracien. Others drawing swords and aiming at Haegan and his small band.

Face carved in rage, the Dark One spun. He focused his gaze, his fury, his wielding—everything—at Haegan.

Haegan felt the warming presence of other accelerants. Darts and bolts peppered the stage but missed the Dark One. A flurry of movements caught his attention, and he realized it was the Auspex wielding, protecting his puppet.

Which meant he was distracted—a good thing. It gave Astadia time to skirt the stone. He glanced at her. "Go!"

Hand on it, she reached up. Her face twisted in grief.

Poired noticeably staggered.

The Auspex shrieked and wailed, throwing himself away from Astadia.

Haegan shot bolts, one after another, pulling Poired's attention from the girl who would be his undoing. Fury tore through the Dark One's face when he caught sight of her. "You dare!" he shouted at Astadia, holding a hand to Haegan as if he were no more than a dog to be commanded. "Dare to attack your own father!"

Astadia kept her gaze low, her eyes squeezed tight, her arm shaking violently as she struggled to drain him. She cried out, quivering in obvious pain, tears streaking her face.

Behind them, Drracien slammed Tili back with a ferocious blast. The steward tumbled and flipped off the stone. He did not rise.

"No!" Haegan lurched.

Poired had turned his full efforts on Astadia. Nostrils flared, he clawed at her. His arms trembled. He wavered.

She was doing it. Draining his embers.

But then she lifted. Agony writhed through her features as she growled.

With a shout, Poired flung her through the air. She slammed into the back of a Drigo. She dropped to the ground like a boulder.

"Kill the Fierian," the Auspex shouted. "Kill him *now!*"

Anger churning, Haegan couldn't see straight. First Thelikor. Then Tili. Now Astadia?

A blast punched him in the gut. Snapped his gaze back to Poired.

"You think to turn the tide? To take me down?" Poired glowered. "Think. Again."

A shape flew at the Dark One, who felt the shift and turned. And was knocked off the foundation by—

"Tili!"

His face was ragged with determination. But it was almost comical. Like one of the stories fed to children at bedtime. Because the Dark One again flung Tili off like a horse shaking off a fly. Angered, he held a hand to Tili and sent embers daggering through his chest.

Tili arched his spine and howled, long and hard.

"No!" Haegan jerked but then stopped when Astadia dragged herself to her feet. She stumbled, but came unyielding, palm held out toward the Dark One. Something in her had changed. Gone were her weakness and hesitation. There was now only violence about her as she stalked closer, her expression one of intent and . . . vengeance.

Poired's shoulders bunched. He tensed. Stumbled. Snapped around. Threw a halo around Astadia's throat, strangling her. She did not yield. Did not stop draining, pulling. Crying.

"Now, Fierian!" Gwogh called.

Haegan twitched. It was not his to do. Or was it? He lifted his hands. A sword flashed around Poired. His head tumbled from his body.

Behind stood Drracien, eyes wide, as if he didn't believe what he'd just done.

Neither did Haegan. He stared, stunned. In that split-second, two things rose to perfect clarity in Haegan's mind: Tili lay on the field in his own blood. Poired was gone.

Haegan went to his knees. Choked back tears. Grief. But then his gaze hit the glittering tear between worlds that hovered over the field.

The Void. Sirdar. Dark shapes loomed around the crackling tear. Sirdarians raced for the Void. So did incipients. Poired had not stepped to safety but others could. Incipients would go through, and in ten, twenty, a hundred years, this terrible day would play out again.

As it registered, all of Baen's Six gathered around the field. They turned to him. Extended their swords. "By Her hand."

Fire flew from the razored edges, straight at—no, *into* Haegan. He breathed it in. Aaesh appeared in the glowing fury of it all. *Finish it, Fierian.*

His thoughts were pummeled by the ravages, the murders, the inflaming, the deaths—Trale, Thelikor, Tili, hundreds on the field. Father ruined by the inflaming. Mother. As She showed him so many lost to the same fate.

No more.

With a bellow that seemed to split his head in two, Haegan obeyed what he saw in his mind. Still on his knees, he slammed both fists into the ground.

Crack! A strange whistling pierced his eardrums. *Clap! Crack!*

Light cascaded over the lands. Incipients were reduced to dust. Mountains trembled, and in the great distance, a geyser shot from the mountain. A cliff wall surrendered and water burst forth, rushing through the lands.

The air sizzled, smoke rising and embers crackling. Then the planet breathed in the silence of redemption.

52

It had taken a week to gather the dead, burn the incipients and Sirdarians who had not been killed in the great purge, and bury the Nine's allies and friends. Curled in the window of the keeping hall, Thiel eyed Haegan, who had yet to awaken since he'd thrown out the wake that destroyed the Void and the lingering darkness of Sirdar.

She tugged her gown over her legs and watched him sleep. As she'd done since they returned to the fortress, which had taken a beating in the great battle. Loneliness tugged at her heart. Cadeif was gone. Father and Mother were planning for the journey back to Nivar. Gwogh and the Council would make for Hetaera to rebuild.

And Thiel wanted to return to Haegan. Or rather, he to her.

A moan drifted from the semi-darkened room.

She shot off the sill and leapt to the edge of his mattress. "Haegan?"

He blinked. Vestiges of sleep hooded his eyes. "Bring Gwogh." His voice came true and clear.

Thiel hesitated. "Why?"

He breathed a smile. "And your father. Hurry."

Confused, but giving him the benefit of the doubt, she went to the door. Opened it and met the sentries' surprised expressions. "Bring Sir Gwogh and King Thurig. The Fierian would see them."

After they agreed, she turned, stunned to find Haegan out of bed and lifting the clothes from the divider that provided him privacy. He disappeared behind it.

"Are ye well?" she asked. "All is well, ye know. It's over. Ye can rest."

He emerged in trousers and a green tunic that made his eyes blaze. "I have spent my life resting. I'm ready to live."

A rap at the door delivered her father, then the elder accelerant into the room.

"Prince Haegan," her father greeted him. "Good to see ye up."

"Thank you," Haegan said. "I have a question to put to you, sir."

Her father hesitated. "Aye?"

"I would have your permission to take Thiel as my bound."

"A little late after giving her the Celahar seal," her father said around a laugh.

Haegan flushed a little. "Aye, but I would have your permission all the same."

"Ye have it, Haegan. I would be a fool to refuse."

Haegan smiled. Nodded. Held a hand to Thiel.

She took it. "What are ye—"

"Will ye have me, Thurig Kiethiel?"

"Aye." Then she saw the determination in his eyes. Glanced at Gwogh. "Oh."

Haegan smiled, lifting an eyebrow as if to ask her approval.

She turned to the older man. "Sir Gwogh, would ye do the honors?"

"Wait just a minute," her father objected. "If yer mother misses this, I'll never hear the end of it."

"My sister as well," Haegan said. "We should gather them. I will not endure another hour without you as my bound."

• • •

Within the keeping walls were three men Kaelyria loved without reservation. One was mentally absent. Another, once in a deep sleep, now danced jubilantly with his new bound. The other had been engaged in tense meetings with the Council of Nine, the steward—his own brother—and Northlanders, who had fled the Rekken.

She stared across the great hall, where revelers celebrated her brother's binding ceremony with the Princess Kiethiel. Dancing. Hennidrile vines. Food. Merriment. While Kaelyria sat with her bound and his family, she wondered if the wake Haegan sent out had done harm to the child she carried. How would she know? What if she lost it? That would ruin Aselan.

"Are ye well?" he asked, his breath warm along her neck, tickling.

"Tired, but well," she said with a nod.

As dancing continued, Kae debating telling him. He was so happy to simply have her alive and back with him, she could not stand to hurt him if she lost the babe.

"Elan," his father said, joining them near the firepit. "I know not how Nivar Hold has fared or what fighting we have left to do when we return, but if we have a home, ye and the princess do as well."

Aselan glanced to her. "Thank ye, Father. We may need that."

As the feasting died down, she and Aselan left the hall and returned to their chamber. She changed into her chemise, taking a moment to study herself while Aselan's back was turned.

It would be awhile before her womb swelled noticeably, but she realized her body *had* changed. Subtly. Almost indiscernibly. But she knew, and it was enough for her.

She rolled a tendril of fire around her fingers, joy rising in a sudden wave. How had it come to be that everything once so black had turned to light? Her wielding had returned that terrible day in the tent, though she knew not why. Was it the babe? Had whatever Cilicien done to her finally worn off? It shamed her how much she'd allowed him to take advantage of her all those months ago. Yet Abiassa had been good. Exceedingly and abundantly good. She started toward the curtained bed.

Aselan turned onto his side, propping his head. "Ye were quiet tonight."

"Much to think on. A lot has happened." She climbed in beside him, kissed him.

He traced a hand along her jaw and neck. Kissed her. Then stared. For a long time.

"What?"

"The Lady is too good to me."

The secret threatened to burst within her. "She is even better than you suppose."

His brow furrowed, the beard twitching beneath his frown as he sought meaning behind her words. Then she moved his hand to her belly. His eyes sprang wide. "Ye . . . ye are with child?"

"Not just any child," she laughed. "Your child."

Laughing, he buried his face in her neck. Kissed her. Then drew back. "Will I hurt ye?"

She rolled her eyes and pulled him back to her.

He arched away, his large hand going to her belly again. "It feels strong already. A boy."

She lifted her chin. "Girls are just as strong."

• • •

One Month Later

NIVAR HOLD, YBIENN

Tili stood before the full-length mirror, eyeing himself. The clang of the smithy's hammer and the rhythmic sawing of lumber echoed outside, evidence of the ongoing repairs to Nivar Hold.

He'd spent the first few weeks after the defeat of Poired with the Council and Crown Prince Haegan, who had already ordered the rebuilding of Fieri Keep. With the Fire King alive but incapacitated, the Council and the Nine's rulers voted for Haegan to take the crown with Kiethiel as his queen. But until his father's death, Haegan refused to take the title of Fire King.

Just as Tili refused to move forward another day without making his own declaration to his father, who held court today, hearing complaints and requests, and giving consent for bindings across the Northlands.

The latter of particular importance.

He snapped down his sleeves. Smoothed the waistcoat. Glancing at the silver circlet he wore, a strict formality his father insisted upon since returning to Nivar, Tili turned from the mirror.

His mother appeared at the door. Her gaze spoke when she did not.

Tili must avoid this conversation. "I will no longer break my promise to her, so do not ask it of me."

"I wouldn't dare." But there was no contrition in her words as she glided across the floor, adjusted the circlet, then rested her hands on his shoulders. "You realize—"

"Aye." He squared his shoulders. Set his jaw. "If ye'll pardon me, I dare not be late."

"I am proud of you," she called softly as he hit the threshold.

Surprise forced him to look back. "Why?"

"You do this at great risk."

"The only risk is losing her." 'Twas not true, though it sounded well enough. Losing his father would gut him. Losing his position as commander of the Nivari . . .

He stalked down the stairs, trusting Aburas had done as asked and would deliver Astadia to the hall at the requisite time. Before the double doors of the great hall, guarded by two Nivari he'd trained, Tili braced. Mustered what little courage remained after the Battle of Ironhall.

"What is this?"

Tili started. Turned. Blazes, she was early. And looked amazing in a clingy green gown. "Ye're early."

"For what?"

Tili straightened.

Astadia hesitated. "What . . . ? Why are you so fancied up?"

"Do ye know what it means to set petition?"

Astadia frowned, her gaze darting over his face, then to the double doors. She widened her eyes. She stepped back, shaking her head. "Tili, you can't. I'm . . . you know what I am. They—it would ruin you."

He slipped his hands around her waist. "What would ruin me is losing ye."

"They'll talk. It'll look poorly on you. I can't let you." Her jaw jutted. "Your brother told me you'd never do this, that you were too smart."

"Aselan said this?"

"Relig."

Tili snorted. "He's often wrong—including now. The petition is already there. I'm to be summoned, but I would not do this if I thought it would anger or upset ye."

"I am upset—they will not be kind. I have killed, Tili. I have—"

"Been forced to do things in the name of survival. As we all were at Ironhall."

"It's different."

"It's not!"

"To them, it will be! I do not want to see you hurt or humiliated." She looked ready to cry, but she wasn't angry. She wasn't yelling. Or pulling knives.

He wished to read her better, because it seemed a thread of willingness ran through her objections. "Will ye refuse me?"

She swallowed. "You shouldn't do this." The thread grew.

"Not what I asked."

She wet her lips. "I would shame you."

"Only if ye refuse."

The doors swung wide and the herald called, "Prince Tili, heir of Nivar and the Northlands."

Tili held her gaze, feeling the stares from the main room. He extended his hand.

Chin trembling, she shook her head.

"Please."

Silence.

Hopes crashed, Tili lowered his gaze, then pivoted. Stalked through the gathered witnesses, gaze locked on the throne where his father sat with his governors. Surprise, consternation, and curiosity vied for dominance on the weathered features. The Caorian wood cane was propped against his throne. Though some had counseled the king to keep it out of sight, Thurig saw it as witness, as a source of pride for the battle that delivered the lands.

Tili clapped a fist over his heart and knelt. "My lord-father!"

"Stand, my son. What purpose has driven ye to such dramatics?"

Pulling his knee and courage from the floor, Tili straightened. There was naught for it but to eat his own pride now. "A petition, my king."

His father chuckled. "Of what sort?"

"For binding."

His father's smile fell. Silence dropped hard on the hall, reminding him of that which devoured the battlefield a month ago. "For whom?"

"Me, sire."

A scowl burrowed beneath his father's crown. "*With* whom?" The rumble in his father's question held warning.

Tili's heart beat an awkward cadence. He had to do this. It was . . . the only way. "I ask to take as my bound Astadia Kath."

Whispers darted through the hall. Naming her assassin, murderer, blood-letter, and even Unnatural. The names were naught to him.

"This cannot be," a governor growled.

"What cause have ye to claim this woman?" his father demanded, taking a lurching step forward. Rejection hung on his brow. "Never once—"

"All our lives changed at the Battle of Ironhall, including hers. She fought for the Fierian, nearly lost her life bringing down the Dark One. I can think of no greater warrior in our lands, nor a truer woman."

"The council calls for Astadia Kath to step forward," one commanded.

Silence thrummed among the tension, which grew with no response to the summons. The governor repeated it. Still silence.

Finally, soft steps tapped behind him.

Tili released the breath he'd held as she came to his side.

His father peeled his glower from Tili and shifted it to Astadia. "What have ye to say, assas—Astadia?"

She pulled straight beside Tili, though her gaze never left the floor. "I would not have him lose his command and his right to the throne for me. Neither do I wish him to lose his family." Her voice faltered. "I know that pain and would not visit it upon anyone."

"So ye do not love my son."

Astadia drew in a breath, held it for several painful seconds, then released it. But never answered.

"Yer king gave ye a question," Aburas growled.

"I am homeless and therefore without king or ruler."

Tili watched his father closely.

The king seemed to be hiding a smile. "Binding with my son makes me not only yer king but yer father-king."

Astadia started, her gaze bouncing between Tili and the king. She opened her mouth. Jerked her gaze away and snapped her mouth shut again. "I beg your mercy, but the politics of court confuse me."

"I know that pain well." His father grinned, turning her words back on her. "Would ye have him, Astadia?"

She huffed. "I . . ."

"Ye hesitate?" he groused. "There are a hundred women who would take him!"

"Then he should take one of his own," she said, her voice cracking.

"Ah, see? Therein likes the poison—he will not have them. His mother and I have not been able to get rid of the troublemaker, despite many efforts." He shook his head. "Now what is stopping ye from saving the queen and I?"

"You and your council would have me branded a murderer, yet you suggest being my father-king." For the first time, she met Thurig's gaze squarely. "Why? Why would you allow me to bind with him?"

"Then ye do not wish to."

"I am not worthy of it." She went rigid, looked at the floor again. "Nor of him. You know what I am—"

"What ye *were*," his father corrected.

"What I have done."

"If ye knew what I had done in my many years, what most in this room have done . . . let us just say, there are things best forgotten. The Battle of Ironhall delivered us from a great evil. And I believe the days ahead need sharp minds, not sharp daggers, to keep us from falling into that pit again." He returned to his throne and met her gaze evenly. "Would ye have my son Prince Tili, Astadia Kath?"

"This is not done!" a councilmember objected.

With an outturned palm, his father silenced them. "Well?"

Astadia shifted. "Aye. I would."

● ● ●

Though the stench had faded, the gift had not. Vaqar sat on his destrier, staring over the waters that once more fed the Oasis of Shandalhar. The salt spray drenched his senses, making it bearable to exist so close to a city. His gaze drifted to the capital.

"Think she's still alive?" Haandra asked from where she stood on the shore with the young captain from the Fierian's contingent, whose raqine splashed and thrashed in the waves. The great beast then lifted from the water, took flight—right toward Tokar, whom he sprayed with water.

Laughing, Vaqar answered the girl. "It would surprise me if Anithraenia survived after all the darkness she spread."

"Not to mention murdering our families," Adassi said.

Vaqar snorted. "We go back there with these senses and we may discover they're not really our friends."

"What are we supposed to do? It stinks in every blazing city, and I don't know how to farm."

"It is time for a new beginning," came a voice from everywhere and yet nowhere.

Vaqar turned, then jolted when he saw a young girl standing at the water's edge surrounded by six overly tall men. There was no need for introduction. He knew her. "Aaesh."

"You have all done well with My gift, used it despite the discomfort it cost you, despite the great price of your loved one's lives." She inclined her head. "I reward your labors with a gift of time."

Vaqar hesitated. "Time?"

"Forever yours," she said with a bright smile. "For you, Vaqar, for leading your people, for continuing on when even your sister threatened to kill you, for protecting the Fierian—for that, I grant you a place among my Six." She motioned to the men with her. "I choose you as a Guardian of worlds and hearts."

• • •

Water rushed from atop the mountain, galloping down over rocks and hills until it crashed playfully at the base, stirring a foamy wake. It then spread out into a broad lake, eventually taking a leisurely southward stroll in a snaking path. It was a stark contrast to the still-blackened fields. And yet . . . green. Sprigs of green pushed up defiantly amid ashes.

"I understand not." Haegan glanced at the meadow where, for the years of his life spent in the high tower, he had watched Jujak in sparring drills. Were it not for the ruins of Fieri Keep, he would think himself lost.

Tucking back a strand of hair, his sister turned a circle. She laughed. "It's so beautiful."

"How can this be?" Thiel asked, joining him with Praegur and Laertes.

"The water," he said, choking back a disbelieving laugh. "The Lakes of Fire—there should be lava there. Not an actual lake."

"Mother would have loved this," Kae said, Aselan coming up behind her and wrapping his arms around her. They would set out for Nivar a week hence.

"I heard talk," Gwogh said from the caravan making its way back to the Keep, "that when you unleashed that wake, it not only destroyed the Auspex and their access to the Void, it broke across the lands. The volcano was sheared away and this spring poured forth with new life."

"Remember the rhyme?" Kaelyria said, placing a hand on her rounding belly, *"Red, orange, gold, and blue; Reshaped the lands, people too.'"*

Haegan gaped in awe at the land, at the words to the poem they'd recited as children. "It never before had meaning," he said, closing his hand around Thiel's as the rest of the words sprang to mind. *"'Now to thrive on holy pyre, They unleash Abiassa's Fire.'"*

Alphabetical
Character Index

Aaesh – Aaeshwaeith Adoaniel'afirema; Abiassa

Aburas – high-ranking Nivari officer

Adrroania Celahar – queen of the Nine Kingdoms

Aselan – Cacique of Legier's Heart; bound to Kaelyria; eldest son of Thurig the Formidable

Astadia Kath – Iteverian assassin

Baen Celahar – first Celahar to take the Fire Throne; assumed name Zaelero as king; fought the Mad Queen

Breab – councilman dining with the Infantessa

Byrin – Aselan's right-hand; member of the Legiera

Cadeif – Ematahri warrior; archon; claimed and protected Thiel years past

Caprit – member of the Legiera

Chima – female raqine; bonded to Haegan

Cilicien ka'Dur – incipient

Deh'læfhïer – mentioned in the Parchments as the defender of the Fierian; Deliverers

Diavel – Poired's black raqine

Doskari – Aselan's late wife

Draorin – Baen's (Zaelero's) right hand; Deliverer

Draorin – colonel with Tili's contingent

Draed – male raqine

Dromadric – Grand Marshal of the Ignatieri

Drracien Khar'val – fugitive marshal; friend of Haegan

Ebose – male raqine; Zicri's brother

Ederac – epitome of evil

Eldin Gwogh – tutor to Prince Haegan; master accelerant; member of the Council of Nine

Eriathiel – wife of Thurig the Formidable; mother of Thiel and her brothers

Etan – Nivari warrior

Falip Wrel – new member of the Council of Nine; replaced Baede

Fhuriætyr – mentioned in the Parchments; the Fierian; also Reckoner

Ghor – Jujak under Graem's command

Graem Grinda – Jujak captain; son of Kiliv Grinda

Griese – one of the Council of Nine

Haegan Celahar – prince of Seultrie; son of Zireli and Adrroania

Hoeff – Drigo; Toeff's twin

Ingwait – elder of the Ladies of the Heart; oversees relational and social affairs

Kaelyria Celahar – princess of Seultrie; daughter of Zireli and Adrroania

Kaiade – Haegan's great-grandfather

Kedulcya – member of the Council of Nine; from Kerral

Kiliv Grinda – Jujak general

Laejan – Jujak general

Laertes – young boy from Caori; one of four companions Haegan joined

Mallius – Jujak lieutenant

Markoo – member of the Legiera

Marz Chauld – Jujak colonel

Medric – Deliverer

Nagbe – boy in the cave during the Contending

Naudus – Nivari fighter; lieutenant

Negaer – general in Zireli's army; commander of the Pathfinders, an elite force of trackers and fighters

Nydelia – Infantessa; Shavaussia; queen of Iteveria

Onerid – Poired Dyrth's right hand

Pao'chk – great healer

Paung – butler at Karithia

Peani Clarentia Ibirel – Relig's bound; daughter of Yaorid

Pharen – male raqine; bonded to Aselan

Poired Dyrth – commanding officer of Sirdar's armies; enemy of all who
    follow Abiassa

Praegur – a Kergulian; one of four companions; marked by Abiassa

Raleng – Ematahri; twin of Ruldan; serves Cadeif

Rekken – foreigners from the north, across the Violet Sea

Ruldan – Ematahri; twin of Raleng; serves Cadeif

Shavaussia – see Nydelia

Sirdar Demas of Tharqnis – Fallen One; Lord of Darkness; enemy of
    Abiassa

Thelikor – Drigo warrior leader

Thomannon – Haegan's manservant in Karithia

Thræïho – mentioned in the Parchments; will fight for the Fierian; also called
    Drigovudd, or Drigo

Thurig Asykth – king of the Northlands

Thurig Eriathiel – queen of the Northlands; wife to Thurig

Thurig as'Kiethiel (Thiel) – daughter of Thurig and Eriathiel of Nivar; one
    of four companions; also called Etelide

Thurig as'Osmon (Osmon) – youngest son of Thurig

Thurig as'Relig (Relig) – third eldest son of Thurig; bonded to Peani

Thurig as'Tili (Tili) – eldest acknowledged son of Thurig

Toeff – Drigo; Hoeff's twin

Tokar – one of four companions; officer of the combined armies

Trale Kath – Iteverian assassin

Vaqar Modia – prince of Tahsca; commander of exiled contingent; brother
    to Anithraenia

Wegna – wise woman in Legier's Heart

Zaelero II –first Celahar to take the Fire Throne; born Baen Celahar; fought
    the Mad Queen and restored the Nine to the ways of Abiassa

Zicri – male raqine; bonded to Tili

Zireli Celahar – king of the Nine Kingdoms; the Fire King

Zoijan – Ematahri warrior

GLOSSARY OF TERMS

Abiassa's Fire – the gift of wielding the Flames, possessed by only certain individuals

abiatasso – the gift in the essence of a person who has the ability to wield

accelerant – one who can wield the Flames

archon – leader of the Ematahri

Auspex/Foreteller – semi-human creature held by Poired for the delivery of messages and orders from Sirdar

Baen's Crossing – village on border between Ybienn and the Nine

cacique – the title used among those in Legier's Heart for their leader

Caori – one of the Nine Kingdoms; capital city is Luxlirien

Choosing, the (aka Etaesian's Feast) – Eilidan custom for bonding rituals

Citadel – the central Sanctuary in the Holy City in Hetaera

Cold-One's Tooth – mountain peak nearest Nivar Hold

cordi – fruit

Deliverer – an ageless minister of justice and discipline; terrifyingly powerful; answers only to the will of Abiassa; also called Lucent Riders, Void Walker, Light Bringer

Destroyers – demons

Drigo – ancient race of giants whose only goal is to serve

Drigovudd – the Drigo in their enhanced state; stories border on myth but they are said to be nearly immortal when in their vudd state

Duamauri – Aselan's icehound

Eilidan – people of Legier; Aselan's people

Ematahri – fierce forest-dwellers; a threat to any traveling the Way of the Throne/Throne Road

Etaesian's Feast – see "Choosing, the"

Fieri Keep – home of the Celahars, who rule from here on the Fire Throne

Fierian, the – a prophesied accelerant said to bring about the destruction of the Nine and the eradication of the Lakes of Fire; greatly feared

Fire King – king who rules the Nine and is most powerful accelerant

Flames – reference to the gift bestowed on certain individuals; sometimes an epithet

Great Falls – a waterfall blessed with miraculous healing every 100 years during the Year of Feasts as a gift from Abiassa

Hetaera – largest city in the Nine; contains the Holy City; close to the Great Falls

hiel-touck – oath used in Legier and Ybienn

Holy City – the seat of the Ignatieri; the largest Sanctuary; contains the Citadel, where accelerants are trained and commissioned

icehound – very large wolves who only exist in cold-weather climates

Ignatieri – holy order of accelerants; refer to each other as The Brethren

incipient – one who can wield but has turned against Abiassa

Infantessa – the queen of Iteveria

Iteveria – twin city to Nydessa, within Unelithia

jav-rod – spearlike weapon

Jujak – the army of King Zireli

Karithia – palace in Iteveria; seat of the Infantessa

Kedardokith – a rite of Ematahri warriors to claim the lives of outsiders; intended for protection; once claimed, always claimed

Kerguli – a race of people from the desert Outlands of the far west

Lakes of Fire – the lava lakes near Fieri Keep; a blessing of Abiassa and connected to the Flames

Legier – largest mountain overlooking Ybienn; home to the Eilidan, a race of mountain dwellers

Lucent Riders – the name given to the Deliverers by the Ematahri

Luxlirien – capital city of Caori

Maereni – Poired's elite guards

moonslight – light of twin moons

Nivar Hold – seat of power in Ybienn; residence of King Thurig

Nivari – Thurig's army; commanded by his son, as'Tili

pharmakeia – a physician who uses herbs and the Flames to bring healing/restoration

Primera – Haegan's planet

raqine – winged creatures widely believed extinct or myth

sentinel – Ignatieri police who patrol Sanctuaries

Seultrie – seat of power for the Nine Kingdoms; capital city is Zaethien

Shadows, the – beyond the grave

Sikir – Aselan's icehound

Silver – name given to Poired's elite incipients

Sirdarian – one of Sirdar

sowaoli petals – flower petals

Tahsca/Tahscan – from House Tahsca off the coast of Iteveria; fiercest seafaring warriors

Unelithia – combined realm of Nydessa and Iteveria

Void Walker – Deliverer or one of the evil counterparts; one who walks between worlds

Ybienn – sovereign kingdom, separate from the Nine; seat of Thurig and his family

ACKNOWLEDGMENTS

Deena Petersen and Shannon McNear, who read every book before it went to print. So appreciate your encouragement, ladies! Thank you!

To you amazing, loyal, fiery readers who have screamed and hollered for this last installment for the last 18 months. Your patience and passion are so appreciated!

My incredible Four Guys—Brian, Ryan, Reagan, and VVolt, who gave me the space to get the story done, the edits plowed, and the map hacked together. Love you, guys!

And to my publisher/agent/friend, Steve, who took pity on my friends, readers, and family when my sleep-deprived self turned in my acknowledgments with only one line. You sure know how to save your authors! *grins*

Ronie Kendig is an award-winning, best-selling author. She lives on the East Coast with her family and a retired military working dog, VVolt N629. Ronie is the voice behind the *Rapid-Fire Fiction* blog. Her action-packed stories transcend genres and grip readers right from the first page. She is very active in the writing community, speaking to various groups, teaching at national conferences, and mentoring new writers.

Connect with Ronie!

Website: *www.roniekendig.com*
Facebook: *www.facebook.com/rapidfirefiction*
Twitter: *www.twitter.com/roniekendig*
GoodReads: *www.goodreads.com/RonieK*
Pinterest: *www.pinterest.com/roniek*
Instagram: *www.instagram.com/kendigronie*

ENCLAVE

an imprint of
GILEAD PUBLISHING

FIERIAN

RONIE
KENDIG

ACCELERANT

RONIE
KENDIG

EMBERS

RONIE
KENDIG

Read the complete
ABIASSA'S FIRE TRILOGY
by Ronie Kendig